Magic Sometimes Happens

Magic Sometimes Happens

Margaret James

Copyright © 2014 Margaret James

Published 2014 by Choc Lit Limited
Penrose House, Crawley Drive, Camberley, Surrey GU15 2AB, UK
www.choc-lit.com

The right of Margaret James to be identified as the Author of this Work
has been asserted by her in accordance with the Copyright, Designs and
Patents Act 1988

A CIP catalogue record for this book is available
from the British Library

ISBN 978-1-78189-175-9

Printed and bound by CPI Group (UK) Ltd, Croydon, CR0 4YY

My love and thanks to C and M and A,
who helped in all sorts of ways.
You light up my life.

Acknowledgements

Once again, it's been a huge pleasure to
work with Choc Lit on this novel.

I'm delighted to be a member of such a brilliant team.

Special thanks to Tasting Panel readers: Kirsten, Jamie,
Elke, Linda, Heather, Caroline, Liz, Jane, Julie & Marsha.

August

⌒ ROSIE ⌒

Once the dead are buried, they stay dead and buried.

They can't come back to life.

They've gone for good.

But as I followed Mum and Dad and Granny Cassie out of the Dorset churchyard, I was still insisting none of this could have happened, that it must be a bad dream.

Any minute now, I told myself, Charlie would come strolling down the road from Melbury, wearing grubby trainers which had walked a thousand miles already and carrying a battered, filthy rucksack fit only for the bin.

We'd have a great big hug. We'd walk back to the house. We'd go into my mother's lovely garden where the Jacques Cartier roses which bloomed for Mum all summer filled the air with scent.

We'd all be talking, laughing – that's except for Dad, who would be shouting: *Charlie, what the hell have you been doing? Where've you been? Your mother has been frantic! Why didn't you send a postcard or an email or at least a text?*

The dogs would all be going mad with joy, the stupid things, and Granny Cassie would tell us to calm down, to stop acting so daft, to behave like normal human beings. But she'd be laughing, too.

Maybe I'd wake up one morning and I would be able to accept it?

But today I couldn't accept it or the part I'd played in it.

So the nightmares would continue, wouldn't they?

I still had the video on my phone. Why did I keep watching it, again, again, again? I couldn't seem to help myself, that's why. Maybe I should share it with my parents? Or would seeing it hurt them even more than they'd been hurt already?

Why hadn't I found the pen?

September

'It's partly the cute accent,' Lexie told me, checking she had emptied that particular closet in our apartment.

The apartment we cannot afford, but Lexie had to have because the views of Minneapolis, of Minnehaha Park and of the Mississippi River are so awesome she fell in love with it, even though she hates to ride the elevators, so she always has to take the stairs.

She says the stair work keeps her in good shape. She's right, it does. She's curvy, sexy, blonde and gorgeous. All in all, she's pretty hot, my wife.

But I digress.

'Let me get this straight,' I said. 'You met this British guy, his accent's cute, and that's the reason you're leaving Polly, Joe and me – your home, your work, your life – to go with him?'

'I'm not leaving the kids.' She threw more stuff into a case. 'I'm taking them with me. We'll stay with Stephen in Saint Paul.'

'He has an apartment in Saint Paul?'

'He has a house, it has a yard,' said Lexie, who has always wanted to live in a real house with a real yard – that's when she's not wanting apartments in expensive blocks in downtown Minneapolis. 'It's on Grand Avenue.'

'When are you moving out?'

'A week, ten days. I'll need to pack all Joe's and Polly's stuff, fix up their rooms at Stephen's place. He said to call a stylist, but that won't be necessary. We won't be there long. Come October we'll be going to Europe.'

'You can't go to Europe. Joe will be in school.'

'There are schools in Europe, Pat. Stephen says they're excellent in Surrey.'

'Where and what is Surrey?'

'It's someplace near London where Stephen's parents live. Stephen has a house there, too. He says there'll be no problem getting Joe enrolled in a good elementary school.'

'Polly isn't old enough to go to school. So what's she going to do?'

'She can go to preschool, playgroup, nursery or whatever they call it over there.'

'You and Mr Wonderful, you have it all worked out.'

'Yeah, we discussed my options, which were—'

'Leave your husband, take his children, but who gives a shit about your husband anyway?'

'I knew you wouldn't understand.' Lex stopped emptying drawers into her case and turned to look at me. 'Joe and Polly, they'll be fine,' she said. 'They get along with Stephen. When we all went to the park last week they had a blast.'

'You took our kids to meet this man?' I thought I must be dreaming. 'You decided you and they are emigrating to some cold, wet island off the coast of mainland Europe to go live with some guy you've known ten minutes? What about your job?'

'Stephen's on a salary which means I'll never have to work again, and there's no need to emigrate. The kids and I will get to go to Europe, in fact we'll have a chance to see the world, to visit places like Dubai and Singapore. But we'll still spend time in Minneapolis. We'll still be Americans, still be citizens of the USA.'

'You don't have passports, Lex. Did you think of that when you were making all these plans with Mr Wonderful?'

'We'll have passports soon. I have an appointment with the Passport Agency downtown on Wednesday afternoon.

We'll go for expedited service and should have our passports inside of a fortnight, Stephen says.'

'Lex, let me remind you there are laws to stop a parent taking children who are US citizens out of the US unless the other parent says okay. There was a case on CBS last week. If you think Joe and Polly will even leave the state without my full agreement, you must be off your head. You try it, and I'll call the FBI.'

'But you don't even like the kids!'

'I love those children! I'd do anything—'

'You love them, maybe. But you don't like their company. They bore you half to death. You know they do.' Lexie pulled the zipper on her case. 'I'll drop this off at Stephen's and sort my other stuff out later, if you don't object?'

'Whatever, be my guest, there isn't any hurry. I don't care if our bedroom stays looking like a member of al-Qaeda came to call.'

'Patrick, please don't be like this? It's not been right between us for so long!'

'What's not been right?'

'We're not a couple any more. You're so wrapped up in your work and students that you don't seem to notice I exist.'

'Lex, don't be ridiculous! Of course I notice you exist.'

'But we never talk. We don't communicate—'

'We're communicating now, and we—'

'I mean we don't talk properly. We don't have conversations, like married people should. We never touch except when we have sex, and that's all we do in bed, have sex. It's been years and years since we made love. Last week, I was speaking with a friend who told me I should get some healing, have some therapy, and now I'm thinking she was right.'

'You mean you want some fifty-dollar shrink to tell you it's okay to walk out on your marriage? Give you permission to treat me like a piece of gum, chewed for a while, spit out?'

'I need to see more clearly, and maybe you do, too.'

'Okay, we'll go get some marriage guidance or whatever. We'll have couples counselling, is that what you're suggesting?'

'It's way too late for counselling,' said Lexie. 'Pat, these past few years I've been so lonely I felt like I had died. But when I met Stephen, he brought me back to life. While I'm with him, he makes me fly.'

Lexie looked at me with big round eyes like the orange cat in that cartoon, the one about the fat green ogre Joe and Polly love. 'You can't deny me the chance to have a life?'

'You can have what the hell you like, Alexis. But I'll never let some opportunist British bastard take Joe and Poll from me. Where are they now?'

'At Angie's place.'

'Why are they at Angie's?'

'I didn't want them to be here while you yelled at me. I'll go pick them up in half an hour.'

'I'll pick them up myself.' I grabbed my keys. 'Does Angie know your plans? Did she agree to have the kids so you and Mr Wonderful could come to life together and go flying in the middle of a Thursday afternoon?'

I didn't wait for Lex to answer me. I was too mad to trust myself to listen.

So I walked out the door.

⌐ ROSIE ⌐

I'd hoped nobody else would have this dress.

But that's the trouble when you shop online. There's some sort of cyber-voodoo that makes everyone end up on the same site and choosing the same thing. I wished I'd asked one of the new designers who have accounts with Fanny to let me have a sample for a day.

6

Why was I there at all? I didn't know. I knew I'd been invited to this wedding, obviously. Jane and I had been at school together and we had been best friends. But last month I had said goodbye to Charlie. So I wasn't in the mood for weddings, as I'm sure you'll understand.

Why do people bother to get married anyway? Why not just have affairs? Out of half a dozen friends who'd sashayed up some aisle or stood under some palm tree or whatever over the past five years, only one seemed happy.

As for all the others – one was having counselling and had fallen for her shrink. One was separated, one divorced. One already had two toddlers and was very pregnant with the third, so *she* had to be certifiable. She needed to be taken somewhere Gothic and Victorian in a padded van. One poor girl was downright suicidal …

I wouldn't have put any serious money on this latest marriage lasting long. Why do I say that? The groom and the chief bridesmaid were snogging in the shrubbery half an hour after the service ended. Or rather more than snogging. She had left her knickers lying underneath a bush, the best man had found them and he was threatening to auction them.

The whole thing was a farce.

The father of the bride had pinched my arse at least three times. I don't think a plastic surgeon with a very exclusive private practice, the owner of a turreted and buttressed pile in Sunningdale, should have behaved like that, at least on his own daughter's wedding day.

The mother of the bride looked really grim and also out of place. Most of the other women there were wearing flowery pastels. But she was dressed in navy polyester. She looked like a stewardess on Geriatric Airlines or maybe a receptionist in one of those old-fashioned Eastern European hotels.

I'm sorry, that was mean of me. Please excuse me while I

go and scratch a sofa or destroy a cushion. I haven't always been so sharp and spiteful. But since Charlie, everything is different ...

As I was thinking about leaving, the best man came over carrying two glasses of champagne and wearing the chief bridesmaid's scarlet knickers on his head. 'Hello, gorgeous,' he began and winked suggestively. 'Where have you been all my life?'

I left.

I'd thought going to Paris for a year – I had come home in early August, several weeks ago – might mean I'd meet a man and fall in love.

Of course I'd been to France before. I'd spent a year at the Sorbonne. But there I'd met just students and students are a different species. Most are quasi-human, only marginally evolved.

I didn't want to vamp my tutor. He was nearly seventy and stank of stale Gitanes. Yes, there were other teachers and some were even borderline attractive, but I didn't want an academic. They didn't earn enough.

Those thirty, forty or even fifty-something businessmen, I'd told myself, *the ones who wear expensive clothes, drive Porsches or Mercedes, they're the ones who'll know exactly how to make a girl feel really special.*

Ha ha ha.

I'd met a lot of rich, attractive Frenchmen, but half of them were married and wanted me to be their *petite amie*, an occasional girlfriend who would show their mates they could still pull. Most of the unmarried ones lived with their *mamans* out in the suburbs beyond the Périphérique and merely wanted sex.

I'd wondered what would happen if I sat upon my suitcase on the concourse at the Gare du Nord, sobbing like Linda

Radlett did in Nancy Mitford's *The Pursuit of Love*, my favourite novel.

A handsome, sexy Frenchman might notice me, perhaps? He'd offer me his handkerchief and take me to have lunch somewhere discreet and very expensive and tell me I was beautiful and fall in love with me?

I thought it was more likely that crowds of British backpackers on bargain weekend breaks would surge and mill around me, bashing me with their enormous rucksacks, while some illegal immigrant tried to snatch my bag.

I wanted so, so much to fall in love. But it never happened, and I finally decided there must be something very wrong with me. I remembered reading somewhere that love is almost always found in the last place you look. But in how many places did I have to look before I found the last one?

So now I was at home in Dorset, moping round the place.

My mother must have got fed up with me because she said why didn't I take a little holiday? Why didn't I go and spend some time in Italy or Spain or California, where it would be sunny?

I didn't fancy Spain or Italy – too many tourists at this time of year – and trying to come to terms with what had happened in a place like California would have been a cliché, don't you think? California's swarming with counsellors and gurus and healers and what-have-you. I'd have found myself in therapy ten minutes after I got off the plane.

I was thinking I should go to London and see Fanny. There was no way I could return to Paris. It would be impossible. But I had a half-formed plan for something I might do in London …

Then I got a text from my friend Tess.

I hadn't heard from Tess for months and months. The last time we had spoken, she'd told me she was thinking about leaving the job she had in London, working as a buyer and negotiator in a reclamation yard. I'd thought she would find something similar, maybe in a bigger, more upmarket company.

But what she'd done was far more interesting than merely change her job. She was in Minnesota with her brand new husband – another happy couple, I couldn't get away from them – a guy she'd met on holiday while she was in Las Vegas back in June, having an American adventure.

I knew she'd gone to Vegas by herself. She always liked to travel on her own. She said it was more challenging and also meant she didn't have to do what other people wanted. She wasn't always saying *yeah, you use the bathroom first* or *yeah, you have the comfortable bed, I love to sleep on nails.*

On her own, she could do as she liked, and always did.

She had often come to see me while I lived in Paris, staying for several long weekends and entertaining all my French friends with her East End Franglais. *Garson, could you bringez-moi duh cwasons, seevooplay, et n'oubliez pas mon pot de jam.*

So first I had the text.

Got married to a Yank met him in Vegas bet u shocked! At home in Saint Paul Minnesota now. Where u these days? TXXX

Then the emails started: ping, ping, ping.

She'd married the American because he was hot. She thought it would be cool to be American herself. Or, at any rate, to be allowed to stay more than three months and spend her husband's money on some stuff. She got lucky there because her rich and famous husband could afford a lot of stuff.

'Come and stay,' she wheedled when later on that afternoon she phoned and we'd caught up. 'We have this ace apartment in the smartest part of town. It's in a block that's got a man in uniform sitting at a desk and opening the door for you. There are two elevators, one for odds and one for evens. It's not some rubbish walk-up.'

'Do you have the space?'

'We have loads of space! You can have your own en-suite. Rosie, you must come. We'll do some serious shopping. Stuff's so cheap out here.'

Some serious shopping. How could I resist?

'I'll be on the next plane out,' I said.

I did feel rather mean, I must admit, leaving Mum and Dad in Dorset at that dreadful time. I sort of felt I ought to stick around, be there for them, remind them they had one child left, that they were parents still.

But Mum said: *go, you need a break.*

Dad said: *your mother's right.*

Perhaps they couldn't stand the sight of me? I sometimes wondered if it would be easier if they blamed me? If they shouted, told me what a fool I'd been, reminded me I knew we should be careful?

They didn't blame me. Or they didn't say so, anyway. I think they blamed themselves. But it was definitely not their fault. It had happened in a foreign country, after all, so what could they have done?

'Business or pleasure?' asked the fifty-something man beside me who wasn't dream of love material, more like someone's lecherous old uncle.

I could see he'd be an armrest wrangler, space invader, one of those who jabs you with his elbow now and then and makes you spill your coffee in your lap. Accidentally, of course – yeah, right. So he could dab at you with paper napkins and have a little feel of you as well. But at least he didn't smell revolting like some old men do.

'Pleasure, absolutely,' I replied. I plastered on my best

Madonna – Mother of God, not Michigan-born super-goddess – simpering semi-smile. 'I'm meeting my fiancé in Saint Paul. We'll be getting married this October.'

'Congratulations,' said Mr Lecherous Uncle. 'So what does your fiancé do and where will you be living – in the States or back in the UK? The ceremony – will it be a big event, in church, a country club, in your fiancé's folks' backyard?'

What is it with Americans? This man was acting as if we'd known each other all our lives. 'The ceremony will be small and private and that's all I can tell you,' I replied.

'Oh, I see. You're Miss Reserved.' Glancing at my hand, he grinned – he must have clocked the absence of a ring – and then picked up his *New York Times*. 'I love your accent, by the way. But if you're fixing to cut it in the States, you'll need to learn to chill a little, right?'

❖ PATRICK ❖

'You need to chill,' said Ben.

'You want to tell me why?'

'You're making something out of nothing, buddy boy. You and Lex, you need time out, that's all. Okay, she has a crush on some guy at the office. Let's call NBC. Pat, she's only telling you she needs a break, like women sometimes do.'

'Yeah, but with my children and some Limey bastard she picked up at Jackson Taylor. Some guy who wants to bring her home to Europe and take my children, too. This Mr Wonderful, he makes her come to life, apparently. She said he makes her fly.'

'She told you that?'

'She did.'

'She reads way too many of those women's magazines.' Ben put another beer in front of me, Japanese this time. 'She needs to take some literature classes, doesn't she?'

'So she can tell me that she's cheating on me in a fancy literary way?' I scowled at him. 'What is it with you and all these dumbshit foreign beers? What's wrong with the stuff they brew in Minneapolis?'

'Man, you need to live a little, beer-wise. Listen, Pat, if Lex talked with a lawyer, she'll know she can't take Poll and Joe out of the USA unless you agree to let them go.'

'I know, and I already told her that.'

'So what's the problem?' Now Ben was speaking in his best calm-down-you-crazy voice, the one I've heard him using on his cell a thousand times to women he's been screwing and to men he's double-crossed. 'Let Lex go play with this new guy. Let her move into his house and fix his dinner, dig his yard. The novelty of pulling weeds for him will soon wear off. She'll see the sense of coming back to you.'

'Lexie's not too great at seeing sense.'

'Then, my friend, you must move on yourself,' said Dr Fairfax PhD, world authority on Steinbeck, Scott Fitzgerald, Faulkner, all those guys, America's most famous living writer, amateur psychologist and by far the richest member of the teaching staff at John Quincy Adams University where we are both professors.

'You've been with Lex since high school,' he continued. 'Perhaps it's time you found somebody new. You should go play the field yourself.'

'I should punch the asshole on the jaw.'

'You know you won't do that. You don't punch anyone, not even me. Well, not since we were grown. You got a lawyer yet?'

'I'll see one Friday.'

'You should see one tomorrow. You need to give this top priority. I speak as one who knows.'

'Of course you do.' I glanced down at my watch and saw I must have had a whole ten minutes of his psychoanalytic time. 'Thank you for the counselling, Dr Freud. You'll bill me later, right?'

'Or you could buy me dinner?'

'I'll fix your laptop next time you mess up.'

'You couldn't fix my last one.'

'You poured your latte over it and it was dead before I even came there. You must have learned in science class – milk and electricity don't mix?'

'I'll know for next time, eh? I'll buy dinner, Pat. I had a royalty statement yesterday and boy was it a good one. Fifty thousand copies sold in hardback in the UK alone, and my agent's shifted Tamil, Georgian and Bulgarian rights as well.'

'Congratulations.'

'I can see you're thrilled.'

'Ben, I always knew you'd make it big.'

Benjamin Lincoln Fairfax. My oldest, closest friend, a kid who had been born in poverty and raised on welfare in Recovery, Missouri, who somehow won a scholarship to Yale and is the author of *Missouri Crossing*, the Great American Novel.

Or one of the Great American Novels, anyway.

Last time I heard, there had already been a few.

Although the book has done so well he doesn't need to work, he still fits in a couple days a week at JQA. I guess he'd miss the pretty female students if he quit. He's now on his third marriage, this time to a foreign woman he picked up while he was on vacation – pardon me, researching his next masterpiece – in Vegas. He doesn't take vacations, his life is one long quest for truth and beauty and he doesn't take time out. Or that's how he would put it, anyway.

They met in Dunkin' Donuts while they were fuelling up on cream cheese bagels and hot chocolate. The girl had been confused by our American funny money. She was trying to buy a single bagel with a hundred dollar bill. So, like the gentleman he always tries to be, Ben helped her out. He bought her bagel and her Dunkaccino, the pair of them got chatting and he noticed she was super-cute, with big dark eyes and long brown hair.

They spent three days in bed. Yeah, more research, Ben's real interested in foreign bodies, they're his specialty. Then they found a chapel and a preacher. Now he's getting all the action he could ever want, or so he says, and feeling very smug about it, too.

I can't see it lasting very long. But what would I know? When I married Lexie, I thought it was forever. When I made my vows, I meant them, every single word, and look how that turned out.

'I can't stay out long tonight,' said Ben, as we ate dinner.

'Mrs Fairfax Three is waiting, is she?'

'Yeah, and let me tell you, I have plans.'

'You mean you're fixing to become a daddy?'

'Get out of here,' he said, mopping up sauce. 'I can't stand kids, as you well know.'

'Why did you bother to get married, then? Why tie yourself to this new woman, after all that shit you took from Mrs Fairfax One and Two?'

'A man should have a wife. Where's the fun in fooling round if you're allowed to do it? You're a married man – you fool around – you feel a little guilty. You get a sense of sin and this adds something special to the pleasure.'

'Perhaps. I wouldn't know.'

'You bet you wouldn't know. When I have a little time to spare, we must take a vacation – just the two of us. I'll show you what you're missing.'

'Who's this girl who's coming to stay with you and Tess?' I asked him.

15

'Why do you want to know?'

'I don't, I'm merely making conversation. I'm also hoping to get you off the subjects of your sex life and all your foreign and translation rights.'

'You're asking if she's hot,' he said.

'I couldn't give a damn.'

'The suspense is killing you.'

'Yeah, it is – by boring me to death.'

'She's one of Tess's British friends, name's Rosie Dawson, Rosie Denton, or some name like that.'

'How long will she be staying?'

'You're interested, aren't you? You can't help yourself. She's planning on three weeks, maybe a month.' He winked at me and grinned. 'I've seen her Facebook albums and let me tell you, big boy, she's a little cutie pie.'

'You mean she looks fourteen?'

'No, I mean great figure, masses of black hair and big grey Bambi eyes. Why don't you come by the apartment, check her out? You could get lucky there. Give Lex something to think about as well – sauce for the goose?'

The look I gave him shut him up for fifteen seconds or maybe even twenty and I figured that had to be a record.

Then somebody called me on my cell.

☞ ROSIE ☜

I must admit that all the airport ground staff at Minneapolis-Saint Paul were absolutely charming and this was an agreeable surprise.

'Welcome to USA, ma'am,' said the guy who checked my alien's passport, stamped it with my date of entry into Paradise and gave it back to me with a big smile. 'You here on business or vacation?'

'On a little holiday,' I said.

'You have yourself a real good time.'

'I'll do my very best.'

I had no problem smiling back at him because he was so friendly. The last time I'd flown into LAX, the immigration people there had glared at me as if I was a terrorist axe murderer trying to get into California so I could cause the Big One and/or eat all the burgers in the state.

I made my way into Arrivals and there was my friend with her new husband, which I must say came as a relief because I was exhausted. My body clock was totally confused.

Tess was jigging up and down and waving like a cheerleader on speed. She was wearing emerald-green jeans, the Chloé top I'd sent her for her birthday back in March and the most enormous thrilled-to-see-you-Rosie grin.

He was a red-haired thirty-something guy in rimless glasses, almost handsome, over six feet tall, broad-shouldered and well-made. So – good face, good body, but whatever was he wearing? Good grief, he was a tartan-shirt-and-bright-blue-boot-cut-jeans fashion disaster. What could Tess be thinking, letting him go out looking like that? I supposed she had to be in love. But there are standards, aren't there?

'Rosie, hi!' Tess threw her arms around me, hugged me tight and then stood back to look at me. 'How are you doing, love?' she added, in the careful way that practically everybody spoke to me since Charlie—

I still find it hard to say the word.

'I'm very well,' I said, and then I thought, *I must work on my Amglish or nobody is going to understand me.* 'I mean I'm good. I'm doing great. I'm not sure of the time, of course. Hello, you must be Ben?'

'Yeah, I guess I must be.' He grinned and winked and shook my hand. 'I love your accent, Rosie.'

'Rosie's posh,' said Tess. 'She went to Cheltenham Ladies'

College and Cambridge University. She got a quarter blue in tiddlywinks.'

This obviously didn't mean a thing to Mr Tartan. 'Posh – I just adore that word,' he said. 'It's so British and ridiculous.' Then he glanced at my left hand and saw what I was holding. A red-and-green-striped apple, a James Grieve from my Granny Cassie's tree. 'You brought that foreign vegetable matter into the USA?'

'Oh – I meant to put it in the bin.'

'She means the trash,' said Tess.

'You'll probably suit orange.' Mr Tartan winked at me again and then began to stroll towards the exit, jangling a giant bunch of keys. Those jeans were flipping awful, so loose around the arse he looked like he was wearing Pampers, and I hoped for Tess's sake that this was not the case.

'Gorgeous luggage,' Tess said enviously, gazing at my shocking-pink-with-gold-tone-hardware bags. 'Where did you get it?'

'Guess?'

'Oh, I don't know – Aladdin's cave?'

'If you mean Fanny's office, yes. It's all Versace – see the tags? You can have it, if you like. I dare say I can get some more or something similar. Fanny's place is full of stuff and there are always new things coming in.'

'Thank you, Rosie, you're a mate!'

'You're welcome.'

'It makes me want to go on holiday. Bermuda, Rome, Capri ...'

'Or Bethnal Green? Tess, will you be coming home for Christmas?'

'Americans aren't big on Christmas holidays. They don't have Boxing Day or anything. So I don't know if Ben—'

'But if you're not working, you could come back for

Christmas, couldn't you? Your relations, they'll all want to see you?'

'Yeah, some of them might.' Tess shook her head and sighed, stopped walking, turned to look at me. 'Mum's still well hacked off because I didn't ask her to my wedding.'

'I can't say I'm surprised.'

'My brother reckons she's taken out a contract on me. If I show my face in the East End I'm going to wish I'd been stillborn. Mum had big plans for my big day, you see. Me in a meringue and limousine, my poor old dad hoiked out of his recliner and made to wear a topper, those awful wedding trousers and a pair of tails, and my nieces bundled up in turquoise polyester.'

'So you sort of ruined everything by getting hitched in Vegas three days after you met Mr Gorgeous?'

'I suppose.' Tess shrugged. 'Yesterday, my cousin rang to ask me when it's due.'

'So are you?'

'No, I'm not – or I don't think so, anyway.'

'Speaking for myself, I'd rather have a nice new handbag, Fendi or Armani preferably.'

'Yeah, me too. I mean, don't get me wrong, I'd like some children one day, just a couple. But I don't want any yet.'

'I don't want children ever.'

'You'll change your mind,' said Tess. 'Your eggs all have a sell-by date, you know. One day something will go click. You'll decide it's time and you'll go looking for the man who'll be the father of your children.'

'Does Ben have any pre-existing children?'

'He hasn't mentioned any.'

'Perhaps it slipped his mind?'

'I'll have to check his bank accounts and see what's coming in and going out. Rosie?'

'Yes?'

'Do you want to talk about it?'

'Why would I want to talk about Ben's bank accounts?'

'I meant Charlie – all that stuff?'

'No, thank you.'

'I hope you got some counselling or therapy?'

'I said I didn't want their counselling.'

'But it must have been an awful shock? Do you get nightmares?'

'Yes.'

'So maybe talking to a counsellor or therapist or even me or Ben would help a bit? I was reading something in a magazine, it was about bereavement and how people deal with it in different cultures and it said the British—'

'Tess, you haven't mentioned it to Ben? I asked you not to tell him. I can't deal with sympathy from strangers.'

'I haven't told him, Rosie.'

'No?'

'I haven't even hinted, cross my heart.'

She didn't add, and hope to die. She glanced towards her husband. 'I suppose we'd better make a move – his lordship's getting fidgety. Rosie, did you mean it about giving me the bags?'

'Of course I did.'

It was so lovely to see Tess again.

We'd only known each other for a year, but I felt I'd known her all my life. She and I could not have been more different if you're talking about background, social class and education. But we understood each other perfectly because in all the most important ways we were the same.

'It's hot out there,' she warned me as we reached the exit and I shrugged into my jacket. 'You won't need your coat.'

'Ninety degrees and counting,' added Ben. 'But let's look on the bright side. At least it isn't raining. It was wet in August which brought out the mosquitoes. Place was a malarial swamp. But the forecast this week's hot and dry. Maybe with a little patchy cloud and first thing in the morning there might be some light—'

'Rosie doesn't want to hear a weather forecast, Ben.'

'Of course she does, she's British.' Mr Tartan winked at me once more and made me want to ask if there was something in his eye? Or if all this winking was a twitch or nervous habit and he couldn't help it? 'What did your Dr Samuel Johnson say?' he added, grinning. 'When two British people meet, their first talk is always of the weather?'

'Yeah, all right,' said Tess. 'He's only showing off,' she muttered tartly. 'He does it all the time. He's always spouting literature and stuff. He even quotes some guy called Robert Frost at our Somali janitor. I mean, who's ever heard of Robert Frost?'

'I have,' I replied. 'He was an American poet, he won lots of prizes and his father's family came from Tiverton in Devon.'

'Well done, my clever phone-a-friend! I know you and Ben are going to get along just fine.'

I wondered if she'd read her husband's book.

✦ PATRICK ✦

It was Lexie calling to inform me what she wanted from me in the way of maintenance for Joe and Polly paid into her brand new bank account on the first day of every month. Then she added if I didn't like it that was just too bad. She had met with her attorney and she knew her rights.

The following day I called my own attorney.

He said unless I wanted to file for divorce in the immediate future, maybe I should cut my wife some slack, see how it all panned out. This British guy, he might be just a wild infatuation. Maybe Lex would realise she had made a big mistake. Maybe she would call to say she wanted to start over.

I figured he might have a point. Whatever had gone wrong with me and Lex, I didn't want to make things difficult between me and the kids.

So I didn't make any kind of scene when on the weekend Lexie, Joe and Polly and the British guy headed to Duluth to stay in a log cabin – or I should say a north-shore-timber-home-with-stone-tiled-bathrooms-panelled-den-and-luxury-wood-burning-stoves. Lexie kindly emailed me the link – on Lake Superior. They were going fishing, swimming, hunting, biking, rafting, hiking and a bunch of other outdoor stuff all in two days. The forecast was still set to heatwave. So I hoped they packed the Factor 50 or whatever, otherwise the kids were set to fry.

When they left, Joe was beyond excited and Lexie said this was because it would be such a novelty for him to go do boy stuff with a guy who actually liked kids, not one who merely tolerated them.

I hoped the Limey bastard couldn't swim. But I guessed the chances were he'd swim as good as any catfish, any mucus-covered bottom-feeder. He was surely bound to do so, coming from a country that's surrounded by the ocean and is full of lakes and rivers, as I seem to remember from studying the geography of Europe while I was in high school. All British people probably had fins.

After Lexie, Joe and Poll were gone, I walked round the apartment. It was far too quiet, like somebody was sick.

I went into our bedroom. It was a shit-awful mess – drawers pulled open, clothes thrown everywhere as Lexie packed her things. I put some of the stuff back in the closets and straightened up the bed.

Then I went into the children's rooms.

Polly's was a riot of pink – pink drapes, pink comforter, pink rug and pink stuffed toys with big sad eyes. It smelled of baby girl. A mix of powder, wipes and something sweet like cotton candy.

Baby girl – I still thought of Polly as a baby, even though she would be three next birthday and was walking, talking, eating anything and everything except the additive-free toddler dinners Lexie bought at great expense from some weird organic-vegan-wholefood store downtown. I held her pillow to my chest, inhaling her sweet scent and almost able to believe it was my Polly in my arms, her little roly-poly body squirming as she struggled to get down to crayon on the walls or go annoy the hamster.

That reminded me – I better not forget to feed Joe's hamster. My son would kill me slowly if The Terminator died. But I was sure the rodent would remind me when it was time to make with the banana and zucchini. Come sundown, I would hear it running on its little wheel and fussing in its cage.

Joe's room smelled of popcorn, schoolbooks, sneakers and it was a shrine to Angry Birds. There was a red backpack, ditto lunch box, ditto flip-flops and a new black hoodie which made him look like some teen hoodlum's behaviourally-challenged little brother. A dedicated follower of fashion – that was Joe. I gave his Red Bird squeeze pillow a hug and felt myself well up.

Where was his red messenger bag we bought last Saturday while we were at the mall? He must have it with him. So it was on the lake shore now with Mr Wonderful. Joe and Mr Wonderful were filling it with rocks and sticks and ring-pulls and a ton of other treasure/trash.

I shut my eyes. I wished my wife and kids were home. I wished it was a lazy Sunday morning when nobody was rushing to get up, head out to work or go to school. I wished

Lex and I were still in bed with both the kids rampaging round the room, Polly trailing her wet diaper, Joe on Lexie's phone shooting at pigs and shouting out his score – and with me not yelling *go away! What does a person have to do to get some sleep round here?*

I offered God a deal.

If he would let me keep my kids, I'd be a better father.

I realised I'd messed up with Joe and Polly. I'd assumed it was enough I'd never been like Dad, who'd used me as punchbag, beat up on me, broken my bones and put me in the hospital. Who'd been too fond of bourbon and had cheated on my mother with a score of trashy blondes, leaving us when I was twelve to go down south, where in due course he ended up in jail where he belonged.

Then Mom worked at half a dozen different jobs so I could go to college, even though I told her I didn't want or need to go to college. I would be a construction worker – plaster walls, pour concrete, mix cement. I would service trucks in a garage. But she was so determined I would make professor in some university that my choice was be a college student or break my mother's heart.

So from this moment on, I told myself, I'd play with Joe and Polly. I'd take them to the park and to the diner and to the museum for children in downtown Saint Paul. I'd push Polly in her bright pink stroller, even though I know she's far too big to have a stroller and she ought to take more exercise. Otherwise she'll end up looking like Miss Piggy's child.

So now and then I would forget the stroller. Polly has to realise she can walk and then she has to do it because it's not an option. She can't be the only kid in high school still demanding to be carried everywhere. I'd take my baby girl to baby gym. I'd get her pumping iron.

As for Joe – I'd answer all his everlasting questions. I'd tell him why the sky is blue, why mommy hens lay eggs, why bugs have great big eyes, why red-brown cows don't give us red-brown milk. I'd play Angry Birds with him and always let him win.

I'd never, ever yell at them again.

I would have a heart-to-heart with Lexie. We would buy a house, a big old house out on the prairie with some land, and she could have her garden, and if she wanted we would have more kids. We'd even have some horses.

How would we afford it?

We'd get by.

Then my cell was ringing and I thought my prayer was answered – blame a Catholic childhood – but it wasn't Joe. It wasn't Lexie saying she was sorry, she had got it wrong, that she'd dumped Mr Wonderful and they were homeward bound.

It was Ben and he was asking me to join him and the British bride and bride's best friend for dinner. I didn't want anything to do with anybody British. 'I'm busy,' I replied.

'Yeah, sure you're busy – watching some hot movie? Or reading Lexie's *Fifty Shades* and picking up some pointers for when she's home again?'

'I'm finishing my grading.'

'No kidding, buddy boy. You're always grading. You're so conscientious with your students it makes me want to piss into your shoes. But listen, did you eat yet? If you didn't, you could come eat here. Let me tell you, something smells delicious.'

'Why, what are you cooking?'

'I'm not cooking anything, Professor. I have Tess and Rosie – she's the girlfriend – waiting on me hand and foot. So right now everything's as nice as ninepence.'

'Pardon me?'

'It's a charming Old World saying dating back to when our British cousins hadn't figured out the use of decimals, when they still had a mediaeval form of currency. Last time I passed the kitchen, T and R were fixing meatloaf, sweet potatoes, collard greens, and I believe there's home-made New York cheesecake for dessert.'

'Your foreign wife, she knows to fix all that?'

'She learns very fast, mate – that's another Britishism – in all sorts of interesting ways. So we'll see you in twenty?'

I realised I was very hungry. I hadn't eaten since the morning and now it was past seven. 'Okay, if you insist.'

'I do, and by the way, Professor, you should do some work on your neuroses. If ever any guy was an obsessive and compulsive grader – man, that guy is you.'

⌦ ROSIE ⌫

I'd heard all about Ben's book, of course. I'd even bought a copy of it when it was on special offer in my local bookshop back in the UK. But I hadn't read it.

Since Charlie's death I'd not read anything except my emails and of course the fashion and the other women's magazines. I had to stay on top of bags and boots and frocks and shoes because it was my job to keep my fingers firmly on the pulse of fashion and to be aware of what was trending.

But now I'd met the author I decided I ought to read his work. I should try to get a handle on this guy who'd married Tess, a girl who probably hadn't read a novel since she was sixteen and still at school, and had been forced to do so then.

There was a bookcase in the living room containing half a dozen copies of Ben's first collection of short stories which had won some prizes and made him a slight literary sensation on both sides of the Atlantic, but had bombed commercially. There were also three whole shelves of various editions of his über-super-duper-worldwide-knockout bestseller *Missouri Crossing* in two dozen languages or more. So, if I had wanted, I could have had a go at learning Portuguese, Swahili or Malay.

I'd read it first in English, I decided. I'd find out if it was as wonderful as everybody – publishers, reviewers and ordinary readers – seemed to think. A man might be a fashion tragedy, but this didn't have to mean he couldn't write a novel.

'You didn't waste a lot of time,' I said, as I made – I had to learn to say I fixed – some coffee for us both in Tess's huge and gorgeous kitchen which was lit by three big chandeliers and even had a wine room leading off it – temperature-controlled, naturally.

The sink was big enough to bath a toddler and a Labrador together. As well as ordinary mixer taps, there were special ones from which you got your water iced. Or – conversely – boiling. It took me quite a while to realise I didn't need a kettle. This was just as well because there wasn't one.

'How did you know you'd be compatible?' I added as I fiddled with the coffee-maker. This was the most complicated model I had ever seen. Ben had bought it. He was into gadgets, obviously. The place was full of them.

'We ran some tests, of course.' Tess was busy making dinner with the basic stuff we'd bought from Target and some speciality stores in downtown Minneapolis earlier that day. She said she had to make some effort because there could be company tonight. Ben had said he might invite a friend. So I didn't count as company? I let it pass.

'Compatibility,' I prompted.

'We did the inkblot stuff.'

'What do you mean – the inkblot stuff?'

'It's sort of like the Tarot but it's more scientific.' Tess looked at me and frowned. 'I thought you went to university?'

'I read Modern Languages, not inkblotology.'

'Okay, you have these cards with different patterns on

them, like those butterfly designs we made when we were little, blobbing paint on paper and folding it in half, you know?'

'I know.'

'So then you look at them and tell the other person what you see. They reveal all sorts of stuff about your personality, your hopes, your fears, your dreams. I don't remember much of what Ben said because he was distracting me. When I have some time I'll go online and find out more. It's probably on Wikipedia.'

She rinsed the collard greens in the enormous granite sink. 'I'll do it when we come back from the mall. After we get up tomorrow morning we're going to the mall.'

'I've been to malls before.'

'You haven't been to this one. It's the Hollywood of the Midwest and it's a total blast. You'll never look at Oxford Street in the same way again. You're going to think you've died and gone to heaven in a golden BMW. Or I did, anyway.'

'I see.'

'You don't, at least not yet.' Tess put down her saucepan and then she grinned at me. 'Actually, I'd like a golden BMW. My Toyota's – it was very nice of Ben to buy me the Toyota – my Toyota's sweet. But if I did that dirty thing he's always going on at me to do in bed but I don't fancy doing, I wonder if I'd get a BMW as well?'

'There's only one way to find out.' I poured the coffee. 'You and Ben, you're not the likeliest of couples, are you – despite the inkblot stuff?'

'What's that supposed to mean?'

'Well, he's a famous novelist, but you're—'

'I'm stupid and he's smart?'

'No, don't be so daft, you're far from stupid, and you know it. All the same, you're not an academic, and I would have thought perhaps ...'

'But it's not like you think,' said Tess. 'We have a lot in common. He grew up in a trailer park where almost everybody was on drugs or in and out of prison all the time. I grew up in a concrete rat-hole of a council flat in Bethnal Green. Ben's brothers are all misfits. My brothers were all born to thieve. Ben's father was disabled in an accident at work and so was Dad when a big lorry wrecked his market stall. The family lived on welfare, just like mine.'

'Oh, right.'

'He's had it hard, you know.' Tess started peeling sweet potatoes. 'Poor white trash, that's what he says they called him when he went to Yale on a scholarship, and he still thinks meatloaf is the height of gracious living, even though he could afford to buy the weight of that one we've been making in Beluga caviar. As for me and him and our relationship – he's experimenting, isn't he? He's trying something new and so am I.'

'So you're not in love with him?'

'Do me a favour, mate? I like him lots. I really do. He's clever and he's generous and he's fun. You'd have to walk a million miles to find a man who's half as good at concentrating on a girl, who makes her feel like she's the only woman in the world – well, at that moment, anyway. When we were in Las Vegas, it was beyond fantastic. But all the time he was with me, he was eyeing up the local babes. I know he has some playmates here in Minneapolis-Saint Paul. I've often heard him on his mobile, whispering and laughing.'

'What if he was talking to a student or his agent?'

'I doubt if he would tell a student or his agent she's got the cutest ass in the Twin Cities.' Tess put down her peeler. 'Or perhaps he might? You can't be sure with Ben. He's shit with boundaries. He couldn't do political correctness if he tried.'

'Well, there you are, then.'

'Yes, but all the same, I know the score.' Tess looked at

me and shrugged. 'I'm Mrs Fairfax Three – yeah, that's what he calls me – and I bet he'll get to Mrs Fairfax Six or maybe even Mrs Fairfax Seven before he calls time out. I've already stashed my diamonds in the bank against a rainy day.'

'He's given you some diamonds?'

'Just a few.'

'But they're nice big fat ones, are they – genuine girl's-best-friends?'

'Yeah, I suppose.'

'Why don't you wear them?'

'I couldn't wear a great big diamond, Rosie. It wouldn't be my style. They're staying in the bank.'

'How long are you thinking this will last?'

'Maybe five, six years?'

'What if you caught him cheating on you now?'

'What, like in bed with someone else? I might have to take some form of action scissor-wise, make my displeasure felt, know what I mean? I don't mind him flirting. But he's not allowed to play away until I give him my permission, until I don't want him any more.'

'What about the babies?'

'Did we mention any babies?'

'Yes, the ones you told me you might have – eggs past their sell-by date and all that stuff?'

'I haven't made my mind up yet. But I don't think he's very keen on children, actually. They might mess with his gadgets. So—'

'Tess, I think your meatloaf might be burning.'

'Oh, shit – I think you're right.' She yanked open the door of the enormous range-style cooker and then pulled out the smoking, blackened pan which now contained a Bible-style burnt offering.

'Well done, Rosie, just in time.' She dumped the pan down on the kitchen counter. 'Blast, I've burnt off half my thumb,' she cried. 'I hate this cooking lark! I'm no domestic goddess, growing my own ruddy basil, making sausages from guts and lungs. If I cut the top off this disaster, do you reckon it will do?'

'Give me a knife and get a plaster for your thumb. Let's see – if I just tidy this side here?' I scraped away some charcoal then stood back from the blackened lump. 'It doesn't look too bad. Maybe I should turn it upside down? Do you think it will be enough for four? Ben's friend, he's definitely coming, is he?'

'Yeah, so it would seem.'

'You going to tell me anything about him?'

'There's nothing much to say. He's called Patrick Riley and does something with computers. Ben says Pat's a tedious number cruncher and couldn't be more boring if he tried.'

'What's he like?'

'You mean in looks or personality?'

'I mean in both.'

'He's tallish, darkish, thirty-fiveish, and – like Ben says – boring. Or, if we're being charitable, intense. He doesn't have a lot to say to me. Apart from *hi, how are you doing*, I don't think he speaks to me at all. Whenever he comes here to the apartment it's to talk to Ben.'

'How does he know Ben?'

'He's from Recovery, Missouri, too. They lived in the same neighbourhood. But Pat lived in a house, not in a trailer, so maybe he was class while Ben was trash? Anyway, they went to school together in some sagebrush swamp. After they grew up they kept in touch and now they teach at the same university.'

'Sagebrush grows in deserts, not in swamps.'

'How do you know that?'

'I went to Cambridge University and got a quarter blue in tiddlywinks.'

'Of course you did. Anyway, as I was telling you, Recovery is one of those dull, nothing-ever-happens little towns where people have to drink cheap alcohol, beat up their wives or shoot each other dead for entertainment. There's damn all else to do. So Ben says, anyway.'

'It sounds like Royal Tunbridge Wells.'

'Yeah, when he talks about Recovery, I am immediately reminded of Royal Tunbridge Wells.' Tess began to fiddle with her home-made New York cheesecake which she'd knocked up from a packet mix and was trying to home-make a bit more by sticking candied lemon slices – which had never been near any lemon – all round the perimeter. 'Did we remember to buy a can of ready-whipped?'

'Yes, it's in the fridge. Or do I mean the icebox?'

'No, you mean the fridge. Americans have fridges now, an icebox is a cooler.' Tess took out the aerosol of cream. 'Okay, rosettes or swirls, what do you think? I told Ben we'd be making stuff from scratch. This needs to look like I made it myself.'

'I'd go for rosettes, then. But don't do them yet. This sort of cream collapses in a puddle five minutes after squirting. I think I heard the doorbell – shall I get it?'

'Please, if you don't mind. I need to make the gravy and turn the sweet potatoes. They're catching just a bit. They always do.'

'You could blame the oven.'

'Yeah, I might.'

I walked off down the passage. What had Tess just said about this guy – that he worked with computers? I supposed that meant he was a geek.

He'd most probably be stooped, round-shouldered from crouching over keyboards endlessly, and either very fat or very thin, all lard or all raw bones. He'd have lots of dandruff and possibly some personal hygiene issues. He'd wear glasses fixed with sticking plaster, badly-fitting jeans, a cheap acrylic sweater …

I unlocked the front door. I opened it and found that I was gazing into the dark brown eyes of the most attractive man I'd seen for years and years.

'Hi,' he began. 'You must be Rosie?'

➤ PATRICK ➤

The dark-haired girl who smelled of something flowery and expensive looked at me like I was something nasty on her shoe.

'Yes, I'm Rosie, and you must be Patrick?' she replied, in a voice that sounded like she should be in a vintage British movie or an episode of *Downton Abbey*, my mother's favourite show. She managed a half smile, like she was a titled lady condescending to a dirty peasant and not liking anything about the situation. 'Tess and I are busy in the kitchen,' she continued. 'Ben is working in the den.'

Okay, I thought, I get it. The famous British courtesy, the elegance of manner which means a British person can be polite and charming while privately deciding you're a jerk and somehow making sure you know it, too …

I headed down the passage to the den where Ben was – working?

You could have had me fooled. I found him lounging like a sultan in his new recliner, watching television and cheering on the Minnesota Twins. A beer in his hand and a half dozen in the pack beside him, he was smug as a raccoon who found a whole roast chicken in the trash.

'What do you think?' he asked me.

'What do I think of what?'

'Our transatlantic friend, of course.' He grinned at me. 'Tess says she went to Cambridge – that's Cambridge

University in England. She's a French and German major. So she must be pretty smart?'

'I guess.'

'She's quite a doll, as well. Great legs, great ass, great hair, and brains and beauty are always a good mix, don't you agree? I can't abide a woman who's all packaging.'

I shrugged.

'Once in a while, she's a little on the sharp side. So maybe there's a squeeze of lemon in her personality? Yeah, I guess there must be. She's mysterious, as well. She doesn't give a man too many clues. Does she like him? Does she wish he'd go jump from a plane without a parachute? Does not knowing what a woman's thinking add to her attraction? Yes, if the woman's cute.'

'I'll take your word for it.'

'You should, because you're talking with an expert. There's a little blonde at JQA, she works in the main library, looks after all the periodicals for the humanities. She's got a viper's tongue, spits like a cat. A guy would need a pair of tongs and goggles before he messed with Coralie. But I'm kind of picking up some signals and I'm pretty sure she's hot for me. She's always—'

'Dinner's on the table, guys!' called Tess.

'She's always none of your concern. You're a married man – did you forget? Redheads, blondes, brunettes and all the other colour permutations, they're off limits nowadays.'

'You missed your vocation, Father Riley.' Ben stood up and stretched. 'Okay, let's go eat.'

'Tess tells me you're at JQA?' said Rosie as she poured a pint of gravy all over her meatloaf, sweet potatoes, collard greens, turning the whole plateful into a disgusting, dark brown mess. The gravy had been made with something Tess gets in the mail, apparently, along with other weird British groceries like Marmite and Maltesers and some stuff called PG Tips, whatever they might be.

'Yes, I'm a professor of IT.'

'My goodness, that's impressive. What exactly do you do?'

'I teach, I lecture, I write scientific papers, I do some outreach work in the community and help develop various kinds of software.'

'You must be very busy.' Rosie started on her meatloaf. 'I do hope you'll tell me more some time?'

Yeah, I thought, *why don't we make a date?*

'What do you do, Rosie?'

'I work in promotions and PR.' It sounded kind of strange the way she said it – *promotions and pay ah* – but kind of cute as well.

'So are you with a global corporation, smaller outfit, working for yourself?'

'I worked for other people until recently. But when I get home again, I'm going to be setting up in business on my own.'

'Fanny won't like that,' said Tess.

'Fanny's going to have to lump it, then. She won't mind, actually. She knows there's heaps of work for both of us.'

Rosie took more greens and sweet potatoes then drowned them in more gravy. It looked gross. Yeah, I know British people love their gravy. I saw a movie one time about a British family on Christmas. It seemed they couldn't get enough of it.

I'd have used the stuff to varnish doors ...

She won't mind, actually.

I always think of sounds in terms of images and tastes and scents and touch, as well as mere vibrations – either pleasing or unpleasing – in the air. Rosie's voice was warm as soft black velvet and made me think of jasmine-scented nights. When she spoke it sounded like somebody was pouring very slowly and seductively from a gallon jug of fresh, sweet cream. I could almost taste the cream, could almost see the matt-but-also-somehow-glossy liquid coiling in a bowl, where it left a momentary trail before becoming part of a smooth pool …

'Tess and Rosie, do you think you could include us in this conversation?' Ben demanded as Rosie talked some more about her PR and promotion plans. Meaning, obviously, talk to him. Or, better yet, listen to him, and speak only when he speaks to you. 'Pat, your glass is empty. What will you have to drink? What about this Napa Valley Merlot? Or will you stick with beer?' He snuck a glance at me. 'I'm sorry, but we're out of gasoline.'

'I'll stick with beer,' I told him. Did he have to mention gasoline, drag all that childhood business up again? Yeah, I guess he did.

He was clearly mad at Rosie. But, since she was company, he took it out on me. *Well, screw you all the way to New York City, you self-important bastard,* I didn't need to say because he would have read it in my eyes.

'Sorry, Ben,' said Rosie insincerely – attagirl – as she ate more meatloaf. 'So anyway, I thought I'd start off small. I'll rent an office somewhere cheap like Camden.'

'Camden isn't cheap,' said Tess.

'It is compared to the West End and all those little streets round Marble Arch.' Rosie speared a cube of sweet potato and then she went on talking with her mouth full, something I would never do because my mother raised me to have manners.

Rosie's mother evidently did not.

'I'm not going after Fanny's high-end clients, Tess,' she added, as she waved her silverware around. 'I'll be starting with the smaller fry, all the little people and sole traders who need my help to sell their stuff and services in these straitened economic times. I'm going to show them how to make a living. The company's called Rosie Sorts Your Life. I chose the name because that's what I'll do – sort people's lives.'

'Maybe you should be a little more specific, Rosie, and say you'll sort their working lives? It's not as if you're offering counselling on personal issues,' said Ben sarcastically. 'Or am I making false assumptions here, and will massage and nail art be included?'

'I'll encourage all my clients to achieve a proper work-life balance,' Rosie told him, looking straight at Tess.

'Balance, moderation – yeah, that's what it's all about,' said Tess. 'It's definitely what you need in life, in work, in shopping, everything. I read about it in a magazine.'

'Shopping, yes – you balance what you need with what you absolutely have to have or go into a terminal decline,' continued Rosie calmly. 'Or you drink a million full fat lattes and turn into a whale, because that frock called out to you and you ignored its cries.'

Then she turned to smile at Ben just like she was the hostess of this party. 'But I think that's enough of me,' she said. 'What are you writing at the moment? A sequel to *Missouri Crossing*, yes? Or something less sensational? Less – what do they call that section in a UK bookshop – Painful Lives?'

This girl, was she for real?

Ben opened his mouth but didn't get a chance to speak. 'Darling, I think everybody's finished. So could you be a love and fetch the cheesecake while I collect the dinner plates?' asked Tess, and he was so surprised he did just that, muttering something to himself as he walked out the door.

☞ ROSIE ☜

When I'd opened the front door to Pat, he hadn't seemed to find the sight of me at all appealing. Why do I say that? He hadn't smiled, he hadn't introduced himself and he hadn't offered me his hand. He'd merely looked at me and then, a couple of seconds later, he'd managed to say *hi, you must be Rosie?*

I didn't say *hi, you must be the geek?*

Yes, he was good-looking, albeit in a serious sort of way. But looks aren't everything and I had bet myself a penny to a pound this wasn't going to be a fun-packed evening.

It's always most annoying, isn't it, when you're in a social situation and you can't work out what's going on? Ben and Pat were friends. They'd grown up together in Recovery, Missouri, Tess had told me, hadn't she – in some sagebrush swamp or other geographical impossibility?

They'd been to the same school. They'd both done well. They must have done extremely well. They must have been a pair of very clever and determined children to have found their way out of that labyrinth of expectation, hadn't lived the lives mapped out for them, did not exist on welfare, beat or shoot their wives or drink themselves to death on bourbon, moonshine or whatever.

Ben had got a scholarship to Yale, which must have been almost unprecedented for a boy who'd grown up in a trailer park. I'd seen those places when I'd been a student backpacker, travelling half asleep on Greyhound buses, driving past depressing, endless trailer cities full of sad, defeated-looking people and dumpster-diving children, townships which had looked like hell on earth.

Abandon hope all ye who enter here.

As for Pat, he must have gone to MIT or Harvard, mustn't he, to be a professor at what was he – thirty, thirty-five? What was all that stuff about the gasoline? It must have been some sort of private joke? But it wasn't funny – not to Pat, at any rate. When Ben had mentioned gasoline, Pat's brown eyes had narrowed and for just one second I'd thought he might get up and walk straight out.

But instead he'd pulled the tab and poured himself a beer, drinking it reflectively and once in a while glancing at me. As if I was something in a zoo. As if he wondered if I could be real and did I bite?

'Patrick, would you like home-made dessert?' asked Ben. As he put Tess's cheesecake on the table, he was almost spitting out the words.

'Thank you,' Pat replied politely. But there was a sharpness in his voice which had not been there before Ben mentioned gasoline.

'The girls made this vanilla cheesecake specially for us,' Ben added. 'Or they went to Target and bought the packet mix – *just add butter and two cups of milk* – in any case. Ladies, you forgot to put the carton in the trash.'

'You styled the finished product with these carefully-positioned lemon slices?' Patrick Riley looked at Tess, then me. 'You individualised the basic concept, right?'

'Yes, of course,' said Tess.

'We might have used a packet mix,' I added. 'But the positioning of the lemon slices always makes or breaks a cheesecake, wouldn't you agree, Professor Riley?'

'Yes, I would.' Pat turned to Ben and shrugged expressively. 'So I guess to call this cheesecake home-made is no lie?'

✦ PATRICK ✦

I hadn't wanted to come by here for dinner. But, as time went on, I found that I was kind of having fun. It was a big novelty, watching such a young and pretty woman *not* making eyes at Ben, *not* listening to every word he said, being in his company yet daring to talk about herself.

But you don't keep Ben Fairfax down for long.

After sulking while we ate dessert, he started up again. It was all about himself, of course. But while he talked she didn't gaze at him in adoration like most women do. She looked at him like I'd look at a wasp, like she wished he'd go away and bother someone else. Or shut up bragging, anyhow.

When he said his agent was negotiating movie options for *Missouri Crossing*, and that Fox was head to head with Miramax, Rosie didn't gasp and say *how wonderful! When would it be at the multiplex? She couldn't wait!* She asked if Ben was going to write the screenplay. Or did he think it might be better left to a professional?

'I could write the screenplay, Rosie,' he said acidly. 'After all, it is my story. I know all my characters through and through and character is story, as I'm sure you would agree?'

'All the same, I've heard it's difficult to write a screenplay. You would probably need to take some lessons in technique.'

She just told Ben he'd need some lessons in technique? She lived? It seemed she did. As we ate second helpings of dessert – the cheesecake made with packet mix, my mother used the same variety, I knew the taste from childhood when a slice of ersatz cheesecake was a treat – I happened to look up and catch her eye.

She smiled at me. I saw her teeth were very white. They were also very even, save for those two at the front. One was slightly crooked and leaned against its neighbour. This was appealing, somehow. Sexy, even – it kind of promised something. I should not be thinking girls looked sexy. It was the sort of thing Ben Fairfax did. He never lost an opportunity to assess a woman's sexiness or otherwise, to mark her out of ten.

Rosie scored a perfect ten, so—

Why was I bothering to think this kind of thing? My personal life was shit. I was about to lose my children. My wife was fooling round and cheating on me like she had the right, like it was all my fault. Getting a divorce was going to be so damned expensive, not to mention break my mother's heart.

But sitting at the table across from Rosie, I felt kind of happy. More than happy, I felt joyful, light of heart. Rosie made me glad.

☞ ROSIE ☜

This isn't really happening, I thought, as we said our goodbyes.

As Patrick thanked us for a pleasant evening, sounding like he meant it, as he shook my hand and said he hoped we'd meet again, I swear he held my gaze for several seconds longer than he needed, and I know I blushed.

What did he mean, he hoped we'd meet again – was he merely being polite to me? Or was he going to try to make it happen?

I shouldn't even think about it happening.

Yes, of course I longed to fall in love. It was on my list of things to do when I got back to the UK. Get my hair cut, get my eyebrows threaded, see my dentist for a six month check-up, renew my car insurance, fall in love. But there's a time and place for everything, and at this particular point in time I didn't need any further complications in my life. I was on sabbatical from love, from life, from fun – from everything.

'I'll see you off the premises,' said Ben, practically pushing Patrick out of the front door. 'But, before you go, come down to the garage and check out my new baby?'

'Yes, okay,' said Pat.

Tess and I cleared up the mess. We loaded up the dishwasher with the first of half a million pots and pans and dishes and started on the silverware and other stuff we had to wash by hand.

Ben wasn't helping. When he came back from showing Pat his baby, he stomped off to his den and slammed the door.

Tess said just to leave him. He was sulking like a moose with antler-ache because we hadn't paid enough attention to his rambling on. This was something authors often did – sulked if no one listened while they talked about their writing. It was down to the artistic temperament. She'd read about it in a magazine. When we went to the mall tomorrow, she was going see she burned his plastic good and proper.

'That'll teach him to be foul,' she said.

I asked why Patrick had seemed a little grumpy when we'd first started dinner.

'He's having problems with his wife,' said Tess.

'Oh – he's married, is he? Tess, you might have warned me.' I dumped a pile of dishes – some silver-banded stuff I thought we ought to wash by hand because the dishwasher would ruin it – in the enormous sink. 'I could have put my foot right in it.'

'I don't think so, Rosie. Your middle name is tact.'

'What's been happening, then?'

'Why do you want to know?'

'I'm only making conversation. We'll talk about the weather if you like.'

'Mrs Riley told him she wants to take their children and go travelling round the world with some British man she met at work. She's a PA, secretary, clerk or something in a multinational that has its US offices downtown.'

'What's she like, this wife?'

'I've only seen her once. We met one afternoon in Barnes and Noble in Minneapolis. Ben was checking out his books and chatting up the shop assistants, asking if they had enough signed copies – authors do that sort of stuff – and so he introduced us.'

'Well?'

'Do you think we should save this bit of meatloaf? Or chuck it in the bin?'

'I'd chuck it in the bin. Tess, you were telling me about Professor Riley's wife?'

'Why are you so bothered about Pat Riley's wife?'

'I'm not bothered, Tess. But you have this irritating habit of starting on a subject then grasshoppering away again.'

'She's just a woman – shortish, cuteish, with natural blondish hair. No prettier than you or me and she'll be dumpy when she's middle-aged. She's got that sort of figure. So she'll always need to diet, exercise, or she'll run to fat. She smiled. She said it was good to meet me and how was I doing? She didn't look like a cow.'

Ben reckoned Pat was broken-hearted, added Tess.

But when he'd looked at me while we were eating cheesecake, I could have sworn I saw amusement in his eyes.

'What's your verdict, then?' asked Tess, as she put the knives and forks and spoons into their purple velvet nests in the big mahogany canteen – a wedding present to Mrs Fairfax Two, apparently. But she hadn't taken it when she and Ben split up. So now it was the property of Mrs Fairfax Three for the duration. 'Professor Riley, Rosie – nice arse, nice face, nice eyes, nice hair, nice everything, in fact?'

'I didn't really notice.'

'Ooh – you did, you liar. I watched you noticing!'

'Tess, he's just a man.'

'You smiled at him as well.'

'I was being polite and British, wasn't I? I always smile at people I meet socially, ask them what they do and all that stuff. It's the way my mother brought me up.'

'Yeah, you do tend to act like Lady Muck from *Downtown Minster* or whatever it's called. You're well embarrassing. But you thought he was attractive, didn't you? You thought he was hot?'

Tess turned from her forks and grinned at me. 'Okay, he doesn't have a lot to say. But we must make allowances. He's been best mates with Mr Gobby Fairfax all his life and Ben can talk enough for both of them.'

As she rattled on, I thought – yes, Pat Riley's arse was very nice. I'd noticed as he left. He had nice eyes as well. Dark and heavy-lashed, they looked like they could smoulder and anyone who crossed him should watch out. As for his hair – jet-black and plumb line straight, he could have had a better cut and style. But it was not receding and it wasn't greying yet.

'He's married,' I reminded Tess.

'His wife's playing away.' She giggled. 'You could get in there while Mrs Riley's being bad and have yourself a little bit of fun.'

'I don't steal other women's men.'

'You wouldn't have to steal him, he's up for grabs. But don't take ages making up your mind. Guys like that don't hang around for long. Co-eds tend to notice when their professor's lonely and they move in fast. Or that's what Ben says, anyway.'

'Ben should know.'

'Well, yeah,' said Tess and sighed. 'I'm sure he does. Ben knows everything. I guess I'd better go and keep him company, that's if I want an upgrade on my ride.'

I found Professor Riley was somewhat in my thoughts, even though he was way out of bounds.

Off limits, as they say.

So, to take my mind off him, I got out my laptop to email Granny Cassie. I often emailed Mum and Dad, of course, two or three times a week. But it was somehow easier to email Granny Cassie. So I sent her a message every day. At ninety, she was probably the oldest iPad user in the world. Or one of the oldest iPad users, anyway.

Hi Granny Cassie
How are you? I hope you're keeping well? Did
you get those new splints and do they help?
Do you think you'll have those operations on
your hands? What does the doctor say?

Tess is spoiling me. She's feeding me with
lots of good home cooking. I'm sure I must
have put on half a stone. I don't dare weigh
myself!

Ben, that's Tess's husband, is quite nice.
He's young and handsome, too. But you mustn't
worry. I'm not going to steal him. He's
absolutely not my type. He thinks he's it, as
you would say.

What shall I bring you from America? They
have some gorgeous dressing gowns in a shop
in Minneapolis. They're very light in weight.
The dressing gowns, I mean. A cherry-red one,
Granny – do you fancy that?

Please say hello to Mum and Dad for me and
tell them I'll be writing real soon, as they
say over here.

Lots of love from Rosie XXX

As I clicked send, I told myself I ought to write to Mum and
Dad tonight. But it was hard to write to them – so hard. I
didn't know what to say and so I waffled endlessly. Or I was
terse and curt with them, and this was just as bad.

FROM: Rosie Denham
SUBJECT: USA
TO: J & W Denham
SENT: 7 September 23:27

Hi Mum and Dad
I hope you're well. I'm having a good time in
the Twin Cities. I'm going to buy Granny a
new dressing gown. What can I get for you?

Rosie XXX

Of course my parents were not well. Of course I wasn't
having a good time. I wouldn't dare. Of course they didn't
want me to bring them souvenirs.

They wanted Charlie back.

When they replied the following day, they told me nothing.
Dad made a few remarks about the golf club, how he was
treasurer again this year and how some of the fairways were
in an awful state. Mum said she was visiting the hospice
every Tuesday and also trying to do something for the young
offenders who were up before the courts repeatedly. But there
was nothing personal. They never mentioned Charlie.

They must hate me, mustn't they, just for being alive?

❖ PATRICK ❖

I slept way better than I had expected and I was almost happy
when I woke on Sunday morning. But it was the fuzzy, half-
conscious, half-unconscious happiness you sometimes feel
when you're just half-awake, before reality kicks in and you
remember everything is not exactly perfect in your world.

I didn't know what I would say to Lex. But I was looking
forward to seeing Joe and Polly. I still planned on being a

better father to my children, even if I couldn't be Lexie's husband any more.

Or perhaps I could?

As I fixed my cereal I was thinking maybe we could take a short vacation, just the two of us? If my mother came to watch the children, if we had some time alone together, surely we could work things out?

As for the British guy – I would delete him from the hard drive of my mind. I would forget he'd mauled my wife. On this sunny morning, I was confident – or almost confident – it could be done.

After I ate breakfast I headed out and bought ground beef, passata, garlic, penne so we could eat Italian when my family came home. I tidied the apartment, put clothes away in closets and magazines in piles – Lex always fussed about my magazines – and took a sack of garbage to the dumpster.

At six on Sunday evening Mr Wonderful brought Lexie and my children home. He didn't ride the elevator up to the apartment. This was wise of him. It's a long drop from the balcony on to the concrete parking lot a hundred feet below.

The three of them looked tired and dirty. Polly had some scratches on her face. I hoped Lex had dabbed on antiseptic so they wouldn't get infected. Joe had ripped his hoodie and his sneakers were in ruins. They'd be going in the trash.

Lex had burned her nose off. She's too fair to go out in hot sun – her parents were a mushroom and a vampire. She had red blotches on her neck and arms. The lakeside bugs had eaten her alive.

'So you'll think about a short vacation?' We were in the kitchen fixing crackers, cheese and additive-free milkshakes for the kids and I was boiling water for the pasta.

'No, Pat,' said Lexie. 'I've done thinking. We're moving out tomorrow after you go to work.'

'Lex, I think we should discuss this further.'

'We have nothing to discuss. I don't want any of that stuff you're cooking.'

So I took the pan off of the hob before I could be tempted to throw it at her head and walked out of the kitchen.

'Did you have a good time at the lake?' I asked my son, who was lying full-length on the couch and playing Angry Birds on Lexie's phone.

'Yeah, I guess,' he said, not looking up.

'What did you do?'

'We rowed a boat. We hiked in woods and Polly fell in brambles. We made a fire and roasted dogs. We did a bunch of stuff.' But he was much more interested in zapping pigs than talking to his father.

Polly bumbled round the living room, sucking on her fingers and dripping chocolate milkshake all over the cream rug. 'Come sit with Daddy, Polly?' I took out some sugar-and-additive-free jelly beans. 'Come read a book with me?'

'Please don't try to bribe the kids with treats and candy, Patrick.' Lex watched from the doorway while Polly toddled over and climbed up on my lap. 'As for books – I need to have a word with you about the reading matter you seem to think is suited to our son.'

'Why, what's wrong with it?'

'Where would I start?' She walked in the room and picked a couple books off of the pile on the coffee table. 'What do have we here?' she drawled. '*Awesome Algorithms. Funky Fractals.* Pat, your son is still in kindergarten. Stephen says that if you start to push a child too early and too hard—'

But I shut my ears to Mr Wonderful's rough guide to raising perfect kids and started reading *Kitty's Birthday Brownie* to my daughter.

Polly listened carefully, her thumb wedged in her mouth, ready to turn the pages of a book she knew by heart and fuss if I should skip a single word.

I read for five, six minutes, then—

'You kids, it's bath time,' Lexie told them. 'Say goodnight to Daddy and go get in the tub.' The children knew that tone of voice and did as they were told.

When I next went to the local bookstore, I decided, I'd find Joe some titles like *Fun with Fire and Flame* and *Easy Electricity – Experiments for Junior Bright Sparks* and see how Lex liked those.

I changed my mind about the house out on the prairie.

'Alexis, if you walk out on this marriage, there'll be no coming back,' I said when she came in the living room again, sitting down as far away as possible from me.

'Who said I wanted to come back?' Picking up a magazine, she started flicking through it.

'Do you want to talk about it – us?'

'As I already told you, there's nothing to discuss. This relationship was never good and now it's over. Pat, it's finished, done.'

'Alexis, we've been married fifteen years. We have two small children. We've known each other since we were in elementary school.'

'Yeah, way too long,' said Lexie, eyes still fixed on her magazine. 'We were kids ourselves back then. We're different people now. It's like we got trapped inside a time-warp. Stephen thinks—'

'Okay, okay,' I said. No way did I want to hear more psycho-shit from Mr Wonderful. 'Give me your new address and I'll redirect your mail. As I said before, I'll make you an allowance for the children. But I'm sure there'll be a ton of stuff they're going to need on top of basic food and clothes and shoes?'

'My attorney will be writing you. Stephen thinks we should do everything through our attorneys from now on.'

49

So this is how a marriage ends, I thought, like a tornado ripping through a house, cracking it and splintering it, leaving only broken promises and tarnished dreams and children who don't need to be upset but who are certain to get hurt.

As Lexie snapped the pages in her magazine, my cell began to ring. It was Ben and hell, he sounded mad. 'Hey, Professor,' he began. 'If you're not too busy freaking grading, come have a beer with me?'

'Why, what's up?'

'I'll tell you when I see you.'

'Mrs Fairfax Three?'

'You got it, buddy boy. I just saw my Amex statement. She went shopping like there's no tomorrow. The screwball girlfriend must have led her on.'

'Meet you at the usual place?'

'Yeah, might as well.'

'I'll be there in ten.'

'Where are you going, Patrick?' Lex demanded as I grabbed my keys.

'Ben wants to meet me for a beer.'

'I thought you wanted to talk about our marriage?'

'I thought you told me there was nothing to discuss?'

'I always knew you'd be like this. When I want to talk, you get up and walk out on me. You go drink beer with Ben.'

'Lexie, don't play games with me. I don't need to go meet Ben, so if you want to talk?'

'You go drink beer. I need to take a shower.'

Did someone write the book on women? Maybe I should read it? Yeah, when I have a million years and nothing else to do.

⌒ ROSIE ⌒

We'd been to lots of stores in Minneapolis already, but Tess said it was time I graduated to the Mall, to the Hollywood of the Midwest.

The Mall of America.

So what can I say, apart from it was very big – in fact, it was enormous. We spent most of Saturday and Sunday there and hardly scratched the surface.

Tess's Amex Gold was melting by the time we left. As we drove back home to the apartment, she was worrying what Ben would say when he found out how much she'd spent, particularly on a gorgeous pair of purple boots we'd noticed in September *Vogue* and bookmarked straight away.

'But surely he will understand?' I said. 'Tess, he must be a millionaire by now and you're his wife and so he'll want you to look good? As Fanny's always saying, the right accessories are so important. There's no point in buying lovely clothes and wearing rubbish shoes. You'll just look cheap. Those boots will be absolutely perfect with your Miu Miu handbag, Gucci coat and Fendi shades. Ben won't want to be seen out with someone who looks as if she gets her clothes from thrift stores.'

Although he always looks as if he shops in them himself, I didn't like to say. *Or if anybody needs a makeover, Ben Fairfax ought to be the first in line.*

'Yeah, maybe you're right,' conceded Tess.

'Of course I'm right.'

'I'm still afraid he'll do his nut.'

'But you might be doing him a favour.'

'What? Rosie, I've just spent—'

'Three thousand dollars, give or take.'

'So how—'

'I saw it on an advertising hoarding as we were driving here. Spend three thousand dollars on your Amex Gold this month and get a zillion trillion bonus points.'

'Blimey, Rosie, damn well spotted you! So he should be grateful, shouldn't he?'

'Yes, of course he should. He'll have enough to buy another gadget at a knock-down price or get it free.'

'Let's get all these babies home,' said Tess. 'We'll have a fashion show.'

'Ben's invited Pat over on Saturday,' she told me, as she tried on all the clothes again just to check they fitted and looked right and wouldn't need to be returned. 'Poor Professor Riley, he needs cheering up. Ben says Mrs Riley's being absolutely vile.'

'Oh, I see.' I tried to sound so casual. But my heart began to thump, because I knew I really shouldn't see Professor Riley. It would not be good for him or me. He should sort his marriage out and I should make some plans about what I was going to do when I got home again. After all, if I was going to sort out other people's lives, perhaps I ought to sort my own?

'What's the matter, Rosie?'

'Sorry?'

'You're a million miles away. You're fidgeting and twitching. You're talking to yourself.'

'I was just thinking – creatively, you know?'

'Oh, about what happens when you get back to London, your new job and stuff?'

'Yes, that's right.'

'If I didn't know you better, I'd have said you were indulging in a happy fantasy about Professor Riley.'

'Why would I fantasise about Professor Riley?'

'He might be dull and not have very much to say, but he's still pretty hot.'

We spent the whole of the next week just shopping – shopping – shopping and then we shopped some more. Moderation, balance, ha ha ha – balance wasn't in it.

I didn't think it would be possible for somebody like me,

who practically lives in Selfridges, in Harvey Nichols and in Harrods, to end up all shopped out. But I was wrong. By Friday afternoon, I had decided I didn't need to see another Gucci bag, Armani frock or Prada belt again. Or for a few weeks, at any rate.

Okay, for a few days.

On Friday evening, Tess announced that in the morning we were going to Red Wing and then on to Winona. The drive would be spectacular, she added, with the trees all starting to turn red and gold and orange in the fall.

I tried to sound excited, even though I'd seen a zillion autumn leaves before. *We do have autumn in the UK too*, I wanted to tell Ben, as he went on and on about the beauty of the Mississippi River valley, how I would be blown away. *We do have leaves*.

'What else is there, apart from leaves?' I asked.

'Shoes,' said Tess. 'There's a great big factory outlet and I need to get myself some Merrells.'

'You have way too many pairs of shoes, babe,' muttered Ben, looking up from tapping on his laptop.

'How can anybody have too many pairs of shoes? I'll need lots of boots for winter, too. You said I'd have to brace myself for winter, for all the ice and snow.' She turned to me. 'Rosie love, let's make a picnic, shall we? Let's leave Ben to write a few more words and earn a few thousand more dollars.'

'I'm surprised you mentioned shoes,' I said, when Tess and I were in the kitchen rummaging in the fridge. 'I thought he was annoyed about your spending?'

'Last night, I did what he's been nagging me to do for weeks. If he doesn't kick up a big fuss when I buy lots of shoes tomorrow, I might do it again. Oh, and by the way, Ben's invited Patrick to come along tomorrow. I hope that's okay with you?'

'Whatever,' I replied and tried to shrug.

'Yeah, I knew you'd wet yourself,' said Tess, grinning at me.

✦ PATRICK ✦

I was looking forward to spending time with Rosie.

Yeah, she could be needle-sharp, but she also had a kind of sparkle. It was like the rest of us were dull, grey rocks while Rosie was a crystal, the sort of girl who made the world a brighter place and hell, mine needed brightening.

Lex had taken Joe and Polly to a good old Minnesota apple-picking, pumpkin-carving, cider-drinking day with Mr Wonderful. Nowadays my wife and kids were staying on Grand Avenue, where the children had new bedrooms – pink and Barbie-ised for Polly, blue and Hero Factory-ised for Joe. Mr Wonderful had got some hotshot stylist round, spared no expense, said Lexie, and the kids were thrilled.

So I would not get to see my children on the weekend unless I made a scene. I was determined I would never make a scene. I would not get drunk and frighten Joe and Polly. I would not be like – *him*.

Ben had a brand new Mercedes sedan and told me I could drive. I suspected this was so he could make out with Mrs Fairfax Three while I kept my eyes fixed on the blacktop, while Rosie was knocked out by autumn leaves? I'm guessing she saw autumn leaves before?

But I love to drive, so I was very happy to be driving Ben's new baby, although it took a while to get accustomed to the stick shift. Why did Ben insist on buying European models with European stick shifts? I guess it was one more way of saying *hey, guys – look at me*.

I soon discovered that driving an S-Class Mercedes is a

bunch of fun. It also made a welcome change from driving my five-year-old sports utility, my mobile trash can full of baby wipes and juice containers, lunch pails, Lex-approved sugar-free candy bars and packs of Polly's diapers.

When we came to Red Wing, Ben said he had to make some notes about the sequel to *Missouri Crossing* and he had to make them now. *While the force is with you*, I didn't like to say. But he's such a jerk. You'd think he was Moses on the mountain, channelling the word of God, the way he talks about his precious writing. It's as if he's taking celestial dictation, as if writing fiction is some kind of sacred thing.

But Tess seemed fine with this and said she had to go buy shoes.

'Why don't you two go look at Winona?' Ben suggested. 'Give the beast a run? I mean the Merc, not you,' he added, as he winked suggestively at me.

'Shall we go see Winona?' I asked Rosie.

'Whatever,' she replied.

'She means *you bet*,' said Ben. 'The British never do enthusiasm. When a British person says *whatever* they mean they can't imagine doing anything more super-duper. Rosie?'

'Yes?'

'If you and this ole boy call at a Starbucks, watch them while they fix your coffee and be sure to ask them for a takeout cup, the sort that has the lid on tight – okay?'

'Okay,' said Rosie, looking puzzled.

'You be on your guard.' Ben glanced at Rosie, winked again. 'This guy can be dangerous, you know. He has – what do you British call it – form.'

'You don't want any shoes?' I asked as we headed off in Ben's new beast, making for Winona. We'd arranged to meet with Ben and Tess again after Ben was through with the celestial dictation and Tess was all shoed out. 'A pair of genuine Red

Wings, they're meant to last a lifetime, so don't you want to get a pair?' I added, when she didn't speak.

'No, I don't think so.' She'd been staring through the windshield, profile sharp against the golden light of afternoon, but now she looked at me. 'I do like shoes. I wouldn't be a woman if I didn't. But I don't need any at the moment. What did Ben mean when he said I had to get my coffee in a takeout cup? When he said you had form?'

'I don't know what he meant,' I lied. 'But I wouldn't pay him any mind. He's always saying oddball stuff. It's part of him, he thinks he's funny. Rosie, do you want to see more leaves? As we were heading over here, there was a ton of green still mixed in with the red and yellow. We get the best fall colour in October, but I know a highway where it should be orange, red and gold with sumac, maple, aspen around now. It would be like driving through a forest fire.'

'I think I've had enough of roads and leaves.'

'Do you like to climb?'

'You mean up mountains? Yes, I do. I was in the mountaineering club at university and we did some climbing in the Alps and Dolomites – in Italy, you know?'

'We don't have any mountains here in Minnesota, but we have some bluffs.'

'I don't believe I've ever climbed a bluff.'

'Let's go climb one now, then. There's no mist today and so we should be able to see for miles and miles.'

'All sounds good to me.'

So, while Ben and Mrs Fairfax Three stayed in Red Wing, Ben in a little coffee shop mainlining lattes and vanilla Danish and tapping on his laptop, and Tess no doubt buying a thousand pairs of shoes, we headed off along the valley of the Mississippi.

Aspen, maple, oak and ash – I didn't think the early fall was quite as beautiful as usual. This was probably because we had such scorching temperatures a week or two ago and the leaves had withered and crisped before they fell. Or maybe I thought this because of Lex, because our marriage had crisped and withered, too?

It was baking hot again today. But soon enough there would be snowfall, with kids riding on sleds, with snowploughs on the streets and snow chains on the cars. Waterfalls would turn to sheets of ice and so it would go on until the spring.

The Merc purred like a tiger, eating up the miles – boy, it was fun to drive! I'd have to write a book myself and get my own some day …

'Where are we going?' Rosie asked.

'We're headed for the Sugar Loaf.'

'What's the Sugar Loaf?'

'A chunk of limestone on the Mississippi River. It used to be some rock, but it got quarried in the nineteenth century and the stone was turned into Winona: sidewalks, public buildings, all that stuff. But it's still impressive, still dominates the town.'

'We could climb this Sugar Loaf? I mean without equipment, ropes and stuff?'

'Yeah, there's a trail, it will be easy.' I turned the air con higher. 'But I ought to warn you, it will be hot up there.'

'I like the heat.'

'You have some sunscreen in your backpack?'

'No, but I don't need it. I'm so dark I never burn.'

'Okay.' I pulled into the parking lot. 'Let's do some serious hiking, then.'

She was pretty fit. She ran up that hiking trail like it was on the level, her legs flashing like Flo-Jo's in the hundred metre sprint. I like to run myself. I don't want to end up overweight and diabetic with a bunch of heart conditions, so I try to spend an hour or two on some form of exercise each day. But Rosie had me beat.

'You're like – who is that girl in Greek mythology, the one who could outrun all of the men?' I asked. Or I should say I panted as I slumped down on a boulder, my T-shirt sticking to my back and chest.

'Who do you mean?'

'You know – the one some guy managed to beat by dropping golden apples? So she stopped to pick them up?'

'Oh, yes – Atalanta.' Rosie scooped her hair back from her face and fixed it with a clip. 'My goodness me, Professor Riley, fancy an American scientist knowing about Atalanta.'

'There's some reason why I shouldn't?'

'No, no reason, but – I'm sorry, that was very rude of me.' She blushed, or maybe she was overheating now. We should have brought some water. 'You weren't very far behind me, were you?'

'You were miles ahead. You'd have scooped those apples up and won the race as well, been sitting on a wall and eating them when I came gasping up. Do you run every day?'

'No.' She shook her head. 'Most of the time, I'm a fat slug. When I'm in London, I roll straight out of my bed into the tube – I mean the subway – and then I sit behind a desk all day. But I sometimes run half marathons for charity and I have to train quite hard for them. I'm lucky, I suppose. I have the physique to be a runner, if not a beauty queen.'

Your physique is perfect, I wished I could say. *You're strong yet graceful. You make me think of panthers and black jaguars. You're so much more attractive than any simpering, bleach-blonde beauty queen.*

We sat there in the autumn sunshine, gazing. The view was beyond awesome, with the river and the forest all spread out before us, like when the world was made.

'You're very quiet, Professor Riley?' She touched my

sleeve, the contact light as gossamer, but it was like a trillion volts passed through me and lit me up like billboards in Times Square. 'I expect you're thinking serious scientific thoughts?' she added, kind of teasingly.

'No, my mind's a blank.' I quit contemplating trees and water and turned to look at Rosie. 'Why don't you tell me something about you?' I asked.

'What do you want to know?'

'Where were you born and raised?'

'In Dorset – it's an English county.'

'Where did you go to school?'

'In Cheltenham, at Cheltenham Ladies' College, it's an English public school.'

'So let me get this right. The public schools in the UK, they're private schools, not open to just anybody, and you have to pay to go to them?'

'Most people pay, but some have scholarships.'

'Did you get a scholarship?'

'No, my family paid. I'm an over-privileged member of the British middle class and so I got to go to boarding school.'

'Boarding school – you mean it was like Harry Potter's Hogwarts?'

'My school was not at all like Harry Potter's.' She laughed and it was – what does that song say – like music playing. 'We didn't study magic spells and stuff. But yes, it was a boarding school with houses, sporting trophies, lots of rules and regulations. Don't you have boarding schools here in America?'

'Yeah, but they're for special kinds of kids – super-rich kids, troubled kids, kids with intellectual disabilities, delinquent kids, those whose parents work or live outside of the USA – or orphans. I hope you're not an orphan?'

'No, I'm not an orphan. Going away to school is what some British children do. It teaches independence, self-reliance, encourages us to have enquiring minds. Or that's the theory, anyway.'

'You studied French and German when you went to Cambridge University?'

'How did you know that?'

'I guess Ben must have mentioned it one time.'

'What else did he mention?' she demanded and her tone was suddenly sharp – there was that squeeze of lemon.

'I reckon that was all.' *Okay,* I thought, *mind your own business, Riley. The lady doesn't want to talk to you.*

But this wasn't CIA in-depth interrogation. I wasn't threatening her with water-boarding if she didn't spill, and I liked to listen to her talk. No, it was more than like. I loved to hear her voice. 'Dorset's where?' I asked, thinking this could not be classified, that Google must know Dorset.

'It's in the south of England, on the coast.'

'You grew up by the ocean – at the seaside, do you call it?'

'Yes.'

'You have brothers, sisters?'

'No,' she said, and it was like a door slammed in my face. 'It's your turn now,' she added. 'Tell me something about you?'

'I grew up in Missouri. I went to high school there. Then I won a scholarship to college here in Minnesota. I've lived in the Twin Cities ever since. I didn't go to boarding school. I've never seen the ocean. I don't speak a foreign language.

'I do understand a few, of course. After all, my job involves messing with sounds and words. But my spoken Spanish is embarrassing. Germans think I have a speech impediment and my French cracks everybody up.'

'Didn't you learn a second language when you were in high school?' Rosie asked.

'Yeah, I took a class in Spanish. I can just about order a beer.'

'It's too late to go to boarding school, but you could see the ocean and improve your Spanish. Or even learn another foreign language.'

'What language should I learn?'

'French is very easy for most English speakers.'

'Say something in French?'

'Je voudrais te baiser.'

'Meaning what?'

'It's very hot up here.'

'Let's go down then, grab a soda somewhere?'

'That would be good,' she said, but didn't get up. She was busy scrabbling and scraping like a rabbit scratching out a hole.

'Hey, you're not allowed to break off bits of Minnesota,' I said sternly when I realised what she was doing.

'Why is that?' she asked.

'It's probably a federal offence.'

'Oh, go on with you – and anyway, it was already loose.' She scrutinised her rock. 'See how it sparkles in the sunshine?'

'The hell with how it sparkles. This is a national monument, you know.'

'You mean like Mount St Helens? I bet it's jolly not. It's just a lump of rock above the Mississippi River.'

'It's a Mississippi bluff.'

'Okay, Professor Riley, it's a bluff. What's this kind of stone, I wonder?'

'I guess it's oneota dolomite. What you have there is limestone made from creatures which were living a million years ago.'

'What about the crystals?'

'They'll be quartz.'

'Gosh, aren't you well-informed?'

She twinkled at me and her eyes were brighter than the sparkles in the stone. 'Mythology, geology, technology and half a dozen other ologies – I'm betting you're an expert on them all.'

'Now I come to think of it, Ben did mention something else about you.'

'Oh? What did he say?'

'You smuggled a suspicious British apple into the USA. Now you want to smuggle out a rock without a permit.' I shook my head and sighed. 'If you're not careful, Rosie, you'll end up in a facility where they re-educate women like you.'

'What do you mean, women like me?'

'Who break the rules.'

'What's the point of living if you don't break any rules?' She stood up now and stretched, her T-shirt riding high, revealing smooth, tanned skin. 'I want this for Dad. He has a collection of bits of foreign stone from all over the world. We – I mean, I – like to …'

'What?'

'Oh, nothing,' she replied. 'Come on, Dr Riley, I'll race you to the parking lot.'

She took off down that trail like she was being chased by wolves. I stood there for a minute, several minutes. I watched her skitter down, dislodging little rocks and jumping bigger ones, a beautiful gazelle of a young woman, full of nervous grace.

Je voudrais te baiser.

You asked her to say something, say anything in French and that was the example came into her head. She didn't mean it personally.

❧ ROSIE ❧

Je voudrais te baiser.

I would like to kiss you. Or that's the polite translation.

What about the stone for Dad? Charlie had brought home all kinds of minerals for Dad. Smooth grey soapstone, striped red agate, polished turquoise – Charlie went on voyages of discovery for one reason only, risking life and suffering extreme discomfort in those last few places where even Coca-Cola hadn't yet set up its stall, to collect rare geological samples for our father.

This was the usual family joke or fiction, anyway.

Dad kept the samples in a china bowl in his study. I wasn't really sure if I should add to the collection, if it would hurt him more than it would please him. But—

'Rosie?'

'Yes?'

'You're about a million miles away.' Pat had caught up with me and now he frowned. 'Do you have something on your mind?'

'I'm fine.' I forced myself to smile at him. 'I'm enjoying getting good fresh air and exercise. I'm having a great time.' It was almost true. But I hadn't meant to have great times. It was not appropriate that I should have great times.

So I didn't know why I felt happy – not laughing, singing, giggling happy, but contented, cared-about and quiet happy. Why, as we went down the trail, I glanced at Patrick Riley and was suddenly overwhelmed with sadness because he wasn't mine.

What business did I have to think of him at all? Why had I told him I would like to kiss him, more than kiss him? It was just as well he knew no French. But it didn't have to be this way. I didn't have to let him get to me. Soon I would be going home and then I could forget him and all the confusing feelings and emotions he aroused in me. Balance, moderation – Patrick Riley's personal attraction genie didn't know the meaning of those words.

I ran on ahead.

But I didn't look where I was going and all of a sudden something slammed right into me. My foot felt like it had been hit with twenty, thirty hammers. My head began to spin and I felt sick with pain. My eyes filled up, spilled over.

I half slumped, half fell on the hard ground. I started crying and I found I couldn't stop. 'I h-hurt my foot,' I stammered when he had caught up with me and asked me what was wrong and I could finally trust myself to tell him. 'These t-trainers weren't designed to run up mountains.'

'Trainers – oh, you mean your sneakers, right?'

He hunkered down beside me, dark eyes serious and kind. I didn't want him to be kind. I wanted him to tell me to get up and not make such a fuss. But he did nothing of the sort. 'They do look kind of flimsy,' he agreed, as if it were the trainers' fault, not mine for choosing them, for running up and down a mountain in them. 'I guess you smacked into that boulder, yeah?'

But I could only nod.

'You think you've broken anything?'

'I h-hope I haven't.'

'You have any feeling in your toes?'

'Yes, just a bit.' I tried to wipe away the snot and tears, scrubbing with my hands. 'I can wriggle all of them and it d-doesn't hurt to flex my foot. I've stubbed one toe, that's all. Let me h-have a moment and then we can go on.'

'You can walk?'

'I'll try.'

'It isn't very far back to the parking lot and it's all downhill. Why don't I carry you?'

'You can't do that, I'm heavy!'

'What do you weigh?'

'Oh, I don't know – about eight stone?'

'What's that in pounds?'

'I couldn't tell you, I'm afraid.'

'Come on,' he said, and now his eyes were dark as night, were hypnotising me. 'You put your arms around my neck ...'

To my surprise, I did as I was told. He picked me up with ease. 'Yeah, it's like I thought,' he said. 'You must weigh about as much as Polly.'

'Polly?'

'She's my little girl.'

'How old is Polly?'

'Almost three.'

'I must weigh much more than Polly, then.'

'Yeah, perhaps you do.' He smiled at me and started walking. 'You definitely have more mass.'

❦ PATRICK ❦

Why did I do that? Why did I carry Rosie? Why did I grab the opportunity to hold her in my arms? I couldn't help myself, that's why.

She stubbed her toe, she said. Okay, she might have hurt her foot. I'm not suggesting she was lying. That old boulder probably hit her hard. But no one cries like that for a stubbed toe. No one gulps and sobs as if their heart is broken when they stub a toe. This was grief, long-standing, pent-up grief, something I knew all about from—

But let's stick with Rosie for the moment.

When we got back to the Merc, I helped her to get in, got in myself. I pushed the key in the ignition, turned the air con up to full. 'Do you want to tell me, Rosie?'

'Tell you what?'

'Why you were crying fit to break your heart back there?'

'I hurt my foot,' she said, but wouldn't look at me.

'What else?'

'What do you mean?' she snapped. 'There – there's nothing else!'

'Oh, come on. You're sad, upset or worried. I can tell.'

'I … well, I'm feeling homesick, I suppose.'

'You'll soon be going back to the UK.'

'I bashed my foot quite hard.'

'Yeah, you hit that boulder at ninety miles an hour, and so it's bound to hurt. But hey, it could be worse – nobody died.'

She kind of choked. Okay, maybe that was crass of me. But I didn't mean to sound unsympathetic. 'Let's go find a drugstore, get some Tylenol,' I added.

'What's Tylenol?'

'A painkiller, it's good.'

'I have a box of aspirin in my bag.' She found it, popped a couple tablets out.

'Do you need water? We could go get water.'

'No, I'll swallow them without.'

'Okay.' I changed the subject. 'You and Tess, you go way back?'

'Oh, no,' she replied. 'We met last year, at one of Fanny's parties.'

'Fanny's who?'

'I think I mentioned her while we were all at Ben's, while I was telling you about my job?'

'Okay, remind me?'

'She was my boss in London. She runs a very successful PR and promotions company. Fanny was at school with my mother and she's always been a family friend. I joined her firm when I left university – got in through the back door.'

'I'm sorry?'

'Fanny offered me a job because she knows my parents.'

'She offered you a job because you're smart. Tell me about this party?'

'Fanny's always having parties. She was giving one to help promote a client's range of gorgeous frocks. She got Tess and another pretty girl to model stuff. We clicked, and Tess came over often when I worked in Paris.'

'You like Paris?'

'Yes, I love it – it's my favourite city.'

'You and Tess, you're very different. I'm a dumb American, of course, but I can hear you speak with different accents, that she's kind of sassy, you're – refined?'

'Yes, I'm posh, and Tess was born in Bethnal Green in the East End of London.'

'So she's a Cockney, right?'

'Good heavens, Dr Riley, aren't you clever to know that?'

'Yeah, my general knowledge is spectacular. I could take on any kindergarten kid and very likely win.'

'You're modest, too.'

'You're feeling better now you took that aspirin?'

'Yes, I am – much better, since you ask.' She sounded quite surprised to think she should be feeling better. 'Thank you very much indeed for looking after me.'

'It was my pleasure, ma'am.'

I saw she'd put her rock up on the dash.

'So now, about that rock,' I said. 'You open up your door and then you pitch it out real hard.'

'Professor Riley, you ain't nothing but a spoilsport,' she retorted, mimicking my accent and sounding like a British female version of Huckleberry Finn.

'Yeah, that's right. But now you listen up. The airport cops find rocks or other items which could be used as weapons in your baggage, you'll find yourself in trouble. People have been shot for less.'

'I can't believe the airport police would shoot me for smuggling out a pebble.'

'Maybe, maybe not, but I sure wouldn't rile them, anyway.'

'The police aren't armed in the UK, you know.'

'You're kidding me.'

'They don't carry firearms unless they're in a siege or something.'

'It would not be wise to take that rock.'

'Okay, okay, you win.' She opened up the door and pitched her pebble. 'Tess and I, we made a picnic. There are cans of Coke and Dr Pepper in a cooler. Maybe you could go and have a rummage in the boot and get a couple out? Why are you grinning, Pat?'

'You belong in *Downton Abbey*, Lady Rosie.'

'Yeah, Professor Riley, I sure do.' She glanced at me and smiled. 'Well, I done told you I was posh.'

'Did you get to read Ben's book?' I asked her as we hit the highway to drive back to Red Wing. This ride was something else. It flew along the blacktop. It would eat up the sixty or so miles we had to travel inside of an hour easily. I could have driven it all day and through the night.

'Yes, most of it,' she said.

'What do you think?'

'It's good. It's very readable, and he tells a strong, involving story. I can see why lots of people like it. At first, I wondered if it would be just a lightly-fictionalised account of a poor boy from the boondocks growing up and going off to college, making something of his life in spite of his pathetic mother and revolting father, but it's much more than that. I hope his real parents weren't as ghastly?'

'Ghastly?'

'Mean.'

'Ben's folks were great. Dirt poor, but they were lovely people, warm and always generous with what they had, and very kind to me.'

'Well, I suppose it's fiction?'

'Yeah, he made it up.' I didn't tell her Ben had painted a living, breathing, all-too-real portrait of my father. But not of my mother – the woman in the novel was a sex-crazed idiot who drank and whored and let her kids go hungry and was nothing like my mother. Ben would not have dared to write a word about my mother. He knows I would have punched him in the head.

Or maybe not, because I don't do stuff like that.

I'm not my father, after all.

'How are you feeling now?' I asked, my flesh still scorched, still burning from the imprint of her arms around my neck.

'Much better, thank you,' she replied.

'You're still in pain?'

'No, the aspirins did the trick. I'm not in pain at all.'

⌒ ROSIE ⌒

Stop it, stop it, stop it.

I pushed my poor stubbed toe against my shoe to make it hurt, to feel the pain, to distract me from the other pain, the pain of Charlie and now the pain of Pat.

I do not, cannot, must not like this man.

I wanted to go home. I wanted to be back in the UK, away from this – this foreign married father, this most unlikely, most unsuitable of men. I wanted to go back to the apartment, to hide inside my room – and yet I didn't.

I wanted most of all to be with Pat.

We left the Mercedes in a parking lot then went into the café where we found Ben and Tess. She looked zonked out but happy, probably because she'd made her plastic melt again. She was surrounded by at least a dozen carrier bags.

'Good time in Winona, guys?' asked Ben, who must have been working all the time we were away, if the half dozen empty coffee mugs and side plates full of crumbs meant anything.

'Yeah, it was okay,' said Pat indifferently. As well he might, I thought. He'd probably been bored out of his mind. I hoped he wouldn't say I'd hurt my foot. I didn't want them all exclaiming over me and Tess telling me to take my trainer off, to let them have a look and all that stuff.

'Rosie?' Tess was looking at me curiously.

'Yes, I had a lovely time,' I told them, nodding like an idiot and smiling through my many kinds of pain.

'*Yes, Ai had a lovely taime,*' she mimicked. 'Ooh, so what have you been doing, then?'

'We saw Sugar Loaf,' said Pat. 'We hiked a trail.'

'We could see for miles and miles across the valley, all along the river,' I continued stupidly. 'We should have had binoculars because the visibility is excellent today.'

'What did I say when you and I first met – you British and your meteorology? *The visibility is excellent today*. You must have had a ball.'

Ben grinned then winked at me. *You really ought to sort that tic*, I thought. *One day you're going to wink at a policeman or a steroid-addled gangster and you'll get your head kicked in.*

'Tess, what did you buy?' I asked.

'Three pairs of boots for me for winter and some loafers and some Oxfords for my husband,' she replied. 'All his shoes are rubbish. Or rather he's a shoe-free zone. He's got a hundred pairs of manky trainers, a load of sad old flip-flops and almost nothing else. As for his tartan shirts and chain store jeans …'

She'd noticed, then.

'… now he's a famous novelist, he needs to be more stylish and *look* like he's successful. So next week I'm going to buy him loads of decent clothes and also take him to an upscale barber, sort his hair out. I'll restructure him.'

'Mercy me,' said Ben.

'You won't know yourself,' said Pat and then he started

laughing and it was the sexiest, the most attractive sound I'd ever heard in all my life.

I was in deep trouble, obviously.

❧ PATRICK ❧

I told Ben no, I wasn't coming up to get a coffee. I had stuff to do.

I let him exercise his wit at my expense for maybe thirty seconds, tell me once again that as a full professor I didn't need to teach at all, let alone grade students. I could hole up in a cosy laboratory with a bunch of other smartass geeks, get on with my research …

I said goodnight.

As I drove to my apartment in my mobile trash can – man, I missed that Merc already, it had been some ride – I put on some Gershwin, my favourite composer, the guy who wrote the soundtrack of my life.

Lexie always teases me for liking old-style music. She says I was born fifty years too late. But when I listen to *Rhapsody in Blue* or *'S Wonderful*, the music takes me someplace I can lose myself, forget myself, stop being me, and sometimes that's exactly what I need to do.

Now I had to get away from Rosie as well as from myself. But when I put on *Rhapsody in Blue*, she strolled into my head. She took my hand and led me to that special place where nothing matters, nothing hurts, where there's no darkness in the soul, where everything is light.

I thought: *am I in trouble.*

❧ ROSIE ❧

'I guess we ought to take you to the hospital,' said Ben, looking at my bruised and bloodied foot. 'You need an X-ray.'

They'd noticed I was limping, even though I tried to hide it. They insisted I should show them what I'd done. Tess had got my foot up on a stool and taken off my trainer so now I was Exhibit A. 'Rosie, honey, what a mess,' she said. 'The nail's split right across and all this blood is coming from the nail bed.'

'Jolly well observed, Nurse Tess.'

'I bet it's agony.'

'Yes, it's just a little sore.'

'Your whole foot is swollen.'

'But that's the histamine reaction, isn't it?'

'I suppose it must be. Do you think your toe is broken?'

'No!' I shook my head emphatically. 'I can move it, even though it hurts, and if I'd broken it, I'm sure I'd know.'

'I think it's like Ben says. You need to go to hospital and get it all checked out. I'll take you to the local A and E.'

'I don't want to go to hospital!'

If they took me to a hospital, if we had to go to A & E, or whatever they call it in the USA – ER – and I had to hear those sounds and see those sights and smell those smells again, I knew I'd have hysterics. I'd become a sobbing, whimpering mess and everyone would think I'd lost my mind.

I don't do hospitals.

'There's no need to go to A and E,' I told them. 'I'll just slob around for a few days then I'll be fine.'

'You'll tell us if there's any problem, if the pain gets any worse?'

'I'll tell you, honestly.'

'You'd better, Rosie.' Tess got up. 'I'll find some antiseptic, clean this up and then I'm going to make some chicken soup.'

'You'll regret you stubbed that toe,' said Ben. 'Tess, do you have a packet mix for soup? Or are you fixing to head out there with your little hatchet, knock some unsuspecting chicken on the head?'

'Why don't you shut up?' Tess threw a cushion in his face.

'You should be aware that violence is the response of undeveloped minds, babe,' he replied and threw it back.

All Sunday and all Monday, I hobbled round the place like some old crone, trying not to hit my poor bashed toe on anything. The bruises soon came out and my whole foot turned black and purple, green and red and indigo and yellow. My heart was hurting, too. So I spent a lot of time in bed, where I ached and felt extremely sorry for myself and listened to the gloomiest, most miserable music I could find.

Tess went to Target, bought a chicken, boiled it up, dismembered it and brought me bowls of home-made chicken soup with greyish, gluey lumps and cartilage and bones in it and sat there while I ate it. So soon I felt much worse.

When I was little and not feeling well, my mother made tomato soup with croutons – a hug in every spoonful. This was purgatory in every swallow.

But it must have done the trick because by Tuesday I was getting better. Or at least my toe was getting better. I was trying to ignore my heart, which thumped against my chest and tried to scramble up my windpipe every time the phone or doorbell rang. I told myself to stop being so silly, that I was far too old to have a crush on anyone – especially a married father anyone.

As for my foot – the swelling had gone down. The bleeding stopped. As long as I wore sandals, I found I could forget my mangled toe and broken nail. 'Yes, I'll come out tomorrow,' I told Tess while we were having breakfast. 'I want to see F. Scott Fitzgerald's house.'

'Oh, there are half a dozen of them, not just one, and they're all – well – just houses, nothing special,' said Tess dismissively. 'Of course, his lordship thinks they're holy shrines. He made me read that book, what is it called?'

'*Anne of Green Gables*?'

'No, that *Gatsby* thing. I've never been so bored in all my life. Ben says it's fantastic, but it's just about some nasty people having a bad time. So, anyway – I thought we might go and have a facial and maybe get our nails done? That'll be a lot more fun than looking at old houses where some weirdo alcoholic used to live. I'm going to the shops this morning, can I get you something?'

'No, I don't need anything at all,' I said. *That's unless you can deliver Patrick Riley gift-wrapped*, I added to myself.

'I'll be back for lunch, then. There's loads more chicken soup wants eating up.'

'Maybe you could freeze some?' I suggested hopefully. 'I'll pour some into Tupperware containers, shall I, stick it in the freezer?'

'No, we'll have it for our lunch today. It's more nutritious fresh.'

Ben was busy in his office, working on his novel. He'd been up since six o'clock that morning, Tess informed me, so he'd be in a frenzy of creation now, and he wouldn't want to be disturbed.

Then she left, most probably heading for the MoA. Did they put something in the air conditioning there, I asked myself. Something that made people need a daily fix of it, and sent them crazy if they didn't get it?

But this gave me time and space to catch up on some work-related reading – okay, to page through Tess's magazines – to do some market research for when I got back to London and of course to think of Patrick Riley.

This was just absurd, ridiculous. I longed and longed to see him. I wanted more than anything to hear his voice again. I told myself to get a grip, stop being so pathetic. He was a married man, at least for now, a father, an American, a scientist, someone who'd despise my frock-fixated, trend-obsessed, shoe-and-designer-bag-mad life.

How could he possibly be right for me?

How could he not?

When I had bashed my foot, he could have told me it was all my fault. I should have looked where I was going. He could have let me hobble to the parking lot. But he had carried me.

He'd smelled of warm, sweet spices. His skin was smooth and tanned by summer sun. His straight dark hair lay like a soft black pelt against his head, and it—

It was just a case of female hormones working overtime.

I made some notes on possible locations for my office, sent some emails off to various letting agents, spent some time on Facebook and on Twitter. Then I googled JQA. Only out of idle curiosity, of course, just to see where Pat and Ben did – well, whatever stuff they did all day.

I let my fingers wander, watched to see what they would do. My clever, clever fingers, they soon found Pat's department. Then they found his photograph, right-clicked on it and saved it to my album.

I read his bio – goodness, what a lot of letters and abbreviations, Professor Patrick Riley PhD. What a lot of publications, fellowships, awards. All that was missing was the Nobel Prize.

There were all his contact details, tempting, mocking me. What should I do? Well, nothing really, seriously stupid – obviously. I considered ringing him. Okay, what would I say? I didn't know.

But then a passing fairy must have checked my balance wish-wise, saw I was in credit and allowed him to ring me.

No, that's a lie. He didn't ring to talk to me. He rang to speak to Ben, of course. I just picked up the phone. But when he realised it was me, not Tess, he asked how I was doing and how was my foot? He hoped it was okay?

'It – it's fine,' I said, or rather rasped, because my mouth had suddenly gone as dry as the Sahara in a record-breaking heatwave. 'It hurt a bit on Sunday, but it's almost back to normal now.'

'That's good to hear,' he said and then he paused for half a heartbeat. 'I was kind of worried when you cried.'

'It was the shock.'

'I guess.'

'Do want to speak to Ben?'

Why did I say that? I wanted him to talk to me!

'Yeah, if he's home, if he could take a break from the celestial dictation? I tried him on his cell, but seems like it's turned off.'

'I'll fetch him for you.' But then I took a chance, dived headlong into shallow water full of rocks and boulders and – I dare say – sharks. 'Patrick, I ...'

But then I paused. What was I going to say? Drop what you're doing and come round to this apartment and *baiser* me to glory, could you? Tie me up and tie me down and then do anything you want with me?

'... I'm sorry I made such a fuss on Saturday.' What a brilliant conversationalist. Dorothy Parker would have been in fits of jealousy. 'I don't often cry.'

'Oh, most anybody would have cried.' Patrick Riley's voice was warm as caramel, a perfect mocha latte on a freezing winter day. 'If I'd run into that old rock, I would have cried myself. You're one brave girl, you know. You did all right.'

I felt myself flush pink with pleasure. Multicoloured butterflies did aerial gymnastics in my stomach. I almost felt myself begin to glow, like I'd been plugged into the mains.

But what had I told myself? All this had to stop and stop right now. 'Thank you,' I said primly, like some Victorian lady saying thank you to a rude mechanical who'd swept the highway free of horse manure so she could cross the road. 'I'll go and get Ben.'

He wasn't in his office after all. I found him in the den, his headphones on and watching baseball on his massive television screen. The den was an Aladdin's cave reinterpreted by some ridiculously nerdish teenage boy. There were gadgets everywhere, wires trailing, stuff on charge, lights flashing, blinking—

'What are you grinning at?' he asked me when I tapped him on the shoulder to distract him from Joe Mauer and the Minnesota Twins.

'I thought you were working?'

'It's research,' he said.

❧ PATRICK ❧

Okay, I told myself, you don't go visit Ben. You don't go anywhere with him on weekends. You don't give yourself a chance to see that over-privileged British girl whose ancestors most likely starved and persecuted your own Irish forebears so they had no choice but to set sail for the New World in rotting hulks.

All I had to do was concentrate on work and sorting out the personal stuff and spend time with my kids.

I saw my own attorney and he wrote my wife's. The kid stuff was arranged to more or less my satisfaction. I'd see Joe and Polly early evenings and have them all day Sunday. There was no room for Rosie in my life. I told her so.

But Rosie paid no mind to me. She walked into my head while I was shaving, showering, fixing breakfast, driving, talking, seeing students, and she never rang the bell or knocked the door, she just came right on in, sat down and made herself at home like she belonged there. When I said she couldn't stay, she smiled and asked who was I kidding, then?

She knew I didn't want her to go.

'What's eating you, Professor Riley?' Ben demanded when I saw him in college on Wednesday afternoon. Why was he in college on a Wednesday afternoon? He didn't teach on Wednesday afternoons. So did he have a meeting with a member of the faculty?

Yeah, I guessed he must, no doubt with that cute and curvy blonde from Idaho who's into Robert Frost – on whom Ben is an expert – and probably into Ben as well.

'What should be eating me?' I asked.

'You look like you bet a thousand dollars on a game of tic-tac-toe and lost. There is a skill to it, you know. You start off in—'

'I'm running late. I'll catch you Friday.'

As I drove out of the parking lot, I played tic-tac-toe and other games with Rosie Denham in my head, and she always beat me, even though I wrote some near-perfect winning algorithms for them all while I was still a high school student and until I played these games with Rosie no one ever beat me, even a computer.

But I figured even Joe or Polly could beat me nowadays.

There were times when I was out of it, had to ask a student to repeat a question, found myself on highways or at intersections without knowing how I came there. This could not go on.

Once a month, I did some outreach work on one of the reservations north of Minneapolis, teaching basic IT skills to disadvantaged kids on a pro bono basis.

Some of those kids were pretty smart and I saw no reason why they should not go to college, be engineers, attorneys, scientists. There were grants and scholarships. You just had to track them down and I could help with that, like my high school teachers once helped me.

I was driving home late Thursday evening when I got a flat. I pulled into a buggy lane – I guessed there'd be no Amish on the blacktop at this time of night – and then got out.

It was getting cold and I was tired. I'd had a very long and busy day and I was looking forward to being home again, even in my empty, dark apartment with my takeout pizza, coleslaw, shake.

It didn't take me long to fix the flat. But as I stowed the jack back in the trunk then cleaned my dirty hands with Polly's wipes, something made me look up at the sky.

Outside of the Twin Cities of Minneapolis-Saint Paul, the night sky is awesome. The hard, white constellations shine so bright. Where was the Bear tonight and where was Cassiopeia? Where were the Northern Lights, the Death Dance of the Spirits?

I recalled one Friday afternoon. I was in school back in Recovery, Missouri. A couple dozen other kids and I were kind of listening to our teacher. I say kind of listening, because we were absorbing rather than attending – hypnotised, I guess you'd call it, literally spellbound while Miss Ellie read:

Many things Nokomis taught him
Of the stars that shine in heaven;
Showed him Ishkoodah, the comet,
Ishkoodah, with fiery tresses;
Showed the Death-Dance of the spirits,
Warriors with their plumes and war-clubs ...

Bada bada, bada bada – as I said the words out loud, I tingled with a toxic mix of good and bad emotions, of shameful memories. I was taunted by my failure to protect the person I most loved. But *The Song of Hiawatha* and the other poetry I learned by heart while I was still in elementary school sure did me a lot of good because it helped me to escape, to block the bastard out. Now I wanted someone who could say those comforting, familiar words with me.

So did I want Ben?

No. Ben hated *Hiawatha*, called it sentimental, racist, pseudo-liberal trash. He said it was a punishment to read it and such garbage should be banned. If Longfellow had been alive today, said Ben, he would have been an adman, writing jingles for suppositories.

Lexie?

No. I didn't want my wife. If I'd started quoting any poetry at Lex, she would have told me to shut up. I wanted Rosie Denham to be here, looking at these bright white stars with me. I wanted Rosie, period. So, eureka – in plain English—

'You okay there, bud?'

A police cruiser stopped behind me and two cops got out. One was short and fat, one tall and thin. They loped toward me looking hard and mean, a practised double act, the one they must have learned in cop school or from *Miami Vice*.

'What's up?' asked the fat one.

'I had a flat,' I said.

'So you fixed it now?' demanded thin cop.

'Yeah, all fixed.'

'You was gazing up into the sky and kind of rockin', like you was in a trance.'

'You was talkin' to yourself.'

'Or castin' spells.'

'Or communicatin' with an alien civilisation.'

'You some kind of voodoo-hoodoo freak, and we don't mean the brand of bike?'

'We mean like in voodoo-hoodoo-juju, all that stuff?'

'I was just taking five,' I said.

'Okay, so now you took 'em, why don't you head on home?' Fat cop had his right hand on his gun. 'You're not in a meditation centre now – ain't no ashrams on the public highway.'

'So you got no call to be here, bayin' at the moon,' said thin cop, fondling his piece.

I remembered Rosie telling me the cops aren't armed in the UK, or they're not routinely, anyway. Rosie would be going back to Britain soon. Rosie should be here with me now.

⌐ ROSIE ⌐

'I thought you said your foot was better?' Tess said crossly.

'It still hurts a bit.'

'I think you should go to hospital and get an X-ray. It won't cost you anything, not if you have medical insurance. You do have insurance, don't you?'

'Tess, I can't come out with you today.'

'Why not?'

'I need to do some work.'

'I thought you were on holiday?'

'I am, but I still ought to think about what I'll be doing when I get back to London.'

'Rosie, honeybun, are you okay?' Tess crouched down beside me and laid her cool hand upon my forehead. 'Do you have a temperature?'

'I don't think so,' I replied and turned my laptop screen away so Tess couldn't see what I'd been googling. My goodness, who'd have guessed there'd be so many photographs of Patrick Riley on the web? Brad Pitt, Aidan Turner, eat your livers. At conferences, giving lectures, looking formal in a business suit, looking casual but stylish, I was pleased to note – yes, I know I'm shallower than a children's paddling pool – in dark jeans and a blue weekend shirt on a reservation near Duluth with a group of smiling, black-haired teenagers – what was that about?

'I'm fine,' I added, when she didn't get up.

'Come out with me, then?' she wheedled. Tess was truly brilliant at doing pleading Labrador impressions. It was her superpower. 'I'll take you to this really ace new restaurant for lunch and put it on Ben's card. You must be sick of chicken soup,' she added, with a little twinkle in her eyes.

'Yes, I am – a bit.'

'Me too,' she said ruefully. 'It's pretty rubbish, isn't it? Cooking-wise, I take after my mother. Dad calls her Lucrezia Borgia, says it's just as well we've got a chip shop on the corner of our road. Me and all my brothers, we grew up on chips and pies. Let's go out and have a decent lunch that's made by someone who can cook?'

'All right, you've talked me into it.' *No more chicken bones and gristle soup for me, hurrah!* 'What are we doing this weekend?' I asked.

'Oh, I thought we might invite Professor Riley round. All have dinner Friday evening somewhere nice downtown? Go out Saturday or Sunday in a foursome? Bowling, cinema, a concert – do you have a preference?'

'Any or all of that's okay with me. I don't know if I could manage bowling, but I don't mind watching you lot.' I shrugged or tried to shrug indifferently.

But it's hard to shrug indifferently when all you want to do is jump up grinning like a loon and punch the air.

A whole weekend!

✦ PATRICK ✦

'Pat, you made such a song and dance about losing your kids: how you were going to fight me, stop me taking them out of

82

the state and set the FBI on me – a whole bunch of crazy stuff like that. But now—'

'What do you mean, I made a song and dance?'

'It's something Stephen says. It means you're moaning, kvetching, just because I've asked you to take care of Joe and Polly for a couple days. My attorney says if you don't want to see your children—'

'Okay, okay, I'll have them.'

'You mean for the whole weekend?'

'Yeah, for the entire, complete weekend. Friday afternoon through Sunday evening, is that what you want? What will you be doing, that's if I'm allowed to ask?'

'We're going to San Francisco. One of Stephen's friends is getting married and partners are invited. It's going to be very smart. Stephen said to go look for a special outfit, has to be designer, and before you say it, he's picking up the tab.'

'How extremely generous of him.'

'Pat, don't be so childish, please? If we both behave like we're adults, if everybody can be civilised, this whole thing will be much easier for all concerned.'

'Yeah, easier for you and Mr Wonderful, perhaps. But maybe it's not quite so fine and dandy for the kids and me.'

I'd thought I might see Rosie on the weekend, find out how she was doing, if her foot was better now. But didn't I want to see my children? Yes, of course I did. So possibly we could head over – no, I couldn't take the kids to Ben's. They'd wreck the place. Polly would leave sticky marks or worse on everything. Joe would go maul all Ben's memorabilia of the Minnesota Twins or break one of his precious gadgets – Ben is the original Gadget Man, yet he calls me a geek – and then there would be blood.

So when Ben called me up, suggested dinner, I said I couldn't make it. Sorry, I was busy. Yeah, for the whole weekend.

'You fixed yourself up with some dates?'

'You got it.'

'Man, I'm proud of you! Who are the lucky girls?'

'Beyoncé's stopping by and bringing Katy Perry. I made a gallon of tequila slammers so we're going to have a blast. I'm watching Joe and Polly. I'd have liked to come—'

'But Lex has spoken.'

I didn't know my kids had so much stuff.

Well, I guess I did. It all lived here not so long ago. It was just seeing it dumped in one great pile on the carpet in the living room that made me double-take.

Stroller, clothes and toys and diapers – *why is Polly still in diapers, shouldn't she be out of them by now, she's almost three* – backpacks, special mugs and plates, special cushions, special pillows, special comforters. I could have stocked a store.

'Be good for Daddy.' Lexie kissed them both goodbye. 'Joseph, don't forget to brush your teeth, and just quit trying to get that loose one out until it's good and ready. Polly, when you need the bathroom, tell your daddy, don't—'

'We'll be fine,' I said, wondering if Mr Wonderful was going to show his face, make my acquaintance?

It soon became apparent he was not. What was his problem? I thought we were being civilised? Did that not mean if we should meet I had to shake the bastard by the hand? Yeah, right, in Lexie's dreams. I'd sooner—

'Patrick, are you listening?' Lexie's voice stabbed into my reflections. 'No fast food – no shakes, no sodas, ice creams, burgers, pizzas, chicken fingers, do you hear me?'

'Yeah, I hear you.'

'No grilled cheese sandwiches for Joe because they're way too high in salt and remember Polly is allergic to anything with soy in it. I think she might be getting a wheat intolerance, too.'

'What is the kid allowed to eat?'

'Oh, a ton of stuff! Most fruit except for strawberries – don't give her any strawberries – most vegetables, all oat-and-corn-and-rice-based products, any kind of salad.'

'So, this wheat intolerance, how do I find out—'

'All you need to do is check that everything you give these kids – I think Joe is getting to be wheat intolerant too – is gluten-free. It will say so on the labelling. Oh, and please don't get them any fries.'

'Say goodbye to Mommy,' I told Joe and Polly.

'Goodbye, Mom,' said Joe, while Polly chewed her thumb and gazed from me to Lex with big round puzzled eyes.

'Do as Daddy tells you now,' said Lexie. 'I'll see you guys on Sunday.'

'You happy to be home, kids?' I asked when Lex had gone.

'I guess,' said Joe and shrugged unhappily. 'But my stuff's all gone, except my bed, and Mom says home's with her and Stephen now. Dad, I want to see The Terminator.'

'Yeah, you go say hey. He missed you, Joe.'

'I missed him, too.'

The Terminator hadn't moved to Mr Wonderful's real house with its real yard. Lex said Mr Wonderful was phobic when it came to rats and mice and hamsters, all those little guys with tails and whiskers.

What a coward.

Joe went to check his rodent out. Polly stood there looking lost, bewildered, and my heart ached for my baby girl. I scooped her up and held her tight, inhaling her sweet cotton candy scent.

'What shall we do?' I asked her as she threaded chubby, sticky fingers through my hair, something she had done since she was tiny. 'We could watch a movie, play a game? Or read a book?'

'I'm hungry, Daddy.'

'Let's go get pizza, then. Joe, what do you say to pizza, ice cream floats and fries?'

'We can get pizza, Dad?' Joe frowned, confused. 'Mommy said no pizza.'

'I'm not Mommy.'

'We can have four seasons?'

'Yeah, Joe, sure we can – or even five.'

'Dad, you're so dumb, there's only four.' Joe managed a wan smile. 'The Terminator's doing great,' he added. 'You took good care of him.'

'Yeah,' I said, 'we're buddies, me and the little guy.'

'Pizza, Daddy?' Polly said, reminding me.

'Okay, let's hit the road.'

After pizza, ice cream floats and fries, we picked up a bunch of movies. Then we headed back to the apartment in the trash-mobile.

We watched *Toy Story*, *Cinderella*, *Shrek*. I told the kids a story, gave them supper – Lex-approved this time. I got them into their pyjamas and then put them to bed.

When I woke on Saturday, I found them piled on top of me like puppies, lying in a grunting, snorting heap. I shoved them off of me. Then we had a pillow fight and then I fixed some breakfast. I decided we would have a super-duper day, as Rosie Denham – why couldn't I stop thinking about Rosie, I already told myself to quit – would maybe put it?

'What do you guys want to do?' I asked them, making with the democratic process but reserving my own right of veto in case they wanted to go play with lions or travel into outer space.

'Be a fairy, Daddy,' Polly told me.

'She means she wants to wear her wings,' said Joe disgustedly. 'They're in her Barbie backpack.'

As I pinned Polly's bright pink glittery wings on to her bright pink sweatshirt, Joe started snickering. 'Poll, now you're a fat pink bug,' he said. 'Poll, you look like—'

'Joe, shut up. What do you want to be?'

'A superhero, Dad.'

So I fixed a Rambo-style bandanna round his head, but drew the line at face paint, which in my opinion makes little kids look weird.

Then we went out to find some action.

We went to a play park, manned a fort. But then it started raining, so we went to three museums, which were pretty cool, since you ask, not like the museums I remembered from when I was a kid. There was stuff to ride on, slide on, hide in, levers to be pulled, bubbles to blow, buttons to press.

We got chicken fingers in a downtown fast food outlet. We drank sodas, milkshakes, we ate fries. Then we ran the calories off in Minnehaha Park.

Joe climbed on stuff and jumped on stuff and threw himself off stuff and generally acted like a tough guy. The fairy didn't join in these activities. She sat on my lap and chewed my shirt cuff, like I guess fairies do.

On Sunday it was cold and cloudy, reminding me that winter would soon be on its way. But it wasn't winter yet – hell, we were barely into fall.

'What do you want to wear, you kids?' I asked when we had eaten breakfast.

Joe of course picked out his usual Angry Birds apparel. But Polly wasn't into wings today. She chose a short-sleeved tee, pink jeans and jacket with little guys like robins, sparrows, bluebirds appliquéd – I think that's the word – around the neck and cuffs. The cuffs themselves were fraying where she'd sucked and chewed on them.

Then we went to the Minnesota Zoo, where both kids had

a ball and I did too, I must admit. Why didn't we come here before? We saw the tiger cubs. We checked out all the big brown bears on Russia's Grizzly Coast. We followed foxes round the Northern Trail. We said hey to the beavers and raccoons.

Then we stopped off at a TGI to get more chicken fingers and more fries and chocolate shakes. Joe ate everything, slurped down his shake and asked for more. But Polly didn't seem to want to eat more than a couple fries and half a chicken finger. She didn't touch her shake.

'Polly, are you done?' I asked.

'Daddy, sore.' She had been fidgeting awhile and now she started fussing with her jacket. Sore – maybe she meant she was overheating?

'Come here, baby.' Polly climbed on to my lap, her thumb wedged in her mouth. 'You want to take your jacket off?' I added when she started pulling at the buttons.

She nodded and went right on sucking. So I eased her jacket off. I saw she had a rash all round her neck and down her arms. When did this flare up? It hadn't been there when I dressed her in the morning, I was sure of it.

Joe checked out his sister's spots and poked them, making Polly cry.

'You cut that out,' I told him.

'But we need to make a diagnosis, Dad.'

'So what's your diagnosis?'

'We should take her to the hospital. Daddy, Polly's sick. When little kids get sick, they sometimes die.'

'Polly isn't going to die,' I said.

'Dad, a rash like Polly's could be a real emergency. Our kindergarten teacher told us. Mrs Daley said that if we ever get a rash, we need to tell our parents right away because it could be serious. Dad, we should go to the hospital.'

Maybe Joe was right? I wasn't seriously worried – yet –

but Polly was still crying and the rash around her neck was red and sore and angry.

What to do, call 911, ask for an EMT?

Maybe not, I thought. I don't want to look like Mr Crazy Panicker.

But if Joe was right, if Poll was sick …

So we left the TGI, drove right on over to the children's hospital, passing near where Lexie's friend had his real house with its real yard on Saint Paul's Grand Avenue. I wondered if – since we were in the neighbourhood – we might have time to vandalise the yard.

Maybe later, I decided, after Polly was fixed up.

I made a total screw-up of getting Polly's stroller organised so she could sit in it. I couldn't make sense of the clips and catches. I was scared that when she climbed on board the thing would fall apart.

Who in hell had engineered it, some wise guy from NASA with a grudge against the human race? But I had to sort the stroller. Polly fussed and grizzled when I picked her up as if she was in pain and, as Joe pointed out a dozen times, she was too sick to walk.

We crossed the parking lot and went into the hospital, were clerked and told to wait. Joe was fascinated by the doctors in their scrubs and clogs, and by the kids with bandages, on crutches or in plaster or with patches on their eyes.

So somebody was happy.

But Polly cried and cried. A candy striper stopped and talked to us, assured us we'd be seen as soon as possible, and did I want to get myself a coffee?

'No, thank you,' I replied. *I wouldn't mind a pair of jeans*, I didn't add. My own were soaked where Poll had wet on me. I hadn't changed her diaper in a while and it was leaking now.

'Hey, Dad – check out that poster!' Joe was gazing round

the place, intrigued by all the artwork on the walls, most of it designed to make you feel much sicker than you did before. 'Men-gin-itis, that's what Polly has – look, you can see the rash!'

I checked out the poster. Bacterial meningitis – a killer of young children – if you notice any of these symptoms …

I didn't know what I should do. Polly had a rash. She was hot and sticky. She might have a temperature. She fussed and fussed and fussed. I thought of going to the desk and making a big scene, shouting that my baby here was dying but no one seemed to care.

As I was considering my options, a nurse came up to us. 'Hi, guys,' she began. 'I'm Sandy Pearson, I work in Paediatrics.'

'I'm Joe, and this is Polly,' said my son. 'Polly here's real sick.'

'We'll soon fix Polly,' Sandy said. Then she took us to a doctor's office, white clogs slap-slapping on the rubber floor.

'Hey, hey, little lady – there's no need for all this fuss!' The tired-looking resident – well, I guess he had to be a doctor, even though he looked about fourteen – smiled reassuringly.

What did he know?

The nurse helped Polly squirm out of her jacket and her tee. Then the doctor looked at Polly's rash. He took her temperature. He checked her pulse and listened to her heart. He looked into her ears and down her throat.

Joe was almost literally fizzing with excitement, like a soda bottle that's been all shook up.

'What's Polly done today?' the doctor asked us.

'We took her to the zoo,' said Joe. 'We saw the tiger cubs and bears and foxes. She liked the foxes best.'

'Did you introduce her to the monkeys?'

'No,' Joe told him, puzzled. 'Why would we do that?'

'The monkeys are our cousins. It's good to visit with our

families from time to time. Swing by and say hello, how are you doing?'

'Yeah, I guess,' conceded Joe. 'When's Polly going to die?'

'Oh, not for years and years,' the doctor said. 'I'm guessing Polly here will live to be a hundred.'

'Yeah?' said Joe incredulously. 'I thought she was dying. The gerbil in our homeroom died. It had a rash as well.'

'No kidding, little buddy. That jacket, is it made of wool?' the doctor asked me, pointing to it.

'I don't know.'

'I guess there'll be a tag?'

I checked the tag and it said wool.

'Okay,' said the doctor. 'Polly doesn't like wool next her skin. I'll let you have some cream. Apply it four times daily and the rash should soon clear up.'

'She won't need any other meds? No painkillers? You don't need to run some blood work to be sure it's just an allergy?'

'No blood work,' said the doctor wearily. 'No other meds. You guys remember no wool next the skin and Polly here is going to be fine.'

'We got it, Doc,' Joe told him, man to man.

The doctor gave him a high five.

I got a prescription and was told to take it to the pharmacy.

As we were walking down the corridor, the candy striper happened by again and asked Joe if he'd like a juice or popsicle? Joe beamed at her and said he surely would and thank you, ma'am. She beamed right back at him and took his hand. I could see her thinking, *a kid with good, old-fashioned manners, someone's raising children right today*. Then she said if I would like, she'd take him to the hospital canteen and meet us there. She also told me where to find the pharmacy, like I was dumb or something and couldn't read the signs.

As I was waiting in the pharmacy, the nurse we'd seen came in. She nodded hi and then went through a door into an office. But she left the door ajar.

'That's the guy through there?' asked someone else.

'Yeah, that's him,' the nurse replied and I could hear the giggle in her voice. 'A case of weekend father syndrome, he was panicking because his baby had a little rash.'

'What was it?'

'Just an allergy. He'd dressed the kid in a wool jacket and she had a lanoline reaction.'

'He should have known, the klutz. No wool next to the skin on babies, it's an irritant.'

'Quiet down, Mary-Lou, he'll hear you.'

'Well, perhaps he ought to hear me? Guys like that, they say they're fathers, but they never change a diaper, never read a tag. They never use their brains.'

'Their brains live in their shorts and they—'

I didn't hear the rest because they realised they hadn't shut the door and now they closed it, snickering.

'Mr Riley?' said the pharmacist. 'Okay, this is a moisturising cream. It's very light and you can use it any time. Just smooth it on your daughter's skin, don't rub, and soon ...'

She rattled on like I was stupid and had never seen a tube of cream in my whole life. I took the stuff and headed out the pharmacy with Polly and her discharge papers, feeling like a fool.

'Dad, is Polly going to die?' asked Joe as I strapped them both into the backseat of the trash-mobile then offered them some bran-rich cookies from a store of sugar, salt and allergen-free snacks that Lex kept on the dash.

'No,' I told him. 'Polly won't be dying yet awhile. You heard that doctor, didn't you? She's going to live at least a hundred years.'

Joe looked so disappointed. I thought he would cry. But the little guy was tired. He'd had a busy day. He'd been to the zoo and to the children's hospital. He'd seen tigers, foxes, doctors, nurses, candy stripers, kids with plasters on their wrists and ankles, kids with pirate patches, just like on TV. He'd have lots to say to Mrs Daley on Monday, wouldn't he?

Oh, and to tell his mother, too.

'Mommy, Mommy, we went to the hospital! Polly nearly died!'

'What?' Lexie stared at me in horror. 'Pat, whatever happened? Did you let her fall, eat something bad?'

'She had an allergy.' I shrugged. 'But I didn't know it at the time. I thought it needed checking out.'

'You took her to the children's hospital?'

'Yeah, we went to the ER and Joe thought he had died and gone to heaven.'

'Please don't talk about my children dying. Pat, you should have called the doctor's office. There's a weekend number in the binder. You say she had an allergy. What caused it?'

'It was a wool reaction.'

'Oh, I see,' said Lexie and did her best school-principal-from-hell impression – folded arms and mouth set in an angry, disapproving line. 'She wore her robin jacket, is that right?'

'Yeah, but she—'

'Patrick, you should know – no wool next to the skin, particularly in the case of little ones and babies.'

'So why do you dress the kid in wool?'

'When she wears that little coat, she also wears a tee with a high neck and sleeves that come down to her wrists. If you ever noticed what your children wore, you would have noticed that.'

'Why don't you put it in the garbage and buy her a new jacket made of cotton or whatever?'

'Your mother sent it on her birthday.' Lexie sighed. 'I never would have bought it. The stupid thing's hand wash, and that's a drag. But Polly really loves it. She loves the birds on it. They all got names. She sucks the cuffs as well – that's why they're fraying.'

Yeah, I thought, it figured. It was the sort of jacket Mom would buy. She loves to get new clothes for Polly, real expensive stuff she can't afford, perhaps because I had a little sister who died of scarlet fever before I came along.

'Good weekend?' I asked to change the subject and hoping Mr Wonderful had fallen off a bridge and drowned to death. Or somehow got himself burned up in a precisely-targeted incendiary attack.

'Yeah, it was great.' At the thought of Mr Wonderful – or so I guessed – Lex became all bright and glowing, and I wondered if I'd ever made my wife light up? I never checked.

'What did you do?' I asked.

'I told you, one of Stephen's friends got married. Come on, kids, it's late and you got school and stuff tomorrow. You should be in bed.'

As Lexie hurried them toward the door, Joe turned to glance at me. 'Thank you for the weekend, Dad,' he said. 'I had the best time ever.'

'Why was that, then?' I was curious to know what I got right and to hear him talk about it while his mother listened.

'Come on, guys,' repeated Lexie. 'Stephen's waiting.'

Let him wait, I thought. I hunkered down so that my eyes were level with my son's. 'What did you like best about the weekend, little buddy?'

'The zoo was awesome, we got fries and shakes, and you took us to the hospital.'

'You bought them fries?' snapped Lexie, adding this new crime and misdemeanour to the charge sheet for, according to the Gospel of St Lexie, fries were the Great Satan.

'You'll take care of The Terminator, Dad?' said Joe as Lexie zipped his hoodie.

'Yeah, sure I will,' I promised. 'I'll see you kids tomorrow after school. We'll bake up cupcakes.'

'I get to put the frosting on?'

'Of course.'

'Joe and Polly, do I have to tell you for the third time?' Lexie glared at me. 'You're doing this on purpose, Patrick, trying to alienate my children. My attorney warned me about devious guys like you.'

She pushed them out the door.

I fed The Terminator, shot the breeze with him awhile. But I have to tell you now that hamsters aren't the greatest when it comes to conversation.

I took a shower and grabbed a beer, lay on the couch and watched some trash TV, missing my kids, my cotton-candy-scented baby, my little tough guy Joe.

I missed Rosie, too – and missing Rosie made me hurt like I had never hurt before. If hearts and minds can truly ache, mine did that Sunday night.

⌒ ROSIE ⌒

I got so excited.

I did my hair and did my nails and gave myself a special lime-and-mango facial that was guaranteed to make me glow. By Friday lunchtime, I was more than glowing. I was almost radioactive with anticipation.

But Patrick didn't come. On Friday evening, there were just the three of us for dinner, which we had at home – a takeout pizza, coleslaw, garlic bread – because there was a game on television Ben wanted to see.

Okay, perhaps on Friday Pat was tired? But surely he'd turn up on Saturday, if only to see Ben? I wasn't going to ask.

I wasn't going to say his name out loud because I knew I'd colour up. Tess was sure to notice and she would laugh and tease me.

But I'm sorry, this was not a laughing matter.

On Saturday I said I had a headache when Ben suggested he and Tess and I should go and check out something scenic, a waterfall or lake or something wet, I didn't catch its name. So he and Tess went out while I stayed home, because for some ridiculous reason I was certain Pat would call me.

I was wrong, of course. I mean, good heavens, psychic – me? I'm just about as psychic as a box of jelly doughnuts.

'What's the matter, Rosie?' Ben enquired when he and Tess came home again with their usual clutch of carrier bags – more clothes for Tess, gadgets for him. 'Your colour's very high. Perhaps you have a temperature? I said we ought to get that foot checked out.'

'She's wearing make-up, stupid.' Tess looked hard at me. 'You going somewhere, are you?'

'No, trying out some samples. Fan wants feedback for a magazine.'

'The eye-shadow's well cool. No streaks, no lines, no creases. It's subtly metallic but not trashy bright. The lipstick's horrible. That kind of scarlet isn't good on everyone and it's not good on you. But it might suit me. I'll go and try it, shall I? You can tell me what you think?'

'Okay.'

'Do you need a sealer? Does it bleed?'

'It doesn't bleed.'

But my heart was bleeding because Patrick clearly wasn't coming and I could have cried and cried.

On Sunday morning, while we were having breakfast and I had got my hopes up high as skyscrapers all over again – *today*, I thought, *he's sure to come* – Ben happened to observe that we would not be seeing Pat because he had to watch his children all weekend.

'Hey, you don't take sugar in your coffee,' Tess said, frowning as she watched me spooning it into my mug. 'It's very bad for you.'

'I fancy something bad for me today.'

'So be a little more adventurous? Sugar, it's just empty carbohydrate. All it will do is make you fat and spotty and give you diabetes. I read about it in a magazine. Let's go shopping, shall we – get a little healthy exercise?'

On Monday afternoon, while we were at the MoA and getting healthy exercise and Tess was buying casual clothes for Ben in Gap and Urban Outfitters – she was taking his restructuring programme very seriously indeed, but wasn't getting any real designer stuff for him just yet because she didn't want to frighten him – her mobile rang.

Maybe it was Ben to say he wouldn't be home for dinner?

That morning, he'd gone into college early for a meeting with the dean – or that was where he'd told us he was going, anyway – smelling like he'd fallen in a vat of aftershave. I'd wondered if the dean was twenty-five and blonde and sexy. I sort of guessed Tess might be wondering, too.

'You mean this week?' she said, sounding surprised. 'Well, I suppose so. Yeah, it's very exciting. We'll see you later, shall we? Yeah, I love you, too.'

'What was that about?' I asked.

'Ben's going to New York tomorrow. He needs to see his publisher.' She slipped her phone into her bag and then glanced up at me. She looked apologetic. 'I'll feel very mean about it, leaving you to entertain yourself, but he wants me to go.'

'Of course he does,' I said. 'Tess, you're his wife.'

'Yeah, I'm Mrs Fairfax Three.' She shrugged. 'I'm

wondering now, if he wants company, maybe I should say take Mrs Fairfax One or Two? One lives in Virginia and Two is in New Jersey. One of them could go with him, perhaps?'

'But don't you want to go?'

'It'll probably be quite boring, listening to Ben and Mr Publisher droning on about Ben's books. I'm not an intellectual, as you know. But One and Two are intellectuals, and Ben and they are still good friends, whatever that might mean. They're still in contact, anyway, especially Ben and Mrs Fairfax Two. She's his literary executor.'

'Why is she his literary executor?'

'Oh, she's a professor in some college. So she knows all about that sort of stuff.'

'She might, but *you're* Ben's wife,' I said. 'I think it should be you.'

'But she's welcome, Rosie. The whole thing sounds a total waste of time and energy. He sends her copies of all his paperwork and emails, photographs, the lot, so she can keep them in a special archive and write his authorised biography, that's when the time is right. I mean, is he up himself, or what?'

'You mean every letter, every email, this woman gets a copy?'

'Yeah, that's what he told me.'

'The personal stuff as well?'

'I suppose so.' Tess looked almost tearful. 'The more I think about it, the more I wonder if this Ben-and-me thing was a terrible mistake. I think I'll tell him I'm not going to New York.'

'Oh, don't be silly, Tess,' I scolded briskly, no doubt sounding like my mother telling off a juvenile delinquent who was up before the bench for stealing fags from newsagents. 'New York City – Bloomingdale's and Barneys, think of it – Ben's Amex Gold and Saks Fifth Avenue, a marriage made in heaven!'

'You might have a point.'

When I mentioned Barneys and Saks Fifth Avenue, Tess brightened up a little. But she was not as excited as I thought she ought to be. 'Tess, what's the matter? Ben's previous wives, they left because their marriages went wrong. Or he left them – whatever. You and he, you like each other, love each other, don't you?'

'Yeah, I know, and yeah, I sort of love him. But I wonder – oh, it's probably nothing. You think you'll be all right here by yourself?'

'Of course I shall. I'll go to the Institute of Arts, to some museums. I'll go and see the Capitol.'

'Oh.' Tess shrugged. 'The Capitol – yeah, right, that will be thrilling. Listen, Rosie, you don't need to do stuff on your own. Why don't you ring Patrick?'

How could she have said his name like that, with no warning, with no lead-up, without giving me a chance to sort my face out, organise my casual response so it would sound as if I wasn't bothered one way or the other?

'W-why would I ring Pat?' I managed to croak at last.

'He's really missing Lexie. So I expect he would be glad to take you out to dinner. Or at least meet up with you for coffee. I'm sure he would enjoy your company.'

'You mean I'd be a sort of babysitter while his best mate Ben is out of town?'

'Well, that's one way of putting it,' said Tess. She looked at me. So had she guessed? No, how could she guess, when inscrutability's my superpower? 'Ben's so worried about him,' she continued. 'He's never been a talker, but nowadays it's like he's an elective mute or something. When they meet up for a beer, he hardly says a word.'

He probably doesn't get a chance, I thought, what with Ben and his relentless bragging about foreign rights and big, fat royalties, me, me, me, me, me.

'You're so good with people, Rosie. Everybody likes you, tells you stuff. Ben is doing his best to help Pat deal with all the Lexie fallout. But, like I just told you, he's not getting very far. Maybe you could get him to open up a bit?'

'I'll try.'

'Good girl – and you know what, talking might help you as well, perhaps? The Charlie stuff, I mean. You ought to talk.'

'I'm not discussing it with Pat!'

'But you could talk to me.'

'I'll think about it.'

'Yeah, why don't you? Listen, we'll be back in time to take you to the airport, see you off.'

'Okay, Tess – that's fine.'

'Okay it's fine that you'll be on your own and okay you'll call Pat?'

'Tess, why don't you go to New York City, burn some plastic, stop fretting about Mrs Fairfax One and Mrs Fairfax Two and Ben and Pat and me?'

'Yeah, all right,' she said. 'But I still think—'

'Let's go and get a coffee. We could have some chocolate muffins, too. Get fat and spotty, shall we? Or get a sugar rush, at any rate?'

What choice did I have?

This was a gift from some kind fairy, and it's rude and mean to turn down gifts. The minute Tess and Ben went off to catch their plane to John F Kennedy, I rang Patrick Riley.

He didn't seem surprised to hear from me, so maybe he'd been warned I'd be in touch? But was he pleased? I couldn't tell. At least he didn't cut me off. He didn't say he had to go and see a student, give a lecture, eat a bagel, snap some gum.

He asked what I'd been doing with myself since he had seen me last. He seemed to listen while I told him I'd been to the MoA with Tess about a dozen times and I was all shopped out, something I had never thought would happen to somebody like me.

'You might be an enthusiast but you're not yet an addict?' he suggested.

'You could well be right.' But Tess was definitely addicted, I continued. She could never, ever get enough of going to the MoA. She started hyperventilating when we drove into the parking lot. She developed cyborg laser vision and her Amex card began to glow.

'She strides around the place as if she's on a mission to save Planet Retail,' I told Pat. 'She's the Arnold Schwarzenegger of the MoA, the super-customer who's armed and dangerous with an arsenal of super-cards. She should get a Purple Heart for courage in the face of overwhelming shopping opportunities. Or free pizza on demand, at least.'

He laughed at that. It was a real laugh. It wasn't forced. I'd stake my life on it. It was the laugh I'd heard when Tess was telling us about restructuring Ben, and it made me feel all warm inside.

'How's that foot of yours?' he asked me.

'It's much better, thank you.'

'You're walking normally again?'

'I am indeed – well, almost normally.'

'You get around okay?'

'I do.'

'So you could take a ride downtown, perhaps?'

'Yes, that might be possible.'

'Maybe you could call a cab? Come meet me for a coffee sometime?'

'Maybe,' I conceded. 'When would be good for you?'

'I'd have to check my schedule. But I figure there must be a window someplace.'

Goodness, were we flirting?

Ten or fifteen minutes later, we arranged to meet when he had finished work the following day and spent time with his children, who he said he saw most early evenings for an hour or two.

So I would be rendezvousing with Professor Riley in a downtown coffee shop at seven on Wednesday evening. Just how many hours away was that? How many minutes? I started calculating – hours, minutes, seconds. There were far too many seconds. If I counted seconds, it was much too long to wait.

❖ PATRICK ❖

What did we talk about?

I don't exactly know. I listened to her voice, is all, and thought how it would be just perfect for my GPS.

As she spoke, I analysed its tones and cadences. I heard it rise and fall, decided it was sometimes clear and crisp as a cold Minnesota winter morning. But it somehow managed to be dark and smouldering too, with the promise of a fire of scented pinecones on December nights …

This was crazy. I was crazy. After all, I was so busy work-wise, setting up a whole new research programme, finding graduate students who could work on it and trying to get funding from industry and commerce.

You don't have the time for complications in your life, I told myself. *You should call and cancel, say you have a meeting or you need to see a student or your children. Or your wife …*

Sometime I had to see my wife and try to sort stuff out, not in an attorney's office or a court of law, but in somewhere neutral like a Starbucks, somewhere semi-public where we'd both have to behave.

Lex was being awkward about access to the kids,

complaining that she had a ton of stuff to do around about half five, which of course was my best time to see them – after I could get away from work, and after they had finished school and pre-school, but before they went to bed. She announced she couldn't be expected to deliver Joe and Poll to the apartment any time it suited me.

'When would be convenient, then?' I asked, when she called me up to talk about it. Or I should say lay it on the line.

'Patrick, don't you take that tone with me.'

'Oh, what tone is that?'

'You know – sarcastic, flippant. If you want this access thing to work, you must co-operate. My attorney says ...'

I let her quote her legal team for several tedious minutes.

Then I asked what time would suit her complicated schedule of beauty parlour treatments, appointments with her personal shopper, therapist, masseuse?

I let her squawk at me again for being so facetious. Then I agreed to fetch the kids from school (Joe) and Angie (Polly), bring them back to the apartment where Lex would collect them at half six, that's after they had dinner.

No additive-rich shakes, no chicken fingers and definitely no fries, some fresh fruit and salad every day, green vegetables and carrot sticks – yeah, yeah, yeah, I got it.

'Oh, and Pat, a couple other things ...'

As she rambled on, I thought, I loved this woman once. But now I didn't even like my wife, for everything about her grated – voice, appearance, manner, attitude. Most everything she said seemed mean and vengeful, like she thought I should be punished. You beat up on your dog, you have to tell yourself the dog deserves a beating, or where does it leave you?

'So, half six,' said Lexie, winding up her monologue. 'I'll expect them to have eaten dinner and be in their outdoor things and waiting in the lobby for me. Or it might be Stephen fetching them some evenings, that's if I'm delayed.'

'Lex, it will be you,' I said. 'I'm not about to hand my children over to some stranger. So until you come fetch Joe and Polly, I mean from the apartment, they will remain with me.'

'You and Stephen ought to meet, be adult and civilised about this situation.'

'I ought to flatten him.'

'Patrick, that's the sort of crazy talk nobody wants to hear, and if you go on being so obstreperous, my attorney says—'

I'd had enough and disconnected.

⌒ ROSIE ⌒

I was far too early – about an hour early, actually.

I ordered a black coffee. But I was so nervous, so wound up, to me it smelled and tasted like soot dissolved in vinegar, even with three sugars in it, and I couldn't bring myself to drink it.

Then, at last, he came.

I watched him as he walked in through the door and as he looked around for me. He was frowning slightly and seemed a little puzzled, as if he had forgotten why he'd come. But instead of finding this alarming or insulting, I found it most endearing. I watched him with increasing pleasure, waiting for his gaze to light on me. When at last it did, he smiled, came up. 'Hi, Rosie,' he began.

'Hello.' Why did he have to say my name? Now my heart was acting like a teenager on heat, thumping like it wanted to burst out of my chest.

'You been here long?' he asked.

'No, only a few minutes,' I replied, or rather lied.

'How's the foot?'

'Oh, it's absolutely fine today!' I told him breezily. No doubt I sounded like the captain of the sixth form netball team.

It was colder in the evenings now. The greens of summer were gradually bowing out and almost every tree was turning russet, red or gold. As Pat sat down, he pulled a black wool scarf – perhaps it was cashmere – from round his neck.

Who buys your clothes, I asked him, but only in my head. *I rather hope it's you and not your wife. I hope you choose. But whoever does it has good taste. A little safe, a little too conservative, perhaps. You could dress ten years younger, which would be closer to your actual age. But on the whole you'll definitely do …*

'I'll go grab a cappuccino. May I get you anything – some cookies, chocolate, candy? Rosie?'

'What?' *Just stop all this*, I told myself. *Stop speculating and come back to reality!* 'What did you just ask me?'

'How about a brownie or more coffee?'

'Thank you, I'm okay.'

He went up to the counter and came back with his coffee and a muffin. 'Do you have plans this evening?' he enquired.

'No, I'm doing nothing in particular. So I'm very open to suggestion.' But this was not a date, for heaven's sake. We were mere acquaintances, mere friends of friends, just meeting up for coffee.

'What kinds of things do you like to do?' he asked.

I watched him as he peeled the greaseproof paper off his muffin, carefully, unhurriedly, not tearing it at all, and I wished he was peeling my underwear off me. *I like to be with you*, I thought. 'What could we do at such short notice?'

'Well … '

He was looking at me now and I could see his dark brown gaze was serious but friendly. I thought he probably looked at all his students in the same approachable but neutral manner. 'Do you like ballet?'

Please don't look at me, I thought. *When you look at me I want to kiss you and that would be a very, very stupid thing to do.*

'I'm not a fan,' I said. 'I can see it's clever and I know all dancers have to train and train and train. But to me it looks like posers prancing round and showing us their pants.'

'Excuse me?'

'Panties, I suppose you call them – knickers.'

'Oh, I see.' He smiled, but it was the sort of weary, rueful smile you give a tiresome child. 'Music, then – do you like music?'

'Yes, I do.'

'What kind of music?'

'Anything, as long as it's not really weird – long silences or people dropping pebbles in a box and calling it a soul concerto, idiotic stuff like that. I like something with a melody.'

'I don't think I've come across the pebbles in the box concerto, so it can't have made its debut in the USA. What about American composers – Aaron Copland, George and Ira Gershwin, Jerome Kern – they do anything for you?'

'I don't know their stuff.'

'It's great. I love it. You should make its acquaintance.'

He stirred his foaming cappuccino, round and round and round, dissolving all the chocolate dust, or most of it. There was a little smudge of chocolate powder on his index finger and I couldn't take my eyes off it. I longed to lick it off.

'So – shall we go listen to something with a melody tonight?' he added, picking up his cup and drinking, dotting foam along his upper lip. It made him look completely edible.

I will come and listen to anything provided I'm with you, I thought. *People banging dustbin lids together, dropping stones down wells, you choose.*

'Who's playing what?' I asked, all cool and unconcerned, or so I hoped.

'The Minnesota Orchestra. A Polish guy's their soloist tonight and he'll be playing the *Emperor* concerto. Do you know it? One of my graduate students told me this man is sensational and I would like to hear him.'

'So would I.'

'Okay, that's what we'll do. I checked the website earlier and there are tickets left. We'll be too late to catch the Mendelssohn this guy is playing first, but we can go in at half time.'

What was this *Emperor* concerto? I didn't like to say I'd never heard of it, that I preferred Bob Dylan, Amy Winehouse and Christina Perri.

Pat drank his coffee, ate his muffin.

'Good to go?' he asked me, putting down his cup and winding his black scarf around his neck.

'Yes, good to go,' I trilled. I was so jealous of that scarf!

'Please could you pass my handbag?' I pointed to the chair beside him where I'd dumped my coat and bag. 'I need a paper hankie. I thought I had one up my sleeve, but it's not there and so I'll need to have a little rummage.' What an idiot, I thought. I must sound like my mother. What must he make of me?

I didn't listen to the *Emperor* concerto.

I was hardly conscious of the hall, the Minnesota Orchestra, the brilliant Polish guy. It was as if they were all under water and everything was muted, blurred – everything, that is, except for him.

Patrick Riley was as sharp and clear as a bright summer morning. As we sat there listening – or in my case not listening – to the Minnesota Orchestra, all my senses were attuned to him.

I heard his soft and regular breathing. There was his right hand upon the armrest, a mere inch or so away from mine. He had attractive hands – of course I had already noticed that – square and capable, with blunt-cut nails, and perfect on a man.

Whenever I could – or dared – I glanced at him. I breathed him in, I almost tasted him. I lost myself in him.

He'd taken off his dark grey jacket and I saw he had a brand new shirt on – light blue cotton with a pale grey stripe. Perhaps he'd bought it earlier that day? There were telltale creases on the sleeves, across the chest, and every time he breathed I saw his ribcage rise, rise, rise, then fall, fall, fall again.

I could smell something faintly cinnamon-scented – was it him? It was delicious anyway, and I wanted, wanted to press my palm against his chest, to feel the warmth of him.

I wanted, wanted to take his hand and—

This was truly awful. I forced myself to breathe more slowly, deeply. I told myself to think of school dinners, trying to find a taxi in the rush hour, hockey on wet winter mornings, putting out the bins. Anything but Patrick Riley sitting next to me, conscious of him breathing in and out and wanting, wanting him …

Then it was all over and everybody started getting up. Pat was putting on his coat and, as he raised his arms, I became aware of the most potent and attractive of all scents to women, that of warm and clean and sexy man.

'What did you think?' he asked me, handing me the scarf I had forgotten.

'Oh, I loved it,' I replied. 'Did you?'

'I thought it was exceptional.' He smiled and made my heart turn somersaults. 'I guess you must be hungry now?'

'A little, I suppose.'

'Do you want to go get a Chinese?'

'That would be great.' I wanted him to take my hand. But of course he wouldn't, I knew that, and it was just as well.

'You'll be going back to England soon,' he said, as they put our dishes of special egg-fried rice, of beef in black bean sauce, of chicken with pineapple and cashew nuts, of sticky ribs and all the other stuff he'd ordered – without asking me, I have to say, which was either very caring, masterful or downright rude of him – on the glass and aluminium table in the most upmarket Chinese restaurant I had ever come across. 'You'll be glad to see your folks again.'

'I suppose so.'

'You don't sound too sure.'

'It will be good to see my family.' I forced a smile. 'But when I get home, I shall be starting my own business, and I suppose I might be just a little bit afraid.'

'I'm sure you'll do just fine.' He forked up noodles, bean sprouts, prawns and rice. No chopsticks for Professor Riley, I observed. They were lying unbroken by his plate. I didn't blame him. I was total rubbish when it came to using chopsticks and I also used a fork. 'How do you like the food?' he asked.

'It's wonderful.'

'It's always good in here.' He scooped up chicken, pineapple, cashews. But he didn't eat – instead, his fork stayed hovering above his plate. 'There must be some guy in Britain who is looking forward to seeing you again?' he added, looking straight at me.

'No.' I shrugged, remembering the best man at that wedding with the bridesmaid's scarlet knickers on his head. He'd been the last to make a pass at me. 'There's nobody at all. Actually, I don't have too much history with guys.'

'You mean you don't like men?'

Well, for goodness sake – direct or what? 'I like men

well enough,' I said. 'I've been on dates. But I've never been especially close to one particular man. I've never got engaged or anything. I'm sure my mother thinks I must be gay.'

'So are you?'

'No – and before you ask me, I'm not bisexual, either.'

I think I must have sounded quite offended because his ears went red. 'I'm sorry, Rosie. Of course it isn't any of my business.' He waved his fork over his laden plate of everything on offer. 'I'm glad you like my choice of food,' he added. 'When the guy came up to take our order, you didn't seem to notice he was there. When he spoke to you, you didn't answer. It seemed like you were in a kind of daydream. So I asked him to bring a bunch of stuff.'

'Oh, good heavens, I do apologise.' I wished the ground would open up and swallow me, digest me. I felt my face catch fire. 'I've always been a dreamer,' I said, or rather muttered. 'My teachers all despaired of me.' But although this was the truth, or at least a kind of truth, I could not remember actually zoning out before.

I forced myself to swallow a half-chewed piece of mushroom. It felt like I was choking on a slug. 'This is all fantastic,' I said brightly, Miss Congeniality herself. 'I've always loved Chinese.'

He didn't speak – instead, looked at me intently, unspoken questions in his dark brown eyes. I met his gaze for maybe twenty seconds. Then I stared down at the table. There was his left hand holding his fork and on his third finger was his wedding ring, which I had never noticed until now.

Or not wanted to notice? Why had I met this man? Why had I rung him? Why was I here with him? I couldn't deal with the emotions I was feeling.

They asked too much of me.

'Rosie, are you done?' I asked.

'I think so,' she replied, putting down her silverware and sighing. 'I'm sorry, Pat,' she added. 'Absolutely everything is totally delicious, but I'm tired.'

No, I told the waiter who was hovering beside us. No, I didn't want a doggie bag. Yeah, the food was excellent. There was no problem with the food or service, but we were running late for something and we had to dash. Yeah, we'd come back soon.

'I'll call a cab for you,' I said when we were on the sidewalk, thinking I can't stand all this much longer. But in another way I'd like to stand it all my life.

'Or maybe you could drive me? I'd appreciate it if you would.'

Did she know what she was doing to me?

No, she couldn't know. But her eyes were bright and she looked feverish and she couldn't concentrate when we were in the restaurant. I swear she didn't listen to that music. She hardly touched her food. She clearly wasn't well. So we walked the couple hundred yards back to the parking lot where I had left the trash-mobile.

'I need to have a blitz on this,' I said apologetically, sweeping candy wrappers and juice containers off the seats to add to the debris and garbage rotting on the floor.

'You should see my Fiesta. It's full of junk, much worse than this. I don't have your excuse because I haven't any children.' She smiled a rueful smile. 'Any mess I make is down to me.'

Yes, I thought, and how.

When we reached Ben's apartment building, I found I couldn't stand to let her go. So I walked her past the dozing janitor, through the empty lobby and then we rode the elevator up to the ninth floor.

I stood there while she rummaged in her handbag – yeah, I was learning Britglish – for the keys.

'Thank you for coming out with me tonight,' she said as she pushed the key into the lock. 'What do I owe you for the concert, meal and stuff?'

'You don't owe me anything at all.' I never let a woman pay. I do have some pride. 'Thank you for your company this evening.' *Rosie, please invite me in*, I begged her in my mind. *No, don't – that would be crazy.* 'When did you say you're due to go back home?' I asked.

'I didn't, but my flight's on Friday evening.'

'So tomorrow will be your last day. Let's meet up tomorrow eightish, shall we? Go someplace for dinner?'

'Tess and Ben are coming home tomorrow.'

'Yeah, I know. The four of us could go for an Italian. Ben doesn't do adventurous with food and so American-Italian is just about as daring as it gets. I'll book a table, shall I?'

'Yes, that would be lovely. Well, it's getting late, and you must have to go to work tomorrow, so I'll say goodnight.'

'Goodnight – sleep well – sweet dreams.'

Why was I saying all this shit? Why didn't I take this woman in my arms and kiss and kiss and kiss her until she begged for mercy? Why didn't I go swim with alligators – that would make more sense?

As I told myself to move, but somehow couldn't get my dumbass legs to understand, my cell phone chirped.

I got a text from Ben.

The CEO of Ryder Books is taking Tess and me to lunch at the Algonquin Friday. Where Dottie Parker and Vicious Circle used to meet – you know? I guess you don't, you ignorant mechanic! So could you see Rosie gets her plane?

As Pat was scrolling through his texts and I was trying to stop myself from grabbing him and pulling him into the flat and tearing off his nice new shirt and making all those plastic buttons ping across the room, I got a text from Tess.

Sorry, sorry, sorry. But we're not coming back for 3 more days. Ben wants to have lunch at this hotel where some old bat called Dottie Parker used to go. He's so excited. This evening, he was almost snogging Mr CEO! I said why don't u 2 get a room, not go to the Algongything hotel? Anyway, Ben's

Then the text broke off.

Twenty seconds later – I was counting and also watching Patrick Riley's fingers typing something, wishing they were tapping out a text on me – my mobile chirped again.

texted Pat and says he's sure he'll take u to the airport, see u off. I hope he will. Did u get to see him in the meantime? Did he meet u anywhere downtown? Did u have a coffee?

Gotta go! TX

'You must go and get some sleep,' I said to Pat.

'Yeah, I guess I must.' He pushed his phone into his pocket. 'Thank you for a pleasant evening, Rosie.'

I don't think I've ever felt so lonely as I watched him walk towards the lift, oblivious of the state in which he left me.

I was awake all night.

At half past seven the following morning, I got a call from Pat.

'Did I wake you?'

'No,' I told him as my heart began to thump.

'Do you have a busy day ahead?'

'Yes, fairly busy. I need to send some emails, write to people who might give me work and then sort out my website.'

Why didn't I say I was completely free, and when and where could we meet up, perhaps for lunch? Where were we going for dinner, was that still on tonight? But I suppose I'm British …

'I expect you're busy, too?' I asked him.

'Yeah, I got a bunch of classes, meeting with the dean, an article to finish, some papers to review – the usual stuff. I'll see you later, shall I?'

'No.'

'I'm sorry? But I thought—'

'I don't have time for dinner, after all.' Why did I say that? I wanted more than anything to see him! So what was stopping me?

I was afraid.

We'd have dinner. He would bring me back to this apartment. So I would invite him in for coffee. Stuff would happen. Or I would do my best to make it happen, anyway.

But if something, anything should happen, where would that leave me? I'd have been a momentary diversion for a married man whose wife might want him back some day, and who was the father of two children. I'd go home and we would never meet again. So why meet at all?

'I have to do my packing,' I said lamely. 'I need to sort things out.'

'Of course you do. Okay, I'll take you to the airport.'

'I was thinking I could get a cab.'

'I'll pick you up about half six to seven tomorrow evening. We can get a coffee and a sandwich at the airport. You have a great day.'

'Patrick, wait, I've changed my mind, I—'

But he had already disconnected.

I moped around the place all day, trying to work and mostly

failing, sending emails, ringing Fanny for advice, fiddling with my website and my blog and drinking pints of coffee.

I was almost on the ceiling by the evening. I didn't sleep at all that night, and I did my packing Friday morning in a coffeeholic haze. I don't remember getting in Pat's Honda or driving to the airport. I only knew I was with him, that's all, experiencing him.

We stood there at the barrier.

'It's been great to know you, Rosie Denham.'

He offered me his hand.

I almost took it. But then I decided it couldn't end like this. I had to taste him, feel him – know if he was warm or cold and if his mouth was hard or soft. If I didn't grab this opportunity, I knew I would regret it all my life. So I took him by the shoulders, pulled him close to me and then I kissed him.

He didn't pull away from me. But that was probably because he couldn't quite believe what I was doing, that I'd grabbed him in a public place and started snogging him.

They called my flight.

He took no notice. He wrapped his arms around me and he kissed me. Almost hesitatingly at first, but very soon his kisses grew fierce and hard and hungry. I forgot the time, the place, for at that moment nothing else existed. The world was made of him.

They called my flight again.

I let him go. Stepping back a pace or two, I ran my fingers through my messed-up hair. Patrick Riley looked at me. What would he say now, if anything? I couldn't tell what he was thinking, could not read the expression in his eyes.

But that's the thing about brown eyes, of course. They don't give much away. My own are grey, transparent. So, when I was little, my mother always knew when I was fibbing. But I bet his mother never knew.

'You need to go.' He pushed his hand into his pocket, found a card and handed it to me. 'Let me know you got home safe?'

'I shall.'

I wasn't going to say goodbye. My lips still smarting from his kisses, I walked through the barrier and went to catch my plane.

A married man, a father of small children – whatever was I thinking? But I couldn't regret what I had done. As I stood in the queue to board, I looked at Patrick's card – plain black and white, no colours, frills or furbelows, but with all the details I would need to contact him again. It was the most precious thing I owned – a holy relic, a magic talisman.

Let me know you got home safe, he'd said.

I remembered reading somewhere that there was no reason emails couldn't be the perfect conduits of the soul and spirit, as effective and direct as any written letters.

They were personal communications, after all.

```
FROM: Rosie Denham
SUBJECT: Back in the UK
TO: Patrick M Riley
SENT: 29 September 18.47


Hi Pat
I'm home again.
    Many thanks for looking after me while Tess
and Ben were out of town and for taking me to
catch my flight.
    You were very kind.

All best wishes
Rosie X
```

```
FROM: Patrick M Riley
SUBJECT: Happy Landing
TO: Rosie Denham
SENT: September 30 16.26
```

```
Hi Rosie
Good to hear you made it.
```

```
Pat
```

That was all he said. How could he be so curt and so dismissive? Those kisses, had they meant precisely nothing? Yes, you idiot, I told myself, that's exactly what those kisses meant – precisely nothing!

So now sort out your life.

October

❧ PATRICK ❦

I couldn't work. I couldn't eat. I couldn't sleep.

I took long walks downtown and sat in cafés daydreaming and trying to figure out what I was doing. Why was I behaving like a teenager? What was wrong with me? I never felt so happy, sad, upset, exhilarated or confused in all my life.

Everyone at JQA knew Lex was fooling round with Mr Wonderful and that the British bastard had my kids because I hadn't put up any fight when Lexie told me she was leaving and taking Joe and Polly.

She shared the details of her new relationship and posted pictures of her Limey lover on her Facebook page. I clicked through half a dozen photographs. I saw the British guy was just a guy – no horns, no fangs, no obvious tail – brown hair, medium build and height, blue eyes and dreadful British teeth.

Then I unfriended Lex and all our mutual friends as well because I didn't need to know them any more.

'Professor Riley, I'm so sorry about you and Mrs Riley.'

'Pat, Melissa's fixing pot roast Thursday. Why don't you come by and join the party?'

'Patrick, if you're ever in our neighbourhood, George and I would love to have you visit with us. Please come by for brunch one Saturday?'

'Dr Riley, may I get you anything – a Danish or a doughnut?'

So they pussyfooted round me, trying to be nice and not to startle me or worry me, I guess, and it was kindly meant.

Julianne, my fifty-something secretary, or whatever I'm supposed to call her nowadays – aide, facilitator, PA, guard dog, she's all of those and more, she guards me like a dragon guards its hoard – brought me cream cheese bagels, salt beef sandwiches, crackers that she made herself.

'You need to eat,' she told me as she brushed some streaks of chalk dust off my sleeve and fussed like Henny Penny.

'Caroline and I, we're always having family on weekends,' said the dean. 'If you ever feel like joining us, we'll make you very welcome. If you got your kids, bring them along. As you know, our Rusty's great with children – very playful.'

Yeah, last time I saw that dog, he played with me so hard he almost took my fingers off. I wouldn't trust him within half a mile of Joe and Polly.

⌐ ROSIE ⌐

I had to forget I'd ever met him.

I also had to rent some office space and build a client list. I had to get my business booming, which in a stop-go recession promised to be challenging.

It took me quite a while to find some office premises. I'd begun to wonder if I'd have to work from home, a shabby rented flat in a not-very-pretty part of Paddington. But then I found a tiny place in Camden, more or less convenient for town, but where it would be possible to park. That's if you were lucky and aggressive and could squeeze into the smallest space.

I needed parking. My Fiesta doubled as my handbag. Pat had been embarrassed by the mess inside his Honda. So, I thought, he'd probably have a heart attack if he could see my clutter-wagon, full of files and plastic bags and samples, sandwich boxes with half-eaten wraps rotting inside and empty coffee cups. The squealing noise I noticed when I braked – maybe I had rats? Pat's SUV had squealed a bit, as well …

But I mustn't think about Pat Riley. He had been a blip – a wild, insane infatuation at a time when I was at my lowest and my most vulnerable. Now I had to get my life on track. Charlie would have hated to see me moping, pining, chasing after married men. I knew I had to start to live again.

I bought some office furniture. I got myself connected. I ordered business cards and stationery. Then I went to see my former boss at her palatial office in a Georgian house near Marble Arch.

'Darling, it's so wonderful to have you back in Blighty!' Fanny Gregory embraced me in a scented, lace-and-silk-upholstered hug. 'It just hasn't been the same without you, has it, Caspar, angel?'

'Fan, it's great to see you.' I kissed Fanny on her perfumed cheek, then said hello to Caspar. The big black greyhound rubbed his handsome head against my hand, gazing up at me with his enormous amber eyes. I do love dogs. They're faithful and they're kind and, unlike some human friends, they don't jerk you around. They don't mess with your head. They don't have wives and children. They don't make you fall in love with them …

'Rosie, darling, what's the matter?'

'Sorry?'

'You're a million miles away. So who did you see, who did meet while you were in America?'

'I saw Tess and met her husband.'

'You're so silly, sweet.'

'What do you mean?'

'I think somebody's made off with your heart. So come on, my angel, tell Aunt Fanny? I hope he's young and charming, smart and witty? You could do with someone smart and witty in your life, someone who could make you smile again.'

'Fanny, no one's made off with my heart. I'm just preoccupied and jet-lagged.' This woman had to be a witch. I'd always sort of guessed and now I knew.

'I think you're in love,' persisted Fanny.

'Well, you're wrong.'

'I'm never wrong, my darling, and you know it. What's he like? I hope he's handsome or at least attractive? I can't bear ugly men. Their looks always reflect their personalities – grudging, warped and mean.'

'Let's get down to business, shall we, Fanny?' I suggested. 'I know your time is precious and I don't want to impose.'

'Oh – it's *don't interrogate me*, eh? Prickle, prickle, prickle, Mrs Tiggywinkle! But, my angel, I must ask you, how's your darling mother?'

'She's okay.' I shrugged. 'Well, of course, she's not okay. She's never going be okay again. But she's sort of coping, keeping busy, as is Dad. They loved the flowers you sent.'

'I wish there was something I could do. I feel so helpless. When I think of all your lovely mother's done for me—'

'Fanny, please, not now?'

'I'm so sorry, sweetheart, clumsy me.' Fanny Gregory came as close to blushing and embarrassed as anyone as armour-plated and detached as Fanny ever could. 'When you see her next, though, will you give her all my love?'

'Of course. So, Fan—'

'So, angel, I shall give you these accounts,' said Fanny, handing me a USB stick and a dozen files. 'You've worked with all these people. So they know and trust you and they'll be very happy to transfer their business to your new company. They'll be more than happy, I imagine. You won't charge as much as me!'

'Thank you, Fanny.' I was touched. I knew she would

encourage and support me while I was getting going. But she didn't have to give me these accounts and we both knew it. 'This is really kind of you.'

'Oh, darling, it's my pleasure. While you've been in America, I've been recommending you to everyone I know. So now I'm going to have to watch my step or I shall do my lovely self out of a job. I'll be flogging *The Big Issue* outside Marks and Spencer. Caspar will be sleeping on a verminous old blanket underneath a railway arch. He won't like that at all. He's used to elegance and luxury.'

'It's never going to happen, Fan.'

'I hope you're right, my angel. So what *did* you do in Minnesota, darling girl, apart from meet somebody very nice?'

'Fanny, please – don't let's start that again.' But I knew I had to give her something, anything before she would shut up about who I had met or hadn't met. 'I met the famous novelist, Ben Fairfax.'

'I know you did, my love. But I meant men, of course.'

'Tess says Ben's a bloke and she should know.'

'But he's not available.' Fanny glanced at me, her blue eyes narrowed. 'Or is he, darling heart?'

'Ben's not available.'

'So he and Tess are desperately in love?'

'I don't think Tess is desperately in love, at least with Ben. But she adores his Amex card.'

'I hope she's buying the right things. Rubies, diamonds, emeralds, they've always been a girl's best friends, you know. They'll come under personal chattels when she gets divorced.'

'You're such a cynic, Fanny.'

'I'm a realist, darling. So you tell Tess from me – earrings, bracelets, necklaces, the settings aren't important, but buy the biggest stones you can afford and always go for quality.

The clarity and cut are more important than the size, unless we're talking rocks as big as hen's eggs, obviously.'

'Ben's already bought her a few diamonds, but I'll mention what you said about the cut and clarity for if she gets some more.'

'You mind you do,' said Fanny. 'Personal accoutrements, that's what she should be buying. No judge in an American divorce court would make her give them back, no matter what. But darling, you look tired, are you well?'

'I've not been sleeping much.'

'It's not surprising.' Fanny's gaze grew gentle. 'But you mustn't blame yourself, my love.'

'It was my fault.'

'It wasn't, and you know it. So you must stop beating yourself up, even though we always ought to do what we do best, and you're especially good at that. Darling, are you moisturising? You have crow's feet coming at the corners of your eyes.'

'I've been out in the sun. It was hot in Minnesota when I first arrived. I went for walks, did some exploring. I climbed up rocks and stuff.'

'It looks like you forgot the factor forty. Angel, I must let you have some samples. I've been sent this lovely range of wonderful new creams and serums. You shall try them out.'

'Thank you, Fan,' I said. 'It's very strange – I've known you all my life, but you never look a minute older. What's your secret? Alchemy, black magic, a portrait in the attic?'

'Sun and water, angel – keep away from both of them,' said Fanny. 'I haven't washed my face since I was twelve.'

Fanny called everybody angel, but she was the angel.

She helped me get my business going, sent me leads and introduced me to all sorts of people who might give me work, and she generally looked out for me.

If I could stop dreaming about Patrick Riley, if I could stop fantasising about getting Patrick Riley's shirt off then running my hands down Patrick Riley's lovely chest, I thought I might have a chance of getting back to normal.

Of course, I'd probably never be quite back to normal – there was all the Charlie stuff and other stuff to sort before I could start thinking about normal. But as October turned into November, I was hopeful I might manage almost-normal soon.

November

✦ PATRICK ✦

I checked my inbox daily, hourly, by the minute, hoping for a message, even one as staid and formal as the one she sent when she came back to the UK.

Come November, you'll be back to normal, I assured myself. But whatever normal might have been, I knew I wasn't it. Unless lying awake all night and wondering what Rosie might be doing, thinking, saying, who she could be seeing and if she might be with some guy and, if this was indeed the case, how I could kill him by just willing him to die, could ever pass for normal.

By November, far from being back to normal, I was getting desperate.

You could write the girl yourself, perhaps?

But what would I say?

Does it matter, idiot? All you need to do is get in contact and say something – anything!

Okay.

I clicked *compose*.

Now write something casual, informal. But don't be too familiar because she won't like that.

Say hi, how are you doing?

Yeah, but also let her know you're thinking warm, affectionate thoughts. You got it?

Yeah, I got it.

FROM: Patrick M Riley
SUBJECT: Missing You
TO: Rosie Denham

Hi, how are you doing?
  I think about you day and night. You're in
my head and in my heart.
  Rosie, we should be together. It's so bad
to be apart.

What the hell? Did I just write that piece of rhyming shit? What was wrong with me? Did I need some form of medication?

I clicked *delete* and opened up an article for which I was doing a review and then I gave the author a hard time.

I felt like I was kind of in a holding pattern.

I went on trying to act normal, or what I hoped was normal.

I headed out to work and came back home to the apartment, which was now a library since Lexie wasn't there to kvetch about the papers, books and magazines. I saw my kids and did a ton of stuff with them. I'd started a new outreach programme on a reservation in Northern Minnesota and it was going well.

But emotionally I felt like I was frozen, that a part of me was in suspended animation in a cryogenic tank. Contrariwise, I also had this feeling it would take one single spark to cause a Three Mile Island-style explosion.

You could say that I was still confused.

Lex had quieted down considerably. Maybe Mr Wonderful was so exciting and inventive that he wore her out? I guess it was a possibility.

The kids had settled into a routine. I read somewhere that

kids of separated parents can be quite adaptable. They can learn and grow and love, develop all the social skills that kids whose parents are together do, and it looked like Joe and Polly fit this paradigm.

I adapted and I fit it, too. Monday through Friday, I picked my children up from Angie's, pre-school, school, wherever. I took them back to the apartment, gave them dinner, read to them a while, we watched a DVD or two.

Once or twice a week they helped me cook. Joe showed quite a talent for making chocolate cupcakes and for decorating them. Polly showed a talent for eating decorations. But Polly was a vital member of our team because she was our quality control. Yeah, we had the process all sewn up. Girl Scout cookie makers, give way to the serious contenders in the home baking stakes!

Later, Lex would pick them up and take them back to Mr Wonderful's real house with its real yard. When I saw them on weekends, we did a bunch of stuff I never thought to do before. We glued. We crafted. We made crazy stuff like wizard wands and monster masks. We had no one saying, *don't you guys get paint on that new rug, eat up all your carrot sticks and then go take your bath.*

The travelling to Europe, Dubai and Singapore had not been mentioned since Lex said she was leaving. So I kind of hoped it wouldn't happen.

Did they get their passports?

Yes, and Joe was beyond proud. Lexie let him bring it to show me and The Terminator. As we sat together on the couch and Polly watched a candy-coloured DVD about a fairy princess, he read out all the noble precepts printed at the top of every page. I have to admit I was impressed. I didn't know George Washington said all that stuff about repairing standards, which as you can guess had Joe confused.

He added that he was the only kid in his whole class

to have a US passport. 'So I guess that means I'm kind of special?' he suggested shyly.

'You always were and always will be special.'

'Do you have a passport, Dad?'

'No, I never needed one.'

'Mom and Polly, they got passports. Maybe you should get a passport, too?'

'Yeah, perhaps,' I said. 'Hey, Joe – did you see The Terminator savage that zucchini? I swear he ate the whole thing in one bite!'

I should get a passport? Why? I didn't think it likely that when Lex and Mr Wonderful went jetting off to Europe or elsewhere, I would be asked along.

So Lex and I, should we be getting a divorce? Lexie didn't mention it these past few weeks and I didn't care to think about it. I had too much work stuff, children stuff and other well-you-know stuff on my mind to sit around in lawyers' offices, chase paperwork, do all the tedious shit you had to do to get divorced.

⌒ ROSIE ⌒

My weeks were beyond hectic.

I was still setting up the business, and this meant chasing clients, making phone calls, sorting advertising, chatting up the editors of magazines and newspapers and taking various people out to lunch. I hoped it wouldn't be too long before prospective clients, editors and advertisers wanting me to help promote whatever they were selling started chasing *me*.

While I'd worked for Fanny and while I was in France, a salary had turned up in my account as if by magic. But that wasn't going to happen now. I had joined the ranks of the ridiculous, the stupid, the cross-eyed optimists, the likely bankrupts. I was self-employed.

I worked myself into a stupor. But still I couldn't sleep. Then I couldn't stand it any more. I sent an email.

```
FROM: Rosie Denham
SUBJECT: Winter
TO: Patrick M Riley
SENT: 18 November 15.45

Any snow yet?
Rosie X
```

```
FROM: Patrick M Riley
SUBJECT: Snow
TO: Rosie Denham
SENT: November 19 09.32

Only flurries.
Pat
```

So much for emails, the conduits of the soul and spirit – right.

✢ PATRICK ✢

Only flurries.

Yeah, succinct and to the point and – well done, Riley – meteorologically precise. But it was not the message I had meant to send, had wanted to send Rosie.

```
FROM: Patrick M Riley
SUBJECT: Snow
TO: Rosie Denham

My darling Rosie
The first snow fell last night.
```

It swirled around the trash-mobile in big white flakes, hitting on the windshield as I was driving home from JQA. It looked like fairies dancing. It was so graceful and so beautiful it made me think of you.

I want so much to see you, kiss you, hold you in my arms and never, ever let you go.

I don't know if you feel the same?

I doubt you do.

So I …

FROM: Patrick M Riley
SUBJECT: Us
TO: Rosie Denham

My beloved Rosie

I hope you're okay?

I guess you're very busy and that's why you don't have any time to write long emails. But nowadays it's getting kind of desperate with me. So if you have a moment …

FROM: Patrick M Riley
SUBJECT: Must see you
TO: Rosie Denham

I can't go on like this. It's killing me. I can't eat, can't sleep. I never needed anyone as bad as I need you …

Delete. Delete. Delete.

'Come by for Thanksgiving, Pat?'

Ben was calling on his cell and he was at his most

persuasive – or insistent or annoying, I could not be sure. It's so hard to tell with someone who is the original Mr Charm. 'You don't want to be alone on Thanksgiving,' he added.

'I won't be alone. Lex is going to Chicago with her Mr Wonderful and leaving Joe and Polly home with me. So we'll be fine.'

I was surprised when Lex announced her plans for Thanksgiving. I'd thought she and the Limey would want to do the whole Thanksgiving-happy-family bit, turkey, pumpkin pie and all, would want to show my children how it was going to be. But it seemed Mr Wonderful was taking Lexie someplace where children were not welcome. So I would get to see my kids, which suited me just fine.

I would fix a real Thanksgiving dinner, I decided. I'd go to Trader Joe's, get quality. We'd have organic-farm-raised, free-range turkey, home-made stuffing, cranberry jelly, green beans, sweet potatoes, followed by my own home-made dessert, not store-bought pie.

When Lex and I first married, I often cooked. I always loved to bake up cakes – still do. I'd make triple chocolate brownies for this holiday. The kids could lend a hand. Then we'd all lie on the couch and stuff ourselves while watching the usual holiday garbage on TV. Or our DVDs of *Shrek* again, again, again. My children couldn't get enough of *Shrek*. I must admit I like those movies. I even got the jokes, or most of them.

Yeah, we'd have ourselves a great Thanksgiving. But it was not about to happen. Tess was planning on a real Thanksgiving dinner too, and we were all invited, which made me kind of nervous …

'Please come by, old buddy, and bring the kids along?' persisted Ben. 'After all, Thanksgiving's much more fun when there are kids around.' This from a guy who hated children and often said he never wanted any of his own?

'You better roll those fancy Persian carpets up,' I told him.

'I'm not worried about the carpets, Patrick. You guys come by and have yourselves a real good time – okay?'

'Okay,' I said. 'But you should put your good stuff out of reach of sticky fingers. I'm just warning you.'

Maybe he and Tess were nesting?

I guess stranger things have happened, right?

⌒ ROSIE ⌒

I'd often wondered why my British diaries felt the need to tell me it was Thanksgiving. But now I was very glad they did. I went into Google and found out more about it.

Gosh, surprise, surprise. I didn't know that it was always on a Thursday. I didn't know you could make all those things from sweet potatoes – pies and cookies, cheesecakes, even candy.

I thought of Pat and wondered what he would be doing, if he'd be alone in his apartment? I wondered if he ever thought of me? Maybe I could ring to wish him happy Thanksgiving? Did Americans do that, send cards, ring round and stuff?

But maybe if his children and his wife were with that other man, he might think I was being sarcastic?

Perhaps I'd send a friendly little email?

But then I told myself to get a grip.

Stop thinking about Patrick, you stupid, stupid thing, and ring your parents. Ask them if they've been affected by the flooding in the west of England, where there've been a hundred landslides, half a dozen cliff falls, and loads of houses, roads and railway lines are under water.

I rang them off and on all day, on their mobiles and on various landlines. I got no replies. By six o'clock that evening, I was panicking in earnest. I watched the news and panicked even more.

So I was beyond relieved when Mum picked up at last. 'Mum, are you and Dad all right?' I wailed, almost crying now. 'I thought you must be flooded out – or worse! Where have you been?'

She told me.

'Oh, of course – the hospice. I'd forgotten it's your day. Where's Daddy, still at work? Yes, I'm fine, but busy, busy busy. Mum, do you fancy coming to visit me in London and staying a few days? Of course I have the time to spare for you! We could have lunch with Fanny. She's always asking after you and Dad.'

Mum said she'd been thinking about a trip to London. But it would probably have to be next year. She had far too many things to do right now, and Christmas would be here before she knew it.

'January, February, March?' I prompted. 'Do you want to pencil in some dates? Oh, Mum – of course you must, it would be lovely! I'd like to see that exhibition, too. We'll do some shopping, shall we, and go to see a show? Yes, it will be something cheerful, Mummy. I'll make sure of that. Give my love to Dad and Granny. Mum, are you all right?'

My mother said all the right things. She assured me she was fine. She told me to take care, to wrap up warm and all that stuff. She said she hoped that I was eating properly and not always snacking, not living off my fat. Since she always said I was too thin, that was her little joke.

But I could tell she wasn't thawing. She was still numb and frozen with grief and misery. I could hear it in her voice. I wondered if she ever would forgive me?

How long it would take?

❧ PATRICK ❦

'There's to be no bad behaviour – right?' I told the kids.

'No running round the place and screeching, no playing dinosaurs.'

Up to the last moment, I wondered if there'd be a change of plan. But no – Lex dumped her children and went to spend the holiday with Mr Wonderful. She left the hotel brochure lying on the kitchen counter. I noted down the contact details then I dropped the brochure in the trash.

We made a batch of brownies for our hosts and then we headed out.

Poll and Joe knew Ben, of course, had known him all their lives. But they hadn't met the current Mrs Fairfax, so they were a little apprehensive. 'She's a real nice lady,' I assured them as we rode the elevator up to Ben's apartment. 'She's a good cook, too.'

Okay, I lied.

'Does she have great tits?' demanded Joe.

'What the hell?' I stared at him, astonished. 'Whatever made you think of asking that?'

'Stephen said that Mommy has great tits.'

Stephen's right, she does – God rot the bastard.

'Joe, don't ever use that word again,' I snapped. 'Or there will be consequences.'

'Daddy, are you mad at me?' Joe looked up at me all anxious and there was a worried little wobble in his voice.

'No, little buddy, I'm not mad.' I hunkered down beside him. 'You don't understand what you just said. But you don't use words like tits in front of Ben and Tess, you got me? You say *hi, how are you,* and that's all. You keep the conversation clean, okay?'

'Okay, Dad,' Joe agreed.

Then the elevator filled up with the most disgusting smell. 'I think Polly's doing a – Polly needs the bathroom, Dad,' said Joe.

I glanced at Polly and saw that she was purple in the face.

Lexie had announced that Polly was now out of diapers in the daytime, so I didn't diaper her before we left – mistake.

'Hey, you guys!' said Ben, opening the door to us and beaming like a chain store Santa Claus. I guess he must have heard the elevator come clanking up the shaft. 'Happy—'

'Hi,' I muttered, scooping Polly up and blasting past him. 'Sorry, this is an emergency.'

We made it to the bathroom just in time.

Tess was a big hit.

She made a special international European American Thanksgiving. There was turkey, British roast potatoes, little savoury pancake muffin hybrid things which she called Yorkshire puddings, British stuffing – it was good.

If she would quit trying to make meatloaf, I decided, and mixing up those soya-sugar-artificial-colouring-and-flavouring-based desserts, I would be tempted to come by more often. Joe especially liked the Yorkshire puddings, which were light and melting, crisp and golden. He ate his three then stole one from my plate.

Dessert was not so wonderful – a store-bought pumpkin pie and Cool Whip – but you can't have everything, and the brownies were a big success.

'Patrick, these are ace,' said Tess. 'They're chocolatey and chewy, just like brownies ought to be. Mine come out more like muffins. Did you use chopped hazelnuts or walnuts?'

'We used pecans, but they're much the same.'

'You must let me have your recipe.'

'I'll send it over. You could maybe send me one for – what did you call them, Yorkshire puddings?'

'I'll write it down for you. It's dead simple, even Joe or Polly could make a batch of Yorkshires. Just make sure you don't use flour with raising agent in it – never works.'

'What is this, *The Happy Homemaker's Half Hour* or

something?' muttered Ben and glowered at me. 'You hitting on my wife, Professor Riley?'

I ignored him.

'I helped Dad make the brownies,' chipped in Joe, who was on his fourth. 'I measured out the flour and cocoa powder, cracked the eggs and stirred the butter in the pan.'

'You sure did,' I said. I suddenly felt a great wave of affection for my son, the Brownie Maestro. I wasn't going to give these children up to Lex and Mr Wonderful, not without one hell of a big fight.

'Do you guys make cupcakes, too?' asked Tess.

'Yeah, we do,' said Joe. 'Dad and I, we bake them up and then we frost them, cover them with jelly diamonds, candy dinosaurs or sugar sprinkles.'

'Sprinkles,' echoed Polly.

'The baby shakes the sprinkles on,' said Joe. 'It's all she's old enough to do.'

'Patrick, is your children's conversation always this high-powered, this dynamic?' Ben got out the bourbon now, poured himself three fingers, slumped down in his chair again and yawned.

'Oh, shut up, you miserybag,' said Tess, who was busy drawing fairies for my daughter on a paper napkin. 'Pat, he's only jealous. Joe and Polly are adorable.'

I glanced at Ben. I saw the novelty of having kids around on Thanksgiving had definitely worn off.

Of course, I couldn't speak for Tess. But it was very plain to me that Ben could not be nesting, after all.

December

ROSIE

Cupcakes, cupcakes, cupcakes – everyone wants cupcakes, don't they?

Yes, it seems they do – and just as well, because I now had seven clients trying to sell fantastic cupcakes, hoping I'd be able to get them deals in supermarkets, catering for private functions and upmarket weddings.

One was exporting monthly shipments to Uzbekistan. No, I didn't make that last bit up. She had connections in the diplomatic service. But sending twenty cupcakes to Tashkent twelve times a year would hardly make her rich or even keep her cat in kibble.

While I was encouraging my clients to build their businesses and trying to show them how to do it – because quite honestly most of these people didn't have a clue – I was also having to tell them to calm down, explain that supermarkets took you over, told you what you had to do and when you had to do it. Then, if you didn't sell in zillions, they dumped you anyway.

You'd do better staying small, supplying local shops and restaurants while I use my contacts to get you advertorial space in women's magazines – that's what I told them. *If you're making something super-special, and if you have charisma (or you're downright weird, but in a non-alarming sort of way), I might be able to get you spots on regional TV.*

You'll also need to learn and change, that's if you're going to keep the punters hooked.

Just like fashion, music, fiction, anything that's man-or-woman-made in fact, cupcakes must continually evolve – be born again repeatedly – otherwise they'd be eclipsed by bran-rich, home-baked dog treats, these were trending.

Yes, it kept me occupied.

'How is it going, sweetheart?'

Fanny phoned me almost every day to ask how I was getting on and give me leads. This was very kind and would destroy her reputation as a gorgon with a tail and horns and cloven hooves as well as snakes for hair if anyone found out. 'I might have a tiny little job for lovely you,' she said one chilly afternoon.

'What job is that?' I asked. 'I don't think I can take another dog treat maker, Fan.'

'You won't have to, angel. Christmas is upon us, darling girl, and – as has been the case each single year since Mary laid her baby in the manger – it's taken everybody by surprise ...'

'Fanny, I'm quite busy. So, although it's always great to hear from you, shall we get to the point?'

'Sweetheart, could you help out with an insy-winsy-tinsy Christmas book tour, shepherding an author around the Waterstones of the Home Counties? This fellow needs a conscientious minder, basically. But his publicist is very busy looking after some extremely boring telly person who is now an author, but who didn't write the actual book and cannot be trusted not to say so to the punters. Gemma phoned me up in desperation.'

'Why does he need a minder?'

'Well, his publicist was very cagey, but from what she hinted I suspect he's banned from driving and she's not convinced he's bright enough to sort the trains. Darling heart, the money's very good.'

'How much is very good?'

She told me.

'I would get expenses, too?'

'Of course.'

'You mean I'd just be driving him around?'

'You'd pick him up each morning, see he ends up where he needs to be, then take him home again each night. Gemma says you mustn't let him near a pub. My love, it's just three days.'

'Who is he?'

'Oh, you won't have heard of him, you're far too young.' Fanny named a famous writer who was eighty if he was a day and whose early books had all been serialised on television when I was a little girl, but the tide of fashion had flowed past him long ago.

'Okay,' I said. 'I'll do it.'

'Thank you, darling heart. You're worth your weight in Prada's loveliest accessories.'

I'd get my Granny Cassie a signed copy of the book.

Malcolm Tyndale Crawley, crime writer and former spy – apparently – turned out to be self-opinionated and demanding but extremely charming.

I thought this must be the legacy of having been a very handsome man who must have pulled the ladies with the twinkle in his eye.

I enjoyed his company because he told me some fantastic stories and was in a good mood all the time. This was probably because although he didn't sell a million books, a lot of lady fans turned up and flirted with him, and he also had a silver hipflask from which he snuck a drink quite frequently.

He didn't criticise my driving, as well he might have done. These days, it was terrible. I was too distracted, too preoccupied with Pat, with talking to him and with doing other stuff with him, to concentrate on roundabouts and traffic lights, on joining motorways.

'It's not generally considered wise to cut up tankers,' Mr Crawley told me calmly as a BP lorry nearly did for my Fiesta and the driver blared his horn at me.

'Sorry,' I said meekly, clicking off the video of that hot afternoon when Pat and I had hiked the trail on the Sugar Loaf. When he had scooped me up and carried me like in a film, and which was always playing on a loop inside my head.

'There's no need to apologise, Miss Denham. I have had a very long and interesting life. I do not wish to end it as a dribbling, incontinent old ruin in some ghastly nursing home in Dawlish. So the awful prospect of going up in flames in a great conflagration on a motorway holds little fear for me. But I would like to think you have a few more years of health and happiness ahead of you.'

'You're right, I need to concentrate,' I said.

'May I give you some advice, Miss Denham?' I was about to drop him off at home for the last time. 'You have been an excellent nursemaid to a very tiresome old man and I feel I owe you.'

'Mr Crawley, you don't owe me anything. Your publisher has paid me.'

'I shall bore you, anyway. Miss Denham, it's quite obvious to me you're either fretting about something in your past and/or you're rather worried about your future. You want something or someone very badly. But you're afraid to reach for what you want. Where's the reckless courage you displayed when we were on the motorway and you put that tanker in its place?'

'Mr Crawley, when did you become a mind-reader and psychoanalyst?'

'I've been both of those for very many years, Miss Denham. I'm currently a novelist and I used to be a spy.' He handed me a hardback copy of his latest novel in which he had written:

> *Thank you for your company, Miss Denham.*
> *Now be brave and go for it – whatever it is you want –*
> *and don't hold back.*
> *Or you'll regret it.*
> *All good wishes for your future*
> *Malcolm Tyndale Crawley*

As I drove home to my flat in Paddington, I thought about what Malcolm Crawley, novelist and spy and amateur psychologist, had said.

You work, you eat, you sleep – or try to sleep. You tell yourself that you're not hurting any more and that you should be grateful, count your blessings – that's what's going to get you through this life. You don't harm anybody, and you hope nobody will harm you.

But if you play that game, is life worth living?

So I wrote an email. Then, before I could delete it or think any more about it, I clicked *send* and off it went.

I knew I'd handed Pat a loaded gun.

✦ PATRICK ✦

The first week of December, we had a foot of snow in the Twin Cities. So everybody knew the winter had arrived in earnest and there would be no respite from snow and ice and bitter, freezing cold until the spring.

Although I usually hated it, this year I welcomed winter. It seemed like it was fitting because it was always winter in my heart.

I got on with my work and plotted my next moves, career-wise, Lex-wise, Rosie-wise and Joe-and-Polly-wise, hardly

knowing if there was any point, or if it was a waste of time
and energy, but plotting on regardless.

Then, as Christmas raced toward me, Rosie's email came.
It seemed that suddenly it was spring.

```
FROM: Rosie Denham
SUBJECT: Merry Christmas!
TO: Patrick M Riley
SENT: 20 December 22.25

Dear Pat
How are you?
   I hope everything is going well in
Minnesota?
   I also hope you have a lovely Christmas and
next year will be very good to you.
   If you have any time to spare, I'd love to
hear your news.

All best wishes
Rosie X
```

```
FROM: Patrick M Riley
SUBJECT: Re: Merry Christmas!
TO: Rosie Denham
SENT: December 22 19.35

Hi Rosie
I'm okay, hope you are, too.
   How's your new venture - doing good?
   You have yourself a very merry Christmas
and a great New Year.

Sincerely
Pat
```

It had no literary merit, but at least it didn't rhyme.

Mom was disappointed not to see the kids on Christmas. As usual, she flew into MSP. As usual, I met her at the airport. As usual, she was thrilled to see me, hugged me, kissed me, told me I was much too thin and needed feeding up.

But the kids weren't in the backseat yelling *Granny, Granny, Granny, Granny, we fixed you some cookies*, and *what did you bring us*, and *we got a monster Christmas tree*, and this made her sad.

'That Alexis, what's she thinking?' Mom demanded as we drove to the apartment, which of course was quiet and had been not been tinselled-up for Christmas. The living room was full of books and papers, magazines and binders lying in great piles everywhere.

'It's like I told you, Mom. She needs some space.'

'Where exactly is she staying now?'

'She's with a friend who has a house.'

'Where is this house?'

'It's on Grand Avenue.'

'I hope the furnace works so Poll and Joe are cosy.'

'I'm sure the furnace works.'

I wasn't going to tell my mother everything. She'd only start to cry and I couldn't stand to hear my mother cry. It took me back to when I was a little kid and times were bad – real bad.

So I didn't tell her Lexie's friend was Mr Wonderful and they were taking Joe and Polly to see Santa Claus at the North Pole, which was temporarily someplace in upstate Minnesota. Lex had told the kids about it and of course she got them all excited before she thought to share this information with their father. I would have looked like the world's biggest, meanest bastard if I'd told them no, they couldn't go.

'So while Lexie has her space, you don't get to see your kids on Christmas,' my mother went on crossly.

'They'll be with us Thursday. Lex says they can come to the apartment and stay over. So you and I can take them to the zoo, the mall, the children's theatre and the park.'

'I hope that girl comes to her senses soon, remembers what she said in church. Pat, is Polly still in diapers? Did you get the turkey yet?'

'I got the turkey.'

'You don't look too good. You hair wants cutting. You're working much too hard. You always did. You need …'

I zoned out of my mother's monologue.

It would be like this for a while, I realised. My poor mother fretting, fretting, fretting, worrying about me and my kids, convinced we must be suffering.

She would do her nut – where did I hear that, it had to be a Tess expression – when she realised Lex was living with a man, information she'd be given by Joe the moment she and Joe met up.

Yeah, I had been suffering.

But no one goes on suffering forever. It's too passive. It gets kind of tedious. Nowadays, I was working on how I could turn my life around.

It started snowing very heavily. I concentrated on the road. After my mother went to bed that night, I made some calls.

⌒ ROSIE ⌒

My mother was determined that this would be a normal family Christmas, the kind we'd always had since I was born.

I wished I could sleep through it in the flat in London, waking up in January when it was all over. But of course I went back home to Dorset.

Dad fetched the great big box of decorations from the attic and we put them up, tacking tinsel garlands everywhere and hanging baubles on the Christmas tree. Mum had cooked herself into a frenzy, making everything from scratch – mince pies, Christmas puddings and a frosted wonder of a Christmas cake, special stuffing for the Christmas turkey, home-made cranberry sauce. The house was soon so styled and Christmassed-up that it looked like something in a December issue of a woman's magazine.

Christmas Eve was gruesome. Mum and Dad were very quiet. My mother was determined not to cry and in the evening Dad got out the usual party games. He'd evidently decided we all had to be jolly, which under the circumstances was impossible.

On Christmas morning, my grandmother and mother went to early Mass. My father drove them into Dorchester. I suppose he hung about outside St Luke's and smoked, or walked around the town while Mum and Granny were in church and praying for us all. I stayed in bed.

When Granny got back home again she seemed quite calm and placid. I'd even say serene. It probably helped that she believed in heaven, that she was certain Charlie was an angel there. My mother probably thought the same. But this didn't help my dad and me.

While Granny dozed and Mum cooked an enormous Christmas lunch I knew we'd have to force ourselves to eat, Dad and I got drunk.

January

✦ PATRICK ✦

The New Year brought the Limey a promotion. I read about it on the company website, where there was a brand new mug shot of his grinning face, complete with crooked teeth.

But I didn't care about the Limey.

I had a ton of plans.

Late one weekday evening as I was about to watch a favourite classic movie before I went to bed, Lexie came by the apartment, out of breath from slogging up the fourteen flights of stairs. She obviously wasn't getting any exercise, that's apart from flying with Mr Wonderful.

'You're not – going to – like this,' she began as she slumped into an armchair, scarlet in the face and gasping like a landed fish. 'But, if you remember, I told you it was possible the kids and I would get the chance to travel? Stephen's job, it takes him to the Middle East and Europe?'

'I remember.'

'He has to do a bunch of work stuff in London, England soon. He'd like to bring the kids and me along. It would only be for a few months. I know you'll be difficult about it.'

'Oh?'

'Yeah, you'll call the Feds, have me arrested for kidnapping your children. But Stephen says it would be a fantastic opportunity for them. It would be educational. They'd get to see the changing of the guard at Windsor Palace, visit Notre Dame and meet the hunchback.'

'I think *you* ought to go to Europe, Lex.'

'Oh – so do you mean—'

'You're right, it would be educational.'

'Why are you laughing, Patrick? What's so funny?' Lexie glared at me. 'I heard they got terrorists in Europe, the Taliban and stuff. It's a very dangerous place. But it's like I always said – you never cared about me or the children.'

'Lexie, you may take the kids to London. If you email me your schedule – general travel plans, which airlines you'll be using, details of where you'll stay in the UK with dates, addresses, cell phone numbers, all that stuff – there won't be any problem.'

'What's the catch?'

'There is no catch. I'm trying to be calm and reasonable about an awful situation. You said you wanted to be civilised. So have you changed your mind and do you want a fight? Do you want me filing for divorce? Do you want a sheriff on your Limey lover's doorstep serving papers? Do you want to file for divorce yourself? Or shall we keep the situation open for the moment – while we're both so busy, anyway – and see how things work out? I'll continue paying maintenance for Joe and Polly into your account. You must let me know if you need more.'

'Patrick, you're impossible. You always were contrary. I'm sure you always will be. Why do you always put me in the wrong?'

'Lex, I don't have time for this.' I got up from the couch. 'I'll see you off the premises. I suggest you ride the elevator at this time of night. But if you want to use the stairs, I'll find a flashlight.'

'I don't do elevators, you know that, but if you don't care about your children's mother getting mutilated, raped and murdered in a dark and dangerous stairwell—'

'Come on, Lex.' I shrugged into my jacket. 'I'll walk you down the stairs. We could both use the exercise.'

Or you could, anyway.

'Oh, don't let me put you out.' She glanced toward the coffee table, saw the DVD case. 'I hope that isn't porn?' she said suspiciously. 'Stephen says men in your situation often use a lot of porn. It's disgusting, jacking off to porn.'

I flipped the case so she could view the artwork.

'Lexie, as you see, it's *Unforgiven*.'

⌐ ROSIE ⌐

You can't miss Pat, I told myself.

Look, you did as Malcolm Crawley said. You went for it, reached out to him. See where it got you – nowhere. All he sent was a three line reply.

What was the matter with the man, could he not read between those lines?

It would seem not.

'Darling, what's the problem?' Fanny asked me every time we met. 'You can tell Aunt Fanny, can't you?'

'I don't have a problem, Fanny.'

'You mean it's a man.'

✦ PATRICK ✦

Okay, I admit it.

I was figuring out how I could get to Europe, too. I told myself it should be possible. My students, graduate students and technicians were the best. Ambitious, dedicated and hard-working, they didn't need me breathing down their necks 24-7. As long as they and I could video-conference, I didn't have to be in Minnesota.

I made more calls. I put out more antennae. I considered leaving academia, applying for a bunch of jobs in industry which all paid twice my salary. I offered to give a course of lectures at some British universities, the ones that had a range of research programmes in my field. I applied for my first passport, expedited service. If nothing else, I thought, when I got to page through all those wise, improving sentiments, I'd elevate my mind.

I didn't dare to hope things would work out. Or not for weeks, or even months. But London University's Queen Alexandra College replied within three days. A professor from Australia who'd been due to visit was sick, had died, whatever. So my own proposal was most timely, there was funding, they would be delighted, it would be an honour, the department would be very happy, there were three post-doctoral students who would be most anxious to discuss – and all that stuff.

When I saw the dean and told him JQA would not be picking up the tab, he said it would be very good to foster some new links with major UK universities, in fact he had been going to suggest it, but I had beat him to it.

'You have a conference in Colorado in the summer, don't you, Patrick?' he continued. 'Where you're planning on presenting some of your new findings and developments in thought-to-text?'

'Yes, Dean, that's right.'

'I get this feeling you'll soon be in demand all over. You'll get invitations to be a visiting fellow inside, outside of the States.'

'Perhaps.'

'Tell me, did you get your passport yet?'

```
FROM: Patrick M Riley
SUBJECT: London
TO: Rosie Denham
SENT: January 14 09.34


Hi Rosie
Happy New Year!
```

        Thank you for the message you sent a couple
weeks ago.
        I'm due to give some lectures at London
University's Queen Alexandra College starting
Wednesday February 6th. I'll be in the UK
around three weeks. So if you're in London,
maybe we could meet for coffee some time?
        I hope your new job is working out.

Sincerely
Pat

⌒ ROSIE ⌒

I felt myself turn into one big grin.

What's all this *sincerely* rubbish? What's so wrong with
love? Perhaps he doesn't love me? Then why's he coming to
London?

Like he says, he's going to give some lectures at Queen
Alexandra College. *Maybe*, said a voice inside my head. *But
he's really coming to see you.*

I wanted to believe it.

FROM: Rosie Denham
SUBJECT: London
TO: Patrick M Riley
SENT: 15 January 15.25

My job is going well. I'd love to meet.
Actually, my laptop's on the blink, so maybe
you could sort it?

All best wishes
Rosie X

```
FROM: Patrick M Riley
SUBJECT: Laptop
TO: Rosie Denham
SENT: January 16 17.45


What's this on the blink? You mean it's
****ed? Okay, I'll check it out. I'll see you
February, looking forward to it.

Pat
```

I wonder if it's possible to be unhinged by joy?

I also wondered about going to meet him at Heathrow. Maybe not, I thought – don't want to look too keen and needy.

'Perhaps,' the voice of conscience whispered, 'you shouldn't meet at all?'

The voice of conscience could shut up.

February

✦ PATRICK ✦

As soon as I was through with immigration, I got out my cell and called her up. 'Hi, Rosie, this is Pat. How are you doing?'

'I – I'm very well.' She seemed to take a great, deep, gasping breath. 'I mean – I'm good. I mean – I'm fine. Patrick, I—'

The way she said my name was like a blessing, even though she sounded kind of like she might be choking. 'Rosie, you okay?'

'I've just run up a flight of stairs. So I'm a little out of breath. Pat, it's great to hear from you!'

'It's great to talk to you.'

'How was your flight? Okay, I hope?'

'My flight was fine. I saw some real bad movies. I ate some awful food. What do they do to eggs on airplanes? How do they turn them into rubber string?' *I want so much to see you*, I couldn't seem to say. 'It would be good to meet some time,' I added.

'Yes, it would be lovely.'

'Then let's do it.'

'Pat, where are you now?'

'Still at the airport. Where are you?'

'I'm at home. Why don't you come round to my flat? I mean, to my apartment?'

'Today?'

'Yes, if you like.'

'How do I come into central London?'

'The most convenient way is train or taxi. Or I could pick

you up? But by the time I get there, you could have been here, if you see what I mean? I think the train would probably be best. You follow the directions to the Piccadilly line. Get yourself an Oyster card and stick on twenty quid, change at Earl's Court for Paddington.'

Get myself an Oyster card and stick on twenty quid – yeah, right. So what was this Oyster card? How much was twenty quid? What was the Piccasomething line? I knew nothing about trains. I'd never ridden one.

I guess I should have read my guide to Europe on the plane, but when I looked it wasn't in my carry-on. I must have put it in my case or left it on the couch back home in Minneapolis.

'What's your address, Rosie?'

'It's 18 Trenton Gardens, ground floor flat. You'll be about an hour on the tube. Or only fifteen minutes, that's if you get the Paddington Express. You'll need a special ticket. You can't use an Oyster card because it's just for buses and the London Underground.'

I took a cab.

⬲ ROSIE ⬳

Okay, I lied to him.

I was not at home and I hadn't run up any stairs. I left my office, and then I drove like somebody possessed back to my flat in Paddington, cutting up black cabs, white vans and silver limousines with tinted windows, and even big red London buses, which was beyond stupid – I knew that.

But I couldn't seem to help myself. I slewed my poor long-suffering Fiesta into a tiny space between some skips and then I raced into my flat, got showered and washed my hair. As I was scrambling into my most flattering pair of jeans, the doorbell rang. I dragged my fingers through my still-wet hair. I flung open the door. I beamed at him. I couldn't help myself. I was so pleased to see him.

Did I say *hello? You found me, then? Did you have any trouble getting here? It's great to see you? I'll put the kettle on?*

No – none of that.

'You said you'd sort my laptop,' I began, still grinning like a loon.

'Yeah, I did. What's wrong with it?'

'It's running very slowly. It takes half an hour to boot up. Okay, that's a slight exaggeration. But it takes a long, long time. It's like it's an old man of a computer. But it's only two years old, and—'

Oh, for heaven's sake, fool – stop blethering on! Say something smart and witty, don't rabbit on about your ruddy laptop! Scintillate, why don't you?

'Ah – um – have you eaten recently?'

'No, not since breakfast,' he replied. 'So maybe you could fix me something while I fix your laptop?'

'Oh – right – it's a deal.'

'This is a most attractive lobby.' He gazed up at the dusty cornicing and then down at the scuffed and scraped and grubby skirting boards, at the piles of junk mail on the staircase, at the universal mess and clutter of communal entrances in all converted houses everywhere. 'But it's kind of chilly.'

I blushed. I felt the blood rush up my neck. I felt it flood my face. 'Where are my manners?' I stepped back a pace or two. 'Do please come inside.'

He followed me into the flat. He stood there in the middle of the sitting room, his luggage heaped around him, looking like a refugee.

'I'm sorry it's so cold in here,' I said. 'My boiler's buggered.'

'Pardon me?'

'My furnace, it's not working like it should. I'm getting plenty of hot water, but the radiators are stone cold. The landlord says he'll send a plumber round tomorrow morning. I do have an electric fire.'

I flicked the switch. This was a big mistake. The flat filled with the stink of burning dust. 'I'm sure you'd like some coffee,' I continued stupidly. 'Why don't you take your outdoor things off and make yourself at home?'

'Where's this old man laptop?' As he shrugged his coat off, he looked like he was trying not to laugh.

'It's on the bookcase over there.' I felt my face begin to glow again and so I went into the kitchen. Making coffee for us both then starting to get dinner meant that I was doing something useful with my hands, and this was just as well.

While I was in the kitchen peeling spuds and coating cod in batter – I was making good old British fish and chips, I was doing my domestic goddess stuff tonight, thanks to Waitrose and the god of freezers – I would not be able to touch *him*.

He came up to the kitchen door to ask me for some passwords and check it was okay to see my personal files and folders.

'If there's a bunch of private stuff in here, perhaps you ought to take your laptop to some guy who doesn't actually know you?' he suggested tactfully.

'It's all right, there's nothing classified. It's just work stuff mostly. You can open anything. Where will you be staying while you're here in London?'

'I don't recall the name of the hotel. But I have the address on my phone.'

It turned out he'd been booked by QAC into a very smart hotel, one of those in a private square just north of Oxford Street near Fanny's office. But as I lit the gas I made my mind up. He wasn't going anywhere for hours.

Or maybe days.

As I was fixing her computer, she fixed me fish and fries and something she called mushy peas. She said they were a British specialty. They looked like the kind of thing a sick coyote leaves in a backyard.

'What do you think?' she asked.

'The fish is excellent, the fries are great, but this green mess is pretty damn disgusting.'

'I bet you haven't even tasted it.'

'You would bet right.'

'Go on, be brave?'

'I guess I'll pass.'

'You ought to try it just the once.' She smiled at me, her lovely grey eyes bright. 'You might find you like it.'

'Yeah?' I took a mouthful. I chewed it, swallowed it, decided I had made a big mistake. 'I never tasted anything so foul.'

'Okay, I'll have yours.' She grabbed a spoon, she scooped it up and dumped it on her plate.

I watched her eat.

I never thought I'd live to see the day when I'd be jealous of a blob of – is there a polite expression for a food the colour and texture of a pile of radioactive shit?

'You could finish fixing my computer while I do the dishes,' she said briskly in that lovely British accent which did weird stuff to my inside and made me feel about thirteen years old.

I could imagine Rosie as a – what is it – Victorian memsahib out in British India, when Britannia ruled the waves – the viceroy's lady, the collector's wife or some such dignitary.

'Yes, ma'am,' I replied and watched her blush. She looked amazing when she blushed. It was like the sun came up on a cold winter morning, like summer roses blooming in the snow.

I uninstalled some stuff she didn't need, like half a dozen browsers she clearly never used and which were slow and useless anyway, ditto a bunch of other applications, then I opened up some folders.

'Why are you keeping all this trash?' I asked.

'What do you mean?'

'You have duplicated files all over, downloads you could probably delete, a thousand photographs you could resize – you surely don't need these three, for example, they're about as big as billboards – and what's with all these images of cupcakes?'

'They're for work.'

'You need three hundred photographs of cupcakes?'

'Well – maybe not three hundred.'

'Why is your antivirus software out of date?'

'I didn't realise it was out of date.'

What is it with these people? Why are they determined to be functionally non-technological? If I'd never heard of William Shakespeare, they would laugh at me and say I was sub-literate. But do they know the first thing about Linux? What is Linux – that's what they would say.

'Do you always leave all this stuff open?' I demanded, moving on.

'Yes,' she replied and shrugged. 'Why shouldn't I?'

'Twitter, Facebook, Gmail – I asked you for your passwords, but you were logged in to all of them. When you're done posting, tweeting or whatever, why don't you log out?'

'Does it really matter?'

'So when you head out shopping or to work, you leave your front door open, do you, keys still in the lock and a notice Scotch-taped to the bell-push saying *hey guys, come right in, take what you want*?'

'Of course I don't.'

'So always, always, always log out of your email, website, Dropbox, Facebook, Twitter – all that stuff, okay?'

'Yes, Professor Riley.'

'I'm not kidding, Rosie. You don't want strangers prowling round your private stuff and spying on you, do you? Or sending dirty emails to your friends who might think they really came from you?'

'No, of course I don't.' She made a rueful face. It was the cutest thing I ever saw, big-eyed and mock-repentant. 'So – both wrists slapped and lesson learned, all right?'

⌒ ROSIE ⌒

'When do you start work?' I asked, as we sat on the sofa cradling mugs of coffee and I so much wanted to kick my slippers off and put my feet up on his lap.

'Tomorrow morning. I have a breakfast meeting with the head of the department.'

'I think it's very mean of them, to get you working straight away. They should let you get over your jet lag.'

'I don't have jet lag. Or I don't think I do. But I've never flown this far before. My longest trip until today was from Salt Lake City home to Minneapolis.'

'How are you feeling, are you very tired?'

'No, I'm wide awake.'

'Shall we take in a movie, then?'

'You mean go to the cinema?'

'Ooh, you're learning Britglish, are you?'

'Yeah, I'm studying real hard. I read a British newspaper on my way over here, so now I'm good and ready for the whole UK experience.'

He smiled, and I thought, *don't smile*. But then I thought, *don't stop*.

'I'd like to hear your London Philharmonic Orchestra conducted by that Russian guy, Jurowski,' he continued. 'I also need to check out Blenheim Palace and Westminster Abbey and maybe Fingal's Cave. Oh, and try some British beer to see if it's as terrible as everybody says. It's warm and flat, that right?'

'I wouldn't know. The only alcohol I drink is wine.'

'I want to see the ocean, too.'

'You've already seen the ocean.'

'I don't think so.'

'You flew over it this morning, didn't you?'

'I guess I was asleep.'

He rubbed his eyes, then ran his fingers through his hair and I was jealous of his hair. Most men tend to make me wince or shudder, and for years I thought I must be gay, even though I didn't fancy women. So perhaps I was repressed?

But I wanted to reach out and stroke Professor Riley, just like I remember wishing I could stroke a marble statue when I was in Florence once on a school trip.

This had to stop before I grabbed him. 'Okay, we'll head out to the movie theatre. We'll go get the tube,' I said.

'You mean we'll ride the subway?'

'I mean we'll take the London Underground.'

'I kept seeing signs for that as I came over here. I thought it must be where your hobbits lived.'

'You mean our Wombles.'

'What in hell are they?'

✦ PATRICK ✦

There's something about popcorn. The burning-sugar smell of it takes me back to necking in the back row of a movie theatre when I was fourteen.

But we adults weren't necking like a pair of high school

students, obviously. We were sitting like two grown-up people, our eyes fixed on the screen, our minds elsewhere. Or mine was, anyway.

I was a married man.

Whose wife had left him.

Who thought he might be falling for a British girl.

Who knew he'd fallen for a British girl.

Whose life and work were in the USA.

Whose kids might from now on be growing up in any country, in Europe, Asia, Africa, even the Middle East.

Who loved his kids and wanted to be in their lives.

Who hadn't felt like this in two decades.

Who knew he was in love, which scared him half to death.

I tried to concentrate. I stared at moving images. I knew there must be voices. But I didn't see or hear a thing.

⌒ ROSIE ⌒

Did we just see a film? What was it called? What happened? I had to know in case he asked me what I thought of it. So now I was slightly panicking ...

'You enjoyed that?' Pat began as we came out of the multiplex into the yellow fluorescent drizzle of the London night.

'Yes, it was great.'

'What part did you like best?'

Somebody save me! Maybe I could faint? But I've never fainted in my life. What do you need to do to faint? I suppose you have to sort of slump? You let your knees give way and then you sink down gracefully, like a ballerina in *Swan Lake*, that kind of thing? I didn't really want to sink down on that dirty pavement, gracefully or not. I was wearing my new coat from L.K.Bennett and my new black boots with three inch heels and lizard trim.

'You first – what did you think of it?' I asked, playing for time and thinking: *please, give me a clue?*

'I'm sorry, Rosie. I think I must have dozed. I – hell, this is embarrassing, but I don't remember much about it.'

'Or anything at all, in fact?'

'Or anything at all.'

'You must be tired?'

'I guess.'

He did look pretty shattered. 'You should go to your hotel and get some sleep,' I told him. 'Let's go back to mine and get your luggage and I'll run you over there.'

'There's no need, I'll find a cab.'

'I'll drive you, Pat. It isn't any trouble, honestly.'

But he wouldn't let me. He collected up his luggage and then flagged down a cab. He promised he would call tomorrow.

'How did you get on today?' I asked him when he rang the following evening, as he'd said he would. A man who kept his promises – this had to be a first. 'What are your postgraduate students like?'

'They're pretty smart, I guess.'

'You mean they're very clever or they wear a lot of Burberry?'

'Excuse me?'

'I was teasing – kidding you.'

'I see.' He didn't sound amused. 'This is the famous British sense of humour, right? What did you do today?'

'I set up two new accounts. I made a lot of phone calls. I had lunch with Fanny and then I spent three hours with a woman who wants me to promote her range of toiletries for dogs.'

'Dogs have toiletries?'

'Of course they do. Deodorants, colognes and styling

products like volumising lotion, hair conditioners for straight or curly, and thickening shampoo. All of them organic, cruelty-free.'

'Yeah, I can see the world has need of all those things. Rosie, may I buy you dinner sometime?'

Say you'll need to check your diary, I told myself. *Say you're very busy.* But I took no notice of myself. 'Oh, that would be lovely!' I exclaimed, delighted.

Now my heart was doing cartwheels and I had to tell it to calm down. 'When would you like to meet?' I asked, still palpitating.

'Well, I need to do some scheduling, but as soon as we can fix a date that suits us both? My kids are here in London with my wife. So I shall want to meet with Joe and Polly. But that will most likely be early afternoons.'

'Did you know they'd be in London?'

'Yes, of course.'

'I see.'

I was so disappointed. He'd come to see his children. Well, of course he'd come to see his children! He was also giving lectures at the university. But, for just one idiotic moment – or, come on, be honest, make that several moments – I'd let myself believe that he had come to London to see me.

There are no wounds more painful than self-inflicted ones. I know that very well. But I'm good at beating myself up. I'm a world-class expert. Why not hurt myself some more?

'Let me know when you have some free time,' I told him. 'We'll do something more exciting than just meet for dinner.'

What did I mean by that?

'I'll call you back with dates and times,' he told me. 'You take care – speak soon.'

The line went dead.

Something more exciting – did she just say that?

What did she have in mind?

I wasn't sure if this was wise. But then I told myself I didn't give a damn about the wisdom of the situation. Yeah, I'd come to this damp little island to lecture college kids on speech-to-text and thought-to-text and see my children – right?

Who was I trying to fool?

❧ ROSIE ❧

Okay, back off, I thought. He's married, he has children. So now cool it, girl, and let's forget excitement. We'll do something public and respectable. I'll take him to the Globe. He might find the architecture interesting, even if he doesn't want to see a Shakespeare play. Actually, you never know – he might. He said he was ready for the whole UK experience, and what could be more UK-experience-wise than Shakespeare?

When he got back to me with dates and times, I found my diary was chock-a-block. I made quite sure of that. We spent ten minutes saying things like *no I can't make Friday* and *I'm busy on the weekend* and *Tuesday isn't any good for me.*

But I still can't understand how we arranged to meet on February the fourteenth. I must admit I hadn't even noticed the shops were full of hideous pink cards and even more revolting stuffed pink animals.

I hoped Pat had failed to notice, too.

❧ PATRICK ❧

When she told me we were going to the Globe to see a Shakespeare play, I had mixed feelings. The Globe – I did some googling – yeah, that might be kind of interesting, to see how an Elizabethan playhouse translated to the twentieth century? As for the Shakespeare play – it would depend.

While I was in high school, we performed a Shakespeare play each fall, and parents came to watch us all make idiots of ourselves. Or anyway, some parents came to watch. My father never did, for which small mercy I was grateful. He would have jeered and mocked and sneered and said I was a faggot, to his mind the worst insult of them all. Then he would have beaten up on me because I was a faggot who had made a fool of him.

I always played a messenger, a herald or – upon one memorable occasion – part of a Scottish forest in brown leggings and a bright green wig. While Ben Fairfax ranted, yelled and strutted as Macbeth, I was festooned with branches. I and some other kids who couldn't act were Birnam Wood that came to Dunsinane.

Tonight it was *The Tempest*. I never heard of it. It can't have been in our school's repertoire. I was prepared to hate it. But I loved it.

At school, we kids – even those who had some acting skills – had hacked and stumbled through the plays, snickering as we spoke the weird, old-fashioned words, which most times made no sense to us at all. But those British actor guys, they spoke them like they all made perfect sense, which obviously they did.

'Thank you, that was great,' I said, as we walked by the river afterward, the words still ringing in my head.

'You really liked it?'

'Yeah, I sure – I really did. Come on, I'll buy you dinner. Where would you like to go?'

'Come in for a while, Pat?' she invited when we came back to her place.

'It's getting late. You need your beauty sleep.'

'You're saying I'm not beautiful already?' Then she smiled flirtatiously at me. 'Do you have an early start tomorrow? A breakfast meeting, is it? You could have breakfast here.'

'Rosie, please don't make all this so difficult for me.'

I could not take this woman in my arms. I could not kiss her on her lovely mouth. Somehow, I had to save my marriage because, if I did not, the chances were I'd lose my kids. But how could I save my marriage when it surely died last fall, when Lex went off with Mr Wonderful? Did Lex and I have any real hope of making up, of even being friends?

'*Our revels now are ended* – is that what you're telling me?' said Rosie in the black velvet voice that warmed my heart.

'I don't mean that at all.'

'*We are such stuff as dreams are made on. Our little life is rounded with a sleep.* Or to put it less poetically, you're a long time dead.' She looked into my eyes. She ran her index finger down my chest and made me shiver with desire. 'Someone told me once: *if you want something, go for it.* But if you want to end whatever's happening now, before it even starts?'

'It's not a question of wanting to end anything. It's about not wanting to hurt somebody who means a lot to me.'

'You mean your wife.'

'Rosie, I mean you, of course.'

'Getting hurt is part of being alive. If I can't deal with being hurt, I might as well be dead. But if you want to go?'

'I want to stay.'

ROSIE

Valentine's Day, my birthday, all my Christmases in one – I felt like I'd won the lottery, the EuroMillions and Olympic gold.

Stop this, I told myself.

My other self said: *why? This is all working out. It's going to be all right. Just trust your female intuition.*

Or should that be my wishful thinking?

Whatever – now I was in far too deep to have any realistic hope of climbing out again.

✢ PATRICK ✢

She made coffee. She was very good at making coffee. She had a cool black coffee-maker, a machine to froth up milk, and the result was perfect every time.

Guys at JQA who'd been to Europe had told me how it was impossible to get good coffee outside of the States. Those guys had lied.

She sat on the left side of the couch and I sat on the right. I drank my perfect coffee. I knew I ought to leave. I knew I wasn't going anywhere tonight.

'What about some music?' she suggested.

'No music.'

'You like music.'

'I don't want any now.'

'Okay.' She started fussing with a bracelet on her wrist. 'I can't undo the clasp,' she said. 'It's stuck, and if I tug I'm going to break it.'

'Let me help?' I took her hand. I held her wrist. The silver clasp was very small, and so instead of touching just the bracelet, my fingers also found the beating pulse on her warm skin. The pulse was fast, as fast as mine.

I'm not especially clumsy. But tonight my hands would not obey me. I gave up trying to undo the clasp. I held her wrist and checked the bracelet out. I turned it round and round, admired the fine engraving. I watched the burnished silver catch the light. 'This is a lovely thing,' I said. 'Where did you get it?'

'It used to be my grandmother's.'

'She died?'

'Oh no, she's very much alive. But she can't wear jewellery any more. She has bad arthritis and her hands and wrists are very twisted, very bent. This bracelet was a present from my grandfather so it's been in the family for years and she said I should have it now.'

She looked at me, her grey eyes luminous. 'Do you think you could try the clasp again?'

I didn't try the clasp. I crossed the Rubicon instead. I kissed her palm and then I kissed her wrist and then the inside of her arm up to the elbow.

There's nothing quite as lovely as the inside of a woman's arm, where the fine white skin is soft as satin, where the pale blue veins are barely visible but, if you should stroke them, you can feel the blood pulsating through them.

'Pat, what are you doing?' whispered Rosie.

'I guess I'm taking liberties with you.'

'I thought as much.'

'So stop me.'

'What if I don't want to stop you? What if I was hoping you would kiss me everywhere?'

'Do you think you'd like it?'

'I won't know until you do it.'

'Maybe I would like you to kiss me?'

'If I do, you might be turned to stone.' She smiled, her gaze hypnotic, pupils huge, the grey almost invisible. 'When I kissed you at the airport back in Minneapolis you stood there like a statue, like you'd been petrified.'

'I guess I was surprised.'

'You mean you were annoyed, upset, embarrassed?'

'No, I mean surprised.' I stroked her hair back from her face. 'I couldn't figure out why you would want to kiss a guy like me.'

'What kind of guy are you?'

'A guy who's crazy because he thinks, he hopes you like him, who's in love with you.' There, now I said it and there was no going back. Did I want to unsay what I just said? I wanted to repeat it.

So I did and then I took her face between my hands and kissed her on the mouth. Then I kissed her neck and then she arched away from me, inviting me to kiss her throat and kiss her everywhere and so I did.

Mr William Shakespeare, you are an accessory, I thought, as I held Rosie in my arms and it felt like she should be there for eternity. It was where she belonged. *I'm holding you responsible, you hear me?*

'You must be tired?' she asked, when ten minutes, twenty minutes later, who was counting, certainly not me, she pulled away and looked at me.

'Yeah, I'm tired,' I said.

'You don't have to go and find a cab or get the tube. You could stay here. The sofa is a bed.' She looked at me, her eyes big and transparent. 'Or you could sleep with me.'

'Rosie, are you trying to seduce me?'

'Do I need to try?'

'A girl like you, a girl who is amazing and fantastic and wonderful in every single way, I guess she doesn't have to try too hard.'

'Then shall we go to bed?' She saw me hesitating. 'Pat, I mean like now, before you check tomorrow's lecture notes or file your tax return?'

'Rosie, have you thought this whole thing through?'

'You're married, you have children, there's every chance you'll go back to your wife and break my heart. But I'd still like to go to bed with you because I know that if I don't I shall regret it all my life – cards on the table, right?'

* * *

I thought I wasn't anything like Ben.

But perhaps deep down I'm just the same? Perhaps I have forgotten what I said in church? Perhaps I never meant it in the first place?

No – I'm not like Ben. When he seduces pretty co-eds, it's all about more conquests, more spraying round the district like a tomcat. It's like the man from Laramie – more notches on his gun.

What I felt for Rosie wasn't about conquest.

So what was it, then?

I couldn't identify it because I never felt that way before. The nearest I had been was when I was a choirboy in Recovery, when we sang Easter Mass. But even that did not come close.

⌒ ROSIE ⌒

I felt like I was drunk, but I was stone cold sober.

I felt like I was floating, as if I was unreal, but I was in the here and now, and everything I felt and sensed was sharp and cut as deep as knives.

Whenever I'd had sex with men before, I'd watched them and I'd judged them. I'd never wanted to engage with them or – as they put it in old-fashioned novels – to give myself to them, except in the most physical, emotionally-disconnected, do-it-for-me way. All I'd wanted was to gain some fleeting satisfaction – to get laid – and I suppose that far from giving, I just took.

But with Pat there was no taking, giving or sexual bargaining. When he kissed me on the wrist, I suddenly knew I was a part of him, that he must be a part of me. We were like a pair of compasses, two separate points but still connected and – although I knew it was irrational or even downright stupid of me to suppose it – I was almost sure we always would be.

* * *

We lay together in my bed and he played with my hair. He wound it round and round his fingers, clearly fascinated by my curls, perhaps because his own black hair was ruler-straight. 'What are you thinking, Pat?' I asked.

'Your hair, I never saw such wild abundance.' He pushed it off my face and held it back. 'Do you ever wear it up?'

'No, never. Or perhaps I should say hardly ever. There's too much of it. I've sometimes had it up for weddings or events. I look as if I have a puffball on my head.'

'I like it down in any case.'

'I hate my hair. It's uncontrollable. When I was child, I wanted more than anything to be a Barbie blonde. I longed for straight, fair hair.'

'Your hair's perfection and I love it.'

'You're a big fat liar, Patrick Riley, but I'll let you off. What else are you thinking?'

'I don't dare to say.'

'Go on, you can dare anything. I'm giving you a global dispensation, a plenary indulgence.'

'You told me one time you didn't have much history with guys. But you must have kind of known some men?'

'Dr Riley, what are you suggesting?'

'I don't have a clue what I'm suggesting. But I want to know, I need to know—'

'You're asking if I've been to bed with lots of other men?'

'I remember what you said when we were in that restaurant in Minneapolis.'

'What did I say?'

'You've been on dates. But you've never gotten close to one particular guy. You've never been engaged. I'm sure you must have had a ton of boyfriends, though – a pretty girl like you?'

'I've mucked around with loads of tossers, yes.'

'Tossers – does that mean—'

'I've known a bunch of wankers.'

'You didn't fall in love?'

'I've always known I couldn't love a git, and most of the men I've known were gits.'

'Gits.' He rolled the word around his tongue. 'You mean they were losers?'

'Yes, but git is stronger, more pejorative. I'm surprised you haven't come across it.'

'I lead a sheltered, academic life.' He looked at me. 'Git – I like it. I must use it. Okay, then – these gits, what did they do to you?'

'Annoy me, try my patience, bore me.'

'They didn't make you care for them at all?'

'Oh, Pat! I think you're jealous!'

'I'm insanely jealous. You can't begin to realise how mad it makes me, not to be your first.'

'I'm not your first.'

'No, you're my second.'

'Yes?' I laughed at him. 'So go on, pull the other one?'

'I beg your pardon?'

'It's another Britishism. *Monty Python and the Holy Grail* – you must have seen that movie?'

'I don't think so, is it new?'

'No, it must be thirty-five years old or maybe more. I saw it first when I was six or seven. We had the video. So you're telling me that you and Lexie, neither of you—'

'Lex and I, we both have Catholic mothers who believe in hell for people who step out of line.'

'I have a Catholic mother, too.'

'You do?' He frowned. 'I thought you British were all Protestants?'

'There are lots of Protestants, but my father's mother – that's my Granny Cassie – she's a Catholic. So she was delighted when Dad met and married Mum. But he wouldn't let Mum bring me up to be a Catholic because he's not religious. I was never christened.'

'Your mom, she didn't insist on that?'

'No, why would she insist?'

'She had a moral duty to insist and to make sure that you were brought up Catholic, as well.'

'She and Granny Cassie sometimes snuck me into church at Christmas and at Easter – does that count?'

'I doubt it.' Patrick shrugged. 'I can see your mother must be more relaxed than mine.'

'It's not that she's relaxed. It's all down to my dad. Nobody, and I mean nobody, is allowed to argue with my father. Pat, why don't you tell me all your secrets?'

'I don't have any secrets.'

'Okay, tell me serious stuff and trivial stuff, like what you have for breakfast, what you do when you're not working, why your ancestors went to America, when and how you met your wife and when you fell in love.'

'I eat cereal for breakfast. When I'm not in college, I do stuff with Joe and Polly. Mornings, I go running. Nights, I try to get some sleep. My ancestors were Irish and Italian peasants who came to America back in the nineteenth century, escaping poverty or even famines, hoping for a better life. Lex and I, we dated all through high school, missed each other all through college, married when we graduated.'

'So you had no other girlfriends? Pat, that's positively mediaeval.'

'Yeah, Ben often says he can't believe that I'm for real. I must be an alien, he reckons, not a human being with ordinary human wants and needs.'

'You're no alien, Dr Riley.'

'How can you be sure?'

'I suppose I shouldn't make assumptions? There might

be room for doubt? Maybe I should do some simple tests to make quite certain?'

'Yeah, I guess you should. I think you'll find the scientific method is usually the best.'

'The scientific method?'

'Okay, you ask your question. You do a little research. You work out a hypothesis. You set up your experiment—'

'I like to learn through play.' I rolled on top of him and started talking dirty and I soon assured myself that Patrick Riley was all human being.

Afterwards, I slept.

But then of course the nightmares came. Mum was sobbing, telling Dad it was his fault if Charlie was in hell, and adding she was sure he'd go there, too. Dad said that was fine by him. He'd probably meet some interesting people. He didn't want to go to heaven anyway, especially if it was full of bores and saints like Mum.

I know my parents love each other. They're devoted, always have been and I'm sure they always will be. Dad would die a thousand deaths for Mum and she would walk through fire for him.

But when people are bereaved and when their hearts are broken, they say some awful things. Charlie dying didn't just divide our lives into before and after. It stopped us saying what we should have said, from comforting each other when we needed comfort most.

I don't know why.

✦ PATRICK ✦

I never knew that you could learn so much through play. Rosie was such fun, so clever, so inventive. I never met a girl – or anyone – with such a great imagination. She was so focused and intent. She made me feel the world belonged to us – and only us.

173

She was also beautiful. The tiny imperfections – her not-quite-California-straight front teeth, the puckered seam from an appendix surgery across her flat, pale stomach, the gravel marks on both her knees from when she must have fallen off her bike when she was just a kid – they made me love her more.

The street light shone into the room so I could watch her while she slept. She lay so still it seemed like she was dead. I touched her arm, her forehead once or twice to make sure she was warm. I listened hard to hear she was still breathing.

Did she always sleep so deeply? Once or twice her eyelids fluttered and she kind of whimpered. Then she was quiet again. I guessed I'd never tire of watching Rosie. Perhaps I'd never get another chance to watch her while she slept?

I figured I would stay awake all night.

⌒ ROSIE ⌒

When I woke up again, it was still early. So early that the everlasting buzz and hum of London were still hushed, still muted, and what sounds there were seemed muffled and apologetic, reluctant to disturb the city's slumber.

The street light shone into the bedroom, leaching everything of colour, turning everything to monochrome, like we were in a 1950s film. Pat was sleeping, lying on his stomach, both arms underneath his pillow, head turned to one side, long, black lashes lying on his cheeks, which lower down were rough and dark with early morning stubble.

I kissed and stroked him until he woke up, too.

'Hey, Rosie.'

'Hello, Pat.'

'Why did you wake me up?' He smiled and kissed me. 'Do you want to play?'

*   *   *

174

'Maybe you could go and put the kettle on?' I said an hour later.

'You go put the kettle on,' he said. 'While you're in the kitchen, you could fix my breakfast, too.'

'Why can't you do that?'

'I'm tired,' he said. 'You wore me out.' He kissed me on my mouth, my neck, my throat. He ran his fingers through my hair. 'Coffee, cereal and toast with some of your delicious British marmalade,' he added. 'Do you have Cooper's Oxford?'

'No,' I said. 'Patrick, do you know that you are nothing but a knuckle-dragging, Neolithic throwback?'

'I love it when you're sweet to me.' Then he grabbed my wrists and pushed me back against the pillows. 'Rosie, do you know that you are funny, clever, sexy, beautiful – the pinnacle of evolution?'

'You're assuming flattery will get you everywhere?'

'I kind of hope it might.' He kissed my nose. 'While you're fixing coffee, maybe you could also fix some brownies, muffins, croissants, jelly doughnuts?'

'Or maybe you could just make do with cornflakes and with me?'

He had to leave for work an hour later. I did, too. While Professor Riley went to do whatever clever stuff IT professors did, I'd go to meet the woman who made shampoos, conditioners and deodorants for dogs. Then I had to find some upscale shops who'd stock these things.

'So shall I see you on the weekend?' he enquired as he ate his cornflakes and swallowed scalding coffee.

'It's already Friday morning,' I reminded him.

'Then I'll meet you after work this evening, shall I?' He was smiling now and with that stubble he looked very, very sexy. 'Show you a good time?'

'What about the children – don't you want to see your children?'

'Yeah, but the kids and Lex are going someplace. York, I think she said. Something to do with Vikings, would it be?'

'So you won't be busy?'

'No – and even if I was I'd change my plans.'

He kissed me one last time and then he went to find a taxi to take him back to his hotel so he could shave and change his clothes before he went to college.

I missed him already.

❧ PATRICK ❧

It was the best weekend. Yeah, she kind of showed me London, but I didn't see it. All I saw was Rosie and, although it drizzled constantly and the sky was stained a miserable British grey, she was always bathed in golden light.

'Let's go out,' she said on Saturday as we ate breakfast.

'Where shall we go?' I asked.

'What sort of thing appeals to you?'

A ton of stuff – but most of all I want to stay in bed with you, I thought and was about to say. But then I decided that perhaps I ought to make a little effort to ride the tourist trail? Be an interested and appreciative guest here in this foreign country?

'Do I need to see the Tower of London?'

'You need to see all sorts of things. The Shard, Madame Tussauds, the London Eye – they're on almost everybody's list. Or we could go on a river trip to Hampton Court?'

'You call your Thames a river?'

'What else would it be?'

'A creek?'

'I know it doesn't rival your mighty Mississippi. But it's wide enough for rowing boats and coracles. So, Professor Riley, do you row?'

'I rowed for college one time. Okay, we'll hire a rowboat or a coracle and go to Hampton Court. Then shall we check out the London Eye, go up the Shard?'

She lied about the coracle. She sent me to the tourist information place to ask where I could hire a tandem coracle to row to Hampton Court. The guys there laughed at me and then directed me toward the pleasure cruiser by the pier.

⌒ ROSIE ⌒

He was just the tiniest bit annoyed about the tandem coracle.

'You're a minx,' he told me as we leaned against the pleasure cruiser's rail and watched the Surrey scenery drift past.

'You're a gullible American.'

'But I never even heard of coracles before!'

'God gave us Google, didn't he? You have a mobile phone? You know how to look stuff up online?'

'I guess,' he said, and then he glanced down at the foaming, dark brown water being churned up by the river cruiser. 'You like to swim?' he asked. 'If you should fall into this creek, you think you'd make it to the bank?'

'Of course – I have webbed feet.'

'I didn't notice.'

'I can't say I'm surprised. You were busy checking out some other parts of me.'

'Maybe I should check them out again?'

He took me in his arms and kissed me – not with passion, but with little teasing kisses, ones that made me tingle from my head down to my toes.

He made me happy – happy, happy, happy. I knew it couldn't last, that – unlike sadness – happiness is transitory. It's just an illusion. But, while I was with Patrick, I felt so warm and comforted, as if I were wrapped up in cotton wool. No, make that cashmere.

Alexis Riley – did he love her still? I wouldn't, couldn't ask him because he might say yes. There was so much I didn't know and was afraid to know. I often wondered about him and his children, if I would get to meet them, or if he would want to keep that part of him a secret, if …

'Hey, earth to Rosie – do you want to get a cappuccino?'

'What?'

'You were a zillion miles away, in some yet-undiscovered galaxy.' He glanced towards the café where white-aproned waitresses were serving drinks and snacks. 'It must be time for coffee?'

✦ PATRICK ✦

On Monday morning, we both overslept.

I woke to hear somebody knocking on the door of the apartment. Someone turned a key, walked in and came into the living room. Glancing at my cell, I saw that it was nine o'clock.

'Rosie? Rosie darling, are you there?' The somebody tapped on the bedroom door. 'Sweetheart, are you up? May I come in?'

'Ruddy hell, it's Mum! We're going to see an exhibition at the Tate. I'd totally forgotten.' Rosie jumped out of the bed, threw on her towelling robe and tied the belt. 'Mummy, could you go into the living room?' she called. 'I'll be with you in a minute, tops!'

'Your mother won't be mad at you?' I whispered. 'I mean, because of me?'

'I think she's twigged – I mean she's figured out I'm old enough to have a sex life. Please could you get dressed? Then keep her occupied while I have a quick shower and wash my hair? Patrick, are you listening to me?'

'Okay, okay, calm down – I'll handle Mom.' I pulled on my jeans and T-shirt, raked my fingers through my hair, then went into the living room to meet with Rosie's mother.

'This is Pat,' said Rosie. 'Or I should say, Professor Patrick Riley.'

'Hello, Mrs Denham.'

I'd learned to say hello to British people. They seemed to kind of like it. Or anyway, they say it all the time. Hello, hello, hello.

'Good morning, Mr Riley.' Mrs Denham looked me up and down and clearly found me wanting. 'I don't believe we've met before?' she added frostily.

'Pat's from Minneapolis, Mummy. It's in Minnesota – in the USA – you know?'

'I've heard of Minnesota, darling.'

Just like Rosie, Mrs Denham sounded like she had escaped from *Downton Abbey*. But her tone was cold and tart, not warm and sweet like Rosie's. It was nothing like her daughter's soft black velvet voice.

She offered me her hand, which was thin and white and brittle-looking, so I shook it carefully. Then I glanced again at Mrs Denham. I never would have guessed that she was Rosie's mom. She was small and blonde, not tall and dark, and she had a sad expression in her light blue eyes. She looked kind of tragic. Or maybe she was cold?

'Mum, I'll be five minutes,' Rosie said and then she ran into the bathroom, shut the door. So I was left alone with Mom.

'When did you arrive in London, Mr Riley?' Mom enquired.

'I came here round about two weeks ago. You don't need to call me Mr Riley. Pat is fine.'

'You're a professor, Rosie said?'

'Yes, at JQA – that's John Quincy Adams University, it's

in Minneapolis. I'm over here in London to give a course of lectures and do some consultation, have some meetings.'

'What's your field?'

'IT – I work on speech-to-text and thought-to-text.'

'How fascinating.' Rosie's mother sounded like she couldn't think of anything more tedious. 'Well, Mr Riley, I don't suppose you'll ever want for work. We're all so dependent on computers nowadays.'

This was going so well ...

But I could kind of figure out why Mrs Denham didn't want to be my mate, as they say over here. Anybody touches Polly between now and when she's forty-five, they'll have me to deal with, and it won't be pretty.

'Rosie went to Cambridge,' continued Mrs Denham. 'She read Modern Languages. She got a very gratifying degree. Languages are so important these days, don't you think?'

'They're useful, anyway. A guy can't easily get along without at least the one.' *Shut up*, I thought, *stop trying to be funny*. 'When did you come to London, Mrs Denham? Did you drive down this morning or were you here already?'

'I caught an early train.'

'I never rode the train. I guess I ought to try it some time.'

'Only if cold stations, dirty carriages and ghastly coffee are your thing, as I believe American people say.'

'You didn't want to drive?'

'I don't do long distance driving any more.'

'You come from Dorset, is that right, it's in the south of England? Dorset can't be very far from London?'

'I'm aware Americans regard a thousand miles as no great distance, but it's different here,' said Mrs Denham.

'How's your weather been in Dorset?' Yeah, lame question, but I could remember hearing someplace that when you first meet anybody British, you should always talk about the weather. It's code for *hi, how are you doing* and *I don't have bad intentions. I'm not about to steal your seed corn, covered wagon, silverware or cow.*

'Absolutely terrible, we've had some awful flooding.' Mrs Denham sighed. 'It's been a dreadful winter. The roads near us have been all but impassable at times, what with walls collapsing and ditches overflowing. The council needs to do more maintenance. But, as I was saying to my husband only yesterday, what with cuts in public spending and – oh, there you are, at last.'

Yeah, the cavalry arrived. Rosie came into the living room, smelling gorgeous, hair still damp, but now she was warmly dressed and booted to go out.

'You're ready, Mummy?' she asked Mom. 'Or would you like some coffee? Do you want to use the bathroom?'

'We ought to leave,' said Mrs Denham. 'Our tickets are for ten o'clock. We'll need to find a taxi.'

'Off you go,' I said. 'You guys have fun.'

'Thank you, Pat. I'll phone you later. Maybe we could meet for dinner?'

'Yeah, sounds good to me.'

'I'll be in touch.' Rosie stood on tiptoes, kissed me briefly on the cheek. But then, quick as a wink, she flicked her tongue across my ear and made me gasp. I hoped her mother didn't hear or see.

'It's been very interesting to meet you, Mr Riley.'

I swear Mrs Denham shuddered as she said my name. But Rosie smiled a secret smile, reminded me to lock the door behind me, and then they headed out.

March

Pat's time in the UK was up.

Lexie and his children had flown home a week ago with Lexie's other man and Pat was expected back at JQA himself.

I wished I'd met his children. I was curious about them. I suppose I could have engineered it. But maybe it was better that I hadn't met them, that I hadn't watched him being Daddy?

I took him to the airport. I wondered what would happen if I made a scene, if I wailed and clung to him and sobbed and acted all non-British and emotional? I did nothing of the sort, of course. When we kissed our last goodbye, there wasn't any tongue stuff. As if by some unspoken, undiscussed but mutual agreement, we didn't do the mouth-to-mouth resuscitation thing. Maybe lurking somewhere among Pat's Irish and Italian genes there had to be some British?

When he went through the gate and then walked on without a backward glance, I felt bereaved. It was like a part of me had been torn out, was lying bleeding on the floor, would die. It was then I cried.

I tried to concentrate on building up my business.

But since Pat had gone away I didn't see the point. I couldn't have cared less about conditioners for dog hair. Or for clever marketing of cupcakes. But I had to earn a living somehow and working for myself was flexible. I wasn't bound by statutory working hours or practices. If I chose, I was allowed to work myself to death.

So did I not hear from Pat? Yes – of course I did. We texted, emailed, called each other all the time. But I could detect no real feeling in his messages or phone calls – no genuine emotion. It was as if we were just casual friends. He talked about the weather – another foot of snow in Minneapolis overnight on six inches of ice, so there would be yet another snow day for the kids – and although he often said he missed me, now he had gone home again I never quite believed him.

What had I meant to him? Maybe I had merely been an opportunity to have some casual sex, a chance to get one over on his wife?

But he'd said he loved me, that he was in love with me.

Well – other men had said the same.

They were just words.

One Friday in the middle of March, the doorbell rang.

I was not expecting anyone. It was four o'clock and I had just come in from work, bringing back a pile of client folders which I meant to work on through the evening.

The flights from Minneapolis, I thought – they land at noon or thereabouts. But flights can always be delayed, so maybe …

Please let it be Pat come back? Let him say he couldn't bear to leave me? Let him tell me he'd resigned from JQA, that he'd found a job in the UK and that as far as Lexie and the children were concerned, we could work something out?

But it was Tess who stood there on the doorstep with a pile of luggage looking like she had been zombified, she was so pale. I stared at her in disbelief and I must admit in disappointment. 'What are you doing here?' I asked, astonished. 'Tess, are you all right?'

'No,' she replied. 'I'm sodding not all right.'

'Why, whatever's happened?'

'Oh, the inevitable, I suppose.'

'You mean you and Ben?'

'Yeah, ten out of ten, my clever friend. How did you guess?'

'Oh, Tess – I'm sorry!' I grabbed a couple of her bags and ushered her inside. 'Come in, sit down, get warm. I'll fix us both a drink, something to eat, then you can tell me all about it.'

'Thank you, Rosie. You're a mate.'

'I suppose it was another woman/women?' I enquired, after I had made us bacon sandwiches and opened some Rioja and Tess was fed and warming up again.

'One particular woman,' she replied. 'I caught them at it, Rosie. I walked right in on them.'

'A student, was she?'

'No, I expect he has it off with students in the comfort of his room at JQA.' Tess glanced up at me. 'I don't suppose I could stay here for a bit? Just for a few days, I mean, until I get my act together, find myself a place?'

'Of course you can stay here.'

'But you're not doing – I mean, you haven't got—'

'A bloke?' I took a swig of red. 'No, don't worry, there's no bloke. You won't be interrupting anything.'

'Thank you, love. Only it's like – I can't go back to Mum's. She'd only crow and say it served me right. Then I might have to kill her very slowly and they can have you for it.'

'Tess, stop worrying. I've already said you can stay here until you're sorted out.'

'I'll pay my way,' she said. 'I'm not hard up. I can afford to help with bills and stuff. Rosie, I don't want to be a burden, like my granny used to say.'

'We'll talk about the money stuff tomorrow morning. Tell me about Ben and this new woman. Who is she, does she work with Ben? What did they do when they saw you?'

'They didn't see or hear me, not at first. They were so

wrapped up in one another and making so much noise they wouldn't have heard a freight train coming through. As for who she was – this will make your hair curl even more.' Tess paused dramatically. 'It was Patrick's wife. The bitch was in my bed and stickying up my sheets.'

What could I say? I was astonished, gobsmacked, horrified. 'I thought she and Mr Somebody were blissfully in love?' I managed to croak at last.

'It would seem not,' said Tess.

'So she was with Ben on – when did you say this happened?'

'Yesterday. I'd gone out shopping, see. There's this big new retail outlet in the suburbs, all designer stuff. I told the bastard I'd be back by seven. But I had a headache and so I went home early.'

'Where were Patrick's children, then – playing with Ben's gadgets in the living room and stickying up your lovely Persian rugs?'

'No, they must have been with Patrick's mum. She's in Minneapolis right now. Mrs Riley Senior was probably meeting Joe and Poll from school or kindergarten or whatever and then taking them to Patrick's place. Mr Whatsit must have been at work, leaving Lex to make out with my husband on the sly.'

'I see.'

'He's such a pig!' cried Tess. 'You should have seen what they were doing, talk about depraved. I bet it's illegal in the state of Minnesota. If it's not, it ought to be, unless you have four legs, live on a farm and don't know any better.'

'What did you do?'

'You mean when I saw Ben and Lexie at it?'

'Obviously.'

'I filled a jug with water and chucked it over them.'

'It was cold water, right?'

'Yeah, it was iced, straight from the special tap.'

'You might have warmed it up a bit.' I started laughing then. 'I expect you've given them pneumonia.'

'Listen, mate, this isn't funny—'

'Tess, of course it's funny! It's hilarious, best laugh I've had for ages. Ooh, iced water – horrible!'

'Yeah,' said Tess and smirked.

'Did they see who cooled their ardour, then?'

'Well, my husband did.' Tess herself was laughing now. 'You should have seen his face and – other stuff.'

'What about the naughty Mrs Riley?'

'She had a blindfold on and had her wrists tied to the bedrail and she was shrieking fit to wet herself, I mean some more.'

'What did you do then?'

'I slammed the bedroom door. I turned the key and chucked it in the bin. Then I cut the cable to the landline, turned off all the central heating, packed a bag, picked up the keys to the Mercedes and drove it to the airport. I left it in the twenty minute parking zone. I didn't buy a ticket. So I expect it's in the pound by now.'

'Tess, I'm proud of you. So would they have had to call the fire brigade or something to get out?'

'They'd left their mobiles on the kitchen table with their keys and coats and bags and stuff. So with a tiny little bit of luck, they're still locked in the bedroom. What a shame.'

'When you told me you were wondering but it was probably nothing? When you were going to New York that time? Do you remember?'

'Yeah.'

'Did you mean you thought that Ben and Lexie might be—'

'I just saw the way she looked at him in Barnes and Noble when we happened to meet that afternoon. It was like they had a guilty secret. I told myself I was imagining things. After all, Ben flirts with every woman under ninety. He can't help himself. He's such a bastard.'

'How do you know that, have you been talking to his mother?'

'You're so funny. I suppose I always knew that marrying Ben Fairfax was a big mistake.'

'You should always trust your intuition, Tess,' I said.

But perhaps I shouldn't trust my own?

✦ PATRICK ✦

It felt so weird to go back to the USA alone.

It was like a part of me was missing. I needed to see Rosie like I needed oxygen. But I also wanted to see Joe and Polly. They'd flown back a week ago with Lex and Mr Wonderful.

My mother came to Minneapolis to see me and her grandchildren, to try to find out what was going on and set us right. She fussed and fretted round me, cooked for me and did my laundry.

She tried to talk to Lexie.

Lexie wouldn't take Mom's calls.

'Patrick, you're not eating properly,' Mom told me, sighing as she took another half-full plate away. 'But I can't say I'm surprised, with that woman giving you the runaround and stuff.'

I wondered about Rosie sometimes, wondered if she missed me, longed for me? I missed and longed for her like I was fit to die. She texted me and emailed me and called me. But all the time she was so formal and polite, I felt she wasn't missing me at all.

I thought about when we had said goodbye back at Heathrow. She hadn't hugged me, hadn't kissed me with a quarter of the feeling she had done whenever we had been alone together. So all that stuff she said about not ever having loved a guy before – had she been warning me? Or was she merely being very British?

The girl was an enigma, a mystery, a riddle.

But I decided I would not believe I'd been a blip, and most times I was optimistic, confident that we would meet again.

The dean was pleased with everything I had achieved in London.

'Pat, you ought to firm up this relationship with London University,' he said. 'Maybe get more people there involved in your research, enrol some graduate students on a programme? Perhaps you could go back to the UK in April, maybe even stay until the summer? I believe there's funding.'

'I'll think about it, Dean.'

I wanted, needed, was desperate to see Rosie, obviously. But I also needed to check out Lexie's schedule, to find out where in Europe, or at least which hemisphere, she and Mr Wonderful were fixing to be next, before I made my plans.

I thought I might go get a beer with Ben. These days Ben was acting kind of strange. He was absent-minded and preoccupied. When we passed a pretty graduate student in the corridor one morning, a girl he often said was hot for him, he never gave her even one glance, let alone a second.

Maybe he was missing Tess?

She had gone to England a few days after I came back to visit with her father, who was sick. Or that's what Ben had told me, anyway. But maybe he and Tess had had a fight? 'Come and have a beer after your classes?' I suggested because he seemed so down.

'I'm not in the mood for beer,' he muttered. 'I got stuff on my mind.'

'Your new book – it's not doing good?'

'My book is doing fine.'

'What is it, then?'

'Riley, will you quit interrogating me!' He rounded on me, glaring. 'You drive a person crazy, you know that? Why are you so freaking cheerful these days? Did you get to see some action while you were in Europe?'

ROSIE

So Tess was sleeping on my sofa bed.

She wouldn't talk to Ben. She wouldn't go and see her family. She did go shopping sometimes, but all she bought was chain store rubbish from the rubbish end of Oxford Street.

'She's such a fool,' she said one evening while we watched tripe on cable and I picked up some pointers on how *not* to do PR, how *not* to market anything.

'Who's such a fool?' I asked. *I must never say that something is faux anything*, I told myself – be it leather, fur or diamonds – ever, ever, ever. It was tacky and it was deceitful. A product should be praised for what it was, and never weasel-worded for something it was not. Well – not extravagantly weasel-worded, anyway. A *little* verbal massage never hurt …

'Pat Riley's wife,' said Tess, sloshing more wine into her glass. 'What the hell's the matter with the woman? She has a lovely husband. He's clever, kind and funny, and he's good-looking, too. It's no wonder Ben's so flipping jealous and felt he had to screw his best friend's wife. You should see Pat with his children, Rosie, talk about a perfect father – and the kids, they obviously adore him.'

A perfect father – right. 'What are his children like?' I asked. Just to torment myself, of course. I didn't seem able to resist it.

'Joe must be five or six, and he's a little charmer. He looks

189

just like Patrick – straight, dark hair and big brown eyes. He chats away and tells you all about his school and hamster and what he wants to be when he grows up.'

'What's that?'

'He can't decide between an astronaut and Spiderman.'

'What about Pat's daughter? It's Molly, isn't it?'

'No, Polly. Well, she's super-cute. She has the same colouring as Joe, but he's quite small and skinny and she's a little dumpling. She sits on Patrick's lap and chews his shirt cuff and snuggles up against his chest and you can see he loves that child to bits.'

'Pat made you feel broody, didn't he?'

'No!' retorted Tess. 'Well, maybe – just a little smidgeon.'

'Why don't you give Ben another chance?'

'Why would I do that? So I can be a literary widow, pregnant at the kitchen sink, waiting for the master to come home from screwing pretty female novel-writing wannabes? Raising all those children he says he doesn't want? I'm filing for divorce. I'm going to sue that bastard for every cent he's got.'

'You've made your mind up, have you?'

'Yes!' she cried. 'Why aren't you on my side?'

'Tess, I'm definitely on your side. But can you afford to hire a really hotshot lawyer?'

'It depends how much they cost.'

'Ben will hire a brilliant attorney – do I mean attorney, is that what they're called – who will make you look like some pathetic foreign gold-digger who had schemed to do this from the start. I mean to run away.'

'Rosie, he was shagging Patrick's wife! It was disgusting. I can't imagine anybody normal enjoying stuff like that.'

'But you have no evidence. That's unless you snapped them with your phone?'

'Of course I didn't, dummy. It never crossed my mind.'

'So now you've deserted him. Or that's what he's going to tell a judge. He might refuse to pay you anything. He might say you've already cleaned him out.'

'Yeah, right,' growled Tess. 'I'd like to clean him out with Dyno-Rod. I'd like to shove a pipe right up his arse and—'

'Yes, okay. Did you remember to bring your jewellery?'

'Yes, of course I did. I got my diamonds from the bank, as well. I called there on the way to catch my plane. Why do you ask?'

'Fanny says the woman always keeps her jewellery and all her other personal – what did she call them – chattels.'

'Good, I'll flog it all on eBay. Jewellery and clothes and shoes and handbags, everything – that'll keep me going for a while.' Then Tess sat up straight, looked hard at me. 'You've discussed all this with Fanny, have you?'

'No, of course I haven't. But she mentioned it some months ago while we were chatting about something else.'

'When you told her I'd got married, eh?' Tess slumped back on the sofa. 'I always knew the woman was a witch. I wish she'd cast a spell on Ben and make his nuts fall off. But in the meantime, I'm going to get my own back.'

'How will you do that?'

'I'll tell Patrick what I saw them doing.'

'Do you think that's wise?'

'I think he needs to know the truth about his shit best buddy and his wife.' Tess got out her Galaxy. I let her carry on.

'By the way,' she said as she was tapping, 'I rang Mum. I'm going home tomorrow. She needs some help with Dad. He's in a bad way, apparently.'

'She's forgiven you for getting married without inviting any of your family?'

'Yeah, I think so. But she also said it's got to be a white meringue, ten bridesmaids in pink taffeta and half a dozen pageboys next time, or she'll hang and draw and quarter me.'

April

❧ PATRICK ❧

The text from Tess, it freaked me out.

I read it twenty, thirty times and even then I couldn't quite believe it. The fortieth time, I did. *Okay,* I thought, that's after I was finished killing Ben in half a dozen cruel and unusual ways, *now you must play it cool.*

What were my options? Do absolutely nothing, file for divorce this very minute, try to find some middle way? Whatever I did next, I was not about to start a fight for custody of Joe and Polly. I doubted I would get it, anyway. Whatever Lexie's failings as a wife, she couldn't be faulted as a mother.

Also, if I started court proceedings, any good attorney Lex instructed would very soon find out that I was seeing Rosie and would drag my name and Rosie's through a ton of mud – or worse than mud.

I consulted with the dean and London University and fixed it so on April 22nd I was due back in London to give a dozen lectures and also do experimental work on thought-to-text at Queen Alexandra College.

I'd be there until July, maybe going back to the US from time to time, but being a mostly cyber-presence back at JQA. I'd get an apartment, I decided, so I could have the kids stay over when they were in Europe.

It would be good to get away from Minnesota where we still had ice and snow and blizzards. Everyone had gotten tired of winter and was longing for the spring, but this must have been one of the coldest springs on record, a mere continuation of a miserable winter.

I emailed Rosie to tell her I was coming to London for the summer. Rosie emailed back to say it would be nice to see me. Oh – *nice to see me* – right.

But when she came to meet me at Heathrow and when I saw her coming toward me, all the doubts I'd had about her loving me, they vanished, and I knew I was home. She looked amazing, black hair wild and curling round her lovely heart-shaped face, gorgeous grey eyes wide, red lips parted in anticipation, long legs doing great PR for her designer jeans. I dropped my stuff and took her in my arms and held her tight, tight, tight for five, ten, fifteen minutes, maybe more.

'I didn't dare allow myself to hope you would come back,' she whispered when at last we broke apart a little.

'I couldn't stay away.'

'Your work, your family, your life – they're all in America.'

'But you're in the UK, and where you are is where I want to be.'

'Oh, Pat – you say the nicest things!'

'The beer is better, too. The last time I was over here, I kind of got a taste for your real ale.'

'You must be the most romantic man I've ever known, Professor Riley.' She socked me on the jaw. Or I should say she would have socked me if I hadn't caught her hand in time.

'Did you drive?' I asked.

'No, my poor Fiesta's just failed its MOT and so it needs some work. I came by train.'

'Let's go get a taxi back to London.'

'Okay. Where are your children at the moment?' she enquired, as I gathered up my stuff and as we started heading for the exit.

'They're in the UK as well. Lexie and the Limey are in London, so the kids are on an outside-of-curriculum vacation.'

'When Tess told you about Ben and Lexie, did you—'

'Give a shit?' I shook my head. 'It was a shock, of course. But I did some thinking as I was coming over here and I realised I was not surprised. Well – not surprised at Ben, at any rate.'

'At Lexie, maybe?'

'Yeah, perhaps. But if she could cheat on me with Mr Wonderful, why not with my best friend? Come on, Rosie, let's go find that cab. We need to make up for lost time.'

So why did I not care?

I should have cared. One time, I'd have beaten up on Ben, like I had when we were little kids back in Recovery and he had gotten me into big trouble with Miss Ellie over missing doughnuts. He'd stolen them and sold them at recess and told our teacher it was down to me. Of course I took my punishment and, after school was out, I flattened him. But afterward I found I was ashamed. I made a solemn vow. I'd never strike another human being, not even my best friend. After all, there was a bunch of other ways to make my feelings known.

Did Mr Wonderful know what had happened between Ben and Alexis? If so, did it trouble him at all? Or was he too busy showing Europe how to manage its affairs?

I took Rosie's hand. I told myself whatever happened next, I would never let *this* woman go.

⌒ ROSIE ⌒

'You're a dark one, aren't you, mate?' said Tess, when we met for coffee in a Starbucks two days later. 'So how long has this been going on?'

'Since he was here in February.'

'So when I was staying at your flat and you said you hadn't got a bloke, that wasn't strictly accurate?'

'Tess, I didn't know if he'd be coming back. After all, his life is in America, and anyway he's married.'

'Yes, and as we both know very well, that never stops them, does it?'

'This isn't just a casual – Tess, I'm not even going to say the word. It's serious. I love him, he loves me.'

'Of course you love him. He's absolutely gorgeous and I must admit I rather fancy him myself. But, my clever intellectual friend – with your degree from Cambridge and your quarter blue in tiddlywinks – as you have observed, the man is married, and he has children, too.'

'So perhaps this means he's really serious about me, is prepared to make a lot of sacrifices so that he can be with me?'

'So perhaps this is his way of paying back his wife? She cheated on him, yes. But what's he doing, if not cheating back?'

'It's not like that at all.'

'Of course it's not. This is a love to last a lifetime. You're Romeo and Juliet. You're Antony and flaming Cleopatra. You're Cathy Whatsername in *Wuthering Heights* and Mr Rochester.'

'Mr Rochester is in *Jane Eyre*.'

'Yes, okay, whatever. Just you be careful, girl. You have your fun and ring me when it all goes pear-shaped, right?'

'What's the matter, Rosie?'

Pat was lying on my sofa. I was lying on Pat. I refused to let myself think any more about what Tess had said.

'Nothing,' I replied.

'You're not usually so quiet.'

'I'm tired.'

'You got a headache?'

'No.' I kissed him. 'But I think I want to go to bed.'

Lexie called to say that she and Mr Wonderful were going on a trip to Düsseldorf. He had meetings with some guys from German banks. He'd be sorting out the world's financial crisis, right? I guess it had to be?

They would be gone three days, said Lex and, when I asked for details of their travel schedule, she announced that they were booked on British Airways and were going first class. Then she added she would sure appreciate it if I'd watch the kids while they were gone.

'Why can't you take them with you?'

'Pat, why don't you want to see your children?'

'I do want to see them. But it's kind of awkward when I'm working.'

'I really don't see why.'

'Okay, I'll take them to some meetings. Maybe Poll could join in the discussion? Joe could swing by at my lectures, too?'

Lexie told me not to be sarcastic because it was the lowest form of wit. Why did I not have a few days off, take this opportunity to show my children some of quaint, historic Britain: castles, turrets, battlements and genuine haunted houses? Stephen said …

I couldn't give a shit what Stephen said. But I postponed a lecture. I told the graduate students I'd arranged to meet that I'd be out of town and I rescheduled all my stuff with them.

I hired a Volkswagen sedan, made reservations for the kids and me at a hotel in Guildford. This was close to where the Limey had a house where he and Lexie and the kids hung out, that's when they weren't at his apartment someplace in the City.

Guildford was allegedly a quaint, historic town convenient

for lots of other quaint, historic stuff. I saw it had a Starbucks anyway. I thought this might be useful because the woman on the desk at the hotel had looked at me like I must be an alien form of life who might bite or sting her on her stuck-up British nose.

So I didn't think this place would be exactly welcoming to kids. But where would kids be welcome? I'd realised the British mostly have no time for kids. Of course, no British people were ever kids themselves.

Lexie and the children met me at a filling station nearly two hours late. No apologies were made for jerking me around, wasting my time. Lexie had a printed list of dos and don'ts. 'You'll need this, Pat,' she said.

I saw green salads, outdoor exercise and early bedtimes, these were all still mandatory. As for fries and shakes and acting like a pair of monkeys in a zoo, yelling, fighting and mad-housing, they were still forbidden. So was drinking water from a faucet – bottled water only was allowed – so that was new.

'It's in case of allergies,' she told me.

'How can a person have an allergy to water?'

'You don't know what's *in* the water here in Europe, Patrick. Stephen says—'

'Lex, I'm sure you have a busy schedule, so don't let me hold you up.'

As Lexie drove, or rather kangaroo-hopped – she clearly wasn't on good terms with British stick shifts yet – out of the parking lot, I dropped her idiot list into the nearest garbage bin.

'What now, Dad?' asked Joe.

'Let's go have ourselves a bunch of fun.'

'Dad, can we be alligators?'

'Awigators?' echoed Polly.

'Yeah, sounds good to me,' I told them. 'Okay, guys, let's go.'

A year back, Lexie had banned alligators. They were not allowed in the apartment. They made too much noise. They flooded out the bathroom and terrified our nearest neighbours who were nervous seniors with a ton of heart conditions.

I doubted alligators were allowed in Mr Wonderful's and Lexie's place – too messy, too much fun?

I thought it likely the kids were starved of fun. So when we came back to the hotel, I let Joe and Polly fill the bathtub and burrow underneath a zillion bubbles, shrieking like a pair of banshees, soaking all the towels and robes and flicking blobs of foam up all the walls.

Meantime, while my children learned through play, I called up Rosie, told her Lexie was back Friday. 'So could I see you Friday evening? Unless …'

'Unless?' she prompted me.

'You'd like to take a day off work and spend some time with me and Joe and Polly?'

'I don't know.'

'You don't know what?'

'Perhaps I shouldn't – no, forget it. Actually, I'd like to meet your children. I'd like it very much. Why don't we meet in – Pat, where are you, anyway?'

'Guildford.'

'Why are you in Guildford?'

'It's historical and Lexie says the kids could use some history.'

'The last time I was there, I noticed a historical McDonald's, ancient Topshop and a venerable Gap. They must all have been there since – well, 1995? Okay, I'll come and find you and then we'll take the children somewhere seriously historical. I know just the place.'

'Where do you have in mind?'

'You wait and see,' she said mysteriously. 'But I can tell you now – you and the children, you're going to be impressed.'

'Come on, Rosie, give me just one little clue?'

'It's not too far from Guildford. It's unique. You have nothing like it in America. If you go into Google Maps, you'll find it. There – four clues – see you tomorrow, right?'

So I invited her to meet my kids.

Why didn't I do this before?

I don't really know, except that she had never mentioned kids, had never said she liked them, didn't like them, wanted any of her own, was seriously into cats. I wasn't sure if she and Joe and Poll would get along.

I guessed I'd soon find out.

She said four clues. I clicked on Google Maps. But then Joe started drowning Polly, so I went into the bathroom, pulled the plug.

When Joe and Polly were dried off and dressed again, we rode the elevator to the restaurant. There, they stuffed their faces – where did I hear that expression, maybe it was one of Rosie's – with a bunch of things their mother didn't let them touch: delicious British fries and chicken strips in neon-orange breadcrumbs – no artificial colours, flavours in the meals for kids, or so it stated on the menu card, but I didn't buy that for a second – and chocolate shakes with sprinkles and marshmallows on the top.

They traded sprinkles – Joe refused to eat the pink ones, Polly wanted all the pink ones – argued over who had got most red ones, agreed that greens were poisonous.

'Listen, guys, I have something to tell you,' I began, as they slurped and blew big chocolate bubbles and made patterns with their sprinkles on their plates. Two pairs of eyes were suddenly locked on mine, daring me to tell them there was lettuce for dessert. 'Tomorrow morning, we're going to meet a lady.'

'Who?' demanded Joe.

'She's one of Daddy's friends.'

'What's she like?'

'She's young, she's nice.'

'She's pretty?'

'Yeah, she's very pretty.'

'She's a guardian ad litem?'

'What?' I frowned at him. 'Where did you hear that expression, little guy?'

'Mom asked Stephen if we'd need a guardian ad litem for us kids if you decided to play dirty.'

Oh, she did?

'What's a guardian ad litem, Dad?'

'It's a person who's appointed by a court of law to look out for the welfare of minors and people who are otherwise incapable. Rosie's not a guardian ad litem. She's a British lady. I'm sure you guys will like her very much.'

I wiped the glop from Polly's face then picked her up and took Joe by the hand. 'Okay, let's go,' I said. 'We got a busy day tomorrow. So why don't we head up to our room and get some sleep?'

All kids are programmed to trip their parents up.

'What happened to The Terminator, Dad?' asked Joe, yawning as I tucked him up in bed.

'He got blown up,' I said.

'Dad!' Joe was suddenly wide awake again and his big brown eyes filled up with tears. 'Why did you let him get blown up? Mommy said you'd take good care of him!'

'Oh, you mean *that* Terminator!' I forgot the rodent. 'When you and Polly came to the UK with Mom, I asked your teacher to look after him. Mrs Daley has him in your homeroom.'

'No kidding, Dad?'

'No kidding, Joe.' I found my cell. 'See here, little buddy – here are pictures of your homeroom – here's the petting corner – and here's The Terminator, safe and snug inside his cage.'

'Dad, can we go see him on the weekend?'

'We're in Europe now, Joe. So I'm sorry, but that won't be possible.'

'Does Mrs Daley know he likes zucchini?'

'Yeah, I wrote it down. Now you guys get some sleep.'

'Tell us a story first.'

'Stowy,' echoed Polly.

'I don't know any stories.'

'You so do!' Joe glared at me and for a moment I saw Lexie. 'Tell about the time when me and Polly got turned into rattlesnakes,' he said. 'When we were on a spaceship and we killed the bad guys with a laser gun and then when we got home again we met with the President and Congress. Dad, what's Congress?'

'It's a bunch of guys in Washington who talk all day and half the night and then they tell us what to do. It's called the democratic process. What colour are these rattlesnakes?'

'Magenta.'

'Huh?'

'It's a kind of purple. Dad, don't you know anything? Anyways, these rattlesnakes …'

Joe told most of the story. Polly listened carefully, snuggled up against my chest and sucking on my cuff. But she was already dozing off as I kissed them goodnight.

'Dad, I'm not tired,' said Joe.

'You need to get some sleep. We're heading out tomorrow early. We'll see something awesome.'

'Did it come from outer space?'

It wasn't such a huge success, the outing with his children.

Or it wasn't at first, at any rate.

I drove to meet them at a big hotel in Guildford. It was dull and dank, one of those gloomy English mornings that cannot be bothered to get light, and threatening rain. People were putting stuff on Facebook saying spring in the UK was cancelled, had failed to install. Where was the flipping sun?

But it was also cold in Minneapolis. Yesterday, they'd had a foot of snow in just one night. I knew because since I had been involved with Pat I'd bookmarked various sites so I could check up on their weather, conduct my own tornado-watch and keep up to date with what was happening four thousand miles away.

Meteorological surveillance – gosh, how sad was that?

I found them waiting in the hotel lobby.

'Joe and Polly, this is Rosie,' said their father.

'Hi.' I smiled at them. 'It's great to meet you guys.'

'Hi, Rosie,' said the little boy politely while the little girl just looked at me, her thumb wedged in her mouth. The children were both gorgeous – dark-haired and elfin-faced with big brown eyes like Pat's. They seemed a little wary. But I suppose it was to be expected. I was a stranger, right? So I could not be trusted?

'Go on, Joe,' urged Dad. 'What did I tell you?'

Joe held out his right hand. I took it, shook it, smiled at him again in what I hoped was a non-threatening manner. He half-smiled gravely back.

'Who's driving?' I asked Pat. 'I'd be very happy—'

'Dad hates to be a passenger,' said Joe. 'Whenever Mommy drives, he tells her *careful of that truck* and *slow down at the intersections* and it makes her mad.'

'Then Dad had better drive.'

Pat's hired family saloon was big and smelled of recent valeting, not of coffee and old sandwich wrappers like my Ford Fiesta. It had proper child seats, too. I hadn't thought of child seats. Children didn't feature in *my* life ...

'You're all right with driving on the wrong side of the road?' I asked as we set off along the dual carriageway.

'Yeah, no problem, everybody else is on the wrong side, too. So I just follow them.'

'You know about priority at roundabouts?'

'You mean at intersections?'

'No, I mean at roundabouts. You have to give way from the right, okay?'

'Roundabouts – so what are roundabouts – I give way from the right – what then?'

What are roundabouts?

We were doing sixty and I was about to panic. But then he shot a glance at me and grinned mischievously. 'Hey, don't look so worried. I read right through *The Highway Code* last night. I got the special interactive version for idiot Americans who never heard of roundabouts. So, where are we headed?'

'It's a surprise,' I told him tartly. 'I'll give you directions in good time.'

'Dad hates surprises,' Joe informed me helpfully. 'Mysteries, surprises, all that stuff – he thinks it's dumb.'

'I don't,' objected Pat.

'Dad, you big liar, you so do. Anyways, you told me there's no mystery that science can't explain.'

'There might be a few.'

Polly was completely silent as we drove. But Joe talked all the time. He summarised the storylines of movies he had seen: *Cars*, *Cars 2*, *Toy Story*, *Toy Story 2*, *Shrek*, *Shrek 2* and *Shrek the Third*.

He seemed to like the stuff that came in series and involved a lot of mayhem and – if possible – machinery. Then he explained about the Revolution, which his class was studying in school. The American Revolution starring Nathan Hale and Paul Revere and all the patriotic, good Americans who drove the wicked, greedy British out – hurrah, hurrah, hurrah – and then they got the Constitution.

'What's the Constitution, Joe?' I asked.

'What's the Constitution, Dad?' asked Joe.

'I'll tell you later, little buddy,' said his father, who was concentrating on the road. As I had already realised when we were in Minnesota, Pat was a good driver. He obeyed all traffic signals, stayed a fraction just below the limit, didn't run red lights and never, ever cut anybody up.

But he did have his children in the back.

So maybe being a parent makes you careful?

But it's like in *Sleeping Beauty*, isn't it? You can have all the spindles burned and all the needles melted down for scrap, but your child will always find the one you missed and prick her finger on it anyway.

'Why have we stopped here, Dad?' asked Joe as he gazed across the sodden, grey-green wastes of Salisbury Plain.

'We're going to check out something even older than your father,' Pat replied.

'A tyrannosaurus rex?' demanded Joe excitedly. 'Or a pterodactyl, yeah?'

'You wait and see.'

We got out of the car and Pat swung Polly up on to his shoulders. I took Joe's hand and let him tug me through the empty car park. I saw him darting glances everywhere, clearly anxious to see dinosaurs.

Then it started raining and, as we left the ticket office and the information centre, what had been a bit of drizzle turned into a downpour. So was this a big mistake? Perhaps. At any rate, Pat wasn't half as impressed as I had been when I'd first seen Stonehenge. In fact, he wasn't impressed at all.

'It's not big enough,' he muttered, scowling.

'Whatever do you mean, not big enough? What were you expecting, something on the scale of the Grand Canyon?'

'No, but I thought it would be more dramatic, awe-inspiring. This is just a bunch of rocks.'

'They're very ancient rocks.'

'All rocks are ancient, Rosie,' he said sourly, as the rain came down in torrents. 'I know what you're about to say. I should be astonished some Bronze Age guys in goatskins dragged them here on rollers made of tree trunks and stacked them up like dominoes?'

'Well, I think it's astonishing,' I said. 'Those Bronze Age guys in goatskins, they had no mathematics, writing, cranes—'

'I never bought that goatskin stuff. My theory is this is the work of aliens from outer space. The rocks were teleported here from distant galaxies one Thursday afternoon after the baseball season ended so everyone was bored.'

'Dad, where are the dinosaurs?' asked Joe.

'Son, nobody promised you a dinosaur,' said Pat.

'Daddy, down,' said Polly.

So Pat put her down. She started pulling at the short green rabbit-bitten turf which was thick with droppings, little hard, black pellets. I hoped she wouldn't try to eat them, thinking they were sweets.

'Let's go and do something else, then?' I suggested.

'What exactly do you have in mind? Checking out more rocks, more grass, more sky?'

'Let's get out of the rain, in any case.'

We headed for the car park.

'Rosie, did you ever go to bug camp?' Joe demanded as he

skipped along beside me in the downpour, swinging from my hand.

'No,' I said. 'What's bug camp?'

'It's a day camp at the zoo. You get to study bugs,' he told me, in the patient tones of someone talking to a simpleton. 'You find out what bugs eat, and what eats them, and how they do a ton of stuff like building bug homes, raising bug kids. Mom says I can go in summer if we're home in Minnesota.'

'I'm not keen on bugs.'

'We have stick insects in our homeroom. They eat leaves, but if they're overcrowded they eat each other's legs.'

'What else do you like to do, apart from study bugs?'

'I like to cook. Hey, Rosie – can you make Yorkshire puddings?'

'Yes, but I usually buy them ready-made. When did you have Yorkshire puddings, Joe?'

'Tess fixed them on Thanksgiving.'

'Well, if you guys come by my apartment some time, I could fix you some,' I told him. Yes, I was determined to learn Amglish. I hoped they were impressed. 'What do you cook, Joe?'

'Oh, a ton of stuff! I bake up brownies, cookies, cupcakes. I'm real good at those. I guess if someone showed me how, I could fix some Yorkshire puddings, too.'

'You could help me make the batter, certainly. When I was as old as you, I used to love a Yorkshire dipped in Lyle's golden syrup – that's like your American maple syrup – or in chocolate sauce.'

'Chocolate sauce – my favourite!' Joe looked up at me. 'I like your hair,' he added. 'Did you put your finger in an outlet? I know that makes your hair go kind of crazy. Mrs Daley showed us pictures one time. You shouldn't put your finger in an outlet. You could die.'

'Joseph!' Pat exclaimed. 'Unless you're paying compliments, you should never comment on the way a lady looks!'

'Patrick, it's okay. The rain has made my hair frizz up. I do look like I've been electrocuted.'

Joe's bemused expression struck me as so sweet – he realised he had put his foot in it, but didn't know how or why – that I began to laugh. Polly stared at me but then she started laughing, too. Joe looked worried for another moment, but soon joined in with us.

'You're a bunch of nutters.' Pat scooped his daughter up into his arms. 'No,' he told her firmly. 'You do *not* eat rabbit poop, you hear me? Let's go get a burger, that's if they have any burger restaurants in downtown Salisbury?'

'Or maybe we should find a sandwich shop, buy the children sandwiches and fruit, not chips and burgers?'

'You sound like my wife.'

'You called us nutters – that's a piece of good old British slang.'

'Yeah, I'm trying to learn a foreign language.'

Polly seemed to like me.

When we went into the café and sat down, she climbed on to my lap. She fidgeted and squirmed and wriggled until she was comfortable. It felt good to have her there, her chubby little body snuggled close to mine.

'You like my new T-shirt, Rosie?' Joe enquired as we ate our burgers in this place whose menu said it made its own from happy cows who'd gladly lived and died for burgerdom, apparently in a meadow full of daisies, if we could believe the illustration on the menu.

'Yes, it's great.' I looked at it more closely. 'Angry Birds – it's H&M new season, isn't it?'

'Yeah!' Joe was delighted I could trace his T-shirt's provenance. 'Mom bought it online. You dig the shades?'

'I do indeed, Joe. Angry Birds in sunglasses are awesome.'
I wouldn't mind a top like that to wear myself, I thought –
ironically of course, as Tess might say.

'I got a shark one with a big red mouth as well,' he told
me. 'But I didn't want a Super Mario, although it was on sale.
I like your top,' he added. 'You look hot in yellow. Rosie, if
you did your eyes in black, you'd look like Alice Cooper.'

'What the hell?' his father spluttered. 'Joseph Riley, what's
with you today?'

'It's all right,' I said to Pat. 'Joe, who's Alice Cooper?'

'A mom, her kid's in school with me.' Now Joe was
blushing like a ripe tomato. 'Sorry, Dad. I know I ought to
call her Mrs Cooper. But she said to call her Alice.'

'Oh, she did?' Pat scowled at him. 'Just get on and eat
your burger, will you, and stop being such a wise guy?'

'Rosie, don't be mad,' Joe whispered.

'I'm not mad at all, Joe,' I assured him. 'I'm very flattered
that you like my top.'

'Where did you get it?'

'Gap.'

'Yeah, I thought it looked like Gap. It's a real cool store. I
got some jeans from Gap.'

Joe and I, we bonded over fashion.

➤ PATRICK ◄

'What shall we do now?' I asked, uncomfortably aware that
they were ganging up against me, which was both good and
bad.

Good because I wanted Rosie and my kids to get along. Bad
because she seemed to be encouraging my boy to give her sass,
and I expect a child of mine to have respect and be polite. A
six-year-old should not be telling any grown up woman she
looks hot, even if she does look hot, as Rosie did today.

'Daddy won't be grumpy long,' she murmured, wiping Polly's ketchup-covered mouth with paper napkins. Then she smiled at Joe, who grinned. 'What shall we do now? Let's have a think. We could go and climb the spire of the cathedral. Or ...'

'Or what?' demanded Joe excitedly.

'We could go to Bath!'

'Go take a bath?'

'No, not take a bath. We could check out something even Daddy will agree is pretty special.'

Yeah? Surprise me.

'How far is it?' I asked.

'About an hour's drive – that's all, I promise.' She spoke to me like I was some resentful adolescent on a family day out who needed talking round. 'Come on, Mr Surly, let's go and drink some water.'

'I can drink water anyplace.'

'But this is special water. It smells like rotten eggs and tastes of blood.'

'You're kidding, right?'

'There's only one way to find out.'

'Come on, Dad, let's go!' Always up for anything disgusting, Joe was already tugging at my hand. So we headed off to Bath, aquaplaning through the everlasting British rain.

I'd heard of Bath, of course. I knew it was a Roman city one time and was a tourist destination now. So what was I expecting? The usual pathetic British shopping mall? Some stubs of columns, maybe? Some piles of Roman rubble? If we lucked out big time, might we get to go inside a dusty, dark museum full of tarnished metal, broken crockery and other trash?

As we parked up, the sun came out. The sky was suddenly cobalt and, to my surprise, beneath white cotton candy clouds there was a gracious city built of glowing golden stone. It looked like something in a movie.

Then we were in the movie.

We trod on the actual paving stones the Romans walked on two thousand years ago. We saw bathing pools of grass-green water from which the steam arose and wreathed around us in wraith-like, spooky spirals. We checked out Roman tombstones, a bronze head of Minerva, a scary Gorgon's mask. We watched as foaming torrents bubbled up from deep inside the earth then gurgled off down ancient Roman drains.

'What do you think?' asked Rosie.

'It's awesome,' I replied.

'Okay, no need to be sarcastic.'

'I'm serious,' I insisted, as I gazed at Roman columns, Roman walls and Roman ...

'Pat, where's Polly?'

'She's right here beside me.'

'No she's not!'

I didn't know what I should do. I stared around in panic, about to get myself a heart attack. But then – oh, thank you, God – I saw my baby. 'Polly, get back here!' I yelled and everybody turned to stare at me.

I'd let go of her hand for just one moment and before I knew it she was kissing cousins with two ducks, would you believe it, who were bobbing on the surface of the larger pool. I grabbed her by the hood. I scooped her up and held her very tight. 'You are not Jesus Christ!' I cried. 'You do not walk on water!'

'Daddy, ducks!' said Polly, pointing.

'Pat, calm down,' said Rosie.

'Why are you British so careless of your children?' I would not calm down! 'These paving stones – they're wet, uneven, slippery – they're lethal for a little one. Why are there no guard rails, nothing to stop a person falling in and never being seen again?'

'There are guides, attendants, and the pool's not very deep.'

'It must be deep enough.' How many cell phones, cameras and eyeglasses could be at the bottom of that pool, that bath of Kermit-coloured water, I wondered, shuddering.

'Polly, stay with Daddy, yes?' said Rosie. 'We would hate to lose you.'

Yeah, understatement of the century. But Rosie had no children of her own, had never had those nightmares when your kids are trapped inside a burning building, drowning in a torrent, and you feet won't move, your arms won't reach, you're paralysed.

How could she understand?

I held my baby in my arms, her head butting my collarbone, her thumb wedged in her mouth. She was tired and soon she would be dozing and drooling on my shoulder.

But Joe was going crazy with excitement, dashing here and there and everywhere and hollering, even though I told him to quiet down a dozen times. I was relieved to see that Rosie held his hand real tight as he did his best to fall into a cistern full of coins.

'Hey, Dad – check this out!' he cried. 'I never saw so many pennies, quarters, dimes!' He loved the deep, mysterious pools of water. He coveted the coins. He adored the spooks and watched enchanted as images of walking, talking ancient Romans bloomed on Roman walls. I couldn't bring myself to tell him they were not for real, that they were projections of actor guys in togas, playing on a loop.

Why spoil the magic? We all need magic, don't we?

After going round the baths themselves, we took tea in the Pump Room, an amazing Georgian space where young, good-looking waiters and pretty college-student waitresses served us tea and perfect sandwiches and jewel-like little cakes.

I thought the British had no time for kids. But it seemed like I was wrong because these guys all made a pet of Polly, joked and high-fived with my son.

I thought how much my mom would love it here. I would bring her over some time, I decided, watch her sip her British tea and nibble cutesy British cakes and tiny British sandwiches served up on silver stands, while a string quartet played music from the shows she loved, and she would—

'Polly, no!' cried Rosie.

I had been distracted for a moment, thinking of my mother. But to my relief I saw that Rosie had just moved the teapot out of Polly's reach.

There are always snakes in paradise.

⟡ ROSIE ⟡

After Polly tried to grab the teapot, Pat took her on his lap and held her there, distracting her from all the dangerous stuff with sandwiches and cake.

The string quartet launched into something bright and jolly, possibly by Noël Coward, and Pat looked at me and shook his head. 'I can't believe this is for real,' he murmured. 'It's like something out of Georgette Heyer.'

'My goodness, you read Georgette Heyer, do you?'

'No, of course I don't. But Mom has all her novels, and I'm guessing I saw this place on one of the covers of her books.'

'My mother loves those books as well.'

'So if they should ever meet, they would have at least one interest in common?'

'Yes, perhaps. Joe, would you like another little cake?' The memory of my mother giving Pat her special ice queen treatment could still make me blush.

'Rosie?' whispered Joe, as Pat was cutting up some bread for Polly. 'Did you lose any teeth?'

'Well – not recently,' I whispered back. 'Why do you ask?'

'I lost a ton of teeth.' Opening his mouth extremely wide, he showed me where three baby teeth were missing. 'I put them in a box with a dead ladybug, a snail shell and a stick insect's head.'

'Joe, will you quit talking about teeth and bugs and stuff and grossing Rosie out?' Pat told him, sighing. 'What will she think of you?'

I thought he was delightful.

If I'd wanted any children – which of course I didn't – I'd have loved to have a Joseph Riley of my own …

The adults ate the cucumber-and-salmon, egg-mayonnaise and ham-and-cream-cheese sandwiches. We all ate the gorgeous little cakes. Pat said everything was good. He tipped the pretty waitress generously. Then I challenged him to drink some water from the fountain in the Pump Room. 'Go on, go on,' I urged him. 'When you come to Bath for the first time, you have to take the waters – it's the law.'

'Go on, Dad,' repeated Joe.

'It's absolutely free,' I added, laughing at his frown.

'It's the stuff we saw in those green pools?'

'That's right – the very same.'

'You'll have some as well?'

'I promise.'

'Spit or swallow?'

'Swallow, definitely.'

'I'll have some too,' said Joe. 'I'll swallow.'

'No, you won't,' said Pat. 'You'll tell your mom I gave you water the colour of Shrek's ass and she'll tell her attorney. You and your sister stick to juice.'

I fetched a couple of glasses from the fountain. He saw the water wasn't green at all and frowned at me. 'You got this from a regular faucet, didn't you?'

'No, it's from the sacred spring. But it's purified and filtered so it's safe to drink. Look over there – the girl is filling glasses for some other people now. What do you think of it?'

'Not bad at all – it's chalky, chemical, but not unpleasant – no rotten eggs, no blood.'

'You can feel it doing you good, then?'

'Something must be doing me good,' he said and gave me a big smile which warmed my heart.

❧ PATRICK ❧

What a day, best time I had in years.

I don't know why I kvetched so much about Stonehenge. When I think about it, little guys in goatskins or whatever moving rocks the size of small apartment blocks is pretty damn amazing.

I guess I hated the rain, the cold, the damp? I was also worried about Rosie meeting Joe and Polly, how it would all work out. But clearly Rosie gets on fine with kids, even if she's careless of them and she talks to them as if they're equals, which of course they're not – they're only kids.

As we headed back to the hotel, I thought: *you have to stop this now. Stop fooling round with Rosie. Stop wasting Rosie's time. She should be out there looking for a husband, for the father of her children, not hooking up with you.*

But I didn't think that I could bear to let her go.

When we got back to Guildford, both the kids were fast asleep. I took Joe and Rosie carried Polly into the hotel. 'Come up and have a coffee or whatever,' I told Rosie. 'I'll get some stuff sent to our room.'

'Dad?' Joe stirred and yawned, opened his eyes. 'I'm hungry, Dad. I want to get a chocolate shake and dinosaurs and fries.'

'Yes, okay.'

'It's not okay,' said Rosie, and she set her mouth the way all women do when they're about to tell a man he's wrong. 'You shouldn't always feed them chips and processed chicken, Pat.'

She was right, of course. I shouldn't feed my kids on junk, use Joe and Poll to make some sort of stuff-you-mate – another Britishism I kind of like – attack upon my wife. They should have a decent, balanced diet of cheese and eggs and fruit and wholemeal bread, not processed shit and shakes and branded sodas, I knew that well enough.

I ordered apple juice and cheese-and-salad sandwiches on wholemeal bread, not white. Joe picked at his and grumbled that he hated dirty bread and that the salad grossed him out. Then he crawled into bed and went to sleep.

As Joe and Polly slept, we talked in whispers.

'Pat, what do you actually do?' she asked. 'I mean at JQA? You've never said.'

'I work on speech-to-text and thought-to-text.'

'Goodness, thought-to-text – it sounds like something out of Harry Potter.'

'It's not magic, Rosie. It's turning brain activity into text on a computer screen. I do stuff with guys from several disciplines – neurologists, computer scientists, psychologists and physiologists. We're developing technology which will mean that one day even people with the most severe impairments – people who can't move, perhaps, can't talk, can't even blink – will be able to communicate with ease and accuracy using just their brains. It's possible to do it fairly clumsily right now.'

'How does it work?'

'You talk to your computer with your mind. Your brain makes brainwaves – yeah, they do exist – and your computer turns them into words. The other guy reads what you said on his computer screen.'

'What's your role in this?'

'I write the algorithms.'

'You're going to think I'm very stupid, but what's an algorithm?'

'It's a method, formula, procedure – whatever you want to call it – a set of rules to follow when making calculations or doing other problem-solving stuff, in my case with IT. Accuracy-wise, the thought-to-text procedures are proving just a little problematic, but we'll get there some day, hopefully quite soon.'

'It still sounds like magic.'

'No, it's science. As for magic, Rosie – that's your specialty.'

I met her glance and wished that she could stay with me tonight. I knew she wished it, too. We needed no computer interface.

But – how does that poem put it – we had space enough and time.

Or at least, we had until July.

May

He hadn't liked Stonehenge.

But he thought Bath was awesome and he loved the British seaside. When we went to Brighton the following weekend, Brighton was a hit.

He had never seen the sea – the ocean, as he called it – except from up on high, through the small windows of an aeroplane, and that was only recently. He had never paddled in salt water, never walked along a pier. He had never heard the susurration of waves dragging on pebbles, never seen the evening sun splash pink and red and gold upon these waves. As a child himself, he had done almost nothing British children take for granted.

So he was determined to make up for it now.

'Cockles, whelks, these things are gross,' he told me. But he ate them all the same because he said he figured he ought to try them once. 'The British can't make cotton candy,' he continued, chewing at it valiantly, but it proved too much even for him, and soon he tossed his candy floss into the nearest bin. 'That was way too sweet, too sticky. It was burnt, as well.'

'Do you have any other observations, grumbles or complaints?'

'No, I guess that wraps it up,' he said and grinned at me. 'Your British chocolate is delicious and your ice cream is divine.'

'Oh, thank you, Pat. It's good to know we got a few things right.'

217

'Rosie, you got almost everything exactly right.' He took my hand and pulled me down beside him on the pebbles. 'We should have met in high school,' he added wistfully. 'Why didn't we?'

'You were destined to be Lexie's husband and Joe's and Polly's father. It was written in your fate.'

'You believe in fate?' He shrugged and seemed to acquiesce, stared for some moments at the white-capped waves, but then turned back to me. He gazed into my eyes, his stare intense. 'But I'm not Lexie's husband any more and I'd love to have some kids with you.'

'You want more children?'

'Sure – I'd like a dozen. I'd love to have a big old house somewhere in upstate Minnesota, full of kids and noise and fun and laughter. But perhaps I couldn't put a dozen kids through college, so let's say four or five. Rosie, maybe one day—'

'See that buoy?' I said before he could go any further. I scrambled to my feet. 'Why don't I race you to it, eh?'

He was surprised to learn I'd never been to Ireland.

'But it's so close,' he said as we drove back to London. 'Why don't you check it out?'

'Perhaps one day,' I said. 'But it rains there even more than it does here, you know – that's why it's called the Emerald Isle, because it's green, green, green. Pat, are you curious about your Irish ancestors?'

'Yes and no – yes because they were my ancestors, no because they must have led shit-awful lives and the whole Irish-British thing is pretty damn depressing. You British aren't too popular with most Irish-Americans, you know.'

'Why's that?'

'You were responsible for so much pain and suffering, that's why. A million Irish people came to the US back in the nineteenth century with nothing but the rags upon their backs, escaping the Great Famine.'

'What great famine?'

'Oh, come on – you must have heard of it?'

'I don't think so.'

'Well, the way they teach it in the USA, the choice was either leave or starve to death, as many thousands did. There were Irish Catholic people lying dead and dying in the streets and in the countryside. But the British let them die – encouraged them to die – kept on exporting Irish wheat which could have fed the people. You didn't study history in school?'

'Yes, but we didn't learn about the Irish. We did the Plantagenets, the Tudors and the Stuarts – Cromwell, Charles I, the Restoration.'

'Cromwell did bad stuff in Ireland, Rosie.'

I didn't want to sour what had been up to then a perfect day. So I didn't ask him what Cromwell did in Ireland. I turned the radio on and got the shipping forecast. I let all those hypnotic, soothing names –Fitzroy, Bailey, Rockall, Malin, Dover – reassure and comfort me.

He said he loved me. I believed him.

But I could see he felt impatient with me sometimes, even though he did his best to hide it. I annoyed him by just being there, distracting him.

I knew his work was very important. It would help to benefit the disadvantaged and disabled everywhere. But I was still jealous of his work, of the fact that he was so wrapped up in it, that I would never be his entire life. I'd always be a part of it, however much I willed it to be otherwise.

Although he never said or even hinted, I got the impression he thought I was lightweight – a very silly, superficial person whose life revolved round handbags, clothes and cupcakes.

I knew he was irritated by my attitude to fashion, couldn't believe how much I was prepared to spend on what was hot. He wasn't mean – far from it – but he wasn't bothered about labels. He always knew exactly what he wanted and shopping bored him rigid. Once he discovered Marks & Spencer menswear, he bought nothing else.

I love shopping – not as much as Tess loves shopping, but I do enjoy it – and of course I love a bargain, particularly a designer bargain. When I saw a rather gorgeous cardigan in a shop in Bond Street – after I had been to talk to Fanny about a new promotion that she said would make me rich – and this rather lovely garment was reduced as well, naturally I had to snap it up. But afterwards I realised I didn't get such a bargain, after all. The girl was chatting to her mate and gave me the wrong change.

'It doesn't really matter,' I told Pat, when I met him later for a coffee and he noticed I was wearing something new. 'I'd have bought it anyway, even if it hadn't been in the sale. I did wonder if the change was right. But the discount was something per cent. So I couldn't work out what I should pay while I was in the shop.'

'Why couldn't you?'

'I don't have that sort of mind, and anyway God gave us calculators. So I don't need to do percentages or long division or any of that tedious stuff I had to do at school. Pat, I'm not going have a nervous breakdown over twenty quid.'

'It isn't cool to be cheated by a store. It's just plain dumb.' He found his pen, reached for my paper napkin. 'Okay, here's the simple way to figure out percentages. Rosie, are you listening?'

Twenty minutes later, I understood percentages at last and realised it was possible to do them in my head. Or some of them, at least. I was amazed.

'Why didn't I get this before?' I asked.

'Whoever taught you math instructed you but forgot to show you how to learn. A teacher shouldn't stand there and pontificate. It's a teacher's job to show his students how to learn. Then they'll understand most anything within a range of capability and they'll go on learning all their lives.'

'I bet you couldn't teach a frog geometry.'

'As I said, we have to work within a range of capability. Rosie, twenty-five per cent of thirty-six?'

'Oh, that's easy – nine.'

'You find it easy now. You couldn't have done it half an hour ago. Fifty per cent of four?'

'It's two,' I said and kissed him. 'Pat, it's you and me.'

What was our range of capability? What did we need to learn? What could we hope to learn, to have a chance of happiness?

'We're good together, aren't we?' I asked later when we were at my flat. He'd seemed distant and preoccupied right through the evening, going through the motions of making conversation, but making me feel like I wasn't there.

'I don't know,' he said.

'What don't you know?'

'You're definitely very good for me. You make me very happy. But I'm no good for you. I think you need a younger guy.'

'You could be right. I'm only twenty-nine but you're already in your fourth decade. You're almost geriatric. But hey, you mustn't worry. I can steer a wheelchair.'

'Okay, put it another way – someone with no baggage, no history, no ties.'

'We all have history. Patrick, do you love me?'

'Yeah, I do – too much to hurt you, now or in the future.'

'I'll take my chance on getting hurt. So let's live for the moment and let's not think about your history.'

I wasn't going to tell him about mine.

Rosie said she had to take a couple days away to visit with her folks in Dorset: her grandmother was sick and she was worried.

My grandmothers were dead and buried by the time I came along and maybe it was just as well. Mom's parents more or less disowned her when she married Dad, and from what I understand his own were trash of the worst kind.

'Yeah, I'll watch Joseph Saturday and Sunday,' I told Lex when she collected Joe and Poll from the apartment London University had found for me. 'We can do some guy stuff. Do you and Mr Wonderful have plans?'

'Stephen's going to take me to the Lake District.'

'Where's that?'

'It's someplace in the north of England, supposed to be real pretty. Wordsworth used to live there.'

'Who was Wordsworth?'

'A famous British poet, he wrote a famous poem about daffodils, the famous British flower.' Lexie looked at me like I was dumb. 'Patrick, could you watch your daughter, too?'

'I don't think so, Lex. Joe and I are heading to the Natural History Museum to check out dinosaurs. We're taking in the Science Museum, too. Polly would be bored. Anyway, I reckon you and Mr Wonderful could use a chaperone.'

Lexie blushed at that. 'Patrick, I – we—'

'What?'

'You kids, go into Daddy's bedroom and close the door behind you,' Lexie told them. 'Joe, you take my iPhone. You know how to find the games. Polly, go play Barbies.' As the kids went off dragging their backpacks, Lexie turned to me. 'Pat, don't be so difficult. You and I – when we were kids in high school, we loved each other, didn't we?'

'Yeah, I thought we did. But people change. Move on, cross boundaries, so there's no going back.'

'What do you mean, cross boundaries?'

'I heard about your afternoon with Ben.'

She looked at me like I had slapped her face. 'How did you know?' she whispered. 'Ben promised not to say a word to you.'

'You forget you had a witness, Lexie, and Tess didn't promise anything.'

'So she told you?'

'She did.'

'But it was nothing! Two old friends, we had a drink together, smoked some stuff and things got out of hand. We didn't mean—'

'I don't care what you and Fairfax did or didn't mean. Or what you and your lovers do, provided you're not jerking me around.'

'You want to file for divorce?'

'No, I'm far too busy and all that stuff takes time. I have a major conference in the summer and I have a ton of work to do.'

'You always put your work before your family.'

'I don't.'

'You do! You always did.'

'As I said, I'm busy. I'm sure your schedule must be crowded too, so I'll let you get on. I'll collect Joe Friday about six o'clock, okay?'

'If you don't watch Polly we can't go to the Lake District,' said Lexie. 'Or not to the place we planned on going.'

'Why?'

'Stephen wants to take me to a smart hotel in Windermere where children aren't allowed.'

'I see.'

'We meant it to be kind of special. We had this little fight around about a week ago. He was tired and I was tired, we both got scratchy and this is his way of making up.' Lexie looked at me with pleading eyes. 'But if you won't watch Polly, seems like we'll miss out now?'

'Lex, don't look at me like that.' I sighed. 'Oh, what the hell – you go have your fun weekend with Mr Wonderful. I guess Poll can do some guy stuff, too.'

⮑ ROSIE ⮐

Granny Cassie was so pleased to see me.

She had been quite ill. She'd had a bad reaction to a new arthritis drug and ended up in hospital. But she was getting better now, was home again and she was very bored. 'So come on, Rosie – tell me everything?' she wheedled.

'All my secrets, Granny?'

'Yes, of course!'

'Why don't you have another violet cream?'

We were eating chocolates. I'd bought them from a shop in Piccadilly. We both knew they were evil, far too high in fat and sugar, so she shouldn't have too many. But they were so delicious that we scoffed them anyway. Mum could read the riot act to us later, after the event – poor Mum.

'How's your new job?' she asked.

'It's going really well. I'm getting lots of new accounts and Fanny's very helpful, always putting work my way.'

'But it's not your job that's made your pretty face light up.'

'What do you mean?'

'You can't fool me, my girl. I've been there, got the silky knickers and the lace suspender belt.'

'Granny, you're so naughty!'

'You're in love.'

'Mum told you she met Patrick?'

'Your mother tells me nothing. She thinks I'll have a heart

attack and die if I hear anything exciting. What do I not know?'

'When Mum came to London, this man was at my flat.'

'You mean in your bedroom?'

'Yes.'

'Oh, I see,' said Granny. 'I dare say that was interesting for everyone concerned?'

'It was beyond embarrassing. Do please stop giggling, Granny. You sound about fourteen.'

'Why should I not giggle if the two of you are happy? As I assume you must be?'

'Pat is an American who lives in Minnesota and he's married with two children.'

'Oh, I see.'

'I don't know what to do.'

'What does he want to do?'

'He hasn't told me, so perhaps he doesn't know. Or perhaps I'm just a blip and maybe he will go back to his wife. Do you think I'm wicked?'

'No, of course I don't, my darling. You're incapable of wickedness. But please don't let him hurt you. I don't want you to be hurt again. You've been hurt more than enough already.'

'Pat isn't going to hurt me.'

'Good,' said Granny. 'What about a game of Scrabble? I could fancy that. You'll have to sort the letters out for me.'

'She's very up and down,' my mother told me when I said Granny didn't seem too bad – in fact, she seemed quite chirpy. 'She's on such a mix of painkillers it's hard to get the dose exactly right.'

I don't know if in this life anybody can get anything exactly right?

But Granny had seemed bright and cheerful when she'd

talked to me. Or maybe she was being determinedly jolly because I had come home? She always knew exactly what to say to me, and sometimes that was – nothing.

But my mother wasn't as intuitive as Granny, wasn't into intuition, never had been, never would be. Mum was into confrontation, self-expression, talking it all through.

On Sunday afternoon, while Granny was asleep and Dad had gone to see a golfing friend about some boring tournament, Mum followed me into the sitting room. I saw she had that look upon her face. The look which was accessorised by *we must have a serious talk* in flashing neon letters on her forehead.

'How are you, Rosie?' she began as I was gathering up the Sunday papers, hoping Mum's interrogation wouldn't last too long and I could have a quiet read.

'I'm fine,' I said and forced a smile. 'I have a bit of indigestion. I ate too many Yorkshires. I can't resist your Yorkshires.'

'You're coping, are you, darling?'

'Yes – are you?'

'I'm asking about you. Do you want to talk about it?'

'No.'

'Do you get nightmares?'

'All the time.'

'You could still have some counselling, you know.'

'Mum, could we change the subject?'

Big mistake.

'That man I met in London,' said my mother. 'Who exactly is he?'

'Patrick Riley. I introduced him to you, didn't I?'

'I mean, what is this man to you?'

'He's just a friend.'

'But he's married, isn't he? I saw his wedding ring. He's an American, as well.'

'Well done, Mum. Ten out of ten for noticing his accent. But don't worry, I'm not having sex with aliens. It's rumoured that Americans are human beings, too.'

'Rosie, please don't be facetious. You know what I'm trying to say. I'm aware that nowadays things must be quite difficult for you, trying to get your PR business off the ground, and—'

'Fanny's being very helpful: brilliant, in fact. She sends you all her love. She said to tell you when you're next in town—'

'Darling, I'm a magistrate.' Mum put on her kind and caring face. 'So I'm very well aware that when a person has a bad experience, it can be hard to cope with normal life. People get confused. Go off the rails a little. It doesn't mean they're bad—'

'Mum, I'm not a teenage hoodie who's been doing drugs because his father beat him when he was a little boy. So please spare me all that Social Services and Probation Officer rubbish?'

'Rosie, listen—'

'If I go to bed with married men, it's because I fancy married men. Or a particular married man. It's not because of Charlie or what happened and it definitely isn't about you.'

As I said it, I regretted it. I knew it was cruel, spiteful, hurtful, all those things. So why didn't I apologise? Why didn't I go and sit beside my mother, hold her hand, tell her that I knew how much she must be hurting and I hadn't meant to make it worse?

I didn't know.

I drove back to London Sunday evening really looking forward to seeing Pat again, to finding something like a truth – a certainty – with him. But whatever Pat was offering, I knew deep in my heart it wasn't certainty.

* * *

He spent a lot of evenings at my flat.

Most of the time, it was all fine. We talked, we joked, we laughed, lay on the sofa entwined with one another, drinking wine and watching tripe on television, mocking idiots on game shows, planning where we could take Joe and Polly when he had them next.

But he had a streak of melancholy in him half a mile wide. He was sometimes silent and so totally preoccupied that I learned to leave him to it, not to ask if anything was wrong or if he fancied going for a drink, to see a film.

He was certainly a workaholic, on his laptop all the time, writing emails, grading coursework, skyping colleagues, students and other academics all around the world, doing his job in Minnesota at long distance, somehow fitting in his London lectures and research, seeing Joe and Polly and also seeing me.

It was just as well I was so busy with my own new company, that my flat was full of samples, folders, files, promotional material (both edible and hopefully-intended-to-be-edible-but-actually-inedible. What were some people thinking? Anyone for birch bark biscuits, pansy cookies, hedgerow harvest pies?), carrier bags and boxes which needed my attention.

I can't pretend he didn't take a lot of interest in me and my not-exactly-Nobel-laureate-level work.

'What's all this?' he asked one evening, walking in to find me sitting on the floor and trying to play a board game which was meant for ten-year-olds, surrounded by a mess of cards and spinning tops and counters and failing to get anywhere.

'It's the next big thing,' I told him. 'Hamleys will go mad for it. Come on, Pat, why don't you play with me?'

'Okay, if you insist. But let's play in your bedroom, not in here with all this garbage on the floor. Those spinning tops look more than capable of doing serious damage to a guy.'

'Pat, this is important! This game could be the next Monopoly or Trivial Pursuit. It could make some people millionaires. One of them might be me.'

'No kidding, Rosie? Maybe I should take a closer look?' He hunkered down, examined all the bits and pieces, read the rules and then he shook his head. He pointed out some fatal flaws of logic. Unless this and this and this were fixed, unless one player cheated, the game would be impossible to win. It always would be stalemate.

'You give that to a bunch of kids without doing a lot more work on it, there will be blood,' he told me. Then he grabbed a notebook. He started drawing diagrams and doing calculations, explaining very clearly what was wrong and how to put it right.

Blood and stalemate.

Pat could fix the board game, but could he fix my life? Or had he stalemated it for good? What if one of the players cheated – what would happen then?

June

I guess in Britain summer doesn't happen?

But it didn't matter. Rosie was the sunshine in my life. She made me smile. She made me laugh out loud. She raised my spirits, and just thinking of her always put me on a high. I told her that I loved her half a dozen times a day.

'But what is it you love about an idiot like me, Professor?' she enquired one evening as I fixed her laptop yet again, explained again why she should choose some stronger passwords so that her accounts would be less likely to get hacked.

'You crack me up,' I said, as she keyed in *patwasbornawankerin1978* and *shrekthe3rdsgreenarse.*

'You mean you find me frightfully amusing?'

'I suppose I must.'

'You mean you guess you do?' She grinned at me. 'Your Britglish, mate – it's coming on a treat.'

'Your Amglish has a way to go.'

'I'm not trying to learn Amglish. I speak seven languages already.'

'Do you – fluently?'

'If we're going to insist on fluency, I suppose it's three. But that's two more than you – and no, computer languages don't count.'

'You're fluent in three languages, you have a quarter blue in tiddlywinks, whatever that might mean – Tess mentioned it one time – you dazzle me.'

'You're such a sarcastic git.'

'I know. Lex and Mr Wonderful are flying up to Scotland on the weekend. Okay if I bring Joe and Poll to visit?'

'Yes, of course. Do bring the children round. I'd love to see them. What shall we do with them?'

'What's Alton Towers?'

'It's a theme park full of noisy rides and shrieking kids.'

'You went there?'

'Yes, when I was ten. Pat, shall I sort something out?' She looked at me enquiringly, head tilted to one side. 'You don't really hate surprises, do you?'

'I guess I don't – but no more rocks?'

'No more rocks,' she promised.

A few days later, she called me on my cell. 'It's all arranged for Friday,' she announced. 'You'll need your passports and a change of clothes, or maybe three for Polly. We'll be away two nights.'

'Why do we need our passports?'

'Why do you think you need your passports, dummy?'

'Where exactly are we going, Rosie?'

'You'll have to wait and see.'

⌒ ROSIE ⌒

I had to face it some time, and going with Pat and Joe and Polly meant I'd have distractions.

'Come on, Rosie, spill?' said Pat on Friday morning when he rang me at the office.

'You'll soon know,' I told him.

'Do the kids need factor forty?'

'Yes, might be a plan.'

'You're such a tease, Miss Rosie.'

'Just a few more hours to wait, Professor, and all will be revealed.'

Although I'd booked it, paid for it, got overdrawn for it, I was still going to give myself the chance to chicken out.

I met them at St Pancras.

Pat was looking puzzled, Polly solemn. But Joe was jigging up and down and grinning, ready for adventures. He had spiked his hair with gel and wore a stylish, brand new denim jacket.

'It's from Gap,' he told me.

'Cool,' I said. 'I like the corduroy collar.'

'It's Sherpa-lined as well. You do rate it, don't you?'

'Joe, I love it!' I'd never known a child so keen on fashion. He was going to be the next Marc Jacobs, Ralph Lauren or Jasper Conran, I would bet my new Armani shades. 'How did you hurt your finger?'

'I cut it on some paper.'

'Ouch, those paper cuts are horrible.'

'Yeah, there was a ton of blood. But Mom got me Batman Band-Aids – look?'

'You said we needed passports. So why are we here in central London?' asked his father, dispensing with the niceties of greeting and cutting to the chase. 'Why aren't we at the airport?'

'Good evening, Pat. It's great to see you. Hello, Polly. What a pretty anorak. I love the pink embroidery.'

'Rosie!' Pat looked ready to combust spontaneously.

'We don't need to fly.' I handed him my iPod. 'Listen for a moment, will you?'

So he did, still frowning. But then, as comprehension dawned, he smiled. 'It's *An American in Paris*. We're not going to Paris, Rosie?'

'Yes!'

'Paris, France?'

'No, Paris, Texas, Pat. Of course we're going to Paris,

France, you clot.' I turned to Joe. 'We're going to catch a very special train. It goes under the water.'

'Awesome!' Joe exclaimed, his brown eyes sparkling. 'Do we get to see some sharks and whales?'

⟩ PATRICK ⟨

She played me *An American in Paris*, my favourite piece of Gershwin.

So she had been listening that time in Minneapolis when we were at the concert hall and I had talked about my favourite music and she hadn't seemed to hear.

Until I came to Britain, I never rode the train. British people do it all the time. But in America, we have about destroyed our railroad network. There've been a few attempts in recent years to change this situation but, apart from in New England, mostly tourists tend to ride the few remaining routes. The rest of us drive everywhere or fly.

As soon as we were boarded, Joe spent several minutes unfolding then refolding the tables which were fixed between the seats and worrying because there were no seat belts and no fire extinguishers, or none that he could see.

'What if there's a train wreck?' he demanded anxiously.

'There won't be a train wreck.'

'Dad, there could so be a wreck! One time I saw a wreck on CBS. It was someplace in Africa. A ton of cars caught fire. Mommy said the people were all fried. I don't want to be fried.'

'There won't be a train wreck,' I repeated. 'Now will you quiet down, relax a while? Chill out, like Polly?'

Polly started yawning soon as we began to move. So her brother let her put her feet up on his lap to lie full-length, and pretty soon she was asleep. That baby would sleep anyplace, I swear. But Joe was permanently wired.

As Joe sat there dismantling and then reassembling Lego heroes in all kinds of different permutations, as Polly slept and Pat read through some academic papers, I looked at his passport.

The photograph was very good. It showed him looking calm and grave and intellectual. My own passport photograph is of an electrocuted hare that's seen a buzzard and knows its time has come.

'You didn't bring a book?' asked Pat, glancing up from something that looked like one long algebraic formula. Do I mean an algebraic formula? Something I could never understand, at any rate, even though I'd sorted out percentages at last.

'I have some novels on my phone, but I don't feel like reading them right now.'

'You look anxious, Rosie. Something wrong?'

'I'm okay,' I said. 'But my ears are popping and it's rather disconcerting.'

'Mine are popping, too.'

'We must be underwater, then?'

'I guess.'

'Joe looks rather flushed. Do you think he needs to take his jacket off? It's quite warm in here.'

'Yeah, might be a plan. But he always goes red in the face when he's excited, and today he's way beyond excited. Hey, little buddy, doing good?'

'I guess,' said Joe. Yawning, he flopped back against the seat. 'Dad, are we underneath the ocean yet?'

'Yeah, the Channel's right on top of us.'

'Where are the sharks?'

'We're in a tunnel.' Pat shut down his laptop, draped one arm around my shoulders. 'Let's all get some sleep now, shall we?' he suggested.

'I can't sleep,' said Joe. 'I'm too excited.'

'You just rest your eyes, then,' said his father.

Joe did as he was told and very soon he seemed to doze. Polly sprawled across his lap, her thumb wedged in her mouth.

As the three of them relaxed then slept, I found that I was almost panicking. Why was I on this train? What was I trying to prove and what would it have mattered if I never went to France again? But then I made a promise to myself. I was going to face my demons. I was going to beat them.

❧ PATRICK ❧

I got some euros from an ATM and then we left the Gare du Nord and took a cab to our hotel, which was halfway down the Boulevard de Magenta. We could have walked the distance easily but the kids were tired, so we piled into a cab.

'Magenta – that's my favourite word!' cried Joe, checking out the street sign as we climbed out the cab. 'Magenta means a kind of purple, Dad. Rosie, did you know magenta means a kind of purple?'

'I do now,' Rosie told him. 'Thank you, Joe.'

'You're welcome.' Joe beamed up at us. 'You guys ever want to know the meaning of a word, I'll try to help you out.'

'Rosie, could you keep the kids here on the sidewalk while I pay the guy?' I asked.

'But you don't speak French. Why don't I sort it?'

'I guess I'll be okay.'

She didn't argue like Lexie would have done. She stood there on the sidewalk with a sleeping Polly in her arms and talked to a now-yawning Joe about their favourite colours while I paid the driver, tipped him, thanked him, said goodnight.

'You're a dark horse, Riley,' she observed as I grabbed our bags. 'I understood you didn't know any French?'

'I know a little, enough to talk to waiters, drivers, clerks.'

'What else do you know?'

'You'd be surprised.'

'*Madame, monsieur, soyez les bienvenus.*'

The grey-haired woman at the desk talked fifty to the dozen and I couldn't follow a single thing she said, because – unlike the taxi driver, who made big concessions to the fact that I was foreign and who was a foreigner himself – she went way too fast.

'So tell me?' I demanded, when after several minutes of chatting and gesticulating and becoming new best friends, Rosie turned to me and handed me a key card. 'No, don't tell me, let me guess. Why's a pretty girl like you in Paris with a baboon like me?'

'It was a gorilla, actually. But Madame also said the kids are gorgeous, and would we like our breakfast in our room tomorrow morning? Or would we prefer to come downstairs because there is a dining room, and is there anything we need tonight?'

'Does this place have an elevator?' I glanced toward the staircase winding high above our heads, three, four, five storeys high. 'Or do I carry these two kids up all those spiral stairs?'

'You'll find the elevator on your right, monsieur,' the woman said in perfect English as she smiled charmingly at me. 'I wish you all a pleasant stay in Paris.'

We had a large white room four storeys up which must have been an icebox in the winter but was perfect at this time of year, high above the noise and fumes of traffic in the boulevard below. There were two big beds with clean white comforters, a very basic bathroom, two long windows with fine wrought iron balconies and a view of spires and turrets and apartment blocks. Doves were nesting on the window ledges and cooing peacefully.

'I hope this is all right?' asked Rosie, looking kind of anxious now. 'It's a room they usually keep for families with children. I thought it would suit us?'

'It's fine,' I said. 'We couldn't ask for better. You know something, Rosie?'

'What?'

'We're going to have a ball.'

⌒ ROSIE ⌒

So did he understand what I had said that afternoon while we on the Sugar Loaf, when I had told him I would like to *baiser* him? *Well*, I thought, *there'll be no opportunities for baisering this weekend – his kids will see to that.*

We started off the night with Pat and both his children in one of the beds, with Joe and Polly piled on top of him like puppies in a basket. I had the other bed all to myself. I should have been happy, I suppose. *At least*, I thought, *I can stretch out in comfort.* Glancing at the squirming, snorting heap across the room, however, in the silver moonlight filtering through the muslin curtains, I had never felt so lonely.

I checked my phone. There were no texts, no emails. So I felt lonelier still. I watched a video on my phone and then replayed it in my head. I tried to doze, still thinking this had been a big mistake and wondering how I'd cope when morning came, how I would walk these streets again?

I thought I'd never sleep. But it would seem I did. As it was starting to get light, I realised there was someone little snuggled up in bed with me and mewing like a kitten in distress. 'What's the matter, sweetheart?'

'Mommy,' whimpered Polly.

'You'll see Mommy soon. I tell you what – we'll call her in the morning, shall we?'

Polly sniffed and blinked.

'But it's not morning yet. So shall we cuddle up again? Shall we shut our eyes?' I shut mine tight and hoped that she would do the same.

She must have done. When I woke up a few hours later, there were small, fat starfish fingers tangled in my hair and she was sucking on a strand of it contentedly.

'Hey, Polly, how are you today?' I whispered. *Pat, wake up*, I thought. *Your daughter is about to realise I'm not her mother and then she'll have a fit.*

But Polly didn't have a fit. She lay beside me, brown eyes open wide, still playing with my hair. 'Poll, what shall we do today?' I asked.

'Go see a puppy?' she suggested.

'Yes, why don't we? There are lots and lots of dogs in Paris so I'm sure we'll find some puppies. There are lots of play parks too, where you can have some fun. Do you like ice cream, Polly?'

'Chocolate sprinkles?'

'Yes, of course.'

'Who said chocolate sprinkles?' asked a drowsy voice.

'We're getting ice cream,' Polly told her brother.

'You are so not getting ice cream for your breakfast!' Joe was suddenly wide awake. 'Dad, get up!' he cried and hit his father with a hard French pillow. 'Polly says she's getting ice cream!'

'Joseph, will you quiet down now?' growled Pat. 'What does a person have to do to get some sleep round here?'

'You say that every morning and it's getting old.' Joe bashed Pat again. 'Dad, tell Poll she can't get ice cream for her breakfast.'

'Polly, go into the bathroom,' Pat said crossly, getting out of bed. 'Rosie, Polly hasn't wet on you, I hope?'

'No, she's fine.'

'I should have brought some diapers.'

'No,' Polly said. 'No diapers.'

'No diapers, Dad,' repeated Joe. 'Mom says Polly is a big girl now.'

After breakfast – rolls and *pains au chocolat*, croissants and delicious coffee for the grown-ups, fruit juice for the children – we went out to see what we could find.

I'd planned a route. We'd head towards the Centre Pompidou where the kids could have a run around and chase the pigeons and look at all the tubes outside that quite amazing building and maybe even go inside, depending on the queues.

Then we'd go to the Louvre where they could see the Pyramid and run around again. We'd sit in a café and eat crêpes. Then we'd get on a Batobus and idle down the river to see the Eiffel Tower.

We'd gradually work our way back home to our hotel along the river walks. Then we would dawdle through the Île de la Cité, along the Rue de Rivoli and through the busy streets of the Marais. Yes, we would walk back through the Marais, and it was going to be fine.

Pat soon decided he liked Paris.

Paris liked him back. It seemed to draw him out, relax him, make him smile more than he ever had in London or in Minneapolis. But Paris is so beautiful I'd challenge anyone to see it on a lovely summer day and not be happy here.

I was determined to be happy.

As Pat relaxed, the kids did, too. I'd wondered if they'd want their mother, if they might get upset, if this whole expedition might be a big disaster. But they seemed more curious than their father, too intrigued by everything they saw to miss their mother.

Polly often wanted to be carried. So she sat on her father's shoulders while Pat and I held hands with Joe and jumped him over bollards, on and off low walls, jump, jump, jump, jump. Children have such lovely hands. Joe's were beautiful, still jelly-boned and small and soft and dimpled. I could not imagine them becoming a grown man's strong, hard hands. When he grew tired of being jumped, he skipped and pirouetted on ahead.

'Stay on the sidewalk!' Pat called after him. 'Don't cross any roads, you hear me?'

'Yeah, I hear you. There's a store that's named for you, Dad.'

'Where?'

'Over there – Pât-isserie!' Joe started laughing, doubling up and practically choking, making Polly laugh as well. I wished I could be six years old again, when life had been so simple, so easy, so uncomplicated, not the mess my whole life was today.

We did all the stuff I'd planned. We went on the Batobus. We took the lift up to the viewing platform of the Eiffel Tower. We stopped for crêpes, for juice, for coffee. It was warm and sunny and we had a lovely day.

At six o'clock, we started heading back to our hotel. Soon we were in the heart of the Marais. We were walking down a narrow street full of shops which sold the most delicious shoes and handbags, but I wasn't interested in shoes and bags today. We were passing jewellery shops and busy cafés and I told myself it was all right, it was okay. This was the way to deal with it, face everything head on and sort it out once and for all. Paris and the Marais couldn't be off limits all my life and anyway, in fifteen minutes we'd be home. It was a mere ten minutes to the Place de la République, soon it would be five, then four, then three, then—

'Dad, I'm thirsty.' Joe tugged at his father's belt. 'Dad, I want a drink.'

'You just had a drink,' said Pat.

'I need to get some juice.' Joe rubbed his eyes. 'Dad, I'm tired. My feet ache and I'm hot. My backpack's way too heavy. Dad—'

'Yeah, okay.' Pat put his daughter down. 'You made your point. Let's go find somewhere in the shade then you can both get juice. Rosie, would you like to get a latte?'

No, I thought, *we need to keep on walking.*

But then I glanced at Joe, who looked done up. We'd walked the poor child off his feet today. 'Yes,' I said and told myself it would be fine, that it would not take long to have a drink. 'A latte would be great.'

It's not hard to find a café in the Marais. There must be a hundred. So Pat wouldn't choose the only one …

Joe was grumbling in earnest now, telling us he had to get a drink or he would die. He sat down on the pavement. 'Okay, Joe,' said Pat. 'You win. Rosie, let's go over there.' He pointed to the only café in the whole of Paris I couldn't – wouldn't – patronise.

'N-no,' I said, 'not that one, it's—'

'It's what?'

'It's not suitable for children, Pat. Look, those men are smoking.'

'The windows are all open and the smoke's blowing away. The place looks good to me, it's in the shade. Rosie, you okay?'

'Yes, of course. I'm fine. I just don't think that café's right for Joe and Polly.' I was trembling, wondering if I'd faint. Why had I done this stupid, stupid thing? I had to get out of the Marais now. 'Pat, I t-tell you what,' I gabbled as my teeth rattled like castanets, 'I'll get Joe some juice from that épicerie. There's a chiller cabinet inside.'

'Okay,' he said. 'But Rosie, are you sure you're fine? You're very pale. You look like something spooked you.'

'I'm all right. Joe, there's a grocery store across the road. I'll get you a juice this minute. Polly, do you want one too?'

➤ PATRICK ✦

I didn't get why Rosie was so spooked.

I asked again. She wouldn't tell me. She got juice for Joe and Polly. Then she took Joe's backpack, grabbed his hand and hurried on. When we came to our hotel she seemed okay again. So I quit asking what was wrong.

As soon as we were home, we put the kids to bed. They were too stuffed with crêpes, brioches and ice cream to want any more to eat today, and all they needed was to go to sleep.

A few hours later, I went to get a takeout. I pointed to the stuff I wanted, pushed a bunch of euros at the guy and hoped I'd got it right.

We ate with all the windows open, watching traffic streaming past us far below. Those French guys, they're a bunch of maniacs. They drive like they're all racing to the hospital delivering a body part for a lifesaving surgery. I never saw a traffic cop in all my time in Paris.

The most romantic thing I ever did?

I watched the traffic on the Boulevard de Magenta. Yeah, I know – pathetic. But in this soft, warm twilight, even watching traffic seemed impossibly and wonderfully romantic, even with two kids lying there grunting in their sleep while we adults ate takeout pizza, garlic bread and coleslaw from a greasy cardboard tray.

It must have been because I was in Paris. It must have been because I was with Rosie, because she looked so beautiful tonight. As the light began to fade, her skin took on a kind of golden glow, her wild, black hair looked like it had a life all of its own and curled around her face because it had a mind to do so, and her big grey eyes shone like a pair of precious stones.

It must have been because I was in love.

'Thank you for a great day out,' I said.

'You enjoyed yourself?'

'You bet I did. The kids did, too.'

'They're lovely children, Pat. You're very lucky.'

'Yeah, I know.'

'I envy you and Lexie.'

'You don't need to envy Lex and me,' I told her softly. 'One day, you'll have children of your own, I promise you.'

'More coleslaw, Pat?'

Sunday was a busy, busy day.

We climbed Montmartre and rode the little boxcar up to the Sacré-Coeur, a church which had a look of our cathedral back home in Saint Paul.

We got lunch in a café where the kids ate stuff I knew for certain they wouldn't eat in Minneapolis. Artichokes and spinach and salami and smoked salmon and a special grilled cheese sandwich which the French call croque-monsieur all went down the same way.

'Poll, is spinach yuck or yum?' demanded Joe as his little sister chewed on a wad of it.

Polly thought about it for a moment. 'Yum,' she said and grinned as bright green drool ran down her chin.

Joe forked up more greenery. 'Spinach is what Popeye eats,' he said. 'It makes you very strong. I guess if I eat spinach every day, when I'm grown I'll be a superhero. Anybody messes with me, I'll be good and ready to punch him on the jaw. I'll grab him by the beard and swing him round and throw him off a cliff.'

'You don't punch people on the jaw,' I told him.

'When you're a man, you might decide to grow a big black beard of your own,' suggested Rosie. 'Then you'll look like a pirate.'

'I shall never grow a beard,' said Joe disgustedly. 'Superman and Batman don't have beards.'

'You'll have stubble, anyway.' Rosie smiled and stroked him momentarily on his soft baby cheeks.

He glanced up from his spinach and gazed at her with adoration in his big brown eyes. Those eyes were bright. Those cheeks were red. A pulse was beating in his neck, bedang, bedang, bedang.

Poor little Joe, I thought, he was in love.

I knew exactly how he felt.

We watched street magicians taking bets and cash from tourist suckers. Then we rode the open tourist bus and saw some more of Paris, the tree-lined boulevards, the Champs Élysées, and I could see why Rosie loved it here. By afternoon on Sunday, I loved it here myself.

'We've worn these children out,' said Rosie.

'Yeah, but it was good.' I swung Polly up on to my shoulders, took Joe's hand. 'One more game of tag?' I asked him when we reached the fountain by the Centre Pompidou.

'Yeah, I guess,' he said.

'Joe, are you all right?' asked Rosie.

'I'm just thirsty.'

Rosie offered him her water bottle. I watched him while he drank most of it down. 'How do you feel now?' I asked.

'Okay, Dad,' he said and then he shot off like a rocket. So Rosie had to chase and grab him by the collar of his T-shirt, otherwise he would have got himself mashed on the road.

We boarded Eurostar to bring us back to London. Joe was tired and fussing. But Polly was still full of life. It must have been the spinach. She annoyed her brother by tickling him and poking him and in the end he slapped her arm and she began to cry.

'You do not slap little girls – you hear me, Joe? You do not slap anybody, right?'

'But she drives me crazy, Dad!'

'Come on, Joe, snuggle up with me,' said Rosie.

So he did. He slept all through the journey and when we arrived in London it was hard to wake him up. I guess he should have had more spinach?

⮞ ROSIE ⮜

We got back to my flat at half past eight that evening.

'Why don't you all come in and have some supper?' I asked Pat. 'Then you can get a cab and take these children home to Lexie?'

'Yeah, okay, sounds like a plan,' he said.

Then he got his laptop out and started scrolling through his emails and the three of us became invisible. Polly toddled round the sitting room, her thumb wedged in the corner of her mouth, touching, patting everything and talking to herself. Joe flopped on the sofa and went straight to sleep again.

I felt his forehead. It was warm, not hot. But his skin was clammy, he was restless, and I had a feeling that something wasn't right.

'Joe isn't well,' I told his father.

'Do you mean he's sick?' Pat glanced up from his laptop, fingers poised above the keyboard, mind a million miles away. 'Or is he just tired?'

'He might be running a slight fever.' I stroked Joe's sticky hair back from his temples. 'He has a rash as well.'

'Rosie, kids are always getting rashes. Polly had one a few months back, turned out it was just a wool reaction. Tylenol – or whatever you call it over here in the UK – that will soon fix Joe. I'll get a bottle from the all-night drugstore on my way to Lexie's place.'

'But Pat, I think—'

'Rosie, could you let me read a couple emails? Then I'll help fix supper. Meantime, please quit fretting about Joe?'

But my feeling this was something bad just wouldn't go away. 'I think you need to take him to A and E,' I said.

'What's A and E?'

'You know – to the ER.'

'I can't take him to the hospital. I don't have the forms.'

'What do you mean, the forms?'

'The little guy's insurance. Lexie has a bag with all that kind of stuff in it and when I have the kids she always makes me haul it round. But when I called there Friday I forgot to pick it up.'

'Pat, you don't need forms! When you're ill in London or anywhere in the UK, you get yourself to hospital. They sort you out. They don't ask you for forms. They don't let children die for want of forms!'

'Joe's not dying, Rosie.' Pat smiled at me all calm and reassuring, as if he were telling an anxious student that his grades were fine and not to worry. 'The kid is tired, is all. He'll be okay after a good night's sleep. But maybe we won't stay for supper. I'll take Polly to your bathroom then I'll get these children home to my apartment, put them both to bed. They can go back to Lexie in the morning.'

Joe was moaning softly in his sleep. I had no experience of children's ailments, didn't know what could be wrong with him, but alarm bells rang inside my head. 'If you won't take him, I will,' I told Pat.

'Rosie, you will not take Joseph anyplace!'

Obviously exasperated with the lot of us, Pat shut down his laptop. Then he collared Polly. They went into my bathroom and he closed the door behind them – and now alarm bells rang inside my head so loud they deafened me.

I didn't care what Pat might think, what he might say,

what he might do. I only knew that someone had to get his son to hospital. So I scooped Joe up into my arms, relieved he was so little and so light – I doubted he weighed any more than Polly – ran into the street, flagged down a taxi, told the cabbie to take us to the nearest A & E.

'What's the problem, Mum?' the driver asked, glancing at me in the rear-view mirror.

'I don't know, but something's very wrong. Please could you hurry?'

He put his foot down hard.

We pulled up outside the A & E at the Royal, Paddington. I realised I had come without my handbag. 'I'm so sorry.' I began to cry. 'I haven't any money on me. I—'

'It's okay,' the driver said. 'You have this one on me.' He got out of the cab and held open the door for me, something I had never seen a London cabbie do before and was sure I'd never see again. 'Good luck, Mum,' he added. 'I hope your little boy will be all right.'

I stood outside the hospital with Joe half-fainting in my arms and knew I couldn't do it. But I had to do it. I had to fight down my own selfish fears. I had to move.

I had to go into a hospital.

So, hyperventilating, feeling sick, I made a dash at it. I ran into the A & E with Joe, sprinting up the steps and charging through the automatic doors which magically opened wide for me and sucked me into hell.

I thought I'd have to wait around for ages. Then, when we were clerked, make up some story that Joe was my son and beg them on my bended knees to treat him, make him better ...

But, as it turned out, I didn't have to say a thing. As I stood there dithering with a practically unconscious child in my arms, half a dozen medical professionals swooped down on us like angels. Joe was on a trolley and they were dashing down a corridor and I was dashing with them. A nurse running beside me touched my arm. 'It's okay,' she told me. 'It's all under control.'

'He's going to be all right,' added another nurse.

I wished I could believe them.

'What's his name?' the first nurse asked me as we reached a cubicle and as they got him on a bed and somebody began to wire him up to various machines.

'Joe, it's Joseph Riley,' I replied, wondering if this was all a dream, or rather nightmare, the nightmare I had had a hundred times before.

'Joe, we're going to make you better,' said the nurse. 'Joseph, can you hear me? Joe, we're going to make you well again. Mum, you hold his hand, okay, and talk to him? He needs to know you're here.'

So I held Joe's hand while doctors in blue scrubs and nurses in blue uniforms and plastic aprons murmured, whispered, took phials of Joe's blood and filled in charts.

'But what's wrong with him?' I wailed, as Joe's eyelids fluttered open, closed and then reopened, as his eyes themselves rolled in their sockets so just the whites were showing, as they cut his clothes off – his Angry Birds black hoodie, his favourite H&M blue jeans, his bleeding jaws shark T-shirt – so they could attach more wires, more lines. 'Please, can't you tell me what's the matter?'

'We don't know yet,' a nurse replied. 'But we need to stabilise him, get some fluid in him, help him breathe.' When the nurse said that, I choked. I practically forgot to breathe myself.

I thought they might send me out while doctors plugged him into yet more bleeping stuff. But they let me stay and hold his hand. 'So I'm not wasting your time?' I faltered.

'No, Mrs Riley, you are not.' The nurse looked at me

kindly, reassuringly. 'You acted on your instincts. You realised your little boy was ill and not just tired or fretting. We mums, we know these things.'

A little time, a lot of time went by. Why do I contradict myself? I honestly didn't know if it was minutes, hours or days. Then they told me they were taking Joe up to the ICU. They needed to do various things to him which I might find distressing. So a nurse would find me somewhere I could wait until I was allowed to see him. I was taken to a room where relatives and friends could sit and fret and drive themselves insane.

I must ring Pat, I thought. *He'll be so worried.* But although I had some change in my jeans pocket, so I could have made a call, there was no payphone in the little room. I didn't have my handbag so I didn't have my mobile. I didn't dare to move in case they came to find me and I could not be found.

Then a doctor and a nurse came in and I could see from both their faces it must be bad news. The nurse sat down beside me, took my hand.

'We've run some tests,' the doctor told me. 'I'm sorry, but your little boy has septicaemia. He must have picked up an infection somewhere and it's quite a nasty one. Mrs—'

'Miss – Miss Denham.'

'Joe is very ill. But you got him to us in good time. If you'd waited any longer, we'd have been in lots more trouble. Now, we're doing all we can, and hopefully we'll—'

'Joe is not my child. I just brought him here. He's—'

What was Pat?

'—he's my partner's son.'

'I see.' The doctor nodded, as if this was the most natural thing in all the world, a girlfriend bringing in a boyfriend's critically sick or injured child. 'We'll need to find Joe's parents.'

'I don't have my mobile.'

'There you go.' The doctor handed me his phone.

By the grace of God or some kind angel, I had memorised Pat's number months ago while I was in America and obsessed with all things Pat, so now I punched the keys.

'Rosie?' he demanded or rather yelled at me when he picked up on the second ring.

'Yes, it's me. Pat, don't get angry, listen carefully—'

'What? I'll give you *listen carefully*! When I get my hands on you – where are you?'

'At the Royal, Paddington,' I said, as calmly as I could. 'You'd better get yourself here quickly. Joe is very ill.'

'What's wrong with him?'

'There isn't any time to talk, just get here!'

'What shall I do with Polly?'

'You'll need to bring her with you, obviously.'

'Why, what's going on? Rosie, just quit being so mysterious and say what's wrong with Joe!'

'Patrick, get here, will you?'

✦ PATRICK ✦

What if that girl had been as dumb as me?

When I carried Polly through the automatic doors, I found Rosie waiting with a nurse. She looked so worried – frightened – terrified – and I somehow knew it wasn't down to being shouted at by me, or on account of I was mad. I wasn't mad now, anyway. I was just plain scared.

They took us to a private room and told me what was happening. By the time they finished, I was ready to fall down and worship Rosie, kiss her feet, and I do declare I might have done so if I'd not had Polly in my arms.

The doctor said that Polly ought to have a blood test, just to make quite sure she wasn't sick, although it was unlikely.

'But will Joe ... will he—'

I couldn't bring myself to say the word, to ask them if my son was going to die. 'We're doing everything we can for Joe,' the doctor told us. 'Please try not to worry, Mr Riley. Joe's in the best place.'

Nobody mentioned health insurance, asked for forms or paperwork. It seemed they were more interested in making Joseph well.

⌒ ROSIE ⌒

All through that awful night we hoped and prayed as Joe tried to decide if he was going to live or die. The grey machines went bleep, bleep, bleep. The thin green lines zig-zagged across their screens. I watched them, mesmerised. *As long as they keep bleeping*, I assured myself, *it will be fine.*

Nurses came and filled in charts, adjusted drips. They took Joe's temperature and wiped the drool off his face and sponged him down because he had a fever now.

Pat tried and tried again to phone his wife. He left a dozen messages, two dozen, but Lexie didn't reply.

Polly dozed on Pat's lap or on mine. While Polly sat or lay on Pat's lap, sucking at his cuff, I held her brother's hand – his little soft white infant hand, the hand which was now bruised and purpled where a line went into it.

They'd given me his ruined clothes. One of his hoodie pockets was full of something light and hard and lumpy. So I emptied it into my lap. I wondered if there might be clues to what was making Joe so ill. I found a dozen pieces of a Lego hero. So would Joe grow up to be a hero, would he grow a beard or stubble, would this little boy grow up at all?

The grey machines bleeped on. Pat's lovely Joe, his hyperactive, never still and never silent child, lay helpless on his back and let the drugs drip into him.

I couldn't find my wife. Sunday went and Monday went and Tuesday came. I called and called and called. But Lex would not pick up. It always went to voicemail.

'She might be out of range?' suggested Rosie.

'Out of range in London?'

'What if she's not in London?'

'She should have had the kids back Sunday evening and it's Tuesday afternoon.'

'Why don't you go home and get some rest? You look exhausted.'

'So do you.' The skin round Rosie's eyes was purple-bruised. It looked like she was in a fight and lost. 'I can't go home,' I said. 'My place is here with Joe.'

'Pat, your daughter needs to go to bed, poor little thing. Go back to your apartment or to mine, take Polly, go to sleep. I'll stay with Joe today and through the night. I'll put my feet up, rest my eyes, and tomorrow morning I'll go home and sleep myself.'

'You'll call me if there's any change?'

'Of course I will.'

I knew I wouldn't sleep. But I guess I must have dozed awhile. I woke to find my daughter lying on my chest and chewing on my bed sheet and to hear my cell phone ringing.

I was wide awake at once. 'W-what's happening?' I stammered, feeling beyond wicked because I'd been asleep while Rosie had been watching Joe. How could I have slept when Joe was lying there so sick? Why was I not in the hospital? What kind of father was I? 'Rosie, is he—'

'It's good news!' she cried.

'Yeah?' I thought I must be dreaming now. 'Rosie, are you sure?'

'Of course I'm sure. Pat, he's out of danger,' Rosie told me, saying every word so slow, so careful that I couldn't help but understand. 'Your son is out of danger.'

'Who told you this?'

'The doctor who's been looking after him. He promised me Joe's going to be all right. They've taken some of the machines away. He's breathing by himself. He's still on a drip, but now he's sitting up in bed. Joe spoke to us!'

'What did he say?'

'He said *hey, Rosie*, then he asked for you. *Where's Dad* – that's what he said.'

'Tell him I'll be right over.'

When Poll and I came to the hospital, Joe was in a little room all by himself. But he was in a children's ward, not in the ICU. Still hooked up to half a dozen monitors and drips, still pale and bloodless, he was lying propped against some pillows, but his eyes were open.

'Hey, little dude,' I said, determined not to cry.

'Hey, Dad. Hey, Polly.' He managed a half-smile which broke my heart. 'The doctor says I was asleep for two whole days?'

'Yeah, that's right,' I said. 'You were real sick.'

'But now I'm better?'

'Almost better.'

'Daddy crying,' Polly said and hugged me round the neck, which made me cry some more.

Doctors came and went and so did nurses, an everlasting blue and green parade. They took Joe's pulse and temperature. They checked on drips, took readings, filled in charts. They spoke with us and told us what was happening in some detail.

But I found I couldn't handle all this information. All I had to understand was Joe was getting better. I kept right on asking them if my son was going to recover, and they kept right on telling me he would.

'He's not unconscious, Mr Riley,' said a nurse, who came to check him out because he closed his eyes and then I panicked, rang the bell. 'He's resting, getting up his strength again.'

'You must go home and get some sleep,' I said to Rosie as we stood at the foot of Joseph's bed and Polly toddled round the little room, patting on things.

'Yes.' Rosie shrugged. 'Yes, that might be a plan.'

'It definitely would – and Rosie?'

'What?'

'Thank you, thank you, lovely, lovely girl, for everything you did for us, for saving Joseph's life. You were our guardian angel.'

Rosie looked at me. I thought she was half-smiling now. But then her big grey eyes filled up with tears, spilled over, runnelled down her cheeks. She turned away. She bowed her head and sobbed, her shoulders shaking. I never saw someone in such distress.

'Hey, don't cry, he's going to be fine!' I took her in my arms and rocked her like I would have rocked a little baby. 'They said so. Did you hear them?'

But she wouldn't stop crying. She sobbed and sobbed as if her heart would break.

'It's relief,' a nurse assured me, coming by to find out what was going on and who was making all the noise. 'I tell you what, why don't you both sit quietly for half an hour? I'll fetch some tea and toast.'

I wonder if there's anything the British cannot fix by drinking tea and eating toast? I kind of doubt it, actually. Rosie certainly seemed better after she had breakfast.

Joe was dozing, so she didn't wake him. She merely touched his hand and then she left to get some sleep herself.

A minute later, Joe woke up and asked where she had gone and then asked, where was Mom?

'I'm doing everything I can to track her down,' I told him. 'I'm sure she'll be here soon.'

It took a while, but finally I got to speak with Lex. She was held up in Scotland, so she said. She and Mr Wonderful took a romantic weekend break in Aberdeenshire. Mr Wonderful had friends who owned a castle there. 'I tried to call you, Patrick,' she insisted. 'But there was a ton of rain and then there was a landslide.'

'What do landslides have to do with anything?'

'The wires came down or some such. So I couldn't use a landline. I couldn't get a signal on my cell. The road was washed away, and – listen, Pat, it's not my fault!'

I told her that I didn't care about whose fault it was, if she'd been held up by a landslide or an avalanche, been swept away by a flash flood or whirled into the sky by a tornado. All she had to do was get her ass to London right away.

⌒ ROSIE ⌒

I had a few hours of troubled sleep then went back to the Royal to see Polly, Pat and Joe. When I saw Pat and saw how tired he looked – he'd aged ten years in just five days – I cried again. I couldn't help myself.

He stroked my hair and told me twenty, thirty times that Joe was doing good. The doctors, nurses all agreed. I'd got him to the hospital in time and he would make a full recovery. So why was I crying?

How could I tell him about Charlie and my nightmare on a loop?

'When will Alexis get here, do you think?' I asked.

'She should be in London by this evening and she'll come straight to the hospital.'

'Then I'll go home. I don't think we should meet.'

'She ought to thank you.'

'She might not see it quite that way.' I shrugged out of his embrace. 'I took you all to Paris. She might hold me responsible for this.'

'I'll make it very plain to Lex it's not your fault. Or anybody's fault. The consultant guy, he told me not to waste my time and energy in trying to figure out what someone did or didn't do. Anyone can get this sort of thing, he said, from a bug bite, graze, an accidental scratch – kids are always getting little scratches – and these can get infected. When you think about it, Rosie, all those tiny cuts and injuries we all get all the time, it's a wonder anyone survives. The important thing is your quick thinking saved Joe's life.'

'The doctors saved his life.'

'They told me three, four hours more, his body would have started shutting down. Then he might have lost his limbs, his hearing or his sight. He might have even died.'

'Three, four hours – that's all?' I whispered.

'Yeah, that's what they said. So Lex and I, we can't thank you enough and we will be forever in your debt. You need me, I'll be there.' Poll was tugging at his T-shirt now and so he let me go and picked her up. 'I'm sorry I got mad at you when you called to tell me Joe was sick,' he added. 'When I think of what I said to you—'

'You were shocked. You probably thought I'd run away with him, had kidnapped him or something, was holding him to ransom.'

'I shouldn't have got mad. I didn't mean to frighten you.'

'You didn't frighten me.'

'I'd hate for you to be afraid, for anyone to scare you.'

'Pat, don't look so worried. I wasn't scared at all.' Although I was so tired and so conflicted, I still managed a small, feeble smile. 'I never could be scared of you.'

'You hold that thought and if I ever yell at you again you tell me to go f— chase myself. I mean it.'

I wasn't scared of Pat, how could I be?

But I was very scared of what was happening to me. I couldn't keep him – I knew that. I'd read the novels, seen the movies, sobbed with Tess through reconciliation scenes between the warring parents at the bedside of their child, seen the joy in both their faces when their child got well.

I'd heard them promise tearfully to be a real family again. I'd watched them crying in each other's arms. I'd heard them ask whatever were they thinking when they'd parted? When they got the chance, they told each other, they would go to see the minister, priest, rabbi or whatever and renew their vows.

Did I want to meet Alexis?

No, because I didn't want to see them being kind to one another, much less making up. Patrick and Alexis getting back together, Joe and Polly living with both parents once again – that would make the perfect happy ending, wouldn't it?

But how would I survive?

✦ PATRICK ✦

Joe was in the hospital a while. At first he made slow progress. But every day he got a little better, had more colour and ate with more enthusiasm. *Polly, don't you touch my chocolate buttons/jelly beans. Rosie brought me those! Okay, you can have one – but only one.* He grew more like the Joe we nearly lost.

Rosie disappeared. I could kind of understand it, see it might be awkward if she and Lex should meet. But I was hurt as well. Joe talked about her all the time. When would he see Rosie? When would Rosie come?

'Rosie, Daddy?' Polly looked around for Rosie, too.

But whenever Joe or Polly mentioned Rosie, Lexie's mouth grew like a hen's butt or a miser's moneybag that had the strings pulled tight. 'I'm your mommy, honey,' she reminded Joe. 'Rosie's just a friend.'

'But Rosie brought me to the hospital. Mom, if Rosie hadn't brought me here, I would have died.'

'Who told you that?' demanded Lexie.

'Daddy,' Joe replied.

'Well, Daddy isn't always right.'

Whatever Lexie said and thought, however – and of course she said a ton of stuff – I was beyond grateful to Joseph's guardian angel and knew I always would be for as long as I might live. If my wife had any sense or feeling, she should have been beyond grateful, too.

But when I explained to Lex, when I told her in much more detail what had happened, all she said was she was not surprised that Joe got sick if that Rosie woman had taken us on dirty British trains. Nobody in Britain rode the trains unless they couldn't afford to travel any other way. Stephen never rode the trains, and Stephen always said …

I considered having a discussion with Mr Wonderful. But it seemed he had the sense to keep out of my way, and I had other, more important matters on my mind, like sorting out my future, a future in which Rosie would play a major part.

As for our son, the afternoon he asked us for his hair gel so he could fix his style, we knew our little guy would be okay.

A few days later, Lexie and the kids and Mr Wonderful flew back to Minnesota. I didn't have a fight with Lexie about taking Joe and Polly home, much as I'd have liked to see them and to satisfy myself that Joe was fit and well.

I knew I'd always get the nightmares. While he was sick, I drove myself half-crazy googling septicaemia, finding out what could have happened, how Joe could have lost his sight, his hearing, his arms, his legs, his mind.

So when Joe and Polly left, I missed them. But I was scheduled to spend more time in the UK. I still had work to do in the IT department at Queen Alexandra College, and – who was I kidding? Shoot, I could have done most of that work in Minnesota. The truth is that I wanted – I needed – to see Rosie.

But she was very busy, so she said. She was working all hours, building up her client list and driving round the country seeing people who could use her PR expertise. 'I need to get this business on its feet,' she said. 'I want to see results.'

Since I also like to see results, I guess I understood.

When she was out of town, we kept in touch by cell. When we managed to meet up again, the magic was still there. Or most of it was there. She seemed as loving and as funny and as cute as she had ever been. But something wasn't right. It was kind of like she was withdrawing, was putting space between herself and me.

'Rosie, is there anything you want to talk about?' I asked one evening, while we were sitting on her couch and she scrolled through her emails. 'You worried about something?'

'No, why would I be? How are Joe and Polly, Patrick? Joe is up to speed again, I hope?'

'Yeah, Joe is doing great. Lexie took him to the doctor's office yesterday. Our Dr Mayer checked him out and seems he made a full recovery. Polly – well, she's fine.'

'That's good to know. Pat, I hate to throw you out, but I'm going to Hull tomorrow morning and I'll need to get up very early.'

I took the hint and left and, as I rode the subway home, I thought – maybe our affair had run its course, that she was tired of me, was thinking it was time she found herself another guy, someone who had no baggage?

There was still so much she didn't know. So much I didn't feel I could explain, had never told a mortal soul. Perhaps she ought to know? I wanted her to know. But if I did come clean, if I should go for full disclosure, would she ever speak to me again? If she wouldn't see me and if she wouldn't talk to me, it would break my heart.

One evening when I called and called, she failed to pick up. All I could get was voicemail. So was this the end, the point at which I should have got the message, when I should have realised what it meant, when a woman would not take my calls?

Or maybe she was sick?

I had just a couple days left here in the UK.

I decided this was not the end.

I went to her apartment and saw at once that something must be wrong. She had been crying. 'What's the matter, Rosie?' I began, concerned. 'Why are you so upset?'

'I've l-lost my phone!'

Oh, sweet salvation, the relief!

'I'm always losing mine,' I said. 'Why don't you call the number?'

'I've called the number half a million times!'

'No luck?'

'It's going straight to voicemail.' She began to cry again. 'It isn't in the office and it isn't in the flat. I've t-turned the whole place upside down.'

'Did you leave it on?'

'I think so, yes.'

'What about the battery – how long does it last?'

'Oh, ages – several days – more than a week, in fact.' She sniffed. 'I charged it up this morning, so—'

'So we have time to find it.' I gave her a big hug and stroked her hair. I hoped her phone *was* on and that the battery *was* fully charged. Otherwise, she'd be looking for a brick. 'Someone kind might find it,' I suggested, fingers crossed behind her back. 'Go into your list of contacts, make a call to one?'

'I suppose they might.'

'But let's not wait for that to happen. We can start to look for it online. What security and tracking applications do you have?'

'I don't have any security and tracking applications.'

'Of course you do. You must. When you first got the phone – remember? When you took out the contract?'

'Pat, my phone is four or five years old. We didn't do security and tracking applications then. We didn't realise we needed them, and I don't have them – right?'

'Okay, okay, don't worry – if your phone is on and no one's using it and running down the battery, I'm sure there'll still be something we can do. But if we can't track it down by GPS, it's just a handset, yeah? You can replace it.'

'I can't replace what's on it.'

'What is that?'

'The last time I saw Charlie.'

'Who is Charlie? Some guy you used to know?'

'Charlie is my sister.'

⌒ ROSIE ⌒

'I didn't know you have a sister?' Pat looked puzzled. 'When we went to Red Wing that time, you told me—'

'I don't have a sister any more.'

'Oh, Rosie, love! What happened?' He led me over to the sofa, sat me down and put his arm around my shoulders. 'Does she ... is she—'

'I can't talk about it now.'

'Then we'll just sit quiet awhile. If you do decide you want to talk, that's fine by me. If you decide you don't, that's also fine.'

If I didn't tell him now, when would I tell him?

When would I tell anyone?

I began to talk.

'I had a job in Paris,' I began. 'I was working for a PR company and having a great time. Charlie had come back to the UK after spending six or seven weeks in Africa. She had been all over, to places like the Congo and Angola and Namibia, hitching rides, staying in people's houses, sleeping rough and doing stuff which gave my parents nightmares.

'But they couldn't stop her going any more than they could stop the world from turning or the sun from rising. Well, unless they'd locked her up in a tall tower or something and thrown away the key. You see, she had to travel. She was born that way, was an explorer as soon as she could walk. She went to London on her own when she was six or seven. She walked into our little local station, caught a train. She ended up in Regent's Park. Mum was mortified because, when two policemen brought her home again, they called in Social Services and Child Protection, put my parents through the third degree. When she was eighteen, Dad started up a Ransom Charlie fund for when he had to go and get her back from somewhere like Somalia, Iraq or Kazakhstan.

'After a week or two in Dorset with my parents, she was bored. So she came to Paris to spend some time with me. We stayed in my apartment. It was in the Marais. We went shopping, clubbing, drinking, partying – did the whole Paris thing.

'One lunch time, we were in a café where I often went with friends or by myself. I loved it, I was comfortable there, I knew the staff and they knew me. It was my local, if you like. On the day I went with Charlie, there was a cool guy I sort of knew at the next table, having lunch alone.

'He started flirting with my sister in that ironic way some Frenchmen do. Soon she was flirting back at him, making out she didn't know much French while he pretended he didn't know much English. So I was interpreting or rather misinterpreting and all of us were laughing.

'I asked him if he'd take a video of the two of us. He said yes, I handed him my phone and he began to film us. Charlie did ridiculous impressions of actresses and singers. We were laughing fit to wet ourselves. Then Jean-Paul said he fancied having ice cream for dessert and did we fancy ice cream, too?

'Charlie said she definitely did. A chocolate glacé with an almond and spun sugar topping, that would hit the spot. She called the waiter over and ordered three ice creams in silly Franglais which made us fall about. She made the waiter laugh as well.

'I didn't think about the milk in the ice cream. I just assumed it would be ordinary cow's milk. But it turned out to be goat's milk. Charlie was allergic to it. She had had a bad reaction to some goat's cheese while we were on holiday in France when we were children and she was sensitised. Pat, it said so on the menu – *lait de chèvre*. Why did I not read the flipping menu before I let her order?'

'Nobody reads everything on menus, Rosie.'

'But I'd promised Mum and Dad that when I was with Charlie I would always check ingredients, would always, always, always read all menus! We knew she wouldn't bother! She never, ever bothered! I was her big sister and so I was responsible! I—'

'Rosie, take your time, okay?' soothed Pat. 'What happened next?'

'The waiter brought our ice cream. Charlie ate a little, but then she started wheezing, coughing – trying to get her breath. It took me twenty, thirty seconds to realise what must be happening, that this was a reaction, most likely caused by milk. The waiter came and thumped her on the back. He must have thought she'd choked on nuts or something.

'As I was begging him to stop and shouting to the guy I knew to call an ambulance, telling him that Charlie wasn't play-acting, that this was all for real, I was searching through her rucksack for her EpiPen.

'The wretched rucksack had a trillion pockets. I couldn't find the pen. I thought, perhaps she doesn't have one? She was very bad at carrying stuff like that around. I suppose she thought – she hoped – she'd never need the thing. Or she was in denial. She hated being different. While she was at school, she—'

I found I couldn't go on.

'It's okay,' soothed Pat. 'When you're ready, when you want to tell me, if you want to tell me—'

'I grabbed my phone back from the guy at the next table. He'd stopped filming when they brought the ice cream, before Charlie started choking, but now he just sat there looking stunned and doing nothing. So I called the ambulance and I must admit it came at once. I explained about the allergy and what had caused it. The paramedics gave her something at the café.

'We got her to the hospital. But by now her system was in shock, she was unconscious and she died ten minutes later, hooked up to a dozen drips, machines. Nowadays, I can't walk past a hospital without feeling sick with terror, panicking and thinking I'll throw up, pass out or both. As for going into one—'

'But you still took Joseph to the hospital. You still stayed with him while he was getting better. You sent me home so I could get some rest.'

'What else could I have done?'

'I already knew you were a heroine. But up to now I didn't know how much it must have cost you to do what you did for Joe. Listen to me, darling, you mustn't blame yourself about your sister.'

'It was my fault.'

'Rosie, it was not your fault.'

'It was, because the pen was in the pocket of her jeans. She'd had it with her all the time.'

Silence.

I could hear it.

Or rather I could hear the thudding of my heart, the drumming in my head. Pat said nothing for a moment. But then, slowly, carefully, he turned me round to face him. 'So how should you have known?'

'It was the most obvious place to look! Pat, I never told my mother, father or anybody else I didn't find the pen. But I should have told them. I should have confessed, not let everyone believe that Charlie didn't have a pen and that was why she died.'

'Do you still have that video?'

'No, I told you – it was on my phone.'

'I mean, you didn't send it to a friend, to Gmail?'

'Of course I didn't send it to friend. I never thought of sending it to Gmail. Yes, I know I should have done it, but I didn't, and it's too late now. Pat, I played and played it, half a dozen times a day. But I never told my mum and dad about it.'

'So they never saw it?'

'No.'

'I can understand why you're upset, to lose something so precious. Perhaps your parents should have seen it?'

'I didn't know if I should show them or not show them, if seeing it would help them or destroy them, and I still don't know.'

❧ PATRICK ❦

I held her while she cried.

'You're not to blame,' I said, once, twice, a dozen times.

265

'Your sister, she was an adult. She should have checked out what she was eating. You didn't have to be your sister's keeper.'

'But if I had only—'

'Rosie, honey, life's full of *if-onlys*.'

'I suppose.' She grabbed a box of Kleenex. 'If Tess had gone to New York City or Los Angeles for her American adventure, I'd never have met you.'

'You would not have known a genuine knuckle-dragging, Neolithic throwback.' She managed a small, tearful smile at that. But still her eyes were sad and, as I gazed into those wide, grey eyes, I found I wanted more than anything to heal the hurt I saw there. 'Most everybody has regrets,' I added. 'Most everybody's done bad things. Or they believe they've done bad things. You did nothing wrong. You and your sister – it was just bad luck, a cruel stroke of fate.'

'I killed Charlie, Pat.'

'You did not kill Charlie. You know you tried to save a life, not take it.'

'But I'm still no better than my sister's murderer, her executioner.'

'You don't know what you're saying.'

'I know only too well.'

'You only think you do.'

I never shared the truth with anyone – not with Alexis, not with Ben.

Of course, Ben's wormed a few details out of me and no doubt guessed the rest. He loves to needle people, poke, prod, pry – loves getting a reaction. It's why he mentioned gasoline when we were having dinner that first time. He wanted me to ask him what he meant – to challenge him. Of course, I didn't. I would not have given him the satisfaction, not in company, not any time.

If I told Rosie, would she hate me? But if she did hate me,

would it matter, if it helped her to forgive herself and if it helped her mend? I owed her, didn't I? *Okay*, I thought, *here goes – confession time.*

'One time, I tried to kill a man,' I said.

'You did what?' She stared then shook her head. 'I don't believe you.'

'It's the truth.'

'Who was this man?'

'My father.'

'Why, whatever happened?'

'Where to start?' I shrugged. 'As you might have heard from Tess or Ben, I was raised in Recovery, Missouri – a dirt-poor town which by some quirk of fate had one good public high school. I had teachers who inspired me, worked with me, encouraged me. So I got an excellent education, in spite of coming from a home which didn't have a single book in it and where the television was always tuned to trash.

'While I was growing up, my mother had a bunch of jobs. She cleaned and did the laundry in other people's houses and apartments, did menial stuff for those few people who were better off than most, the doctor and the lawyer and the judge, their wives and widows. She waited tables in the local diner, worked the register in grocery stores. But it hadn't always been like that for Mom. When she graduated high school, she became a college student in St Louis.'

'So what happened?'

'She met with a rodeo rider at a county fair. She fell in love. So she dropped out of college, married Dad. But he was from the wrong side of the tracks. She found her parents didn't want to know her anymore.

'She didn't care. She was in love. She had a little money of her own and put down a deposit on a house. But while my mother worked her fingers to the bone, Dad stayed home and drank.'

'He didn't work at all?'

267

'Sometimes he did casual labour on construction projects, pouring concrete, hauling rocks or lumber. But he was usually too drunk to work. The only reason he got out of bed most mornings was to raid my mother's purse and head out to the liquor store. When he had the energy, he beat and kicked my mother and took a strap to me.'

'Oh – like in Ben's book?'

'Yeah, just like that. One time, after he'd beat up on my mother bad, so bad she couldn't go to work, so bad that she was in the county hospital for weeks, I thought, *I'm going to kill him.*

'I was eight or nine years old. So although I was a kid, I knew what I was doing. While he was asleep one afternoon and Mom had started back at work, cleaning some old lady's house downtown, I found the can of gasoline he kept in the garage and poured a slug of it into his bourbon.'

'But, Pat – you only meant to make him ill? You didn't really want to kill him, did you?'

'Yes, of course I did.'

'Why did you think he'd die?'

'My class had done a project on combustion engines. We all wrote reports on how they worked. Miss Ellie warned us gasoline was very flammable and not to mess with it. I'd watched big kids spilling lighter fuel in puddles, setting it on fire so that the water seemed to burn.

'One day as I was heading home from school I thought, *if Daddy drank some gasoline then lit a cigarette, it would be like – kaboom! He would be lit on fire and he would die and how great that would be.*'

'So when you poured the petrol in his whiskey—'

'He realised straight away. He took a mouthful but he didn't swallow. He spit it out and then accused my mother, who'd just walked in the door, of trying to poison him. He got her by the throat. She was choking, crying, pleading, didn't know what he meant, her eyes were bulging in her head, she looked like she would die. So I fessed up.'

'What did he do?'

'He beat up on me so bad that I passed out. So then he had to take me to the hospital. He told them I was climbing out a window on the second floor and fallen on the concrete in the yard.

'While I was in the hospital the nurses made a pet of me. They gave me treats and candy. They told me I'd been hurt real bad but I was going to mend. I had to be a little soldier for my daddy's sake because he was so worried about me.

'I was afraid he'd punish Mom for giving birth to me, and I was right – he did. Today, she has almost no hearing and she can't see out of her left eye. The tears I've cried for Mama, Rosie! All the grief I've felt for my poor mother – more than any kid should have to do.

'So there you have it. If you want to see a real-life murderer, a real-life executioner, or would-be executioner, all you need to do is look at me.'

So Rosie looked.

'All I can see is somebody who got a life and made himself a big success in spite of everything. Anyway,' she added, 'what you did as a child would surely not be murder or attempted murder, even if your father had drunk the poisoned bourbon, even if he'd died?'

'What's your definition of attempted murder, Rosie?'

'I've never thought about it.'

'So think about it now?'

'There has to be intention. There needs to be a plan?'

'You got it, more or less. I looked it up a year or two ago. I'm not sorry, Rosie. If I'd killed the bastard, I would have run round singing. When I hear he's dead – one day he has to be – I'll make a point of dancing on his grave.'

'Where is your father these days?'

'I'm not exactly sure because he left when I was twelve and headed off down south. Last time I heard, he was in jail someplace in Alabama – got ten years without parole.'

'What did he do?'

'He robbed a store. He sprayed the clerk with Mace and blinded him. But he'll have suffered worse than blindness while he's been in jail. Trash like him, they have it hard in prisons in the USA, and that makes me glad. You think I'm wicked?'

'No! You were a child who was afraid a cruel man would kill your mother and I'm not surprised you hate him. But one day you might decide you've hated long enough? Maybe you could let the wounds inside you heal, like the ones you got from beatings did? Maybe you could make your peace with him?'

'It's never been about what Daddy did to me. But while my mother lives and while I watch her startle when a drunk walks down the street and while she still gets blackouts because he hit her far too many times, I never shall make peace with him.'

'What if he contacted you and asked for your forgiveness?'

'I would not enter into dialogue.'

'When he dies?'

'It's like I said – I'll go dance on his grave.'

'You won't. You'll wish you'd seen him one last time. You'll wish you'd made your peace. My sister died. Pat, it matters when a person dies.'

'You loved your sister – that's what matters. You're beating yourself up for failing Charlie. But that's not the problem, because deep in your heart you know you didn't fail your sister. You're sad because a person you loved very much is dead. I think you should forgive yourself, don't you?'

'Perhaps I'll try. Pat, do you feel better now?' she asked.

'Yeah, I do.' It was the truth, I did. It was like a burden

had been lifted. I kissed her on the forehead. 'Thank you for hearing my confession.'

'It's no problem. Thank you very much for hearing mine.' Rosie looked at me. 'I expect you're hungry now? If you give me your mobile, I'll phone up for a pizza.'

'Let's get pizza later. Let's track down your cell. We might not have much time.'

⌒ ROSIE ⌒

'You're going to need a magic spell,' I told him.

'So let's find one, then.'

It took him twenty seconds flat to find and then download an application which he said could send commands to my lost phone and get it to respond. 'I don't see how,' I muttered. 'It sounds like something out of Harry Potter. *Accio phone* – that sort of thing? You command, my phone obeys?'

'Yeah, that's certainly the plan,' he told me, tapping on his keypad. 'So now you keep your fingers crossed, you knock on wood, you stroke your lucky rabbit's foot and you believe in magic.'

As I watched him tapping, I thought about the gasoline. I thought about the frightened little child, the one who wanted more than anything to help his mother, who confessed to save his mother, knowing he'd be beaten half to death as a result. I understood that this was courage. I also understood I should be kinder to *my* mother. If and when I got my phone back, she'd be the first person I would ring, and from now on I would be nice to Mum, however much she patronised and irritated me and told me how to live my life.

I would not forget that she'd lost someone precious, too.

'How's it going, Pat?' I asked.

'We're almost done.' He tapped more keys, looked up at me. 'Okay, I guess it's sorted.'

'You mean you've tracked it down?' I stared at him, astonished. 'You've really found my mobile?'

'No, not yet, it's going to take a while. So now we wait. Why don't you go put the kettle on?'

The first email arrived five minutes later as we were drinking coffee, followed by another message, then another, then three more. Then—

'Gotcha!' Pat exclaimed and punched the air.

'You've found it?'

'Yeah, I found it.'

'You really can do magic!'

'Well – magic sometimes happens.'

'You are amazing, you know that?' I was so excited I spilled coffee on my lap. 'Where is it, then?'

'You had the good news, here's the bad.' He glanced up from the screen to look at me, his brown eyes serious and kind. 'I'm sorry, Rosie. If we're to believe the GPS, looks like your cell will be impossible to find.'

'Why's that?'

'See here.'

He turned the screen to show me and I could have wept. The GPS had pinpointed a London landfill site. 'But how on earth did it get there?' I wailed.

'Maybe someone stole it from your bag or pocket while you rode the subway, saw it was an older model, threw it in the trash?'

'No.' I cursed myself. 'I bought some sandwiches for lunch and ate them walking down the road. I stuffed the empty wrapper in my bag, but then I pulled it out again and chucked it as I passed a bin. I must have thrown my phone away as well. Oh, I'm such an idiot!'

'Anybody could have done it, sweetheart. Do you want me to erase the card?'

'Yes, if you could?'

'You're sure?'

'I'm sure.'

'It will take a minute, couple minutes. I'll need to—'

'No.' I grabbed his hand. 'I've changed my mind.' I couldn't bear to think of Charlie being lost, erased. I thought that maybe one day someone working on the landfill site might find my phone, might even fire it up and track me down.

Magic sometimes happens, after all.

As we lay in bed later that night, I made a wish. I made three wishes, actually. I wished a university in the UK would offer Pat a job he didn't feel he could refuse. I wished his wife and children would also come to live in the UK with Lexie's bloke. Then – if Pat and Lexie should decide to try again, if they renewed their vows, if they divorced, whatever – I might still get to see him now and then.

So much for unrealistic expectations.

I wished he'd stay another week or two, which would not be unrealistic, would it? Or too greedy? Yes, it would.

'I'll come back,' he promised, as I sniffed and rubbed my eyes. 'Rosie, darling, please don't break your heart? I'm not worth it, surely?'

'You're worth everything to me!'

But I knew he had to go and, two days after he had found my phone, he flew back home to Minnesota.

July

My work at London University was done. My flight was booked and, two days after Rosie lost her phone, I flew back to Minneapolis, where I was congratulated by the dean and told I'd been a great ambassador for JQA.

So I did one thing right.

While I was on the plane, I thought about that video on Rosie's phone. She'd told me to erase the card, then said not to erase it. I wouldn't have erased it anyway, even if she'd said to wipe it, just in case she'd changed her mind again. I didn't want to break her heart.

I was sure there had to be a way to get that video back. So all I had to do was find the way. When I was home again, I scrolled through all my contacts, looking for the numbers of people who might help me, and finally I found the very one.

I called a friend who had connections with the CIA.

'Yeah, it might be possible,' he told me, after I explained. 'I might know a guy who knows a guy. But a private contract – it would cost a bunch of money. We're talking big bucks here.'

'What, thousands, millions?'

'It would be ten thousand dollars minimum, and in cash.'

'If you let me have some contact details, I'll go on from there.'

'No, I'll meet you for a beer some time. I don't want to put this stuff in emails or tell you on the phone. You never know who's listening.'

'Maybe we could meet later today?'

'Yeah, I guess,' he said. 'It's been a while. So tell me – you mislaid the secret of eternal life?'

'I want this data found.'

'Okay, okay, but listen up – before you give your money to this guy, you need to know that he won't offer any guarantees. Also, if he manages to track your data down, he could take his time to hand it over – might be months or even years. The fact is, he might never hand it over, but don't even start to think you'll get your money back.'

'I'm prepared to take the risk.'

'You're prepared to take a reckless gamble and very likely lose. These spooks play by their own rules, not by yours.'

Lexie and my children were still living with the British tosser in his mansion on Grand Avenue. Joe was full of what was going down in its backyard. 'There are a bunch of foxes, Dad,' he told me. 'We got squirrels, too. One time Polly said she saw a snake.'

'What colour was it, green?'

'I guess. Or it could have been magenta? Polly wasn't sure. When I told Mom about the snake, it freaked her out. She said she's going to call the pest exterminator guy. She wants him to come by and deal with all the vermin.'

Awesome, I decided. *Maybe he could deal with Mr Wonderful as well?*

'Dad, she's going to have the foxes killed!'

'You don't need to worry, Joseph. Foxes are real smart and so are squirrels. When the pest exterminator's truck shows up, they won't stick around to be exterminated.'

'What about the snake?'

'The snake will slither off into the grass.'

'You're sure?'

'I know it.'

'Did you ever get to hear from Rosie, Dad?'

'She emailed me this morning, asked after you and Polly and sends you lots of love.'

'When will we see Rosie?'

'I don't know, little buddy. Rosie lives in Britain and we live in America, four thousand miles apart.'

'When we are on vacation, perhaps we could go visit Britain again?'

'Yeah, perhaps we could.' I changed the subject. It can't be good for little boys to see their fathers cry.

A few days after I came home, Lexie called to ask if we could meet.

Angie would be happy to watch the kids, she said.

I guessed she must want money – more of it. Or even a divorce? Maybe Mr Wonderful had been down on one knee, made her an offer that she could not refuse?

'Perhaps, if it's about our situation, you should speak with your attorney?' I suggested. 'Then I'll speak with mine.'

'This is purely personal,' she said. 'So we don't need to go through our attorneys.'

'Do you want to come by the apartment?'

'No, we'll meet on neutral territory,' she replied.

So I named a coffee shop in downtown Minneapolis.

'Yeah, sounds good,' she said.

'Okay, I'll see you Tuesday after work.'

Lexie had her hen's butt face on.

'What about this Rosie?' she demanded, making Rosie's name sound like a swear word. 'Joseph talks about her all the time. It's all Rosie's hair and Rosie's clothes and Rosie's cool apartment and Rosie's Yorkshire puddings. I'm sick and tired of Rosie, Daddy's British friend.'

'But you have a British friend, Alexis. Why can't I have one, too?'

'I don't get Stephen to turn your kids against you.'

'Rosie hasn't turned your kids against you.'

'Why is Joe fixated on this woman?'

'Joe is not fixated, Lexie. They just like each other, get along. Rosie never met you, and while Joe and Polly were around she never mentioned you – fact is, she never mentioned you at all.'

'I guess she knew she didn't need to mention me if she already had you by the balls.' Lexie worried at a fingernail. 'I thought you wanted to make up with me?'

'I never told you so.'

'Last fall, you said we ought to see a counsellor.'

'You told me it was way too late for counselling. Do you want to get a latte or a cappuccino?'

'A latte and a brownie – I missed lunch today.'

I went up to the counter, ordered, waited while they fixed the coffees, glanced at Lexie now and then. I saw that she was looking very tired. Maybe she was overdoing things, exterminating vermin, digging weeds in Mr Wonderful's backyard and servicing the guy who made her fly?

'How is life in general, Lex?' I asked.

'It's okay, I guess.' She sighed. She crumbled up her brownie. 'But I must admit it's sometimes not too great. The kids are so demanding these days, always wanting this and that and cluttering up the place with Barbies, Lego—'

'What about the guy who makes you come to life?'

'Next month, he'll be going to Dubai alone.' Lexie sounded like she had the words pulled out of her with forceps and was trying not to scream. 'We're not so good together any more. Stephen is a—'

'What?'

A louse, a slug, a piece of shit?

Come on, Lexie, let me hear you say it?

'A serial marriage-wrecker. He's done this before, you know. Put the moves on married women and convinced them they should leave their husbands, go with him. Rhoda at the office called me up a week ago. It seems he has some history. I think he must be seriously disturbed.'

'Or perhaps he's seriously dumb? But maybe that's unfair. After all, there's no way he could be as dumb as me.'

'Oh, Pat!' She looked at me and I could see her eyes were bright. 'Patrick, we were lovers once. We could be lovers still. We have two awesome children. We could put all this behind us, couldn't we? Strike the past out for our children's sake, if not for our own?'

I could see she needed to be comforted.

She needed me to take her in my arms, to kiss her better, to tell her it would all work out, to say we could pretend the past few months had been a nightmare and we had woken up and everything was fine again.

But although I could remember how I felt about her once and was even kind of sorry we could not go back and be the way we were, there was no way I'd want to do what she suggested.

I had no desire to punish Lex, I swear. But when she left me for the British guy then went to bed with Ben, she smashed up something precious. However much I wanted to repair it – and part of me did – I knew deep down it couldn't be repaired. It might have been repairable one time.

But there was Rosie now.

⌒ ROSIE ⌒

'Patrick, don't you care?' I asked him when we next spoke on the phone. Gosh, I loved my new and whizzy smartphone! It organised my life so well that I could not imagine how I'd got along without it, even though the battery lasted only half a minute. 'You must surely care a little bit?'

'Yeah, I care about my kids and how we're jerking them around. But as for Mr Wonderful and Lexie, Ben and Lexie – no, it doesn't bother me at all. I guess I always kind of wondered about Lex and Ben, even from the time we were in high school.'

'Or maybe you knew they liked each other? But since Lexie was your girl and Ben was your best friend, perhaps you trusted them?'

'Perhaps I was a clown? Whenever we and Ben and Mrs Fairfax One or Two met up, there'd always be this kind of flirting going on. Ben would compliment her on her outfit, notice when she put her hair up, tell her she looked great, and Lex would blush and simper, make big eyes at him.'

'What's Ben's problem, Pat?'

'The world's a great big toy store full of dolls. They come in every colour, shape and size. He wants them all.'

'Why does he bother to get married, then?'

'If he's single – if Tess isn't going back to him, and if she has any sense she won't – chasing other women is allowed. But if he's a married man and if he has a mistress, she can be his guilty secret, his little bunch of fun.'

'Perhaps it's just as well he has no children.'

'None we know about, in any case.'

'I'm glad I don't want children.'

'But you get on great with Joe and Polly, Rosie! Why—'

'What's in it for me, apart from getting fat and being sick and having swollen ankles? Then there'd be the sleepless nights, the toddler tantrums, teenage mutinies. I think I'll pass.'

'You like my children, don't you?'

'Yes, of course I like your children, Pat. I love them, they're amazing. But they're still like Labradors.'

'My children are like dogs?'

'Yes, in the sense that I love other people's dogs to bits. My mother's are all gorgeous. But, given the choice, I'd rather have designer handbags.'

'I think you'd be a perfect mom.'

'I think you're projecting and seeing what you want to see in me, not what's really there.'

'I must admit that sometimes I don't get you, Rosie Denham.'

'I don't get men at all. You're married, so am I your little bunch of fun?'

'Darling, you're my life.'

❖ PATRICK ❖

I'm glad I don't want children.

I so wished she did. I wished she wanted mine. So was this the same withdrawing I had sensed before and was she warning me to keep my distance? She did not get men? I sure as hell did not get women …

'Pat, are you still there?' she asked.

'Yes.'

'Joe and Polly – don't misunderstand me – they're a pair of charmers, and you know I think the world of them.'

'They think the world of you.' Then, recklessly, I played my wildest card. 'I know they'd love a baby brother, baby sister.'

'Polly's still a baby.'

'You're great with kids, you know. Why don't we think about it? I get a divorce from Lexie, then maybe we—'

'Patrick, you're still married. You already have two children. Maybe we could change the subject?'

Yeah, okay, point taken, ask her something safe, non-controversial – don't interrogate this woman, you know she won't stand for it. 'What's the weather like in the UK?'

'It's gorgeous, warm and sunny, perfect.'

'I heard you have a heatwave?'

'Yes, it's quite a novelty, and of course it's lovely to go out without a waterproof, umbrella, all that stuff. But it's not all good. The sun brings out the fashion tragedies – khaki shorts and socks and sandals on the hideous old men, see-through cotton trousers on the women and too much wrinkled cleavage on display.'

'You won't be young forever, Rosie.'

'But I hope I'll always have the sense to dress my age. I don't want to frighten little children, do I? Be a great big blot upon the fashion landscape?'

'I must come direct from Fashion Tragedies R Us.'

'You don't, and if you ever got it wrong, I'd put you right.'

⌒ ROSIE ⌒

Why did I have to be so mean? Why shouldn't poor old men let their old knees enjoy some sun? Why did I say such stupid, spiteful things?

I suppose because I missed him like a part of me. I'd never understood that cannot-live-without-you stuff, but now I understood it all too well. While he was away from me, I had to remind myself to eat, to sleep, to breathe.

Perhaps he was the same? Maybe he forgot to eat, to sleep, perhaps he had to tell himself to breathe? Whatever – after one long phone call during which I cried and cried and said I couldn't live without him, I received a text.

We can't go on like this. I'll see you Thursday.

I met him at Heathrow and, when we kissed, it was as if I'd never kissed a man before. I could hear angels singing. The people milling round us stopped to stare and, in a place where people kiss each other all the time, we still managed to cause a small sensation. A group of Japanese with phones and video cameras must have been recording because, when we came up for air, they beamed at us and bowed. It was well embarrassing. We'd be up on YouTube next, I thought, and all our friends would soon be having fits.

But I so didn't care. When you're in love, you just don't care.

'All this jetting round the world, it must be costing you a fortune?' I began, as he took my hand and we headed for the exit.

'This is the first time the college didn't pay.' He stopped and looked at me, gazed deep into my eyes. 'Rosie?'

'What?'

'I don't know what you did to me or how you did it, but you make me happy.'

'You make me happy, too. How long will you be here?'

'A week, that's all. I'm going to a conference in Colorado soon. I'm doing presentations, chairing meetings, so I need to do some preparation. But I can afford to take a few days off.'

'Let's make the most of them.'

'It's a lovely morning,' I announced, when we woke up naked and perspiring in my stuffy flat, in the dusty, stifling heat of London, which stank of petrol fumes and frying burgers like it always does in summertime. 'Let's go to the seaside.'

'Oh.' He looked at me, mock-rueful. 'I guess it's not mandatory I should eat more whelks, more cotton candy?'

'We're not going to Brighton.' Now I made my mind up – no more hiding him away. Whatever happened next, I wanted Dad to meet him. I wanted Mum to get to know him and – I hoped – to like him. I wanted Granny Cassie to meet and like him, too. 'Pat, let's go to Dorset.'

'Now?'

'Why not?'

'Okay, we'll go to Dorset.'

Rosie's home was the last word in cute. It was all honey-coloured stone and fancy chimney pots and smart white paint. Its windows sparkled in the summer sun.

I didn't know these places could exist outside of storybooks. I would not have been surprised to find it was made out of sugar candy. It looked like something from that movie, what is it – *The Hobbit* – except that it was kind of cuboid, or at least not round. But, as I pulled the parking brake, I still expected Bilbo Baggins and a couple other hobbits, dwarves or some such to walk out the door.

'It was just a little bailiff's cottage once,' said Rosie, as I stared. 'But it's been gentrified. Dad's had some rebuilding done and there's a new extension at the back. Mummy's got her dream Nigella kitchen at long last. But most of it looks like it must have done for two, three hundred years.'

'It's like something from a fairy tale.'

'Yes, isn't it?' She turned to smile at me. 'One day, maybe we'll bring Joe and Polly here? I rather think they'd love it.'

'Yeah, I guess they would. But they might try to break off pieces, thinking the whole thing was made of gingerbread. Rosie, are your parents home?'

'Dad will be at work in Dorchester. Mummy's probably helping at the hospice. Or maybe she's in court.'

'Your mom's a judge?'

'She's a JP, a Justice of the Peace, a voluntary magistrate. I don't know what you call them in America? Maybe you don't have JPs?'

'We do. They marry people. Rosie, if your mom and dad aren't home, maybe we should come back later?'

'Granny will be here. She's probably dozing in the sitting room pretending that she's not asleep at all. *I don't sleep in the day*, she says. So come on, let's go and wake her up.'

When Rosie opened the front door, a ton of dogs flowed out. I don't much care for dogs, I must admit. But these four big black ones all seemed well-behaved and courteous. They didn't bark at us, jump up or try to knock us down.

They were all delighted to see Rosie whom they greeted with affection, dancing round, wagging their tails and obviously hoping for some hugs, which of course she gave them. They nodded toward me but kept their distance. I decided we might get along.

Granny was the littlest old lady I had ever seen, smaller even than a Chinese grandmother and they're often tiny. She had the brightest, bluest eyes and soft white curling hair and dimples in her rosy cheeks. She was as cute as fifty buttons and I loved her from the start.

'This is Professor Riley, Granny,' Rosie said, after Granny woke up from her doze and after they had kissed. 'Pat, this is my granny, Cassie Denham.'

'Hello, Mrs Denham, good to meet you, and do please call me Pat.'

'Hello, Pat.' She offered me her hand. She eyed me up and down. She smiled, kind of flirtatiously. 'It's nice to meet you, too. I'm sure we'll get on like a house on fire. Rosie always has good taste in friends.'

What a big improvement on Mommy's attitude toward me, which could not have been any more chilly if it tried!

I took Granny's little hand and held it for a moment and it was like I held a bunch of warm, dry bones, a newborn kitten or some other tiny, fragile creature, curled up on itself. She must have bad arthritis, I decided, and it had to be quite painful. But I got the feeling Granny was the kind of person who never kvetched or grumbled. She was far too curious and interested in life. I could see it in her bright blue eyes.

'I'll go and make us all some tea,' said Rosie.

'I'll come give you a hand.'

'No, you stay here with Granny, Pat. She loves meeting new people and she would like to talk to you, I'm sure.'

'I would indeed,' said Granny. 'So you come over here and sit down on the window seat where I can see you. You must be an American?'

'Yes, ma'am, I'm from Minnesota.'

'What is Minnesota, a city or a state?'

'It's a northern state in the Midwest. It's mostly agricultural, but there's some industry as well. Minneapolis-Saint Paul, where half the population lives, is a big conurbation, and – Mrs Denham, do you know the USA?'

'I'm very sad to say I've never been there and I won't be going now. They wouldn't let me on a plane in case I died on them. It's my heart, you see.'

'I'm sorry.'

'Oh, my dear, there's no need to be sorry! I've had a long and active life and always been a busy little bee. It's my turn to put my feet up now, and most would say a good thing, too.'

She twinkled merrily at me. 'So, America – is it like on television, like in all the films? Does everybody have a gun? Do you have a gun yourself and did you bring it with you? Do you have it on you now? May I see it, may I check it out – is that what you American people say?'

'Ma'am, I never owned a gun. I never wanted one.'

'Oh,' said Granny. 'What a disappointment.'

I almost apologised before I realised she was kidding me.

She said she'd heard of Minnesota. She remembered now. The teacher showed them on the map when she was just a little kid in elementary school. Hiawatha came from Minnesota, didn't he? She knew some of the poem.

She was beyond delighted when I said I knew it, too.

When Rosie came in with the tea stuff, we were getting

nicely reacquainted with Hiawatha's childhood, reciting line for line;

'*From the full moon fell Nokomis –*'

'*Fell the beautiful Nokomis –*'

'Patrick, what on earth is going on?' Rosie stared at us like we were crazy. 'What are you two doing – casting spells?'

'We're reciting poetry, my darling,' Granny said. *We're resoiting powetry* – that's how it came out. 'Pat, I don't recall the next bit. Maybe you can help me?'

'*She a wife but not a mother.*'

'Yes, that's right,' said Granny and she beamed at me.

I felt like I was home.

But why did Rosie look so sad? Why did her eyes cloud over? Oh, shoot – I probably imagined that.

⌒ ROSIE ⌒

'She likes you,' I told Pat while Granny Cassie had a doze and we washed up in Mum's new kitchen. I don't know why my mother has a dishwasher. All her precious china is always washed by hand. 'She thinks you're *virry noice*.'

'That's good to know. I'd hate to get on Granny's bad side.' Pat grinned at me. '*Virry noice* – yeah, that's exactly how she speaks. But I can't place her accent. It's not at all like yours.'

'Granny is a Brummie.'

'What's a Brummie?'

'A Midlander from Brummagem. I mean Birmingham. It's a big industrial city in the heart of England.'

'How did Granny Cass fetch up in Dorset?'

'She met my grandfather while she was a land girl during the last war. They were very different. He was posh and she was working class. Grandad loved the countryside and she came from a city. He was a farmer's son but she had never seen a cow and she was terrified of horses.'

'But they still fell in love.'

'They did – and stayed in love. When Grandad died, poor Granny cried for weeks. She never came to terms with being widowed. She still remembers how it feels to be in love.'

✦ PATRICK ✦

When Dad and Mom came home, I swear the temperature dropped down by ten, fifteen degrees. There were stilted British introductions – *hello*, *hello*, *hello*. Then we all ate dinner – spaghetti bolognaise. I guess most everybody in the world must eat spaghetti bolognaise, even if they live in seaside cottages with roses round the door?

Dad was courteous, shook me by the hand, said he hoped we'd had a pleasant journey and how did I like Dorset? But he said it in a most reserved and very British kind of way. It didn't sound as if he meant a word.

Mom was just reserved.

But Granny made me feel like I was welcome. 'Come on, Pat, dig in,' she said when Rosie brought dessert – a dish of raspberries from the garden and a jug of yellow cream. 'I like to see a man with appetite.'

Oi loike ter see a man with appetoite.

I loved her accent.

After we had coffee, Granny said she'd like to go to bed. So Rosie's mother helped her up the stairs. Dad said he was going to his office. He had some work to do.

'Poor Granny never moans about her aches and pains,' said Rosie as we cleared the dinner stuff away. 'But she gets so bored and so frustrated.'

'What does she do all day?'

'She reads a bit – not books, just magazines. She's fond of crossword puzzles. She listens to the radio. Dad bought her a laptop a few years ago. She absolutely loved it. She emailed all her friends – well, all three of them who weren't afraid of new technology – and she surfed the net. But she finds it really hard to use a keyboard now.'

'Why don't you get speech recognition software – speech-to-text?'

'We tried it and she hated it. She said you had to talk so flipping slowly, like someone off the BBC Home Service – Radio 4 to you and me – for it to understand you.'

'The older stuff was hard to use. You had to say the words one at a time, make sure you kept them nice and separate, or your computer wouldn't understand you.'

'Yes, that's what she found.'

'But SRS is getting better. Nowadays the user can talk normally, can run the words together. If you have an accent, chances are you'll still be understood. If Granny used the new continuous speech recognition software, I figure they'd get on. Maybe I could – but she's very elderly ...'

'Maybe you could what?'

'I could enrol her in a research study?' The more I thought about it, the more I thought that this might be a plan. 'She could be very useful. It's hard to keep a senior in a study. Seniors tend to get fed up or they get sick or ...'

'Die.'

'I didn't like to say so, but – yeah, seniors die.'

'Pat, I think you're brilliant!' Rosie dumped the crockery on the counter then hugged me round the neck. 'Granny Cass loves to be doing things. She's been busy all her life, and she finds it so annoying being so disabled.'

'Let's enrol her on a study, then – and better yet, make her a pin-up.'

'A pin-up?'

'Yeah, why not? She could be a centrefold in *Senior Computing Times* and a great big inspiration to old ladies everywhere. There'll be lines around the block to ask her out on dates.'

'You are an idiot, you know.'

'I thought I was a Neolithic throwback?'

'Yes, that too.'

⌒ ROSIE ⌒

'Rosie, don't be silly,' Granny said as I did bedtime duty Friday evening, giving Mum a break. 'I'm ninety, don't forget. I'm no use to anybody now.'

'So you don't want to help?'

'I'm sure this man can't need my help.'

'You like him, Granny. You told me he was nice.'

'I think he's very nice.'

'If you think he's nice, why won't you help him?'

'But does he really want me to – what was it – enrol in a study, is that what you said?'

'You'd be an enormous help to him.' I crossed my fingers. 'Granny, there's no reason older people should be cut off from everything. All they need is someone of their own age to encourage them to use computers, to use the World Wide Web – and that's what Pat wants you to do.'

'Well, if I'd be helping Pat?'

'Yes, you would, and he'd be very grateful.'

'He's very handsome, isn't he?'

'I think so.'

'I always like a tall, dark man.'

'I know.'

'He looks a bit like Grandad, doesn't he?'

'Yes, just a bit. Granny, you've gone very pink. I think you've taken quite a shine to Pat.'

'Oh, go on with you. I'm well past all that kind of thing.'

We stayed three days. Rosie had appointments, meetings in the coming week, so this was all the time she had to spare. But it was time enough for me to be under the microscope, to make me feel I was some kind of parasitic bug.

Yeah, Rosie's granny was a charmer. But Rosie's parents were a different story and I found it hard to talk to them. I did not speak their language. I did not know what to say.

So when Rosie's father talked, I listened. I tried to ask appropriate questions, tried to show an interest in his work. But he is an accountant and so it wasn't easy, in fact it was real hard.

I also tried to talk to Rosie's mother. But it was a total waste of time. She didn't want to talk to me. 'I love your roses, Mrs Denham,' I began on Sunday morning as Rosie, Mom and I ate breakfast in the sunny garden.

'Do you, Mr Riley?'

'They have a great perfume.'

'Most roses do.'

'What's this pink one called?'

'Jacques Cartier.'

'He was a French explorer, wasn't he, claimed Canada for France? He mapped the gulf of the St Lawrence and he found a cure for scurvy?'

'Did he really?'

'He also took a cargo of what he believed had to be gold and diamonds back to France. But turned out he found quartz and iron pyrites.'

'My goodness, Mr Riley, you're a mine of information. I know Jacques Cartier only as a rose.' Then Mrs Denham got up from the table. 'If you'll both excuse me, I have lots of things to do.'

'Sorry,' Rosie mouthed at me as Mom went in the kitchen door.

'It's okay.'

'It's *not* okay.' Rosie grabbed a flower, started pulling it to bits and dropped the shredded petals on the grass. 'She's being very mean. She's never chatty, but she's so rude, so horrible to you.'

'It's no big deal, and anyway I kind of understand. You're her daughter. I'm a big bad wolf, a married man who's trying to corrupt your innocence.'

'Ha – fat chance of that with Mum around.'

Yeah, fat chance indeed. Mrs Denham put me in a bedroom as far away from Rosie's as she could. I guess she figured if there was any sneaking down the landing in the night, she could rush out her bedroom door then whack me with a baseball bat. Or cricket bat in this part of the world.

As if I would abuse her hospitality – my mother raised me better.

Monday morning, Rosie's father headed off to work while Rosie and her mother did girl stuff at the beauty salon. Rosie's mom insisted Rosie got herself a haircut. So I drove to Dorchester, bought and then installed new speech-to-text on Granny's laptop and showed her how to use it.

I would have expected a ninety-year-old senior to be slow. But Granny learned real fast. She turned out to be the kind of student I like best to teach, who's keen to figure out solutions for herself, to understand a principle, apply it.

She asked her teacher searching questions, too.

'Do you love my granddaughter?' she began as we took five minutes, drank the coffee I had fixed.

'Yes, ma'am, I do.'

'Any chance you're going to marry Rosie? I wish somebody would.'

'I'm already married. I guess I'll soon be getting a divorce. But I don't know if Rosie would want to marry me.'

'Why don't you ask her some time and then you might

find out?' Granny looked at me with bright blue eyes which seemed to see into my soul. 'My late mother-in-law – a lovely woman – she was Rose Denham, too. She fell for someone who was married.'

'Do you know what happened?'

'He left his wife, they were divorced – no easy thing to do in those days, let me tell you, it caused all sorts of ructions – and then he married Rose.'

'They were happy?'

'Yes, extremely happy. I don't think I ever knew two people who were better matched.'

'I guess they got lucky, then?'

'You could say that, although I'd say in this life we often make our own luck, wouldn't you?' Granny met my gaze. 'I was lucky, too. I married Rose's son, a man who loved me, whom I loved, and you can't get much luckier than that. Rosie loves you, Pat. You say you love Rosie. So—'

'Mrs Denham, should you be encouraging a married man to make eyes at your granddaughter?'

'Mr Riley, do you need encouragement?' Granny's blue eyes twinkled. 'I have you down as a decisive sort of man, so please don't prove me wrong.'

⌒ ROSIE ⌒

So summer had arrived at last.

A British player had won Wimbledon and another Briton was about to win the Tour de France. The beaches were all packed with people trying to develop melanoma, ice cream sales had rocketed and everyone was having a good time. But, like in the Buddy Holly song from years ago, it was raining in my heart and I could hardly bear to let him go.

I was almost sure he felt the same way about me.

But almost isn't certainly, and I found I couldn't make

assumptions, couldn't quite believe it would work out between us, not with Polly, Joe and Lexie in the frame.

'What are we going to do?' he asked on his last day in London, as we stood on the concourse at Heathrow.

'You could get a job in the UK?'

'I think I must.' He ran his fingers through my hair. He often said he loved my wild, electrocuted hair and for the first time in my life I loved it too. 'I get offers all the time from industry in Europe and the USA.'

'But you like working in a university.'

'Yeah, I do. But it's comparatively badly paid. I could get to like the money I would earn in industry.'

'You'd sell your soul to industry?'

'I'm going to think about it. Yeah, I love my work at JQA. But I sometimes feel I'd like a job that's nine to five, something that allows me to take time off on weekends. After all, there's more to life than work. But first, I need to sort things out with Lex.'

'Of course you do.'

Alexis Riley, the mother of his children, the woman he had loved for years and who would always be a part of him.

Do you really want me, Pat?

I found I couldn't bring myself to ask him. I wasn't going to cry and beg and plead, force him to choose – how could he choose?

'It's been good this week,' I said.

'It's been more than good – much more.'

'But all good things must end.'

'Yeah, so my mother always said, but I figure mothers don't know everything.'

'Let me know you got home safely?'

'Yes, of course.' He took my face between his hands and gazed into my eyes. 'I'll find a way for us to be together.'

'How?'

'I'll sort something out. Rosie, you and I – it's permanent. It's going to last forever.'

'I know what permanent means.'

'That's good.' He kissed me once, he kissed me twice, he kissed me one more time and then he went to catch his plane.

✦ PATRICK ✦

It was just as well I had my work. It stopped me going crazy. I was glad I had a bunch of stuff for Colorado to prepare, a ton of calls to make, a dozen meetings I had to organise.

'You're hoping you're on track to win the Nobel Prize with all this thought-to-text shit?' Ben demanded, when he called to say he had forgotten what I looked like and to ask if we could meet up for a beer – fancy Japanese, no doubt. Like there aren't a dozen breweries here in the Twin Cities.

'No chance,' I told him. 'I'm just a mechanic passing spanners to the experts – neurologists, physicians, biochemists – guys who understand the bunch of neurons that make up the human brain.'

'It's a deep and devious mystery, the human brain. You can't reduce it to a bunch of neurons, however hard you try. So, this beer, then – when and where?'

'I don't have time.'

'Come on!'

'I'm very busy.'

'Nobody's too busy to down a beer or two – not even you, Dr Obsessive and Compulsive Grader.'

I did have time to down a beer or two. I had not seen Ben for what seemed like a century. But I didn't have any inclination to hook up with him now.

I didn't know if I ever would again.

There were long, long phone calls. Pat said he was willing, more than willing, in principal at least, to work in Europe. But there were Joe and Polly to consider and of course he needed to see Joe and Polly.

'Rosie, could you relocate to Minnesota?' he suggested. 'There must be a ton of PR opportunities here in Minneapolis-Saint Paul.'

'There's this little problem, Pat. I don't have a green card.'

'Why don't you apply for one?'

'I doubt if I would get one. I don't have any special skills. I'm not married to a US citizen.'

'Perhaps you could become a US citizen yourself?'

'I wouldn't want to lose my British nationality.'

'I heard you can't do that. You could build a bonfire outside of Windsor Castle on November 5th, let off a bunch of firecrackers, call your Queen Elizabeth all sorts of dirty names, but if you're born British, you can't become un-British.'

Lexie must have told him that. She must have been discussing it with Mr Wonderful then passed this information on to Pat. Maybe she was hoping her boyfriend would apply for US citizenship himself, had made a few enquiries of her own? What else had Lexie said to Pat? Did I want to know?

'I must go and see a client,' I told him.

'Yeah, I meant to ask you, how's it going? Whose lives are you busy sorting now? You're meeting interesting guys, I hope, but not too interesting?'

'I'm working with a lot of authors these days. I'm organising signings, getting interviews for them in magazines and newspapers and on radio and television. I'm involved with the relaunch of someone who's quite famous. Or he used to be.'

'Oh – who's that?'

'You won't have heard of him.'

'Why don't you try me?'

'It's Malcolm Tyndale Crawley, he writes crime and mystery fiction, used to be a spy.'

'I know the guy you mean. I met him one time.'

'Goodness, did you?'

'I bought a book of his when he was signing in a Barnes and Noble, must have been while I was still a student. It was *The Russian Cross*, as I recall. I know it was a keeper, so I must still have it someplace.'

'Patrick, you're astonishing. Do you know everyone, know everything?'

'Rosie, honey, it's a little world. So you'll think about it, will you, working over here?'

'Yes, I suppose I might.'

➤ PATRICK ➤

She supposed she might.

Okay, big deal. I tried my darnedest not to get excited. But perhaps I took too much for granted? Maybe I was trying to railroad Rosie into making a decision she didn't want to make?

I came into my office at JQA one evening to catch up on some paperwork and meet with a graduate student who was having problems with a project.

I did not expect to see Ben Fairfax.

What would he be doing here this time of night?

But I could make a guess why he was strolling down the corridor toward me, at his side a very attractive junior female colleague, and grinning like he won the Super Bowl.

'Hey, Professor! How's it going?' he began.

'Good,' I told him. 'You okay? Mrs Fairfax Three – I hope she's well?'

'Yeah, yeah, Tess is fine. She's in the UK right now, she's visiting with her folks. Pat, did you meet Adeline before?'

'I see you in the line for lunch occasionally,' I said. 'You're working late?'

The female colleague glanced at Ben, and then she glanced at me, and then she said she must be going, and she scuttled off.

'Cute ass,' said Ben reflectively. 'I always was a sucker for a callipygous woman.'

'A what kind of woman?'

'You illiterate mechanic – like I told you, one with a cute ass.'

'Tess, will she be in Europe long?' I asked.

'Maybe two or three weeks more, I guess. Hey, come in my office, will you? I got stuff to tell you.'

'Oh?' He was surely not about to tell me how he'd screwed my wife at his apartment? But I followed him into his office anyway.

It smelled of books and sex.

'Grab a seat,' he told me, gathering up a bunch of hardback volumes – new translations of *Missouri Crossing* into Aramaic or Aleutian? They all had his picture on their covers, anyway.

A new picture, too – his hair was cut and styled and gelled, and he was wearing something that looked as if it came out of an upscale store, not from a rummage sale. He had the same shirt on today.

'You'll get a coffee, yeah?' he added, walking over to a shiny chrome machine. 'I just got this new Italian baby and boy, she does the business.'

'What do you want? I'm meeting with a graduate student later. He's coming into town to see me, wants to talk about his project.'

'Man, forget the student, will you? Come on, buddy, chill a while, take a seat, relax?'

'I can stay five minutes, tops.'

'Yeah, okay, okay.' He prowled around the room. It was like he was a preacher working on a sermon in his head. Then suddenly he rounded on me, stabbing at me with his index finger. 'So, get this. A guy's been working on the screenplay of *Missouri Crossing*.'

'I thought you told me you'd be writing it yourself?'

'Yeah, it was suggested. But I'm busy working on my current novel so I don't have too much time to spare. Anyway, the money men have done their stuff. The whole thing's been green-lit. There's going to be a movie! We got some very special folks on board, including someone who is mega-famous to play me.'

'You always said the hero isn't you.'

'Well, he's kind of me.'

'Who is this famous actor?'

'I can't tell you his identity. It's still embargoed. But I've met with him and I can tell you that the guy is A-list and hell is he excited!'

'Great,' I said, and wondered who was going to play my father, if anyone could do the bastard justice, which I rather doubted.

'You and Lex, you'll both be at the premiere,' he added, picking up one of the books and starting to page through it.

'I can't wait,' I said. 'I'll get to meet a bunch of movie actors and other famous authors, a ton of VIPs?'

'You bet.' He glanced up from the book to look at me. 'You forgot to say congratulations.'

I saw how he was smiling his holy-cow-I've-made-it-God-in-heaven-how-I've-made-it smile, and suddenly I couldn't stand to carry on with this charade a single moment longer.

'You and Lex,' I said. 'I know.'

'You do?' He turned his smile off like he just turned out a flashlight. 'Who told you, Tess or Lexie?'

'Does it matter?' I stood up to leave. 'You are a piece of shit.'

'Yeah, I guess I must be.' He sighed, but then he smiled again, and this time it was his old smartass, boy-I'm-brilliant smile, the one he keeps for younger female journalists and attractive graduate students. *I am irresistible. I am hot sex, come fly me.* 'But I'm not the first, you know,' he added. 'Lexie has been cheating on you since she was sixteen.'

'What did you say?'

'You heard me.'

'You're a liar.'

'It's the truth, I swear. Patrick, my old buddy, I might be a piece of shit but I'm a shit who always tells the truth. It's what novelists do. We tell the truth. Lexie is a tramp and she's had lovers by the score. As for those two kids – I doubt they're yours, and I—'

It was like I hit a bowling pin. One second he was on his feet, the next flat on his back. His eyeglasses flew up into the air, the book he had been holding spun out of his hand, and he lay there on his Persian carpet, blinking up at me.

'Get up,' I told him.

'Why, so you can knock me down again?'

'Get up, I said!'

'Okay, but let me take it nice and slow, in case I got me a concussion?' He rolled on to his side and maybe thirty seconds later he managed to sit up. 'Wow, that was some punch,' he added as he rubbed his jaw. 'Pass me my eyeglasses?'

'Say please.'

'Please, Professor Riley.'

I picked the glasses up and saw that they were broken. 'Do you have a spare pair?'

'They should be in the top left drawer.' He pointed to his desk and then he struggled to his feet. 'Man, those babies cost eight hundred dollars and that's without the lenses.'

'I guess they were insured. So who did Lexie—'

'Oh, the usual suspects – jocks, homecoming kings, class presidents and later guys at work. Then the more attractive, more successful, richer fathers in the PTA. Guys with glitz and glamour who were up for one night stands.'

'Why did I not know? Why didn't I notice anything?'

'You were always working. The ladies don't like playing second fiddle to a guy's career. I tried to warn you, didn't I?'

'When did you try to warn me?'

'It must have been last August, last September, when Lex took up with Mr Wonderful, or what the hell you call that British guy. I said you'd been with Lexie way too long and you should find somebody new, go play the field yourself, instead of storming round the place and being mad at everyone.'

'I was mad at Lexie and her lover. I was desperate my kids should not be hurt. But you're saying Joe and Polly aren't my children?'

'Maybe, maybe not – so how does any father know?' He smiled a slow and sly and secret, clearly wince-inducing smile. 'When Joe and Poll were born, you didn't get a DNA test, did you?'

'So you're telling me that you—'

'No, of course I didn't, haven't – Pat, calm down. I went to bed with Lexie once, and that's the honest truth.'

'You're not the father of my children, swear to God?'

'You have my word. Pat, you only have to look at them to see we're not related. Hell, I shouldn't have said what I just did. Those kids, they have your face, your eyes – they're yours, poor little bastards.'

'Yeah, I guess they must be.' Suddenly, I felt so sick, so

tired. I wished I hadn't hit my friend, betrayed myself, done what I'd told myself I'd never do, no matter what the provocation. 'Or maybe I don't care who fathered them. Joe and Polly – they're my children, even if their mother fooled around with other men.'

'Of course you would say that. You might be a smart-guy scientist, but you're a romantic too, and romantics don't do very well in this cruel world. Pat, like I just told you, Alexis is a tramp. She'll go with anyone. She isn't worthy of you, never was and never will be. You should head off back to the UK and tell that Denham woman she's—'

'She's none of your business!'

'Yeah, okay, let's change the subject. I was thinking, maybe I should call up Tess and tell her that I'm fixing to have some therapy for sex addiction? The guy who's going to play me in the movie, he was saying while he was in therapy—'

'You don't need any therapy. You're a two-bit serial adulterer, plain and simple. You never could resist it when it's offered on a plate. You're never going to change.'

'So I guess I'll have to live with it?'

'I guess you will.' Now I could see the damage to his face was quite impressive. When he went down, he must have caught his cheekbone on the corner of his desk. 'But, whatever – I should not have hit you. I apologise. You want to hit me back?'

'I'll take a rain check.' He rubbed his reddening cheek and jaw and winced. 'So I was telling you about this movie. They're looking at locations and casting all the minor parts right now. I was thinking I could maybe play a little role? A bartender, perhaps? The younger version of the father? When he was young, your daddy must have been a real cool dude? A magnet for the chicks? He worked the fairgrounds, didn't he, and rode the rodeo? I'd have to dye my hair, of course. Your father's hair was black.'

I walked out of his office and was halfway down
the passage when I heard his voice again. 'Hey, Professor
Riley?'

But I kept on walking and didn't turn around.

'You mustn't feel too bad about what happened in my
office! It's all great material! I'll put it in a book!'

FROM: Patrick M Riley
SUBJECT: Back in the USA
TO: Rosie Denham
SENT: July 23 17.35

Hi Rosie
Miss you, darling.
It's so bad without you.
Call you soon.
Pat XXXX

FROM: Rosie Denham
SUBJECT: London
TO: Patrick M Riley
SENT: 23 July 23.31

Dear Pat
I miss you, miss you, miss you.
I love you, love you, love you.
Rosie XXXXXXX

⌒ ROSIE ⌒

I missed him like an eye, a hand or some other essential part
of me.

I wondered about setting up in business in Minneapolis.
That would be a challenge, wouldn't it, and might even be

fun? Fanny had American clients and American connections and I knew she'd help.

So I googled green card application and I looked at websites for the IRS and other US government agencies. I found it wasn't like the door was open and America was saying *welcome, Rosie, come on in and stay how long you like.*

I should have been a fashion model of distinguished merit. Yes, that's exactly how the relevant website put it. Or a famous and successful artist or an entertainer, those occupations would have been just fine.

I should have been Victoria Beckham, David Hockney or Kate Moss.

I didn't think I could fix that omission overnight.

✤ PATRICK ✤

Ben called me up the following evening.

'I don't wish to speak with you,' I said and disconnected.

So he called again and then again and then again.

'What do you want?' I muttered. 'No, strike that from the record. I don't have time to talk. I'm very busy.'

'Pat, we need to meet, you need to listen to me – please?'

'Why would I need to listen to a piece of shit like you?'

'There's a ton of stuff you ought to know.'

'So tell me on the phone.'

'Patrick, please don't be like this?'

'Patrick, please don't be like this?' I mimicked. 'You know you sound exactly like a girl?'

'Yeah, I sound exactly like a girl. The usual place, about half eight, okay, and I'll be buying.'

'You got that last bit right.'

'Well?' I demanded as Lou-Anne-our-waitress-for-the-evening

set the glasses on the table, smirked at Ben then sashayed off again.

He was looking good in a white dress shirt and dark business suit, not a pre-restructuring plaid horror or bright blue denim jeans. His silk tie was loosened and the top button of his shirt undone, like he was an executive in a multinational company who just had a busy day and had earned his rest and relaxation. Tess had reinvented him – at least the outward part of him – pretty comprehensively, I guess.

He suited a black eye and swollen, purple-yellow cheek. He wore his injuries with flair and pride. He looked like he was in a fight and won, because his whole demeanour shouted *yeah, but you should see the other guy.*

'You and Rosie Denham,' he began, as he poured the wine – an expensive Californian Merlot, I observed, he must be feeling guilty still. 'You and that British girl—'

'—are none of your business, like I told you yesterday.'

'Patrick, listen – hell, it hurts to talk, feels like I did twenty rounds with Lennox Lewis or Muhammad Ali. I swear I never knew you had it in you, to smack a guy like that. I saw whole galaxies – no, make that whole universes.'

'Good.'

'Hey, come on, old fella, don't let's bear any grudges.' Ben's hand was on my sleeve. 'You and I, we go way back, remember? We've been best buddies from the time we were in diapers, all through kindergarten, grade school, high school—'

'You have anything to say, I mean aside from yarning like an idiot, because I have a ton of stuff to do?'

'Okay – cut to the chase. You and Rosie, you have something great between you. So hang in there, buddy – don't be tempted to make up with Lex, and don't lose what you have with Rosie.'

'What are you today, some sort of covered wagon counsellor, moonlighting from the pages of a trashy magazine?'

'I'm a piece of shit. But, like I told you, I'm an honest piece of shit and I'm your friend. Okay, I screwed your wife. But that was after you and she were through – I'd never have done anything while you were still a couple. You know that.'

'You want me to be grateful you held off?'

'I want you to understand that if you let the British woman go you will regret it all your life.'

'Fairfax, you're a prairie schooner charlatan, is all.' I stood up, found my backpack. 'You know nothing about anything.'

'Riley, I know you.' He grabbed me by the belt and pulled me down again. 'I know your history. I know your nature. Lex was never right for you, but Rosie – you and she are perfect.'

'We know – we did a quiz in *Cosmopolitan*.'

'Pat, I'm serious! The afternoon last fall, when you and Rosie climbed the bluff, you came back all lit up, the two of you, in spite of Rosie getting hurt. She must have been in agony – that foot, it took some beating – but hell, the woman glowed! As for you, old buddy – as God is my witness, I never saw you look that way before.'

'I don't know what you mean.'

'You do, and as for Lex – don't trust that girl. She'll be out to get you now. She'll punish you for daring to be happy with another woman.'

'Why would she do that? You should stick to writing novels, Ben. You know damn all about the real world.'

☙ ROSIE ❧

I was working hard, so very hard.

But I wasn't making any money.

'Why's that, then?' asked Tess.

'Goodness, I don't know.' I shook my head. 'I'm charging people reasonable fees. I have a lot of clients now and most of them pay up on time. But even so I'm barely breaking even.'

'You could ask your dad for some advice?' suggested Tess. 'Your old man, he's an accountant, right?'

'I don't want to ask my dad. He'd only tell my mother I was struggling and then they'd both start bossing me around and knowing best.'

'Why don't you ask Fanny, then?'

'She'd tell my mother, too.'

'So that leaves me. Let's have a dekko at your books.'

'Do you know the first thing about books?'

'I've done Dad's for years.'

Tess was brilliant, I have to say – just absolutely brilliant.

She knew about dull stuff like cash flow, profit margins, all that if-I-earn-a-pound-but-spend-a-pound-and-five-pence-I'll-be-miserable rubbish.

Or upon reflection perhaps it isn't rubbish?

'Okay,' she told me several hours later. 'This is what you have to do. Stop buying fancy stationery from little local firms. Get it printed by the guys online for half the price. Stop buying flowers to decorate the office. If you want some greenery, get yourself a spider plant like everybody else. I'll bring you one of Mum's. She's got a dozen of the things. She won't miss one.'

'I don't like spider plants, they creep me out. I could get a fern or two, perhaps? A well-behaved Dryopteris might give the place a certain ambience?'

'Ferns aren't tax-deductible,' said Tess. 'So I'm very sorry, but you can't have any ferns. Stop taking people out to lunch, as well. You can't afford it.'

'When you run a business, you have to take your clients out to lunch.'

'No you flipping don't.' Tess glared at me. 'Rosie, sweetheart, there's no way a baby firm like yours can justify a spend of eighty quid on lunch. Your clients, your customers, your punters – they're all busy people, yeah? I reckon they'll be happy with a sandwich and a coffee from the local Starbucks. You don't need to take them to the gastropub or tapas place.'

'But Fanny has expensive stationery. Fanny has fresh flowers in her office. Fanny always entertains her clients. When you're trying to build up a business, don't you think it's sensible—'

'—to sit there half the afternoon and nibble baby squid, *patatas bravas* and stupid little strips of belly pork? To drink a bottle of – flipping heck, girl, look at this receipt! What did you order, Chateau Mouton Rothschild '86?'

'How do *you* know about Chateau Mouton '86?'

'Oh, Ben has three bottles of the stuff. They're an investment, not for drinking. You were saying?'

'I don't like cheap wine. So I won't insult prospective clients by offering them plonk.'

'Who are these clients, then? All members of the aristocracy, the House of Lords?' Tess gave an exaggerated sigh. 'I dare say you skirt around the money stuff, as well. After all, it's vulgar to talk money, isn't it?'

'I can talk money!' I retorted.

'But I bet you have to force yourself. Rosie, honey, you're so bleeding middle class it hurts. You're so into doing what is charming and respectable. How many of these tossers you take out to lunch get back to you and give you work?'

'At least two thirds – well, give or take.'

'You mean just over half, which isn't good enough, you know. It should be all of them. You spend your time and money on these people. So you want it to be worth your while. You want them to give you their accounts. You're trying to run a business here, for heaven's sake – not a drop-in club for losers who have nothing else to do and all day to do it. Listen, Rosie – power, water, petrol, software, postage – you're not keeping proper records, and you need—'

'Tess, before you tell me what I need, I'll pop across to Starbucks and get us both a latte, shall I?'

'Yeah, and get some chocolate muffins, too. We could be here all night.'

❧ PATRICK ❧

I thought about what Ben had said.

It galled me to admit it, but I knew he was right about me being a romantic. Rosie was the centre of my world. What I wanted most in all this world – more than money or consumer goods, success in my profession – was to spend my life with Rosie. So I tried to see a way.

My kids – I wanted, needed to be with my kids, of course. But I wanted, needed Rosie, too. It would be impossible to choose between them, and I hoped I'd never have to do it.

A few days after I met with Ben, I took a call from Lex. She said she wanted to meet up. We needed to discuss the kids. 'Their shoes and clothes and school, you know?' she added. 'Polly's day care, Joe's computer camp?'

'I'll give you fifteen minutes in the place we met before next Friday afternoon.'

'Fifteen minutes, Patrick – is that all your family is worth to you?'

'So how long do you need?'

'I guess fifteen, twenty minutes will be fine. Patrick, I don't quite know how to say this, but—'

'What is it?'

'You're still mad at me?'

'No, Lexie, I'm not mad. But, like we both know, we don't have any future as a couple. So I'm trying to be civilised, which is what you always wanted, right?'

'You're still with that woman?'

'I don't wish to discuss it.'

'Oh – okay.' She sighed and then she disconnected. I was surprised to realise I felt – nothing. No anger, no regret, no irritation, no desire to hurt or wound or throw a pan of pasta at her head. I'd changed, moved on, and there was no way I could go back to being how I used to be, to feeling how I used to feel.

It shocked me somehow. I felt like I was grieving for somebody who died. I guess that somebody was part of me.

Lex was running late.

But she was never very punctual, so I was expecting that and I had brought my laptop. I got myself a latte, was drinking it and working through my emails when she came in hot and flustered, gasping like she ran a marathon and saying she couldn't find a place to park.

'Sit down, get your breath back.' What was the etiquette for people who were friends and lovers once but weren't friends or lovers any more, although they didn't hate each other, didn't wish each other any harm?

Did we air-kiss, cheek-kiss, shake hands or do nothing?

The seconds ticked on by and we did nothing.

'What would you like?' I asked. 'A cappuccino, brownie, smoothie? Do you want a sandwich, croissant, muffin?'

'Just an espresso, please. I need to watch my weight.'

Yeah, you do, I thought. *Your thighs have gotten heavy and you've thickened round the waist. You ought to climb some stairs.*

But then I felt mean.

I went up to the counter where the dumbest snail of a barista in the universe was serving, so I stood in line a time. When I got back to our table in a quiet corner, Lex was looking worried. She was fussing with a paper napkin and tearing it in shreds. Did she still think I was mad, in spite of what I said?

I wasn't mad at all. I didn't care what Lexie thought, what Lexie did, what Lexie felt or said. She would never jerk my chain again. So talking with my wife was easy, after all.

We discussed the kids, Joe's school and Polly's day care. It appeared that Mr Wonderful was no longer so keen to drag my wife and children all around the world with him. There would be occasional trips abroad. But from now on, Lexie and the kids would spend most of their time in the Twin Cities.

'You were telling me about some conference when we talked a while back?' she continued as she stirred more sweetener in her coffee which I saw she hadn't touched.

'Yeah, it's on thought-to-text, on all the new developments in experimental software. Delegates are coming from all over – Europe, Asia, South America, the Middle East.'

'Where is it?'

'Colorado.'

'You'll be busy getting stuff together?'

'I need to do some preparation, yeah. I'm scheduled to give a couple lectures and various presentations. I'm chairing several meetings.'

I expected her to make some smart remark about my work, how she knew it was important, more important than my family, how I cared about my work more than I ever did about my wife and children, how it was the reason we broke up, all stuff I heard before. But I got a shock. 'I'm sure you'll do it very well,' she said.

'It's kind of you to say so. Thank you, Lex.'

'Good luck, although I don't suppose you'll need it.'

'Lex, I'm sorry, but I have to leave. I need to see a student.'

'Okay. It's been good to talk.' She stood up, found her purse. 'Pat, I hope we'll meet from time to time? Just the two of us, I mean, as friends?'

'I hope so, too,' I said and was surprised to find I meant it.

We said goodbye, shook hands. But then she stood on tiptoes and kissed me on the cheek. 'Goodbye, Pat,' she said. 'You take care, now.'

'You take care as well.'

'I shall, and listen, Pat – if we can both be sensible and calm, we don't need to have a great big fight.'

'Of course we don't,' I said and then I thought: *one day when things have settled down, I guess it's possible we might be friends again?*

'We're adults,' continued Lex.

'We are.'

'We're parents, too. We love our kids. Whatever we decide to do about our own relationship, we want the best for them.'

'Of course we do. Lex, I have to get back now, but I'll be in touch about the money, schooling, day care, regular access – all that stuff. I can't imagine there'll be any problems.'

'I'm so glad it's working out,' said Lex.

'Yeah, so am I.' As I watched her walking out the door, I thought, *I loved that woman once.* I was so sure our love had died. But she was so sweet today, so reasonable, so generous. She was the Alexis I had loved.

Perhaps a little spark of love remained?

⌐ ROSIE ⌐

```
FROM: Patrick M Riley
SUBJECT: Cool it!
TO: Rosie Denham
SENT: July 26 15.27
```

Rosie, I've been thinking about us.

It was so great to be with you. But now I'm home again, I realise my life is here in Minnesota with my wife and kids.

Lex and I are going to try again.

It's time for you and me to draw a line. You take care now.

Pat

I had half expected it, of course.

But when the actual email pinged into my box at half past nine that evening, while Tess and I were having a late dinner at my flat, I was so shocked that Tess kept on repeating *stay with me, Rosie, darling* like they do on *Casualty*.

Then, not like they do on *Casualty*, she revived us both with Chardonnay. It was lucky she was there for me, or heaven alone knows what I might have done – run mad and torn my garments and my hair, or something equally Victorian and ridiculous?

We must have made a very touching tableau. It was like she was my maid or mother and I was a nineteenth-century virgin whose fiancé had been killed in Africa or up the Khyber Pass. I could have posed for one of those revolting every-picture-tells-a-story sentimental paintings depicting fainting women, weeping children, howling dogs, entitled *Dreadful News*.

Two or three days later, I still couldn't believe that Pat had told me it was over, that it was – how exactly had he put it – time to draw a line. Well, I *could* believe it. He was safely home again, back in the USA, and it turned out I'd been what I always feared I'd be – a temporary diversion, after all.

'I'm not worth it, surely?' he had asked me.

Well, he got that right.

It was the follow-up that really hurt.

```
FROM: Patrick M Riley
SUBJECT: Okay?
TO: Rosie Denham
SENT: July 30 13.34
```

Rosie – haven't heard from you in days.
  Please let me know that you're okay?

Pat XXX

```
FROM: Patrick M Riley
SUBJECT: Talk to me?
TO: Rosie Denham
SENT: July 31 14.59
```

Rosie, you're not picking up my calls on your new cell. Did I get the number wrong? Do you have a problem with your laptop, too? On the blink again?

Pat X

A casual email asking if I was okay. The mention of my laptop, was it on the blink again? So he must have realised he'd blown it, had decided he might like to see me if he came to London, if he wanted casual sex. *We will be forever in your debt. You need me, I'll be there.* Did I dream it, or was that what Patrick Riley said?

He clearly hadn't meant a word of it.

❧ PATRICK ❧

It looked like I messed up. Rosie didn't reply to emails. When I rang her cell phone she refused to take my calls. Or I was calling the wrong number. She ignored my texts.

I guess if I *was* calling the wrong number, the person who was getting all my stuff would be deleting it? The chances were they wouldn't call me back.

I was worried now, so worried that I called her parents on their landline. When her mother finally picked up, she sounded very cross. But she didn't sound distressed. So that was a relief.

'No, Professor Riley, Rosie isn't here,' she snapped, like she was talking to a disobedient dog.

'I'm sorry to disturb you, Mrs Denham, but she isn't taking calls from me. Please could you assure me she's okay?'

'She was very well four hours ago. Mr Riley, if my daughter wished to speak to you, I'm sure she'd get in touch. This is a very antisocial time to ring, you know. It's the middle of the night.'

'I'm sorry if I woke you.'

'You did, and now I'll find it very difficult to sleep without some form of medication.'

'As I said already, I'm sorry to disturb you, Mrs Denham.'

'Goodnight, Mr Riley.'

August

⌁ ROSIE ⌁

'Just go on ignoring him,' said Tess. 'The man's a total jerk.'
She glugged down more red wine and poured a second glass for
me. *'Laptop on the blink again* – my arse.' She glanced towards
my laptop, which was fine. 'Look, there's another text.'

Darling, won't you write me?

'Delete?' I asked.

'Of course delete, you muffin-head.'

So I clicked delete obediently then took another gulp of
my Shiraz. I'd bought four bottles from the Waitrose in the
Edgware Road on my way home and meant to drink them
all. 'Tess, do you ever hear from Ben?'

'Yeah, this week he's been emailing and texting fit to bust
a gut.'

'What does he say?'

'Let's have a look.' Tess found her phone and started
scrolling. 'Oh, the usual rubbish you get from stupid tossers
who realise they've messed up. *When will you be coming
back to Minnesota, darling? Miss you, babe! Honey, won't
you call me up some time?'*

'My goodness, you can tell the man's a novelist. I hope he's
copied all that stuff to whatsername, the woman who'll be
writing his authorised biography.'

'So do I. After all, his fans deserve no less. But before this
latest lot, I hadn't heard a dickybird for months. He didn't
answer any of my texts. He didn't seem to care when I took
off. But now it seems he's changed his mind. I thought that
was a woman's privilege?'

'I never thought I would be dumped by email. I thought at least he'd ring me. Men are all such cowards.'

'But we need them, don't we, for when our girly bits need servicing? Men have the perfect tools to do the job.' Tess sighed. 'I know Ben Fairfax is a git. But for a couple of lovely months, I thought he was the one. I thought meeting him in Vegas had to be my lifetime highlight, that he was Prince Charming, my happy-ever-after.'

'You didn't think that at all.'

'I sort of did, when I was drunk.'

'The trouble is you can't always be drunk. Well, you can, but it's not good for you. It's difficult to put on your mascara while you're drunk.'

'What are we going to do?' asked Tess. 'I'm getting old. I have all these fine lines around my eyes. Or when I smile, I do. I've got others coming round my nose.'

'You haven't any on your actual nose.'

'Of course I haven't any on my actual nose. You'd have to do some serious skin-neglecting to get lines on your nose. I've never seen a wrinkled nose, have you? Well, not on anybody under eighty, anyway.'

'Let's start another bottle,' I suggested.

'Yeah, why don't we?'

'Damn those Yankees, eh?'

'I'll get the alimony first then I'll damn ruddy Ben. Maybe we should find ourselves some British guys? I know this cool club in Dagenham—'

'No, Tess – no guys. British, Yankee, aliens from outer space, none of them are any use to us. Okay, there might be good ones out there somewhere, special pebbles on life's great big beach. But you'd need to shift a million tons of worthless shingle before you found a gem.'

'Oh, come on, it's not as bad as that. You're being very glass-half-empty now.'

'Yes, that's right, I am – but at least I haven't dropped the glass and broken it. I haven't cut my fingers on the shards.' I shook my head and sighed. 'That Y chromosome, it fouls up almost everything. Tess, I promise you, I'm done with men.'

'What are you going to do then, work and work and work like Fanny, end up rich and powerful and alone?'

'It might be a plan. But Fanny's not alone in any case. She's got her gorgeous Caspar and probably half a dozen lovers, too. The last time I saw Fanny, she had a great big knuckle-duster of a brand new ring on her right hand and great big smile on her face. Tess, forget the alimony. You don't need Ben's money.'

'Yes I do.'

'You don't. You're not a parasite, a feeble-minded gold-digger who preys on ghastly men. Listen, sell your diamonds. Get a flat and come and work for me.'

'You mean in your PR business?'

'What else would I mean, you muffin-head yourself?'

'You're serious, are you?'

'Yes, of course I'm serious. Tess, you're smart. You're sharp. I think you could be brilliant at promotions and PR.'

'Why would you think that?'

'You come from a family of market traders, right?'

'Yeah, people who sell cauliflowers and spuds.'

'Then you worked for a salvage merchant, didn't you?'

'Yes, but I—'

'So you could sell stuff for my clients, couldn't you? Cauliflowers or antique bathroom fittings, selling's in your blood. You're used to doing deals?'

'I suppose. Okay, I'll come and work for you. Tess and Rosie sort your life, eh? Yeah, let's drink to that. When shall I start?'

'What about immediately?'

❧ PATRICK ❧

I still can't believe I was so dumb.

After all I tell my students, after I tore Rosie up about her carelessness, I messed up spectacularly. I'm a full professor of IT, and what did I do? When I went to get Lex her espresso, I forgot to log out of my email application.

So any burglar could walk in and shit over my stuff.

So any burglar did.

While I was at the counter, Lex wrote Rosie. She sent the message through my email application and then she deleted it from my Sent folder and from my Deleted one as well.

So I wouldn't see it on the app because it wasn't there.

So I would not suspect a thing.

How did I work out what must have happened? A week after I met with Lex, my email application failed. It was usually reliable. But once in a while it got the screaming heebie-jeebies and packed up.

So I had to go into my Gmail. My app sent and received all of my messages through Gmail and Gmail doesn't delete anything.

So as I was looking for something else, I found it. There it was as large as life and twice as toxic in my Sent Mail folder.

```
FROM: Patrick M Riley
SUBJECT: Cool it!
TO: Rosie Denham
SENT: July 26 15.27


Rosie, I've been thinking about us.
   It was so great to be with you. But now
I'm home again, I realise my life is here in
Minnesota with my wife and kids.
```

Lex and I are going to try again.

It's time for you and me to draw a line.

You take care now.

Pat

⌒ ROSIE ⌒

I was surprised to find how much it kept on hurting.

But I knew I had to work on that, get over it. So I did cool and capable, at least during the day. While I was with Tess, we even had a laugh, a girly giggle. I pretended I was fine.

I also knew Tess would be good. But she was more than good. She was persistent and determined and she also worked extremely hard. She chose not to understand when anyone said *no*. She just kept on at them until they gave in and said *yes*. She didn't waste her time on niceties or idle chatting. She put her offer on the table and demanded an immediate response. She got more done in twenty minutes than I did in an average working day.

Whenever Tess picked up the phone, she sold – catering to private functions, interviews to local radio stations, a range of articles to magazines. I reckoned she could sell a brand new range of vegan wholefoods to a pride of lions in the Serengeti National Park. So I was not especially surprised when she had no trouble selling cupcakes made in a client's kitchen up in Leicestershire to Harrods.

'We're winning, aren't we, mate?' she asked me, beaming as she disconnected after she had closed a deal on a range of cushion covers I'd been trying to sell to national chains for weeks and weeks.

'Yes, we are, all thanks to you,' I said. 'Tess, could you go to Manchester tomorrow?'

'Who or what's in Manchester?'

'A woman who makes special jams and marmalades and stuff – her lemon curd's sublime. She wants to sell stuff locally.'

'Why would she sell it locally when she could probably sell it nationwide, if it's that brilliant?'

'Well, precisely, Tess – and that's why I'm sending you to see this lady. You could get some sales locally and encourage her to be a little more ambitious, couldn't you? She's got all the necessary certificates, so she—'

'Yeah, I know – so she can sell to shops, at markets, to the general public. I'm a market trader's daughter, right?'

'Of course, I was forgetting. Okay, I've tasted all the stuff she makes. Mum has tasted it as well and if my mother passes anything it must be close to perfect.'

'I'll have her jams in Fortnum's by tomorrow afternoon. Or I'll have some orders, anyway.' Then Tess looked at me with narrowed eyes. 'As for the other rubbish in your life – you're dealing with it, are you?'

'I suppose.'

'You mind you do. You tell yourself a hundred times a day – that man is worthless, that man is a waste of oxygen, that man is bad.'

'All right, all right.'

I did get through the days okay. Tess helped enormously. She was both inspired and inspiring. She was full of energy and she was determined to make Tess and Rosie Sort Your Life a big success. She decided she would be a self-made millionaire. After all, if somebody like Ben could do it, she announced, she was going to do it, too.

So on the whole the days were fine.

But at night I cried into my pillow. I sobbed my heart out for a faithless, fickle, cruel man. I acted like the sort of idiot woman I despised.

'I'm sorry, Pat,' said Lexie, when I called her in a white-hot rage which frightened even me and told her to get round to the apartment now, this very minute.

No, she couldn't bring the children.

They could stay with Angie.

'But there was no other way to do it,' she began.

'What do you mean, no other way to do it? Lexie, don't just stand there, come inside, don't give the neighbours a free show.' So she came into the living room. I closed the door. 'Okay, now tell me – no other way to do precisely what?'

'I want to try again.'

Then Lexie looked at me with big round eyes, and I saw the cute preteen – the pretty, sexy co-ed – the girl in bridal white – the radiant, happy mother in the downtown birthing centre with first Joe then Polly in her arms – the wife I'd thought was mine until we both sat dribbling in our wheelchairs on some balcony in Florida.

The woman I once loved. But, if Ben Fairfax wasn't lying – and this now seemed more than likely – I'd been a fool to love. The evidence had been in front of me for years and years and I had been too dumb to see it. I'd thought nothing of it when Lexie headed out to basket-weaving, quilting or whatever classes, all dressed up and smelling like a lily. When she took a ton of whispered calls from a new girlfriend, a teacher at Joe's kindergarten, some guy selling cabins in the woods …

'When you sent that message, what would you have done if Rosie had replied to me while we were in the coffee shop – if I'd read an email from her there?'

'I hoped she would. I hoped you would. I figured she would write you straight away and tell you to get lost. Or say *please don't do this to me, I love you, we can work it out* – a bunch of stuff like that. Whatever, it would draw the battle lines.'

'So why did you delete the message?'

'Pat, I wasn't thinking straight! When you went to stand in line, I saw my chance and grabbed it. But afterward I realised I'd been stupid. So that's why I deleted what I sent.'

'I think you lost it big time.'

'No, I was confused. I knew whatever happened next you would be mad at me. But I also knew you wouldn't kill me in a coffee shop.'

'Huh – I might have done.'

'When you called me up, you were so angry. But now you're so calm again. I wish you'd yell at me.'

'You don't.'

'I do!'

'I recall when you first told me about Mr Wonderful, you left the kids with Angie so they wouldn't hear me yell at you.'

'I thought you'd yell. I thought that leaving you would wake you up, would make you think about the two of us.'

'So you were testing me, like Jesus being tested in the wilderness? Let me tell you something, Lex – you're crazy. I was crazy too, to love you like I did, when you cheated on me all the time from when we were in school.'

She gaped at me.

'You knew?' she whispered, looking stunned.

What could I do but shrug?

'You knew, but you did nothing?'

What could I do but shrug again?

'I'm so sorry, Patrick. I wish it hadn't been like that. If I could turn the clock back—'

'But you can't.' I grabbed my carry-on. 'Okay, so now we understand each other and I have to leave.'

'Where are you going?' Lexie blocked my exit by standing

with her back against the door. 'Oh, to that conference – I forgot you have a conference. But you could change your flight. Listen, Patrick, we must talk. Go somewhere on our own for a few days, just you and me. Angie won't mind watching Joe and Polly. Pat, you don't have to go to Colorado.'

'I'm not going to Colorado.'

'But I thought your conference—'

'I'm not going to the conference.'

'What? I never knew you miss a conference, and this is an important one, you said so, it's all about your work. I know how much you love your work. You've always been so focused on—'

'Lexie, if we didn't have two kids who need some sort of mom, however useless, I'd seriously consider strangling you. So don't push it, baby. Get out of my way.'

'I love it when you're masterful.' Lexie trailed one finger down my chest and gazed at me with big cute-kitten eyes. 'Listen, honey, we could start again. Okay, we had a falling-out. When we were first married we were kids. We hadn't been around. But now we're stronger, wiser. Pat, you can't run out on me. It was starting to work out between us, you know that. When I said I was glad about it, you said you were, too.'

'I meant I was glad we sorted out the maintenance, agreed that we both wanted what was best for Joe and Polly.'

'You don't want me back?'

I dropped my carry-on. I took her by the shoulders. I moved her to one side and then I grabbed my case again. I walked right out the door and pressed the button to call the elevator.

'You leave, you'll never see your kids again!' she hollered after me. 'I'll tell the judge you and that woman did some stuff to them. You hurt them, traumatised them. You—'

Then the elevator came and I got into it.

I caught the evening flight to London out of Minneapolis-Saint Paul and landed at Heathrow the following lunch time. There were no taxis, so I rode the subway – big mistake, the train broke down.

I could not find Rosie anyplace. I went to her apartment. She was not at home. I went to her office. She was not at her office. It was all closed up. I tried to call. She would not take my calls. So I went back to where she lived. I sat down on the step and then I waited – and I waited – and I waited.

Passers-by most probably figured I must be a beggar. Travel-stained, dishevelled and unshaven, I guess I looked the part, and all I needed was a dog.

'I can't believe you have the nerve,' she said, when she found me slumped down on the step at ten o'clock that evening.

I was starving, having eaten nothing since the usual plastic airline breakfast. I was dying for a drink of water. I'd wanted to lie down under a tree in one of London's parks and go to sleep. But I'd been too scared to move in case I missed her coming home and so I'd sat it out in the hot, dusty London sunshine.

Consequently I was dry as London dust myself.

She glared at me. She has the most amazing eyes. Slate-grey, black-fringed, they're deep as forest pools. Their gaze can be as hard as granite or as soft as gossamer, can chill, can warm, can burn.

Now, her gaze was burning into me.

'May I come in a while?' I asked, standing up then almost falling over because I was so hungry, jet-lagged, dehydrated and my feet had gone to sleep.

'No, you may not,' she snapped. 'If you don't go away right now – I mean this very minute – I'm ringing the police.'

'Rosie, I flew all the way from Minnesota.'

'So fly back again.'

'Okay, but will you come and get a coffee, talk to me? There has to be a shop along the road, so we—'

'Patrick, I don't want a stupid coffee! I have no desire to talk to you! I've just driven home from Birmingham. The traffic was horrendous. I want to go to bed.' She found her cell. 'What part of *go away right now* do you not understand?'

'I do understand you, but please don't call the cops.'

'Why shouldn't I?'

'You need listen to me – please?'

⌒ ROSIE ⌒

You need to listen to me – please?

'Why's that?' I asked.

'So I can explain what happened.'

'I don't wish to hear your explanation. It doesn't interest me.'

'Rosie, may I have a drink of water?'

'I suppose so.' I unlocked the door. 'But stay here on the step. I'll fetch you one and bring it out. Then you must go.'

As I filled a glass, my heart was racing. It had been so easy – well, comparatively easy – to hate him while he wasn't here in London.

But when I saw him standing right in front of me, tired and dirty and unshaven, obviously exhausted, looking like he'd hitch-hiked from Heathrow, which I suppose he might have done, I wanted to invite him in and feed him and do – other things. Okay, okay, okay. I never thought that it would be as difficult as this to tell a man to go to hell.

'Rosie, it was all a big mistake.'

'But I think you were right to finish it. After all, it wasn't working out. Long-distance friendships seldom do.'

'You know you don't mean that.'

'I don't mean what?'

'You and I, we have a way to go before we're finished. We have our whole lives.' As I gave the glass back, I decided I would risk it. So she called the cops? So I got arrested and then I was deported? So I lost my job at JQA? I took her by the shoulders. 'Rosie, I'm so sorry—'

'Yes, I know.' She turned her head aside and wouldn't look at me. 'You didn't mean those things you said. You've changed your mind. You want to try again. I've heard all that before from other men. You're such a bunch of bastards, cowards, opportunists, shits. You men say women cheat, lie and deceive, but you—'

'I didn't send that email.'

'What?' She clearly hadn't been expecting this. She jerked her head up, met my fuddled gaze, her own eyes blazing. 'What are you trying to say?'

'I did not send that email!'

'But it came from your account! Of course you sent it! Do you think I'm stupid?'

'I didn't write it and I didn't send it.'

'Then who did?'

'Rosie, give me five? Just five little minutes, please?'

'All right – five minutes. You'd better come inside.' She sounded like her mother, the Justice of the Peace. She checked her watch. 'I'm timing you.'

'I know.'

'Do you want a coffee?'

'Yeah, that would be absolutely great, but may I use the bathroom first?'

'I suppose so. Get yourself a towel and have a shower. You damn well need one.'

'I'll take more than five minutes to get myself a shower.'

'You won't, because I'll turn the water off.'

It took some persuading, but finally she started to believe me.

'You mean you didn't log out of your account?'

'I didn't log out of my account.'

'Patrick, you're – I don't know what to say.' She shook her head at me and sighed, all what-are-men-like, as women love to do. 'After that big lecture you gave me about security and stuff? You left your own door open with a message Scotch-taped to the bell-push, saying *come right in*?'

'I did.'

'You're such a fool.'

'I know.'

'You're the biggest wanker in the world.'

'I know that, too.' I leaned across the kitchen table and kissed her on the mouth. 'Now you slap my face, like in the movies.'

'Oh, Pat, you're such an idiot!' She shook her head again. But she was smiling now and it was like the sun came out after a storm. 'I don't want to slap you anywhere.'

She let me kiss her and finally she kissed me back and we got up and walked into the living room and sat down on the couch and kissed some more.

I stayed the night.

'When's that conference in Colorado?' she asked the following morning. 'I suppose it must be fairly soon?'

'Yeah, it must be tomorrow,' I replied. 'Come on – lie down again for half an hour? It's only twenty after seven. You don't need to get up yet.'

'What precisely do you mean, Pat, it must be tomorrow?'

'Today, tomorrow, yesterday – I lost all track of time.'

'But you're going, aren't you?'

'No.'

'You must!' She stared at me. 'You're doing presentations, chairing meetings. People will have come from anywhere and everywhere to hear you.'

'Rosie, I messed up with Lex. She said I always put my work before my family and she was right. I want you to understand that you come first with me.'

'It's not a question of coming first, you halfwit.' She grabbed my shoulder, shook me, glared at me. 'You can't let all those people down! This is your career, your work, your destiny, it's why you're on this earth. You have to go!'

'I can't be there in time. My first presentation is tomorrow morning, ten o'clock.'

'So you can get a flight today. How long does it take, nine hours or so? You'll be in Colorado around teatime. Or by late this evening, anyway, even if it isn't possible to fly direct. See, Patrick, how the planet spins to fall in with your schedule? Go and pack your stuff, get dressed. I'll drive you to Heathrow. You can get a stand-by ticket.'

She was out of bed and pulling on her own clothes now. 'Come on, Pat – get up!' she cried. 'We don't have much time.'

'I'm not going, Rosie.'

'If you don't, you stupid man, I shall never speak to you again!'

'But you're much more important than a conference. Don't you get that? Don't you understand?'

'I'm flattered, obviously.' She looked at me as if she thought she never saw someone so dumb. 'But you have work to do, important work. So go and do it and then come back to me.'

I could see she meant it. So I got out of bed, pulled on my jeans, reached for my shirt. 'I love you, Rosie Denham.' I collected papers, pulled on socks and fastened buttons, pushed my laptop in my carry-on. 'You're fantastic, fabulous, amazing—'

'Yes, yes, yes. I'm everything that's wonderful. You've got your passport, have you?'

'Yeah, I think so. Rosie, some day we must have a baby. What does Shakespeare say? You would be the cruellest she alive if you went to your grave and left the world no copies of yourself – something like that?'

'This baby might take after you, not me – have you considered that small point?' She grimaced, grabbed her keys. 'Okay, Pat, you've got your stuff? Let's go.'

She pushed me out the door.

I got on a plane.

I came to Denver.

I don't remember anything about the presentations or the meetings. My papers seemed to go down fairly well, as far as I could judge. But I was in a kind of daze throughout, and one day later I was on a flight back to Heathrow.

ROSIE

While he was away, I did some thinking, told myself I wasn't playing fair.

When he returned, he must have realised I'd been making some decisions about us. 'Rosie, what's the matter?' he began. 'What did I do now?'

'You shouldn't have come back to the UK.'

'Why not – you got somebody new?'

'Of course I haven't got somebody new.'

'That's a relief.' He took me in his arms and hugged me

tight. 'Okay, I have a schedule. I'm getting a divorce. I want to marry you. We'll get a place in the US or the UK or both. We'll have some kids. What do you say?'

'I can't,' I told him.

'Marry me?'

'Marry you, have children. I can't do it, Pat.'

'Oh, right.'

He tried to look as if he wasn't bothered one way or the other. But I could see I'd hurt him by being so abrupt. 'Patrick,' I continued urgently, 'please don't think it's you, that it's—'

'You mean it's like you said. You don't want children. I know some women don't – a woman's right to choose and stuff.'

'I'd love to have some children! Your children, Pat, they're gorgeous. I'd love to have a little Joe or Polly of my own.'

'So there is some reason—'

'Yes.'

But I didn't want to talk about it. I hadn't told my female friends. I'd never told a man that as a woman I was a big disaster both mentally and physically, totally messed up.

'Rosie,' Pat said gently, 'these days there are treatments, therapies. If money is the problem, then I will find the money. I'll leave JQA tomorrow. I'll go work in industry, in research and development. As I believe I told you, I get offers all the time.'

'Money won't solve anything.'

'You're sure it won't? I know it can't work miracles. But lots of it can solve a bunch of stuff.'

'It can't solve this.'

'So will you tell me, Rosie?'

'No.'

'I think you ought to tell me.'

'Why?'

'I love you very much. I want to help you. So please share

this with me?' He looked at me, his dark eyes loving, kind. I realised I owed him. I couldn't let him think I didn't want him, when I did so very much, more than my life itself.

'When it gets dark, I'll tell you,' I replied. 'It will be easier, talking in the dark.'

The darkness came too soon, but I had promised.

'When I was fourteen … I'm sorry, Pat, it's difficult for me.'

'Just take your time, okay? Did someone hurt you?'

'Yes, you could say that.'

'What happened?'

'Dad and I were driving home one January night. He'd picked me up from meeting friends in Dorchester. It was sleeting and the road was like a skating rink. We hit a van coming the other way. Or so they told us later. I don't remember even seeing the van. Dad was cushioned by the airbag, but he still broke half his ribs, his collarbone and both his legs.'

'Your own airbag, Rosie – it must have saved your life?'

'I didn't have an airbag. This was fifteen years ago when only driver airbags were routinely fitted. Anyway, a bit of tin or plastic – something sharp – sheared off the dashboard and then sliced into me.'

'Oh, Rosie, honey—'

'The surgeons did a brilliant job. I had half a dozen operations, but today I don't have any scars except the little one across my stomach.'

'Your appendectomy – I noticed that.'

'It's not an appendectomy. It's where they sewed me up again the last time.' I turned to face him, forced myself to look at him. 'I don't want to say this, Patrick. But you need to know that I'd have loved to have your children and if I could have one wish, just the one …'

I said the next bit quickly. 'My uterus was shredded. The doctors did their very best to put it back together. But by the time I was eighteen I'd had four years of problems. I researched it all and I decided the obvious solution was to have a hysterectomy. My parents, all my doctors – they tried to talk me out of it, of course. They made me have six months of counselling. I told the counsellor repeatedly I'd never wanted children. Yes, I said, I understood what I was asking them to do, and in the end they did it.

'But all I really wanted was for the everlasting pain to stop. I didn't want more months or years in hospital. I didn't want to risk a pregnancy which might kill me, the baby or us both. So when I let Charlie die, I took away my parents' chance of grandchildren as well.'

'But Rosie, like I said, there must be treatments? If you still have your ovaries, there might be—'

'Stop it, Pat!' I turned away. 'I'm not going down that route because I know I'd hate it! Doctors harvesting my eggs, then renting someone's womb – it's not for me. So if you need more children, you'd better go and find another woman, someone who can have them.'

'I don't want another woman. I don't need more children.' Gently, very gently, he turned me back to face him. 'Rosie, darling, you must look at me while I say this.'

'Okay, I'm looking.'

'All I want is you.'

✥ PATRICK ✥

I did what all the British do in times of grief or crisis.

I went into the kitchen. I put the kettle on and found the teabags and made a pot of strong, brown British tea. As I stirred in milk and sugar, I thought, yeah – it would have been amazing to have a little Rosie. But it was the woman

332

that I wanted, not an incubator. Rosie was the one I loved with all my heart, with all my soul, and I tried for half an hour or more to get her to see that.

'Rosie, I'd give anything, do anything at all, for you to have a baby of your own,' I said and meant it. 'But if it's not to be, it's not to be, and we can live with that. We'll still get married, yeah?'

'Whenever anybody mentions babies, I always say I'd rather have a handbag.' She smiled a small, brave, hell-we-can't-do-anything-about-it-so-we-might-as-well-accept-it smile, so weak and watered down that it was almost homeopathic. 'Last week, I saw a beautiful Armani one in Harrods.'

'Let's go get it, then.' I put my mug down and stood up. 'Let's find a cab, go buy it now.'

'Pat, I'm joking, can't you tell? You Americans, you scientists – you're all so flipping literal! You never know when somebody is teasing. I don't want a sodding handbag, and—'

'Okay, forget the handbag. Anyway, you have a ton of handbags. Your closet's full of them.'

'But on second thoughts, a girl can never have too many handbags, and I'm a fan of multiplicity …'

'There's only one of me.'

'That's a blessing, I suppose. I don't think I could handle two of you if it's for life.'

'So is that a yes, you'll marry me? You'll wear my ring?'

'I would be honoured and delighted,' she replied.

'You're not – what do you say – having me on?'

'I wouldn't joke about a thing like this.'

'Let's go shopping, then.'

August

One Year Later

⌒ ROSIE ⌒

It took a while to sort our lives out, for Pat to be divorced, for Alexis and her legal team to do their very best to bankrupt him, even though the state of Minnesota has no-fault divorce laws and frowns on mean, vindictive stuff like that.

I didn't care what Lexie wanted in the way of property and money. As I told Pat often, Lexie could have anything she liked, provided I had him.

She'd broken up with Stephen and was apparently good friends with Ben. Maybe, after Tess had been unhitched from Ben, Lexie would be Mrs Fairfax Four? It seemed quite likely.

'I'm so glad you're marrying an American, my angel,' Fanny told me. 'Marry him and then become American yourself and start a PR business over there, while Tess runs your UK operation – they'd be smart moves, my darling. Obviously, Americans will love your British accent. You'll clean up. What about his children, do you get on with them?'

'I love them, they're fantastic. I'm going to be a brilliant stepmother. I won't have to do the disciplining, buy the shoes or go to all the PTA events. I'll just have all the fun.'

We decided on a quiet wedding in a small hotel in Dorset.

Pat's mother wouldn't come. She said it wasn't right for Lex and him to be divorced. She'd talked to Father Conley who agreed it was a sin and thought it likely Pat would go to hell. Of course, his Jezebel would go there, too.

'You couldn't talk her round?' I asked.

'I wouldn't waste my time and energy. She's an old-style Catholic – once married, always married. She never would have left my father, even though he kicked a million different kinds of shit out of us both.' He shrugged. 'It's the way she's made. Some people, they like certainty.'

'I'm one of them.'

'You are?'

'I'm certain about you.'

So on the day it was my grandmother, my parents, some relations, Pat's children and our friends, including Tess and Fanny, who were as thick as treacle nowadays.

Joe and Polly bounced around and grinned like naughty pixies from the moment they got out of bed. My mother made a special effort to be nice to Pat, and actually she almost managed it. The children had begun to melt my parents' hearts, so I was fairly confident that soon we'd all get on.

Charlie wasn't there, of course, which grieved me …

After Pat and I were up and breakfasted and dressed – there was no bridegroom-not-seeing-the-bride or any of that superstitious nonsense – we escaped from everybody else and walked around the garden where Mum's Jacques Cartier roses had been flowering all the summer. I don't know how she managed to persuade them to do that. Other people get one early flush and then the season's over, more or less.

'You two, are you coming?' called my father from the kitchen doorway. 'You're going to be late!'

'Daddy's fussing,' Patrick murmured. 'So I guess we should go have this wedding? But, before we leave, I need to give you something.'

'What?'

'It took a while to get it back.' He handed me a memory

stick. 'I didn't check it out, of course – it's private – but it should all be there.'

'Oh, Pat! You mean it's—'

'Yes,' he said. 'I thought you'd like your sister to be here with you today.'

About the Author

Margaret James was born and brought up in
Hereford and now lives in Devon. She studied
English at London University, and has written many
short stories, articles and serials for magazines.
She is the author of sixteen published novels.

Her debut novel for Choc Lit, *The Silver Locket*, received
a glowing review from the Daily Mail and reached
the Top 20 Small Publishers Fiction List in November
2010 and in the same year a Reviewers' Choice Award
from Single Titles. *The Golden Chain* also hit the Top
20 Small Publishers Fiction List in May 2011.

Margaret is a long standing contributor to Writing
Magazine for which she writes the Fiction Focus column
and an author interview for each issue. She's also a creative
writing tutor for the London School of Journalism. *Magic
Sometimes Happens* is Margaret's fifth novel with Choc Lit.

More Choc Lit

From Margaret James

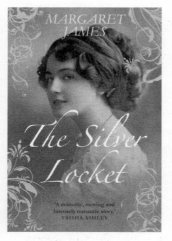

The Silver Locket

Winner of 2010 Reviewers'
Choice Award for Single Titles

If life is cheap, how much is love worth?

It's 1914 and young Rose Courtenay has a decision to make. Please her wealthy parents by marrying the man of their choice – or play her part in the war effort?

The chance to escape proves irresistible and Rose becomes a nurse. Working in France, she meets Lieutenant Alex Denham, a dark figure from her past. He's the last man in the world she'd get involved with – especially now he's married.

But in wartime nothing is as it seems. Alex's marriage is a sham and Rose is the only woman he's ever wanted. As he recovers from his wounds, he sets out to win her trust. His gift of a silver locket is a far cry from the luxuries she's left behind.

What value will she put on his love?

Find out about Rosie Denham's ancestors in the Charton Minster series! This is the first novel in the trilogy.

Visit www.choc-lit.com for more details including the first two chapters and reviews, or simply scan barcode using your mobile phone QR reader.

The Golden Chain

Can first love last forever?

1931 is the year that changes everything for Daisy Denham. Her family has not long swapped life in India for Dorset, England when she uncovers an old secret.

At the same time, she meets Ewan Fraser – a handsome dreamer who wants nothing more than to entertain the world and for Daisy to play his leading lady.

Ewan offers love and a chance to escape with a touring theatre company. As they grow closer, he gives her a golden chain and Daisy gives him a promise – that she will always keep him in her heart.

But life on tour is not as they'd hoped. Ewan is tempted away by his career and Daisy is dazzled by the older, charismatic figure of Jesse Trent. She breaks Ewan's heart and sets off for a life in London with Jesse.

Only time will tell whether some promises are easier to make than keep …

Find out about Rosie Denham's ancestors in the Charton Minster series! This is the second novel in the trilogy.

Visit www.choc-lit.com for more details including the first two chapters and reviews, or simply scan barcode using your mobile phone QR reader.

The Penny Bangle

When should you trust your heart?

It's 1942 when Cassie Taylor reluctantly leaves Birmingham to become a land girl on a farm in Dorset.

There she meets Robert and Stephen Denham, twins recovering from injuries sustained at Dunkirk. Cassie is instantly drawn to Stephen, but is wary of the more complex Robert – who doesn't seem to like Cassie one little bit.

At first, Robert wants to sack the inexperienced city girl. But Cassie soon learns, and Robert comes to admire her courage, finding himself deeply attracted to Cassie. Just as their romance blossoms, he's called back into active service.

Anxious to have adventures herself, Cassie joins the ATS. In Egypt, she meets up with Robert, and they become engaged. However, war separates them again as Robert is sent to Italy and Cassie back to the UK.

Robert is reported missing, presumed dead. Stephen wants to take Robert's place in Cassie's heart. But will Cassie stay true to the memory of her first love, and will Robert come home again?

Find out about Rosie Denham's ancestors in the Charton Minster series! This is the third novel in the trilogy.

Visit www.choc-lit.com for more details including the first two chapters and reviews, or simply scan barcode using your mobile phone QR reader.

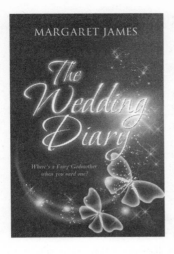

The Wedding Diary

Shortlisted for the 2014 Romantic Novel of the Year award

Where's a Fairy Godmother when you need one?

If you won a fairy-tale wedding in a luxury hotel, you'd be delighted – right? But what if you didn't have anyone to marry? Cat Aston did have a fiancé, but now it looks like her Prince Charming has done a runner.

Adam Lawley was left devastated when his girlfriend turned down his heartfelt proposal. He's made a vow never to fall in love again.

So – when Cat and Adam meet, they shouldn't even consider falling in love. After all, they're both broken hearted. But for some reason they can't stop thinking about each other. Is this their second chance for happiness, or are some things just too good to be true?

Rosie Denham makes an appearance in The Wedding Diary and there are also links to the Charton Minster trilogy.

Visit www.choc-lit.com for more details including the first two chapters and reviews, or simply scan barcode using your mobile phone QR reader.

More from Choc Lit

If you enjoyed Margaret's story, you'll enjoy
the rest of our selection. Here's a sample:

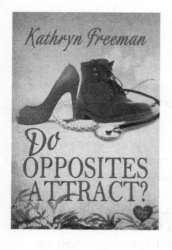

Do Opposites Attract?
Kathryn Freeman

**There's no such thing
as a class divide – until
you're on separate sides**

Brianna Worthington has
beauty, privilege and a very
healthy trust fund. The only
hardship she's ever witnessed
has been on the television.
Yet when she's invited to see
how her mother's charity,
Medic SOS, is dealing with the
aftermath of a tornado in South America, even Brianna is
surprised when she accepts.

Mitch McBride, Chief Medical Officer, doesn't need the
patron's daughter disrupting his work. He's from the wrong
side of the tracks and has led life on the edge, but he's not
about to risk losing his job for a pretty face.

Poles apart, dynamite together, but can Brianna and Mitch
ever bridge the gap separating them?

Visit www.choc-lit.com for more details
including the first two chapters and
reviews, or simply scan barcode using
your mobile phone QR reader.

Follow me follow you
Laura E James

You save me and I'll save you

Victoria Noble has pulled the plug on romance. As director of the number one social networking site, EweSpeak, and single mother to four-year-old Seth, she wrestles with the work–life balance.

Enter Chris Frampton, Hollywood action hero and Victoria's first love. His return from LA has sparked a powder keg of media attention, and with secrets threatening to fuel the fire, he's desperate to escape. But finding a way forward is never simple. Although his connection with Victoria has lasted the test of time, has he been adrift too long to know how to move on?

With the risk of them breaking, will either #follow their heart?

Doctor January
Rhoda Baxter

If you keep looking back, you might miss what's standing right in front of you ...

Six months after a painful break-up from Gordon, Beth's finally getting her life back on track. She has faith in her own scientific theories and is willing to work hard to prove them. She's even beginning to see Hibbs, her dedicated lab partner, as more than just a lousy lothario in a lab-coat and goggles.

So when Gordon arrives back from America without warning and expects to be welcomed back into Beth's arms, she's totally thrown. She also quickly begins to see that Gordon isn't the man she thought he was ... Hibbs has always held a candle for Beth, but he can only wait so long for her to realise there's more to life than being patronised and bullied by the one who's meant to love and protect her.

Will Beth foresee the explosive nature beneath Gordon's placid surface before he destroys everything she's worked for, both inside and outside the lab?

Visit www.choc-lit.com for more details including the first two chapters and reviews, or simply scan barcode using your mobile phone QR reader.

CLAIM YOUR FREE EBOOK

of

Magic Sometimes Happens

You may wish to have a choice of how you read *Magic Sometimes Happens*. Perhaps you'd like a digital version for when you're out and about, so that you can read it on your ereader, iPad or even a Smartphone. For a limited period, we're including a **FREE** ebook version along with this paperback.

To claim, simply visit ebooks.choc-lit.com or scan the QR Code.

You'll need to enter the following code:

Q091409

Introducing Choc Lit

We're an independent publisher creating
a delicious selection of fiction.
Where heroes are like chocolate – irresistible!
Quality stories with a romance at the heart.
See our selection here:
www.choc-lit.com

We'd love to hear how you enjoyed *Magic Sometimes
Happens*. Please visit our website and give your feedback.

Choc Lit novels are selected by genuine readers like yourself.
We only publish stories our Choc Lit Tasting Panel want to
see in print. Our reviews and awards speak for themselves.

Could you be a Star Selector and join our Tasting Panel?
Would you like to play a role in choosing which novels
we decide to publish? Do you enjoy reading romance
novels? Then you could be perfect for our Choc Lit
Tasting Panel. Visit our website for more details.

Keep in touch:
Sign up for our monthly newsletter Choc Lit Spread for
all the latest news and offers: www.spread.choc-lit.com.
Follow us on Twitter: @ChocLituk and Facebook: Choc Lit.

Or simply scan barcode using your mobile phone QR reader:

*Choc Lit
Spread*

Twitter

Facebook